Til Pie

For Lene

Revised edition March, 2020.

ONE

Monday, 22ⁿᵈ September.

He didn't need to hear this all over again. He just wanted shot of this guy and to get back to a quiet office.

"You know there is drought in the area. Building a canal to divert water from the Guseni River to a reservoir in Bakooli city can only make things worse. Think of the consequences for those who live in villages and depend upon the already limited supply of water from the river for their cattle. Many cattle have already died and now the villagers themselves are in danger. You must alert your authorities in Dublin to the consequences." The Danish hydrologist droned on as Bartley urged him toward the door of the Irish Embassy.

"Yes, well I'm very glad you called in to let me know all this, Mr. Andersen. I will make sure that our foreign aid division in Dublin is informed of your concerns..." He made to open the door, but the Dane was not yet finished.

"And just because Emmanuel Gabi is back in his old job as Minister for the Environment does not mean he is not corrupt. He is not a man to be trusted. Certainly he does not care if the cattle herders starve in their villages because their cattle are dead. In any case he says they should be cleared out of the Guseni area so that it can be turned into a wildlife reserve. Hah! Can you believe that? Can you believe a man like Gabi is interested in wildlife? No, he has another quite different agenda and soon I will have all the evidence I need to expose him. Then you will see that you should have nothing to do with him or his canal. Gabi is only interested in money. He is not the kind of man who would think twice about breaking the law before allowing anyone or anything stand between himself and a fortune. If you help him now it could prove very embarrassing to your government when the true purpose of his plans becomes public."

Bartley placed a hand on the Dane's shoulder, gently easing him onward. "I'm sure the Prime Minister knew what he was doing when he reappointed Minister Gabi," he offered, "and as I said earlier, if he can trust him, then things can't be as bad as you fear. But don't worry. I will make sure Dublin is kept fully informed." They were standing outside, but Andersen once more insisted, "If you only knew what I have already learnt..." His voice tailed off seeing a distracted Bartley looking up at the darkening sky and obviously no longer paying attention. He sighed resignedly. "Well, thank you for seeing me today, Mr. Ryan. Goodbye."

"Mmm, yes, goodbye." Bartley returned from far away.

A guard opened the front security gate of the embassy compound allowing the Dane out onto the street. Bartley felt a drop of rain on his shoulder and looked up again. The oval blue escutcheon with a gold harp on the embassy wall caught his eye. "Ambasáid na hEireann – Embassy of Ireland" framed the edge in gold lettering. Not for the first time, he wondered how of all the Irish embassies throughout the world he had ended up here in the Embassy in Kutaba, one of the most desolate and underdeveloped countries of all of Africa? He groaned inwardly as an acute jolt of pain shot across his temple adding to the acid misery of his churning gut. His hangover was truly kicking in. Treading lightly, he returned to his office where the clutter of papers spilling out of his in-tray now prompted an involuntarily audible moan.

A sudden rattling against his window alerted him that the threatened storm had really begun in earnest. He could see the rain drumming down on the road outside, massive drops bouncing a muddy brown and all but obscuring those caught unawares and hurriedly scuttling for shelter into the nearest makeshift shops and shebeens. One single, lone figure trudged obliviously onward. Bartley could just make out his Danish visitor whose only concession to the downpour appeared to be a satchel raised quite ineffectively to cover his head. He disappeared from view behind a parked

Nissan 4x4. He did not notice, and Bartley did not see, the ragged, barefoot figure emerge from the rear of the car and begin to follow him.

****

The Embassy of Ireland in the Republic of Kutaba was one of Ireland's longest established embassies in Africa. For decades it had ticked over as a quiet, primarily symbolic, outpost serving the needs of the large Irish missionary population that had arrived to spread the Catholic catechism. It had been the kind of place where the demands made of its diplomatic staff were few and necessarily leisurely. Those were the days before e-mail when communications with HQ in Iveagh House in Dublin were via the weekly diplomatic pouch that took days before arriving. This relaxed pace had no doubt gone some way to compensate for the vicissitudes of life in a torrid climate where the most basic services were often lacking. Nowadays, of course, the workload had increased dramatically. One reason was the multiplication of visa applications from the myriads of Kutabans seeking to make their way permanently to a better life in Europe. For the most part they claimed to be visiting family or simply travelling as tourists - the latter a stretch for those on a verifiable income of at most a couple of thousand US dollars a year. However, another factor responsible for the growth of the workload was that in these millennial days the emphasis was constantly on the *business plan* and *going forward*. Every embassy was expected to assume a commercial, business oriented role. Even in a place like Kutaba it was expected that the Embassy should make a considerable effort to promote - or at least be seen to promote - and to facilitate Irish companies seeking to expand their overseas activities. Thus, although Bamgboshe, the dilapidated capital of Kutaba, might seem an unlikely location for investment opportunity, Bartley found he had to spend an inordinate amount of his day and sapping energy trying to prevent naïve Irish would-be entrepreneurs from being ripped off by Kutaban scam artists selling shares in non-existent diamond fields and other exotic rich-quick schemes. It was rather a thankless role, but such was his lot as *First Secretary,* the second in rank of the Embassy's three diplomatic officers.

The matter the Dane, Andersen, had raised fell outside Bartley's usual gamut of work. The canal to which he took exception was a part of a recent Irish Aid initiative seen to be a tentative first step that, if successful, could well lead to establishing a fully-fledged programme of development aid to Kutaba. This was something that the country's government was keen to encourage and which the Foreign Aid Division of the Irish Department of Foreign Affairs wanted to promote. But it had first to be demonstrated that Kutaba could utilize any aid offered effectively and efficiently. And that meant it had to be clear that no funds could possibly be diverted into the private bank accounts of local government ministers or senior officials. Although Bartley had no more than a nominal watching brief over the canal project, he was well aware that in Dublin there would be no welcome for the Danish expert's assessment. He also knew that his Department normally took a dim view of anyone reporting negative news.

His stomach rumbled. He had not noticed the Ambassador's wife standing just inside his door. "Bartley, the car..." she began with no introduction, "The new Mercedes, Bartley. You know it has been sitting at Customs in the rail yard for two weeks now. Adrian wants it cleared and delivered so we can check it before we fly out tomorrow night. It will be such a relief to have a decent car. The old Landcruiser may be fine for moving things around or for going up-country, but it is hardly appropriate for the Ambassador to be seen arriving at receptions in that old wreck with a dented front bonnet and the Irish flag hanging practically upside down. What with the cutbacks, you know Adrian had to fight very hard to get sanction from the Department for a new car. It really is quite unacceptable that it should still be sitting for so long in some yard somewhere downtown. God knows, anything could be happening to it."

Bartley peered blearily at Brigid Clendenning who by now had already retreated back into the corridor. He wondered whether it was the odour of stale alcohol infused with sweat which no doubt permeated his office that made her step back or perhaps had she heard his tummy rumble? Not that Brigid ever approached too near for, despite her years of honing the necessary social skills as her husband climbed the diplomatic ladder, she appeared totally unable to hide her spontaneous look of distaste whenever their paths crossed. Bartley could not fail to notice this, but surely it wasn't his fault that he had inherited his father's awkward, gangling frame? Admittedly, the comb-over that showered a permanent layer of white specks of scalp over the collar of his suit did nothing to recommend him. Rather the wispy straggle served only to emphasize the purplish blotches of his face. He knew those blotches well from daily encounters in the mirror and knew too that this morning they would have taken on an angry blaze while his eyes behind the grease-clouded lens of his glasses must appear almost to the point of bleeding. Focusing more clearly he could just make out the involuntary wrinkling of Brigid's nose.

Whenever Brigid or her husband raised the subject of cars there seemed always to be a hint of accusation that it was Bartley who was responsible for the damage to the ancient Landcruiser. True, it had been his misfortune to be the passenger when the bonnet was stove in. He had been returning from one of his infrequent trips up-country and was half dozing in the front passenger seat allowing Fumbe, the Embassy driver, to build up to 140 kph on the last long stretch of tarmac road before they hit the confusion of trucks, donkey carts, bicycles and the baggage-laden human tide that choked the approaches to the capital, Bamgboshe. A baboon had suddenly darted out onto the highway right in front of the car. Fumbe had reacted instantly with the instincts of one born and raised in a country where life is cheap, but material possessions zealously protected. He had therefore made no attempt to avoid the baboon by braking or swerving in a manner that would have endangered the car. He continued straight, pedal to the floor so that when the car's front bull bar made contact with the baboon there was sufficient momentum to hoist the unfortunate animal upward to rebound off the leading edge of the bonnet and then, with a further thump, crash off the side wing. Later, with the blood and the coarse baboon hair washed off, the damage was found to be more cosmetic than structural. Admittedly, the bonnet no longer locked securely and a piece of rope was attached to the front to prevent it yawning open. Also the baboon - while not quite impaling itself on the car's flagstand to which the national tricolour was attached on formal occasions – had with its second bounce landed on the metal pole and flattened it. It now jutted out dangerously on the horizontal.

Despite this, Ambassador Clendenning still insisted that Fumbe mount the flag whenever he travelled in the car. He seemed oblivious to the bizarre appearance or the potential hazard the flagstand presented. Indeed, on one occasion the Bulgarian Ambassador's wife had been forced to take to her considerably overburdened heels when, having just alighted from her own car and stooped to adjust herself, the Irish Landcruiser had come sweeping forward with its flagged spike like a drunken picador threatening to disembowel her. Doormen at the establishments the Ambassador graced with his presence now knew to keep well back when his car approached.

Despite himself, Bartley inwardly admitted to some sense of responsibility and guilt for the damage. The report he had given the Ambassador, and the one that he had sent to HQ in Iveagh House, indicated the speed at which Fumbe had been driving to have been a conservatively responsible 80 kph. Still, today, he could not help feeling more than a little annoyance that Brigid should come to him about liberating the new car from the Bamgboshe rail depot. After all he was the First Secretary, the number two in the Embassy, whereas such a task should fall to the next most junior officer, the Third Secretary, Michelle Finn, who had recently been drafted in from Dublin to help with the increased workload.

"Err, good morning, Brigid." His voice came out an involuntary strangulated croak. He considered perhaps rising from his seat, but then thought the better of it since Brigid had by now stationed herself well outside. "I think Michelle knows exactly what is happening. I'll have a word with her, see if she can move things along and get her to let you know."

"Well Bartley, Michelle is helping me prepare for the Ambassadors' spouses' monthly meeting and luncheon this afternoon. You know it is my turn to host and Michelle has been very useful. In fact, she is an invaluable help. So the Ambassador, Adrian, and I think it would be best if you were to take an interest in the car. A personal approach is the only way to get a result, so it really is a question of you going down to Customs this morning and having a word with whoever is in charge."

The last thing Bartley wanted was to go down to the Customs office in the rail station and stand around watching some official root round in his desk drawer pretending to be looking for an inky rubber stamp that would not be found until an appropriate *gift* had been proffered. Meanwhile, any hydration remaining in his system would be leaching slowly out in the humid heat. Also, he thought and not for the first time, since when had the Ambassador's wife been put on the official payroll and authorized to issue instructions? And this nonsense about *we* all the time, as if she had actually discussed this with the Ambassador. The fact was that Clendenning was more interested today in Bartley coming up with a draft programme for a planned visit by the Irish Foreign Minister than anything else. He would not take kindly to Bartley blaming his wife for not having some decent ideas to present.

And as for that other one - Michelle Finn? Bartley seethed that once again he should be landed with something he believed she should be doing. She seemed to have a knack of moving things in his direction while at the same time enhancing her standing with Adrian and Brigid. She had arrived only some months previously, shortly after the Clendennings, and had immediately made a favourable impression on each. Petite and slim, with long blonde hair and an array of fashionable and climatically appropriate power suits, Michelle was a mix of intense self-confident ambition and jolly hockey sticks enthusiasm that seemed to fit in well with the Clendenning's image of a promising junior officer. It was disappointing that her arrival had seen no appreciable let-up in the amount of paperwork daily swamping Bartley's desk.

Acknowledging the futility of arguing, he nodded, prompting a high-pitched yelp. He had forgotten the crick in his neck, but Brigid was already striding off and appeared not to notice. He lifted his phone to call Grace, the receptionist, to arrange that Fumbe drive him down to the Customs.

Although Fumbe was technically the Embassy's all-purpose driver, he was regarded de facto private chauffeur to the Clendennings, a fact impressed upon Bartley angrily at an early stage when he had sent Fumbe to collect a note at the Foreign Ministry without first making sure that neither of the 'first couple' needed him. It had been in the course of Clendenning's dressing down, after the driver had returned and Brigid was late arriving for her afternoon origami class at the Japanese Ambassador's residence that Bartley had first begun to address Clendenning formally as *Ambassador*. While the latter had insisted that the office staff call him "Adrian", and even Goodness, the office cleaner, referred to him as such, Bartley drew secret pleasure in using the title whenever they found themselves in disagreement. *Ambassador*, he felt, conveyed just the right amount of sardonic respect.

Thinking of Fumbe, he decided he should ask the driver if there was any recent gossip about Minister Emmanuel Gabi. Fumbe seemed always to have a take on every scandal and scandal-linked personage and Gabi, Bartley knew, was certainly a colorful character, but it did seem to be going too far for his Danish visitor to accuse him of corruption. Yes, there had been some scandal that had led to his resignation only a few months earlier, but was that not related to his alleged involvement with some married woman? Surely if the Prime Minister had reinstated him so soon, everything must be alright and above board?

TWO

It would be some while before Fumbe was free. Bartley shakily lifted his mug of now tepid coffee and took a tentative sip. It made him gag. Goodness, who was responsible both for cleaning the office and making coffee, had a knack of adding extra astringency to the brew. He placed the mug down again to the side of his desk carefully trying to avoid further spillage over his already sticky keyboard. Even at a distance the aroma of burnt coffee prompted another wave of nausea. He now imagined steel bands of tension cutting into his forehead. The heaviness in the air, the humidity and the heat only added to his hung-over discomfort.

Again, the hangover was entirely his own fault. He was barely back a week from leave in Ireland and already he had broken his resolve to cut down his alcohol intake to allow his liver some chance of regenerating itself sufficiently for him to begin taking anti-malaria medication. Going dry would alone be worth it if warded off a repetition of last June's fever. On that occasion he had come close to becoming one of the Embassy's own 'Death Abroad and Repatriation of Remains' cases. Sobriety, he also reasoned, would keep him more alert and better able to negotiate through his anticipated confrontations with Clendenning. It seemed that the latter, since presenting his ambassadorial credentials six months earlier, had done little other than find fault with his First Secretary. It had become a case of one bollicking after another.

Thoughts of the Ambassador served only to exacerbate his nausea and he tried to push them to the back of his mind to return to the task to hand. Leaning forward and squinting at his computer screen, he called up the draft outline of the programme for the Minister's intended visit. The Irish Foreign Minister, David Canavan, had decided to visit Africa and would be arriving in Kutaba in early November before continuing on to Uganda. His stay in Kutaba was scheduled to last two days and nights, but apart from the dates, no other detail had been worked out. All that Bartley had to go on was a presumption that the Minister might spend one day in and around Bamgboshe and another up-country. Getting any commitment from the Kutaban Foreign Ministry as to what meetings or events might be arranged for the Minister had so far proved impossible. Bartley had already called twice to the Ministry in this connection, each time making small talk for at least half an hour with the two secretaries while he waited in the European Director's outer office.

"You long time in Kutaba, Mr. Ryan?" they asked. "You like Kutaba? Much rain, yes?"
"One year – more - in Kutaba. Yes, I like – very friendly, warm not like my country. Yes, much rain, also like my home, but here more heavy." All too often in Kutaba he found himself responding in his own weird version of pidgin. He wondered why? Perhaps, subconsciously he had decided it might make him more intelligible to the local population. At least, he thought, he was not one of those who resorted to shouting.

After finally being ushered into the European Director's Office and being offered the obligatory cup of over-sweetened tea with condensed milk, the Director's preambular greeting never varied.

"Well, my dear Mr. Ryan, you know we sincerely appreciate that the Irish Foreign Minister intends to visit Kutaba. We attach considerable importance to our friendship with Ireland and to the special ties between our two countries." The Director's English, in contrast to that of his secretaries, was impeccable and his accent hinted more than a little of some expensive British public school. "Since the time your first Irish missionaries arrived in our country, Ireland has had a particularly fond place in our hearts. Why, even Prime Minister Okeke himself was educated by Irish priests. He is personally very much looking forward to the visit and to meeting with your Minister. Most unfortunately, however, his diary commitments - and indeed those of Foreign Minister Roble - for the dates in question are already very heavy and I still have to clarify with the PM's office when he might be available. It really is quite regrettable that until we do so there is little information that I can offer at this point."

Dublin was not yet asking to see a draft programme. Indeed, for such a visit it would be unprecedented to have a firm programme arranged at such an early stage, but Ambassador Clendenning was a lot less patient. He was about to head off on his first vacation. Six months precisely after arriving in Bamgboshe he was eligible for leave and he was sticking strictly to his entitlement. But he was insisting that Bartley present a full draft programme for his approval before he left. Bartley predicted he would demand more, undoubtedly fruitless, visits to the Foreign Ministry. He did not relish the prospect of further language mangling sessions with the cheerful secretaries, followed by more sweet tea and clichéd compliments from the Director. But now, an urgent, frantic, gurgling in his belly accompanied by a burning sensation in his bowels reminded him of the National Club's Sunday curry lunch that had preceded yesterday's extended drinking session.

Why was it in Africa, he wondered, no matter where expatriates congregated to drink and bemoan their lot, that their clubs invariably served a curry of dubious quality for Sunday lunch? The answer, of course, was that Sunday was when expatriates gave their domestic staff the day off and ate out. But the clubs, too, were short staffed on Sundays. Their cooks prepared a curry on Saturday night that could be laid out as a self-service buffet by a minimal number of waiters the following day. Bartley himself gave Sundays off to Aida, the tall, emaciated housekeeper whom he had inherited from his predecessor's predecessor. It was rumoured that she was related to some senior, but unidentified, government minister - which could explain why she had never been fired. Certainly, her housekeeping and cooking skills offered no reason for keeping her on.

On Sundays therefore, Bartley had little option other than the National Club's curry. He could, if he wanted, try the elaborate buffet lunch in the newly refurbished four star Bamgboshe Hilton ($50 plus tip, both in US currency), but he preferred the Club not just because it cost a fraction of the Hilton, but also because it offered a sense of camaraderie among those who turned up like himself, week in, week out, at the long wooden bar where they whiled away the afternoon when there was nothing else to do either in the dusty heat of the dry season or the depressing, grey light and battering rain of the wet season. It was in the Club that he usually met up with Otto, his corpulent counterpart in the Dutch Embassy.

The two had lunched together again yesterday and carried their plates of curry to the bar where they ordered a couple of cans of imported Heineken beer. They were still in their seats drinking locally brewed Hippo beer (the bar's supply of Heineken having run out after their first round) when, shortly before six o'clock, Fiona appeared. In her mid-thirties, tall with black, spiky hair and considerably overweight, Fiona was an Irish volunteer in a local primary school and depended largely on Bartley and Otto for a social life. Not technically a member of the Club, she never seemed to have a problem getting past security at the gate. Without asking, Bartley ordered her a beer and signed her in the guest book that lay at the end of the counter. He felt vaguely guilty that he had not earlier thought to phone to invite her to join them.

Fiona brought a renewed vigour to the drinking session and it was almost nine-thirty by the time Bartley realized he would have to go home if he was to sober up for work the next day. It was thus he who called a halt to the proceedings and headed out to his little Toyota Rav, which again somehow auto-piloted him around the potholes and muddy pools of Bamgboshe toward the colonial style bungalow that he called home.

The following day now, peering hazily at the screen in front of him and listening to the ominously continuing squirting in his belly, Bartley realized the curry could not be totally held to blame for the state of his innards. Local beer was notorious for its varying quality and even Hippo, considered by expatriates as generally reliable, could often contain a mismatch of yeasts and chemicals guaranteeing an explosive outcome. Those who complained of the proverbial *bad pint* of Guinness in Ireland had never tried a dodgy Hippo. He decided it was time to move toward the bathroom - slowly, avoiding sudden movement. Before he could put the thought into action his phone rang.

"Good morning, Bartley. It is Fumbe. Grace is telling me you want to go to rail station Customs depot. The Ambassador says I can drive you, but we go now. I must be back in one hour only. Mrs. Brigid is needing help with lunch. Ambassadors' wives they are coming today. I will bring the car now to you at the side door. It is raining very hard".

Feeling a veritable tsunami washing over his innards, Bartley promised to be down in a moment. But first, leaning slightly forward with his hand already tugging at his belt, he slipped out the door and down the corridor toward the loo. He emerged some five minutes later, purged for the moment at least, and ready for whatever the rest of the morning might throw at him.
Or so he thought.

THREE

The rain had indeed started again in earnest as Bartley came out the side door of the Embassy where Fumbe was parked waiting for him. A torrent of water was flowing past, swirling around the car as he tried to step over. He did not quite make it and his right foot landed in the water filling his shoe with dark, putrefying silt. He hauled himself into his seat with a curse. Inside, he was met by a blast of chill air from the air conditioner that Fumbe had turned up full in an effort to clear the fogging windscreen. He shivered, pulled off his shoe and emptied it onto the rubber mat as Fumbe pulled forward and through the gate out onto the street. Here, the road from the boundary wall of the Embassy as far as the butcher's shop opposite was submerged in a pool of water though which two women of indefinable age were trudging, their backs bent to accommodate their loads of massive bundles of firewood. Their bright tie-die dresses were already trailing in the flood and Fumbe slowed so as not to splash them. At that same moment the green Nissan Pathfinder that had earlier been parked on the street abruptly pulled out and raced down toward them. The women halted. One turned her laden back against the brown wave the car must throw up, but the other attempted to dash across to the dry side of the road. She just about made it when she slipped shedding her load. The Nissan swerved to avoid her but crashed into the wood with a crunching wallop that sent branches flying over the bonnet. It then slewed to a halt sideways across the road.

The driver and his passenger, both in army uniform, got out to inspect the damage. From where Bartley sat he guessed there should be little or none. But that seemed to do little to calm the passenger, obviously an officer, whom he could see shouting as the woman tried to pick herself up.

Suddenly his foot lashed out and he landed a brutal kick to her side sending her sprawling back down. He then motioned to his driver and made to get back in his car, but stopped first to stare over at Bartley still waiting to get out on the street. Bartley felt uncomfortable under a lingering scowl that was all the more threatening for a long blue scar disfiguring one whole side of the soldier's face.

"Crazy man! See how these soldiers beat our people." hissed Fumbe, but Bartley did not respond, as much unnerved by the angry glower as by the soldier's act of brutality.

The woman was off the ground and with her companion was stooping to gather up her scattered load. They did so wordlessly with an air of resignation. Not for the first time, Bartley wondered how he would have survived if circumstances had been different and he had been born a Kutaban? He could not imagine that he could ever hack it as a peasant. The rain lashed down even more heavily. It battered on the roof drowning out the roar of the air-conditioner still running full blast. Huge drops rattled machine-gun-like off the bonnet forming an opaque curtain of water beyond which the road ahead was all but invisible.

The downpour eased just a little by the time they reached the rail station and drove past its grand main entrance. Despite the building's state of dilapidation it was still rather impressive, although somewhat out of place. The façade boasted solid stone blocks with tall columns and steps rising to a high, covered porch. It had been designed by some colonial architect with a sense of grandeur that he had doubtlessly been unable to indulge in his home country. But if its style was already at odds with its location even as it was being built, it was even more so now. A rickety row of open stalls and shops had been tacked together on either side and these somehow lent it an air of being uncomfortable, even embarrassed, by its shabby, low class neighbours. Almost without exception, the shops specialized in the sale of cheap suitcases and bags. This was the part of town to which everyone came to buy luggage, no doubt a consequence of the station having been the main transport hub in the old days. Other streets in town were similarly known as the place to go for any one particular type of goods. Thus, for example, there was one street selling nothing but paint and paint products, another car tires, another plastic buckets and containers. Before going on leave, Bartley had come down to the station and bought his mother a Louis Vuitton bag. In trying to haggle down the price, he had insisted to the shopkeeper that they both knew the bag was fake and not a real Vuitton. The shopkeeper had immediately countered that it was, however, a *genuine* fake. They had settled on a price of forty American dollars, way too much, as Bartley well knew.

They skirted round the row of shops and turned into a narrower street, deeply cratered by heavy trucks constantly making their way in and out of the rail yard. Here and there isolated islands of tarmacadam were all that remained of the original road surface. Another 100 metres along, they came to a barrier formed by a long slender tree trunk resting on an oil drum at one end with a rope to raise it tethered to a tall post at the other. A red-painted cargo container stood on concrete blocks alongside the barrier. As they drove up a guard stuck his head out through an opening cut into the side of the container. Seeing the car, he hurried through the rain with an AK47 under his arm to the driver's window where Fumbe explained their business. Bartley handed over his diplomatic ID and the guard looked closely at the photo and then at Bartley before handing it back to Fumbe. He walked round to the front and shouted out the car registration number in the direction of the container, presumably to a more senior colleague inside who did not wish to get wet and who was entering the details into some form of log book. The guard then moved over to the post and started to pull on the rope, raising the makeshift barrier.

The rail yard into which they drove was a confusion of ancient brick and mud-plaster buildings to which a hotchpotch of extensions, annexes and sheds had been added in response to need at different times. Beyond them was a vast corral of stacked containers that had been trundled slowly and cumbersomely by train up from the coast. Fumbe navigated his way toward one of the larger buildings that bore signs of recent whitewashing. Unfortunately, if the fresh paint had been applied in an attempt to consolidate or to bind together the crumbling plaster, it had failed and the walls themselves looked in danger of imminent disintegration. Bartley sighed. This was where he had already spent many fruitless hours on too many occasions, waiting to be dealt with and patiently trying to comply with the conflicting demands of Kutaban bureaucracy while interpreting the hinted suggestions of some informal gift for the various officials. He had thought that Michelle's arrival would spare his ever having to return, but here he was again.

He hoped a copy of the note from the Foreign Ministry confirming the Irish Embassy's entitlement to take duty free delivery of a car had at last made it this far The Ministry claimed the note had been delivered to Customs promptly by hand by one of its drivers well over a week earlier. But even if Customs had received it, the note still had to be collated with a file of other papers – the bill of lading, the statement of conformity, specifications of manufacture, invoices and proofs of ownership and so on. This file would have been placed at random in any one of a number of steel cabinets stuffed full of similar buff folders and yellowing documents. If the file could be located - meaning if Bartley made someone's effort worthwhile - the question would then arise of whether the responsible official could be persuaded to agree that all the different bits of paper were in order and that none was missing.

At the door of the building a tall, smiling man in a blue shirt with dark blue epaulettes recognized the dented bonnet of the Landcruiser pulling up. As Bartley climbed out and sidestepped a puddle to approach, he held out his hand in greeting.

"Mr. Bartley, dear friend, how is the Irish? You are welcome."
"Officer Saleh." Bartley nodded and they shook hands, changing grip after the first touch to grasp palms in the local style – the *gunslinger* handshake as Bartley liked to think of it.

"Come in, Mr. Bartley", he repeated, "I have been expecting you. Yes I think everything is *almost* in order for your car. I will send my man to check the file. Please, seat. I will send him. But excuse me, first I have some work I must finish"

Bartley's shoulders dropped as if reflecting his inner feelings of despair. He had noted the emphasis on *almost*. It sounded like there might be one or more palms still waiting to be greased.

The smiling official took his seat behind a battered metal desk and began to tap loudly with two fingers on a large typewriter while Bartley sat in silence on a hard wooden chair. He wondered was there anywhere else in the world that still used typewriters? Or were they employed in Kutaba simply to torture him with each strike of the keyboard resonating in his still pounding head? After five minutes, the official reached forward to the top of the machine and, with a jerk that caused a whirring sound against the roller, pulled out the paper.

He was in the process of separating the top sheet from the blue carbon copies underneath when the door of the office was flung open. A tall fair-haired figure, head bowed to avoid hitting it on the doorframe, strode in.

"Ya little fucker, Saleh, where's my goddam pipes?" The accent was drawling American, John Wayne as a blonde Marlboro man.

The official leapt to his feet and retreated behind his chair.

"Sir, I am sorry. They are not yet here."

"Of course they're fucking here. Y'all just too fucking incompetent to get your shit together to find 'em. You and me, we jus' going out now have a look-see till we find them. Right?"

The American only now noticed Bartley.

"Is this little bastard givin' you the run-around too? Don't take it. Ya need show these guys who's boss. C'mon, Saleh, get your ass outta there."

"Mr. Bartley, please wait." The official was shaking. "I must go, but I will come back very soon. Also my man will be coming back with all papers that you need."

Bartley could only nod as Saleh followed the American out. He sat, alone, occasionally looking at his watch, but there was no sign of the officer or his minion's return. Finally, there was a light tap on the open door and Fumbe stepped in.

"Mr. Bartley, already it is late. I must be going to Madame Brigid in the Residence for the lunch. I am sorry if you cannot come now. Perhaps you can take a taxi to the Embassy. There are many taxis in front of the station."

"Alright, Fumbe, that's fine. I don't know when this guy Saleh will be back. Some big American just barged in and pulled him out."

"Ah, yes. I saw a big man, he looks American. He has soldiers with him and the people here looked frightened when he came. They are still here."

"Alright, Fumbe, you better head off. I might call a friend to see if he can pick me up."

The rain had stopped and a blistering sun had come out as Bartley finally emerged from the Customs office and made his way on foot around the steaming puddles toward the front barrier. Saleh had eventually returned, but after some rooting around in various drawers and cabinets announced that the rubber stamp needed for the final clearance had gone missing. Could Bartley return tomorrow?

It was almost one o'clock and Bartley had been sitting on a bum-numbing chair for more than two wasted hours. In truth, he had all along accepted the inevitability that he would not be taking possession of the Mercedes anytime today. He had acknowledged as much when he had called Otto to suggest lunch at the Club and his friend had agreed to collect him. As he made his way to the gate there was no sign of the bullying American or his military companions, but he could see the Dutchman's silver BMW X5 parked outside. He climbed into the back alongside Otto. The car still smelt expensively of new leather.

"So, Bart my Irish friend, apart from an entertaining morning down here, what have you been up?" Otto asked with a grin that turned at once into a frown upon catching sight of the reddish mud oozing from Bartley's shoes onto his new beige carpet.

"Jeez, the floor..."

Seeing Otto staring at his shoes Bartley quickly changed the subject, "I hear Emmanuel Gabi is back in government."

"Yes, he's back. It seems all is forgiven. He's too powerful for the PM to leave out in the cold. He's got back his old job as Minister for the Environment and Natural Resources, which is good news."

Bartley looked quizzically at his friend. "So how is that good news? I've heard it suggested that he is corrupt?"

"Really? That's absurd." Otto waved his hand dismissively with a knowing smile, the carpet already forgotten.

Mondays were usually quiet inside the Club. The emergence of the sun had already encouraged the usual gaggle of white expatriate wives and their toddler children to congregate on the plastic loungers and chairs set out on a threadbare lawn around the ancient swimming pool with its faded, blue, cracked tiling. Dotted among them was a sprinkling of wealthy local matrons wearing chunky gold earrings and necklaces, sipping Pepsis. A waiter was delivering plates of chips to one of the groups and children came screaming in, seagull-like, to snatch a chip and then run off with further yelling to splash in the shallow end of the pool. Several nannies in less flamboyant clothing scuttled round trying to retain some measure of control.

Bartley and Otto circled the edge of the pool and headed toward the main Club dining room. One particularly boisterous urchin wielding a long fat chip smothered in ketchup collided into Otto's stocky frame. The chip dropped from his hand, glancing off the cuff of Otto's sleeve, leaving a red smear. The child stopped and briefly surveyed the chip on the ground. Then, overcoming his surprise, he simply pirouetted round and flew back to swoop down on a replacement. Otto looked at his soiled cuff and at the fleeing culprit's back making a visible effort not to chase after him and dump him in the deep end before remonstrating with his matronly mother.

Benjamin, the Club's ancient head waiter offered a half bow to the pair as they entered. He took in first the sauce Otto was still trying to dab off his sleeve with a large white handkerchief and then Bartley's mud-caked shoes. The Club insisted on a high, if somewhat dated, dress code within the dining room and bar. Benjamin had been serving here for almost forty years and retained fond memories of the style and formality of the old colonial days. He considered himself the guardian of what remained of those standards. But while Bartley and Otto might not have quite made the cut some decades earlier, they were both wearing jackets and ties which sufficed to gain entrance in these modern times. Besides, these two were Monday regulars and the Dutchman was a generous tipper. For their part, the two appreciated the personal service provided by the shuffling old boy in his immaculately white but frayed jacket and black bow tie.

"Sirs, beer?" the latter asked, slipping a chair under Otto's bulk while leaving Bartley to settle himself opposite at the corner table to which he had shown them.

"I don't suppose you have any Heineken stashed away here, have you Benjamin?"

"Sir, sorry – the Heineken done finish. Perhaps next week the container is coming. Sirs would like Hippo?"

Bartley and Otto looked at each other. Supplies of Heineken and other imported 'luxuries' often ran out, but today each of them was all too wary of another one-on-one session with Hippo beer. Even Otto, with his formidable digestive capabilities, had been suffering throughout the morning after yesterday's lunchtime-to-evening session.

"No Benjamin, thank you. I think a couple of your mega gins should nail it for us today. And two fillet steaks. Make sure you tell the cook just to slide them on and off the skillet. I think we need lots of fresh blood today to go with the gin."

Otto liked to take control, but Bartley did not mind. He guessed that this habit of Otto's had been acquired along with his perfect, American-accented, English when he had served as a junior in Washington. He did, however, regret Otto's insistence on the steak being served raw. There was little difference between a fillet steak and any other kind of steak in

Bamgboshe. The meat was all poorly butchered, essentially hacked off the carcass in chunks and consumed 'fresh', in other words as rapidly as possible before it went off. The concept of hanging meat to age and tenderize simply did not exist here and even if it did, this would be near impossible without a constant supply of electricity and a cool room to prevent it turning green. However, the worst of it all was not the tough sinewy texture, but rather the fact that it played host to a whole range of parasites potentially lethal to someone of Bartley's constitution. Like most foreigners therefore, he preferred his steak thoroughly incinerated to a point where it resembled crisped charcoal.

They were finishing their steaks, or rather Otto was forking down his last gory mouthful while Bartley's fillet showed evidence of no more than several cautious incisions, when the third round of large Gordon's was delivered. Otto was in high spirits resulting from the pleasing horizon afforded by the imminent and final departure of his Ambassador. He was looking forward to a period of being his own boss until a successor arrived.
"I reckon you're also looking forward to a spell with your Ambassador out of town?" he asked.
"Yes, I guess so..." Bartley answered with a somewhat preoccupied air.
"What do you mean *I guess so*? What's up with you?"
"Nothing, I was just thinking I really don't have that much to complain about." Otto looked at him sceptically and he continued, "It's just when I think of the kind of life we have and what some of these Kutabans have to put up with. Well, take this morning, for instance..." and he proceeded to recount the incident of the army officer and the woman on the ground as he kicked her.
"An army officer, you say, with a scar running down his face like so?" Otto demonstrated as Bartley finished. "That sounds like Major Mbuta. He's Emmanuel Gabi's sidekick. It's funny you should run into him since we were talking about Gabi earlier."

Bartley's phone rang at that moment before Otto could elaborate.

"Bartley, it's Michelle. Where are you?"

"Michelle, hi, I'm having lunch, err, with a contact." Otto looked over at this last and raised his glass in a toast.

"Give her my love," he whispered, "and tell her she's welcome to my teepee anytime."

"Shhh," Bartley covered the mouthpiece and shook his head. Otto grinned and quaffed his gin.

"So what's up Michelle?"

"Adrian has been looking for you for ages and told me to find you. He wants to know what you've done this morning about the Minister's visit."

"Hell, I spent the whole morning down at Customs on Brigid's orders trying to liberate his car and I could hardly do two things at once, could I?" He found Michelle's tone somewhat exasperatingly self-righteous. "So how was Brigid's lunch for the ladies? I hope you enjoyed it?" He could not help throwing this in.

"It was very successful," Michelle sniffed, "but Adrian wants you back in the office immediately."

"Alright, alright, tell him I'm on my way."

As Bartley put away his phone, Otto chuckled.

"Trouble back at the ranch?" he grinned, "If you need to go, I'll pay here and settle up with you later."

"Thanks, I'd better run," Bartley agreed, realizing even as he did so that allowing Otto to pay the bill would involve an unjustifiably generous tip that he could otherwise have avoided.

He considered his still half-full glass of gin, but decided it wiser to leave it. Instead, he headed off to the scrimmage of taxi drivers congregated outside the Club's front gateway. The drivers surrounded Bartley as he emerged on the street, each insisting he had the most modern and comfortable vehicle at a cheap price. Bartley held out his hands in an attempt as much to steady himself against the effects of lunchtime gin as to gain some control over the noisy confusion.

"Air conditioning, who has air conditioning?" he shouted.

One short, lean driver had knifed forward between his colleagues and come right up to within inches of Bartley's face.

"Sir, me. Clean car. Radio. Air condition. This car." He pointed down the line of battered, blue painted taxis, guiding Bartley over to one while the other drivers protested. The car was indistinguishable from the other wrecks alongside. It was stifling hot inside with protective plastic seat covers that scorched Bartley's back as he settled in.

"Air conditioning?" he asked again. The driver had already started the engine and was pulling out onto the road. He leaned forward picking something off the floor on the passenger side, then half-turned to Bartley offering him both a grin and a chrome handle to wind down the window. "Air condition, sir."

There was no point complaining. This was Kutaba where you had to make do with what life offered you. But sometimes it was hard to reconcile the cheeky cheerfulness of someone like this taxi driver and the gratuitous cruelty of someone like the army officer he now knew to be Major Mbuta, friend of Minister Emmanuel Gabi.

FOUR

As a rule the Embassy's diplomatic staff came in by the back door rather than go through reception running a gauntlet of waiting visa applicants. The danger was that whenever a white face passed through, some impatiently irate supplicant would pounce. Michelle was sitting in the little back kitchen and saw Bartley quietly slipping in. She called his name but he did not stop. She sighed, knowing he expected her to follow him.

She watched him plonk down behind his desk. Sniffing the odour of gin, she took in his dandruff flecked collar and resolved to make no effort to go easy on him. To date he had failed to offer sympathy or support on any of the occasions she had felt slighted or belittled by Clendenning or his wife. Not for the first time in dealing with Bartley, she surprised herself by adopting a school-mistress-telling-off-errant-pupil demeanor.

"Adrian left just a few minutes ago. He told me to tell you he couldn't wait any longer for you to come back. He's not happy with your long lunch breaks and says you should in future tell him where you're going whenever you leave the Embassy.
"He was expecting you would have a draft programme for the Minister's visit to show him before he went out and he wants us both to meet him at nine tomorrow morning. You're to have a draft ready for us to run through. He also has a number of other things he wants to discuss before he goes on leave."

The leery frown with which this news was received showed that she had succeeded once again in getting his back up. There seemed to be little possibility of their ever having an easy-going relationship unless, of course, she might possibly join his coterie of hard drinking buddies. No chance of that, she thought as he waved her away with a curt *Thank you.*

Bartley sighed as she closed the door. It wasn't Michelle's fault that he had to try putting together a programme for the Minister's visit knowing that any such effort at this stage was entirely futile. The Kutaban Foreign Ministry was unlikely to agree or confirm any proposals until closer to the Minister's arrival and even then most of the detail would not be finalized until the very last minute. He had tried patiently to explain this to the Ambassador: the mindset of Kutabans simply did not lend itself to worrying unnecessarily about events that might or might not take place at some future date; it was difficult enough to deal with today.

Clendenning had bristled when Bartley told him. He accused him of simply making excuses to cover for his own lazy incompetence. In the Ambassador's mind it was totally inconceivable that the Kutabans would not wish sit down immediately to copper-fasten every last detail. Still, he was slowly coming to the realization that he had received more courtesy and consideration in his previous postings. Could it be that the Kutaban Foreign Ministry did not after all feel bound by certain standards of civilized behaviour? Or was it that his First Secretary was somehow complicit in a plot to undermine him when the Minister arrived? He turned apoplectic when Bartley unwisely protested it was *fucking outrageous* to suggest there was any such possibility. In the end of course, he had forced Bartley to apologize for his language and get on with the job.

What Bartley had put together was a rough itinerary for the Minister's visit. If necessary he could pass it off as something he had dutifully worked out with the Foreign Ministry. Since Ministerial visits invariably followed a set formula, the visit to Kutaba was unlikely to be too much different. When the Kutabans did finally get their act together, he would present any changes they might suggest as being the result of unforeseen circumstance. Meanwhile, he knew the Kutaban Protocol people would be more than happy to allow him get on with the donkey work, aware that when it came to the crunch they would do whatever the hell they wanted. The Protocol Service would have it in mind too that if the Embassy took responsibility at this stage for arranging the logistics of the visit, it should also end up paying the costs, thus saving them from being out of pocket.

Just to be on the safe side Bartley decided to send a copy of his draft to the Ministry that afternoon. It did not matter the Ministry would pay it no heed, but it would put him in a better position when he met Clendenning in the morning to say he and the Ministry had already progressed to *sharing a common draft.*

But two hours later he was struggling to deliver the draft. First, every attempt to e-mail the document through to the European Director's office had encountered a mail service error message saying the address was unobtainable. He had then asked Grace to fax it through. No sooner, unfortunately, had the covering page been transmitted than the power went off. There was a problem starting the generator and when the electricity finally did come on, it turned out all lines through the local exchange were engaged or out of order.

"Forget it, but thanks, Grace. We're wasting our time for the moment. It's probably better you get back to the reception desk. If you try again later, you might be lucky and get a line out."

"Inshallah," she had muttered with little enthusiasm.

Not Inshallah, more a case of AWA, Bartley thought blasphemously, *"Africa Wins Again."*

He scarcely had time to sit down again when Grace called to say Fiona was in reception and wished to see him. He said to let her through and a few moments later she breezed into his room.

"Really, Bartley", she began, "what kind of Embassy is this? I've been in reception for over ten minutes and there was no-one there behind the counter. What if I were an asylum seeker or an Irish citizen with the police waiting to arrest me and pull me off to some hellhole prison? You guys wouldn't have helped. You wouldn't even know I'd been here. Some bloody consular service this is."

Bartley looked at Fiona. He could hardly imagine any local policeman wanting to take on a woman of Fiona's size. Her punk haircut alone would frighten off any Kutaban policeman who would probably mistake her for some evil juju priestess. Despite himself and the frustrations of the day, he smiled, cheered by her arrival.

"But I see obviously that you are not being pursued by any policeman, so what can I do for you, Ms. Scott, now that you are here?" he asked.
"Well, what about a new passport? I've lost the old one. Or had it stolen. Or maybe I am about to sell it. Seriously Bartley, I've had a wretched day. Another of the girls in my class is pregnant. She's only thirteen, for God's sake. And another one was crying because her father is marrying her off and she won't be coming to school anymore. I'm pissed off and just need a drink and thought you might be interested?"

He was not. In fact, the last thing he needed was another drinking session. He felt like going home and collapsing onto his sofa to sleep off lunch. On the other hand, Fiona was a friend, one of the few he had in this town. She was good company and he felt he could be open and let down his guard when she was around. It worried him only slightly that she had more than once hinted she might like to take their friendship somewhat further, but he believed he had successfully flagged that this was not an option. Although he was fully aware he was no alpha male, and certainly his prospects for any other romantic liaison in Bamgboshe were just about zero, he still lived in hope that someday some newly arrived long legged blonde might arrive in the Swedish Embassy and fall instantly in love with him. Meanwhile, just as he much enjoyed Otto's company, so too he enjoyed Fiona's. At this very moment he welcomed her ability to distract him from the overwhelming nuisances of the day.

Ruling out another session in the Club or a visit to one of the bawdy local drinking shebeens, he proposed they head back to his house where Aida, having finished her token housekeeping duties for the day, would have left out some food. His home promised no great luxury, but at least it did offer some peace and quiet.

Fiona agreed with a degree of eagerness that made Bartley wonder for a moment whether it would be necessary perhaps to be more specific about the precise nature of their friendship as he saw it.

They arrived at the house some half an hour later. It was a former colonial officer's bungalow, situated near the old town centre not far from the Embassy, but the early evening traffic delayed them. They stopped in front of the entrance, Bartley in his Toyota Rav and Fiona behind him in her decrepit Suzuki Vitara, waiting for the watchman to waken to their arrival and open the gate. The street might sometime long ago have been quite attractively lined with neat bungalows and elegant villas built for colonial civil servants and merchants, but nowadays Bartley's was one of the few to survive. True, most of the front garden had been removed and a shop selling refrigerators and air conditioning units had been built on the site. At least the shop partly shielded the house from the constant blare and rumble of passing traffic on the busy road outside. It lay to the left of Bartley's gate while to the right was an oriental carpet shop, its wares displayed in a haphazard jumble behind a large dusty window. A narrow driveway led between the two shops before widening into a parking space big enough for three or four cars. White paint peeled off the walls of the bungalow which had a narrow covered verandah running the length of its front. The verandah was bordered by a wooden balustrade to which someone had nailed a series of wooden uprights to support wire mesh netting to keep out mosquitoes. A matching screen door at the top of several steps sat off to the nearer end.

Bartley stepped out of his car and felt his shoes gluing into soft mud. One reason he liked this house was because a line of tall trees planted to the rear of the refrigerator shop shaded his front from the worst of the sun and kept the verandah comparatively cool. The downside, however, was that the sun did not penetrate long enough to burn off the surface rainwater, a problem exacerbated by the driveway being slightly lower than street-level and thus allowing excess water from the main road to empty into his parking area. Fiona was behind Bartley as he mounted the steps and opened the screen door. Despite wearing open sandals, she seemed not the least bothered by the greasy conditions underfoot.

As they entered through a second door directly into the living room, Bartley peeled off his jacket, draped it over the end of a battered sofa. A pile of books was propped under one corner where it was missing a leg. He made straight for the kitchen. Aida had left two pots sitting on top of the stove, one with boiled rice and the other containing a brown stew of unidentifiable meat. He lit a flame under the stew as Fiona opened a cupboard and delved into a case of red wine, one of the few survivors of a large consignment that Bartley had shipped down with his belongings from Dublin. She lifted out a bottle and waved it at him, seeking his permission.

"Sure, let's try it," he agreed. "That case seems better than the last one where half the bottles were corked, so better drink it before it also goes off. You open the bottle while I heat up Aida's version of Babette's Feast."

They sat down at a table off to the side of the living room. Bartley had ladled some of the heated stew over cold rice onto two plates and they both picked at it halfheartedly. The wine turned out considerably better than the food. This was one bottle at least that had not yet turned to vinegar. While they ate, Fiona recounted her day at school. It had begun with a bad tempered argument with her principal over the conduct of a couple of male teachers. Bartley listened as Fiona's sense of anger and frustration brought back to mind some of his own feelings from that morning.

"...and so these teachers are picking up the girls after school and telling them that if they want good grades that they have to show some *appreciation,* if you know what I mean?" Fiona tailed off. "Right, Bartley?"

"Yeah, they have to fuck them. It's Kutaba, what else can you expect?"

"Christ Bartley, what a thing to say... What's wrong with you?"

"Sorry, it just hasn't been a great day for me either. Bad enough that I had a hangover this morning, but then I have had both the Ambassador and Brigid, that bloody wife of his, on my case about one thing or another all day. Clendenning's not an easy guy to keep happy. Even before he came here I heard he had a reputation in the Department of Foreign Affairs for having a foul temper and for manic mood swings. But, god, he's even worse than I expected. Though I guess it isn't just him. You know you talk about your girls, but there's shit everywhere here. Today, for example, I saw a senior officer of Kutaba's elite army just kicking a defenceless woman when she was lying on the ground. No, I guess it's not only your teachers that are fucking people around. It didn't help that I wasted a few hours in bloody customs stupidly expecting the guys to do their job when I should have known they were all just waiting for a backhander. Some bastard American came in and gave them hell, but you just have to wonder if it really is their fault they won't do their work until they get a bribe. It's a messed up country. I really can't say whose fault it is, but definitely those of us from the so-called developed world aren't totally without blame."

They both fell silent. They had finished picking at their plates of unappetizing stew. Bartley stood up, shook his head.

"Let's move out to the verandah. It's cooler out there." He lifted the bottle of wine to eye level and poured what remained into their glasses. Asking Fiona to carry these outside, he returned to the kitchen with the empty to dig out a second bottle.

When he came out, Fiona was already sitting back on one of the two ancient steamer chairs that Bartley had inherited with the house. The wine glasses stood on a low table between them alongside a rather soiled looking packet of Rothmans cigarettes. On the ground sat two citronella candles that she had lighted as a deterrent to any mosquitoes that might slip through the numerous tears in the wire netting.

"I brought you a present", she nodded toward the Rothmans packet as Bartley raised his eyebrows and sat down. "Fancy a wrap?" she asked.

He knew that Fiona was an avid devotee of marijuana, locally known as dagga, and that Kutaba had a reputation for growing some of the finest, a fact that may well have influenced her choice of destination as volunteer. She was apparently on sufficiently friendly terms with one of the cigarette sellers who traded from a stall in front of the Hilton to know that these all ran an under-the-counter trade in ready rolled marijuana cigarettes, appropriately called "wraps". He had shared a wrap with Fiona on several previous occasions and rather enjoyed the sensation, so unlike the joints of tobacco lightly sprinkled with low grade cannabis he had smoked in his university days.

Fiona extracted a tightly rolled cigarette out of the carton and lighted it. The twist of paper at the end flared momentarily as she took a first, long drag. She settled back and took a couple more puffs before handing it to Bartley.

"So tell me more about the Ambassador. You were saying that he has a bad rep?" Fiona sensed the possibility of juicy, insider gossip. She blew out some last remaining smoke.

"Well, I guess he hasn't liked me from the start." Bartley paused at the recollection of their first meeting at Bamgboshe airport. The Ambassador had been unable to hide his distaste upon being welcomed by his First Secretary in a soiled light blue seersucker suit. He had bought it as part of his new wardrobe in preparation for his African posting. It seemed like a good idea at the time and the department store assistant, who had probably never been further south than Mallorca, had assured him that it would be perfect for a tropical climate. Furthermore, it was guaranteed to keep its shape without ironing even after washing. Perhaps if Fiona or some other woman had been on hand, he might have been better advised, but as it was, the suit in which he had greeted his new Ambassador hung limp and rumpled off his stooped, skinny frame. His efforts to sponge off various stains had not helped. Indeed, he reflected ruefully and not for the first time today, his overall appearance - his unkempt comb-over of wispy blonde hair and blotchy forehead – left much to be desired. He really should do something about his appearance, but wasn't sure where to begin.

"He's always had a reputation for being a bit of a flake," he continued, "but that can fairly much go with the territory in Foreign Affairs. It doesn't help of course that he is sixty-three and that Bamgboshe will be his last posting. I heard he was really disappointed to land up here. It's only four years ago that he first became Ambassador – in Foreign Affairs it's what we call getting the "Cardinal's Hat". He got Portugal, but usually you wouldn't get a cushy post like Lisbon for your first Hat. Posts like that as a rule go to experienced Ambassadors who have been round the block and are now being put out to grass. Lisbon was a surprise and I guess he thought he could only go up after that. Being told he was being sent here to Bamgboshe apparently came as a bit of a shock. I heard he flew home from Lisbon when he was given the news and that he tried to get in to see the Minister about it."

Fiona inhaled deeply and handed him the wrap.

"He's an awkward man who expects everything to go just as he expects it. Kutaba is the last place he should be. He doesn't realize that you need to go with the system here rather than fight it. For example, he's already demanding that the Kutaban Foreign Ministry agree a full programme for our Minister's visit in November when anyone else could tell him that the Kutabans don't do this sort of thing until the last minute. Just to keep him happy until he goes on leave, I have to invent some nonsense that's a complete waste of my time."

"Hey, if your Minister's coming, how about arranging for him to visit my school?" Fiona imagined herself hosting the Irish Foreign Minister. It would be a story to tell back home. "After all," she added to bolster her case, "I'm the only Irish volunteer left in Bamgboshe. And I've been teaching some of the kids Irish dancing. We could put on a little show?"

"Yeah, maybe," Bartley was non-committal and they both fell silent.

They ended up smoking two wraps and emptying the second bottle of wine. The smell of dagga mixed with the fumes of citronella. There was a gentle wind stirring the tops of the trees that reached down to cool the verandah, causing the candles occasionally to splutter.

Bartley yawned. It had been a wearing day and he guessed that the wraps on top of the wine together with all that gin at lunchtime had gotten the better of him. "I think I'll head off to bed," he stood up and stretched out his arms. "I have to face Clendenning first thing in the morning."

"Bartley, do you want me to stay?" Fiona blurted it out, startling him. He hesitated. She was a friend, a good friend, but when would she realize he had no wish to sleep with her? Much as he liked her, he just didn't fancy her. He could be sure her sudden offer was not entirely a spontaneous reaction to drugs and alcohol. It might, after all, be necessary to reiterate more bluntly the nature of their relationship as he saw it. But not tonight.

"Eh, I don't know, Fiona. I mean sorry. It's going to be tough enough tomorrow and I really do need to get some sleep."

"Yeah, sure me too, I have a big day tomorrow." Fiona tried to cover her embarrassment. "We have some bigwig Minister for the Environment visiting the school to launch the Green Schools Initiative I've been working on."

"Not Minister Gabi?"
"Yeah, that's the one." She finished off what remained of her glass and stood up. She rocked back, slightly unsteady on her feet and groped in a

bag for her car key. "But, don't forget what I said about your Minister visiting my school."

It took Bartley a moment to register that she was speaking about the Irish Foreign Minister and not Gabi. "OK, maybe it would be a good idea," he offered, but his mind was on the coincidence of Gabi's name coming up yet again.

Fiona had found her key and looked around, seeing the Rothmans pack on the table. "Best leave those here in case I'm stopped on my way home." She giggled, her earlier embarrassment already forgotten. She leaned forward, half stumbling to offer a kiss. She missed his cheek and landed instead on the side of his forehead. She giggled again more loudly.

Bartley watched her climb into her Suzuki and spend the next few minutes executing a clumsy multi-point turn before managing to get the car facing in the direction of the gate at the far end of the drive where the watchman stood patiently waiting.

When she was gone, he picked the debris off the table and carried it inside. He wondered for a moment what to do with the Rothmans pack. On his way to the kitchen he stopped to slip it into a used manila envelope that he saw lying on the sofa. He then wedged the envelope between some books on his shelf. He emptied the ashtray in the bin by the sink, yawned and stumbled off to bed.

He stretched out under the covers. Yes, he had better get some rest before meeting with Clendenning in a few hours' time. As he drifted off into unconsciousness he wondered if perhaps he should feel a little sympathy for the Ambassador. After all it must have been a severe shock to learn he was swopping Portugal for Kutaba: Bamgboshe was no Lisbon and the muddy red Bamgboshe River that flowed full at this time of year was no Tagus.

But in his dreams he found himself standing in front of the glass partition in the Embassy's reception area with Clendenning sitting opposite. The Ambassador was saying, "No, you can't come in. Your visa application has been refused." Then he turned away showing a blue scar running down the side of his face.

FIVE

Tuesday, 23rd September.

Bartley had been preparing himself for his meeting with the Ambassador when Grace walked in. He was taken aback to see her displaying signs of agitation. This was most unusual for her. She had been with the Embassy for over twenty years and had seen generations of Irish diplomats come and go. Somehow she had endured their individual idiosyncrasies, occasional outlandish demands, fits of pique and bad temper. She was the institutional memory of the office, far more effective than any archive and an immediate reference point for any officer confronted with an unfamiliar problem. Almost as round as she was short, her hair almost entirely grey, she had a presence and a glint in her eye that discouraged all but the most foolhardy Irish diplomat or local visa applicant from taking issue with her. He wondered what could have upset her.

"Bartley, there has been an accident outside. I was coming in our gate when a goat was knocked. The car it also missed me. The goat it is lying there now, but it is dying and people waiting outside are angry. You must come."

Reluctantly, Bartley stood up and followed her. He did not know what good it would do for him to go out to examine a goat that had been run over by a car, or "knocked" as Grace put it. However, it was best not to ignore any incident that upset the queue of visa applicants waiting outside the Embassy's gate. Passing Michelle's room, he glanced in, but there was no sign of her. So, there was no chance that he might delegate the matter.

They found the goat right in front of the gate. It was lying on its side and anyone could see its back was broken. Its belly was horrifically swollen and it was struggling to roll over to push itself upright on its front legs. Each time it tried to heave upward the back legs refused to follow and it fell back on itself. The queue of visa applicants had been joined by several curious onlookers and there was angry shouting directed against two young boys standing in front of the butcher's shop opposite. They were using the goat as target practice and one of them sent a stone skimming across the road that hit the goat full in the belly. The onlookers roared at the boys who were in fits of laughter, but as soon as they caught sight of Bartley coming out of the Embassy they took to their heels.

After being struck by the stone, the goat appeared to give up on any further attempt to stand. It lay in the white dust of the roadside twitching in pain, its eyes staring in terror. There was little that Bartley could do. No-one, including himself, wanted to touch the animal, but he felt he could not just leave it there, suffering indefinitely until finally it took its last breath. He looked at Grace and then at Jonas, the gardener, standing beside her. Could Jonas perhaps move the animal out of the way, he suggested? Apparently not – Jonas was afraid that the mere act of his touching it would make him financially liable for compensation should the owner turn up. Bartley pondered the problem while the crowd muttered angrily.

"OK, there's a vet down the road isn't there Grace? Jonas run down the road and ask the vet to come quickly."

"Sir, what you want me to do? We must not touch goat."

"Then go down the road and get the vet to come!" Bartley repeated.

Jonas looked at him blankly, not moving.

"Jonas, go get animal doctor down by here!" Grace pointed down the road and Jonas, at last understanding, took off with unexpected speed.

Fortunately the vet, a very young and earnest looking Indian whom Bartley had seen in the neighbourhood from time to time, was walking out his door as Jonas arrived and he agreed to come at once. He first stepped quickly into his surgery to collect his bag and then the two came hurrying along to the Embassy.

"This goat has broken its back," the vet confirmed. "The swelling of its belly indicates also some massive internal injury. It is inevitable that it should die, but whether within minutes or after an hour or more of agony, only God can tell us. I would suggest it would be humane to put the animal to sleep." He looked at Bartley expectantly, before adding, "Reluctantly such a humane gesture would cost money. It is the drugs for an injection, you see?"

Bartley nodded and waved at him to go ahead, agreeing to pay. It took the vet only a moment to ready a syringe and approach the goat, placing one hand surprisingly tenderly onto one side of its head while simultaneously burying the needle deep behind its neck. He continued to hold the head and make soothing sounds after removing the needle.

The crowd watched quietly as the goat took a final breath, as if sighing, before turning still. Bartley found he was strangely touched and sad. It was only a goat, but somehow the manner of its death and its endurance of pain summed up much of what he felt about Africa, where life was often hard and painful and almost always all too cheap.

He paid the vet $25 from his own pocket, guessing that making an official expenses claim, *$25 for mercy killing of goat* was hardly going to be taken too seriously by the bean counters at home – any such claim he might submit would probably end up doing the rounds of Iveagh House as the latest joke offering from the deranged denizens of the Embassy in Kutaba. He wondered if any of his colleagues, returning to work from lunch in some expensive restaurant ever had need of a vet to euthanize a goat lying in front perhaps of the wrought iron gate of the Villa Spada, the elegant Irish Embassy in Rome, or the discreet porte cochere of 12 avenue Foch, the Embassy in Paris?

"It's typical of course that the driver who hit the goat just drives on without stopping." he sighed.

"Oh, he did stop...just in time before the car also knocked Professor Ballo. Then the soldier got out and argued with the Professor. Then the Professor drives away and the big car that knocked the goat followed after him."

"What? I don't understand, you mean Professor Ballo – the politician - he was here?" Bartley looked at Grace, "What has he to do with this?"

"It was when I was coming in," she explained, "I saw Professor Ballo walking to the gate when the green car, a big Nissan, came up very fast from this side. I think the Professor saw it coming and he runs back out of the way, but the goat is eating some rubbish here and it is frightened so that it jumps straight in front of the car. Then the soldier he comes to speak to Professor Ballo. The Professor looks angry and he argues with the soldier. The soldier is also angry and even I am frightened because he looks so dangerous, you know because he has a big scar on his face. After a minute he goes back to his car and drives off fast and Ballo leaves also."

Bartley was more confused, but further questioning of Grace shed no more light on the incident. He was intrigued by the suggestion that Professor Ballo, the leader of the main opposition party PDAK, the People's Democratic Alliance of Kutaba, had seemingly been about to visit the Embassy. But what was even more mystifying was that someone who sounded very much like Major Mbuta, of whose existence he had been unaware until the day before, had played a role in the drama and that for some reason after speaking to him, Ballo had apparently changed his mind about his visit. Would Mbuta somehow want to frighten Ballo as Grace suggested? Had he perhaps warned him away? But Bartley was already late for his meeting with Clendenning and pushed any further speculation out of his mind

The Ambassador made no comment on his late arrival as Bartley sat down at the small conference table set at one end of the room in front of the wide iron-framed windows. The blinds had been partially closed over to shield the room from the glaring rays of the sun and heat magnifying through the glass. Clendenning seemed to keep the blinds like this all the time even on dull, rainy days. Bartley liked to think he looked at home in this world of semi-darkness, a malign, long-haired Dracula-type figure needing protection from daylight. The Ambassador's once modern desk itself also appeared to share a vampire's sensitivity to light in that that a combination of sun and humidity had rendered it a wizened, peeling hulk of cracked veneer that had become unglued at the edges offering endless sheltering crannies to any cockroach suddenly exposed when a sheaf of papers was removed. The conference table, in contrast, had a faux Georgian look to it, although the curved legs, as Clendenning had remarked upon first seeing it, were from a completely different era and style. It had been manufactured in the Office of Public Works carpentry workshop in Dublin and shipped out at some considerable expense to Bamgboshe. It was hard to tell if it was intended to serve as an advertisement for Irish design or simply to provide employment for some Irish chippie. Whichever, no-one seemed to have considered that the table was bound to look dramatically out of place in a jerry-built office block in Kutaba.

Clendenning had put together a formal agenda and had Grace print copies that he passed to Bartley and Michelle. Bartley looked at the list of items and tried to concentrate. He was still confused following the incident at the gate and the mysterious non-visit by Professor Ballo. Or was it a lingering after-effect of the two *wraps* shared with Fiona? He was grateful the blinds were closed and hoped the gloom would hide his bloodshot eyes.

"Let's get through this quickly." started the Ambassador, "I want to go over to the residence this afternoon before Brigid and I depart on leave. First item: The Mercedes. Well Bartley, I hear you were off trying to take possession of our new car yesterday?"

It was tedious going as Bartley explained first about the car and then sat through as Clendenning reeled off a list of other chores to be attended to in his absence, most of them various reports being demanded by HQ, foremost among them being the report on the Embassy's progress toward implementing SMaP. SMaP, Strategic Management and Planning, was the latest *tool* expensively foisted on the Department of Foreign Affairs and Trade by some management consultancy. Its jargon seemed deliberately arcane and Bartley had even less idea of what the Embassy was supposed to do with it than he had about what *progress* there was to report.

"Now, we come to the final item on my list." Clendenning resumed. "I am rather disappointed, Bartley, that you appear to have made little or no progress on the draft programme for the Minister's visit. Perhaps it will help if I set out for you some of the more obvious elements of the programme. It goes without saying that there should be the usual courtesy calls on the PM and Foreign Minister, but I would propose that the Minister should make a trip up country to Bakooli Region. It would be interesting to show the Minister our canal project there and I would quite like to see it myself."

This was the canal that had upset the Danish expert. The plan was to tap part of the flow of the famous Guseni River that meandered through the vast Guseni wilderness that covered most of the Bakooli Region. It was intended that the siphoned-off water would consolidate supplies to the existing reservoir that was having difficulty in meeting the demands of the fast growing population of Bakooli city, the regional capital. Admittedly, the canal project appeared to have met with some delays and setbacks, but Bartley could see how a visit by the Minister could lead to some positive press coverage, providing, of course, that no-one came forward with some criticism. He hazily recalled some report on this morning's radio news that a Danish citizen had been seriously injured in some sort of incident in Bamgboshe yesterday morning. It would be too much to hope for, he speculated, that his Danish hydrologist had been put out of action?

The canal project was in fact quite important, for if it were to prove successful and demonstrate the ability of the Kutaban authorities to work in partnership with Ireland it could well lead to the full blown aid programme that Dublin was contemplating. Coupled with the Minister's visit going well, an announcement could be imminent. The Kutabans were of course aware of this, but that did not necessarily mean they would bother to pull out all the stops to make Canavan's visit a huge success. That was what worried Bartley, and indeed Ambassador Clendenning too. Keeping Minister Canavan happy would be no mean feat. He had the reputation of being the most notoriously hard-to-please Minister in a number of years.

Bartley guessed that Clendenning had also heard the story that, during a dinner on the occasion of a recent visit to Paris, the Minister had actually reduced his host, the Irish Ambassador, to tears with his openly voiced criticism of the food and quality of service at table. If this could happen in France, what chance did they have in third world country like Kutaba? This could go some way to explaining Clendenning's impatience with the visit programme. But Bartley wondered whether the Ambassador was taking too much of a risk by proposing to take the Minister to Bakooli? Perhaps driving through the African landscape might prove an adventure that would appeal to the Minister, but there was too much that could go wrong.

"I think it would be useful," Clendenning continued, "if you, Bartley, were to visit Bakooli within the next week or two to prepare the ground. Since Brigid and I will be on leave over the coming month, I have no objection to Fumbe driving you. It's a long road trip and we will, of course, have to arrange for the Minister to fly up. That's something else you could look into.

"There is one other thing. Reluctant as I am, I am afraid you had better also make contact with Fr. O'Driscoll since he's the one Irishman we have on the ground in Bakooli. I doubt if we can avoid having to arrange that he be somehow involved in the Minister's visit."

Bartley knew little about O'Driscoll except that the Ambassador disapproved of him. Despite apparently only having met him once, Clendenning made no secret of his having found the priest to be more than a little scruffy and in some way disreputable.

"While I have some fear that O'Driscoll might well say or do something that could embarrass the Minister that is a risk we will have to take simply because he is one of the very few Irish missionaries left in Kutaba and certainly the only one in Bakooli."

Clendenning had a point. Whereas Irish priests and nuns in Kutaba had once been numerous, there were now no more than a handful scattered throughout the country. Indeed, this was a phenomenon throughout quite a few countries on the African continent. The missionaries' role in laying down a *footprint* for modern-day Irish volunteers and aid workers to follow had long since become an essential component in any speech about Africa by Irish Ministers or Presidents - that and the inevitable reference to sharing the experience of colonization with our black brothers. Any Irish Foreign Minister worth his salt, or vote, would always insist upon meeting as many Irish missionary priests or nuns as possible. His office would later follow up with each priest's or nun's family and relatives in the voting register saying that he had made a point of visiting the good Father/Sister out of regard for his/her marvelous work and concern for his/her welfare. The Minister would spell out importantly his personal commitment, and that of the Department under his leadership, to ensuring that the security and wellbeing of Irish missionaries and indeed of all of Irish citizens overseas was of the highest priority.

The Ambassador had fallen silent, seemingly wrapped up in his own thoughts for a moment, then he looked at Bartley as if only remembering his presence. "Actually, there is something else," he began. "I hear that Professor Ballo is again trying to stir things up in Guseni."

Bartley jolted to attention.

"You know he's always going on about people's rights there being trampled on. Well now he's apparently started complaining that the government is guilty of human rights violations against nomadic pastoralists in the area – something to do with some proposal to turn part of Guseni into a national park. I don't think there's much merit to his claims and my colleagues here certainly are of a view we can put them down to no more than a publicity seeking rant by the leader of a failed political party."

Bartley considered attempting to interrupt to tell that Ballo had been seen outside the Embassy only this morning, but the Ambassador was in full flow.

"That's something else to bear in mind. There's no reason to include a crackpot like Ballo in plans for the Minister's visit. In fact, it would be best to keep him entirely out of the picture. You can just forget about him, but in the unlikely event that you come across him down in Bakooli just make sure you keep him at a distance."

"I'll do that." Bartley agreed. Too late, Professor Ballo was already on his mind.

SIX

As they left Clendenning's office, Bartley turned to Michelle. "I think we should sit down to decide how to divide this lot between us. Let's go to my office."

Michelle looked at him, "Sorry Bartley, but you may remember that Brigid is expecting the arrival of other Ambassadors' spouses at the residence again this morning." Her tone was regretful, "She asked me to call over as soon as I was finished with Adrian."

"What's she organized this time? Another origami display?" Bartley made no effort to hide his exasperation.

"That's hardly called for. I'm sorry you feel that way, but I really have to hurry over to help out. I'll be back after lunch. If you still want to talk, we can do it then."
Bartley sighed. Yet again Brigid had priority.

Fumbe was hovering outside his office.
"What's up, Fumbe?"
"The Ambassador and Mrs. Brigid, they say I am free this morning. I am wondering if you want to go now to pick up the Mercedes. Maybe it is ready. Also, have you heard that the man you had to visit yesterday, that Danish man, he is in hospital. He is very hurt. I think they will have to fly him to Europe."
"What? I heard something on the radio about some Dane. What happened, do you know?"

"Someone robbed him in the street. I am thinking it must be soon after he has left you. They say a poor man - a street beggar - stole his bag, but first he beat him very badly. He is lucky he is not dead."

"God, poor guy!" Bartley recalled his last view of the Dane clutching his bag above his head in the rain. He regretted his earlier uncharitable thought of how convenient it would be if he were out of the way for the Minister's visit.

"So, we should go to Customs?" Fumbe interrupted the thought.

Bartley first looked at his watch.

"Yeah. Alright. What do you think we need, Fumbe? We've already looked after the Foreign Ministry, what do you think our friend in Customs wants?" He trusted Fumbe's advice in matters of local protocol and tradition, particularly as regards how big or how small a *gift* was appropriate at any given time.

"Mr. Bartley, you should not be asking me these things. This is not my way. A man in Kutaba should do his work. He is paid. It is dishonest he should look for more. But I think one bottle Black Label Johnny Walker will make our Customs man very happy."

"Fine, you go off first and buy Mr. Johnny Walker at the diplomatic store, then come back to collect me and we'll head off." He fished some dollars from his wallet and handed them to Fumbe. He wondered, not for the first time, how he could claim a refund for the whisky. He would have to give a reason for making a claim against the purchase receipt that Fumbe would give him, but he could hardly write *Bribe for Customs Official* or *Gift for Customs*. Dublin did not seem to appreciate that the Embassy in Kutaba could not function without the frequent oiling of greasy palms. The Department made no provision for such payments in its accounting procedures. Probably he would once more have to foot the bill for this item of extra-curricular expenditure from his own pocket. Or, he considered, he could perhaps make up the loss by paying some future bar bill for himself and Otto. He might then legitimately submit a claim for *offering hospitality* to a useful contact among the Bamgboshe diplomatic corps. Making a mental note to remember, he picked up his phone. He should call his friend Alex in the French Embassy to see if he could supply some economic data he could work into the SMaP report. For some reason the French seemed very keen on details of the economy.

It took longer than expected for Fumbe to fight through the traffic to the hard currency store reserved for diplomats on the far side of town and return to the Embassy with the Scotch. He handed it over to Bartley who hunted around in his desk for an envelope large enough to slip in the bottle. He mused that Scotch, and specifically Johnny Walker Black Label, along with the US dollar, might be the real currency of Kutaba. He would prefer a good Irish Jameson's, a superior whiskey in his view, and a suitable Irish-made product for promotion by the Embassy. But Irish whiskey as yet remained as rare and unrecognized in Kutaba as the Euro. Be that as it may, armed with Johnny Walker robed in his buff coat, he headed out with Fumbe to drive back hopefully for a final time to Customs.

Upon arrival everything went as well as he could have hoped. Officer Saleh was smiling and had obviously recovered from his encounter with the bullying American the day before. He was wearing the same blue shirt with armpits stained as dark as the epaulettes pinned to his shoulders. He oozed a distinctive odour of unwashed sweat. He ushered Bartley in, waved him to a seat in front of his desk and, after a brief and mutually flattering exchange of pleasantries, allowed Bartley present the manila envelope: a *small token* of the Embassy's gratitude for his much valued assistance.

Saleh beamed and gave Bartley the good news. A search of the office had turned up the missing rubber stamp which he held up with a triumphant flourish before proceeding with no little ceremony to a blurred staccato of paper stamping. He reassembled the various components of the file, closed it over and pushed it to one side, patting the cover in appreciation of another job well done. He kept back three flimsy sheets, an original and two copies from which he removed blue carbon copy sheets and handed these over to Bartley. It seemed that these were all that the Embassy needed.

Fifteen minutes later, Bartley was sitting in the driver's seat of the Mercedes, following Fumbe in the Landcruiser to the exit. Bartley drove somewhat hesitantly, unused to the controls and very much aware of the newness of the car. Thick brown paper still lay in the foot wells protecting the carpet underneath. Strangely there seemed to be little of the leather, new car smell he had expected. Rather there was a strong odor that was all too reminiscent of the hum wafting off Officer Saleh in his grubby shirt.

There was, inevitably, one final hiccup. They had stopped at the exit barrier and a security guard had come out to examine the flimsies. The papers, he said, were in order but he had received no phone call from inside the yard to say that the car should be allowed drive out today. Bartley felt frustration spilling over and was preparing to vent his rage when Fumbe slipped up in front of the security officer cutting off his view of Bartley in the driver's seat.

"My friend, you are right," Fumbe was saying. "We should go inside to discuss this phone call. It will be good. We can arrange everything."

Saying this, he grabbed the guard by the elbow and steered him to the container hut. As the guard turned away Fumbe looked over his left shoulder and motioned to Bartley with his right hand, his thumb running meaningfully back and forward against his fingertips. Bartley hurriedly dug in his back pocket and took out a few crumpled notes, singling out two $5 bills. He got out of the car and caught up with Fumbe standing in the doorway of the hut, his hand still behind his back. Bartley slipped him the notes and then retreated back to the car. Sometimes local pride demanded that the foreigner paying a bribe should not be a witness to its actual giving - an act to be conducted between locals only.

It was hardly more than a minute before Fumbe and the guard returned. The latter beckoned to one of his juniors to raise the barrier and came forward to shake Bartley's hand.

"Sorry for the delay sir. I now have a call to release this vehicle."

Bartley took the proffered hand and smiled, making another note to add a further $10 to the bar bill he intended to rack up for some future expenses claim.

Fumbe drove in front with Bartley in the Mercedes nervously trying to keep up behind. This was not the way he drove his dented Rav. He drew confidence from its knocks and bruises. They testified to his being unafraid to make physical contact whenever a taxi, bus or truck tried to barge him aside. When the traffic snarled up in Bamgboshe's fume-filled streets and drivers forced their way from one lane to another Bartley never hesitated to edge aggressively forward to defend his space. It gave him especial pleasure to be able to face down local drivers and successfully play them at their own game, forcing his way from one lane to another if only to gain a single metre of progress in the constant traffic jams that brought everything to an almost complete standstill.

However, driving the still pristine Mercedes was another matter. It was as if everyone else on the road smelt the newness of the car as much as his nervousness. He drove in dread of the slightest scratch. Other cars kept cutting in front of him, pushing him to the side so that it was not long before he lost sight of Fumbe ahead. Then, at one point when he thought he had almost made it safely to the Embassy, a large police motorbike pulled abruptly in front to cut him off, its rider waving him onto the side of the road. From behind came the sirens of an approaching convoy. The policeman began waving more frantically, motioning that Bartley should pull the Mercedes deeper into the muddy morass that bordered that stretch of roadway. A moment later two further motorbikes whizzed past, lights flashing and sirens blaring. There followed a drab green pickup with four soldiers standing in the rear, their bodies wedged against a central crosspiece, holding automatic weapons pointed to either side to protect a black Range Rover with dark tinted windows directly behind. It was flying the national flag of Kutaba and Bartley recognised it as one of Prime Minister Okeke's official cars. Closely behind again came a gold coloured Landcruiser and a second pick-up of soldiers. When they had passed, the motorbike blocking him sped off leaving Bartley to struggle back on to the road amid the returning surge of traffic.

If he expected a word of thanks or congratulation upon delivering the car safely, he was disappointed. When Clendenning came down to inspect, his face immediately flushed upon spotting what appeared to be a deposit of cooked rice surrounded by oily smudges mushed into the pale leather of the back seat. His temper did not improve when Fumbe suggested by way of explanation that the car had most likely been used for the last while as a shelter by the night watchman at the Customs yard.

SEVEN

Tuesday, 30 September.

Bartley leaned back in his chair as Michelle entered the office. He had taken things relatively easy since the Clendennings had left, but reckoned it was time that he and the Third Secretary looked at finalizing some of the practical arrangements for the Minister's visit. To be fair, he had not been entirely idle over the days. Through Fumbe, he had arranged that the proprietor of the local dry-cleaning shop carry out a partially successful removal of the Mercedes' stains and smudges that had so enraged Clendenning. Admittedly, there was a certain amount of discoloration of the leather as a result of the over-enthusiastic application of some cleaning fluid, but apart from that, there was little evidence remaining of the watchman who had first enjoyed its leathered luxury. Bartley had composed and dispatched a tersely worded letter of complaint to the Head of Customs in the matter. He expected no reply or other result, but hoped the mere act of writing a complaint would somehow mollify the Ambassador when he returned.

He was looking forward to today's lunchtime Independence Day reception hosted by Botswana. The food on offer might not be entirely to his liking – plantain and goat stew or soggy samosas would inevitably feature – but unlike last week - when he attended the Saudis' and been offered nothing stronger than orange juice - there should be lashings of gin and tonic or at least some cheapish wine (served at a room temperature of 30 degrees Centigrade). But first, he had to do something about the Minister's visit. There were a number of other pieces of work he had recently let slip and he felt he better move on these today, particularly as he and Fumbe were due to drive to Bakooli tomorrow and he would be absent for the rest of the week. In particular, he had put off thinking about the essentially dull, and to his mind quite fruitless, exercise of completing the myriad of reports that Clendenning wanted sent to HQ. He was well aware that the Ambassador would blow a gasket if the reports were not sent in before his return. He could not really put them off much longer.

It was with this in mind, that he had asked Michelle to call into his office for a chat. She arrived and plonked herself wearily onto a chair across from him. He wondered whether she too was finally succumbing to the heat. She flipped open a notepad, but this too seemed to take an effort.

He smiled. "Hi Michelle, thanks for coming in." Yes, she definitely looked lethargic and somehow vulnerable.

"I just wanted to talk about setting in motion some of the arrangements for the Minister's visit. You may have seen that Dublin sent the final confirmation of dates yesterday. There's been no change.

"We should begin with making immediate contact with the Hilton to try to arrange at least a suite for the Minister and a sufficient number of other rooms to accommodate all of the accompanying officials. I'd like you to deal with this while I'm away. I'm a little concerned that there might be a problem because I've heard the World Bank has a delegation arriving in town around the same time. You know what World Bank and UN delegations are like. They're always massive and there'll certainly be several times more World Bank people coming than there'll be with our Minister. Also, they're likely to demand the best rooms, which the Hilton will probably give them seeing as how everyone thinks a World Bank delegation outranks any Minister from a small European country, especially one like Ireland. Although, I guess there's some truth in that. In any case try to get the best you can,"

He paused to look down at his notebook in which he had scribbled a list of the different reports they needed to send off to Dublin.

"OK, let's have a look at SMaP...." he began.

About half an hour later, they had almost finished going through his list and agreed – at least he hoped they had agreed – on how they would divide up the work, when the phone rang. It was Grace at reception to say that Professor Ballo, the leader of PDAK, *Peedak* as she pronounced it, had just walked in the door and, learning the Ambassador was on leave, had asked to see Bartley.

Ballo's presence posed an immediate dilemma. Bartley had been intrigued when Grace had told him about seeing Ballo outside the embassy the day the goat got hit and one part of him welcomed the possibility of finding out what that had been about. On the other hand he was conscious of Clendenning's injunction to keep Ballo at arm's length. Prudence cautioned the latter, but he could hardly refuse to see the man now he was here.

He had never met Ballo and really knew quite little about him apart from his being leader of PDAK, a party claiming to be representative of all Kutaba. In truth the party was associated almost exclusively with the Guseni people, by far the largest ethnic group in the south. In an attempt to downplay any aspirations that the Guseni might have to asserting a separate identity, the area from which they took their name had several years earlier been incorporated by the government in Bamgboshe into the newly created Bakooli Region, Bakooli being the name of the fast growing city on northern border of Guseni. Bakooli was run and controlled by outsiders who were members of Prime Minister Okeke's KNP, the Kutaba National Party.

Ballo and his PDAK claimed to seek no more than increased autonomy for Bakooli Region and to replace the incumbent Governor, Francis Awale, and his cohort of party officials with indigenous locals. Prime Minister Okeke and his KNP countered by accusing PDAK of pursuing a private agenda that would ultimately see Guseni breaking away to form a separate, independent state. The KNP further claimed there was a lack of support for PDAK's agenda – whether for more autonomy or independence – among the Guseni people themselves. In proof it pointed to PDAK's poor showing in both national and regional elections. PDAK, for its part, put this down to widespread intimidation and harassment of its members that prevented it from competing fairly against the KNP.

Before having Ballo brought in, Bartley quickly reminded Michelle that he would be travelling in the morning. He suggested they catch up with each other when he returned at the weekend.

As she made to leave, Michelle collided in the doorway with the politician who was already being ushered in by Grace. Bartley rose and moved quickly forward as if to steady Ballo. Michelle looked uncharacteristically flustered and stood to one side as Bartley introduced them both. She looked embarrassed, showing a side he had not seen before.

Bartley of course recognised the politician from seeing him at receptions in various Embassies and hearing him speak in the national Parliament on the rare occasions that the Prime Minister convened the assembly and allowed the opposition a very brief opportunity to present a suitably respectful critique of government policies. Ballo, appropriately enough, had a professorial air. Short and trim, he wore a western style dark suit. His hair was completely grey and as neatly groomed as his matching goatee beard. But despite his mild-mannered, bookish appearance, his public image was of a passionate politician, bravely expressing his views, heedless of the inherent dangers of invoking Prime Minister Okeke's wrath.

At the same time, he apparently knew his boundaries. He was known never to go too far in his public criticism. He had never been suspended from Parliament, far less arrested and thrown into jail to join a number of other erstwhile opposition colleagues. More than a few of his closest allies had been accused of "anti-constitutional activities" and been rounded up. Now, two years later, they were still languishing in prison while the state prosecutor continued to compile the case against them. Ironically, until it was decided precisely what charges were to be brought, they were unable to begin preparing their defence. Meanwhile, the Minister for Justice regularly assured the international community that he was giving priority to gathering evidence to allow for the earliest trial date. But the process seemed to drag on interminably and there was still no sign of their appearing in court anytime soon.

Bartley had removed his glasses and was using a somewhat frayed paper tissue to wipe the coating of skin flecks off the lens.

"Mr. Ryan, I must thank you for seeing me at such short notice. I only regret that I missed seeing your Ambassador and wishing him and Madame a pleasant vacation before they left. But, I think your Ambassador has not been here in Kutaba too long?"

"No, six months."

"Ah, a short time. And you, of course, are here longer?"

"Yes..."

"Well, then you must be aware of some of the difficulties facing an active politician not belonging to the government party in my country. As you know I represent the people of Guseni – Guseni is the original name for what is now called part of the new Bakooli Region, but the real Guseni is still there, unchanged. It is wild open countryside where my people have raised cattle or camels for generations. Sometimes there is great hardship when the rains fail, but our people have learned to adapt and live with nature. But now there is a plan, a plan that Minister Emmanuel Gabi is proposing to turn the traditional Guseni land into a wildlife park for tourists. You know this will result in my people being cleared into one small area where their way of life will not be sustainable. But perhaps you have heard of these plans?"

"Well, yes, as a matter of fact, I have heard some things, but don't have any great detail."

"But perhaps you have heard of a Mr. Paul Andersen, from Denmark, who is an expert who has looked at the problems of Guseni?"

"As a matter of fact I met Mr. Andersen some time ago, before he was mugged in the street and had to be shipped home."

"Yes, that was unfortunate. It seems he was in the wrong place at the wrong time and was attacked by some hooligan beggar. But what did Mr. Andersen tell you about Guseni?"

"Not much really. Just that he was unhappy with the canal being built to take water from the Guseni River."

"Yes, that is an issue of concern for me also. Water has become a problem again for my people these last few years. We need to find new sources. We need to dig new wells. I am sure Mr. Andersen told you this and much more."

It sounded more like a question than a statement and Bartley wondered what Ballo was driving at. He had already decided not to let on about what Andersen had said about Gabi.

"Not really, no."

"Ah, indeed, perhaps not, but I should, however, not take up too much of your time unnecessarily. My purpose in coming here is simply to alert you that there is need for concern over Minister Gabi's plans. I have reason to believe he will seek assistance, financial and other, from one of our donor countries in Europe. If you, or rather your government, is approached in this matter it is important that you are aware of the problems that the plans would have for my people. I would ask that you do not commit to anything without full consultation and I would, of course, be grateful if you would keep me informed of any development." He paused, seemingly to think for a moment and then, placing the flat of his hand on the desk and leaning close in toward Bartley, continued. "I will say this to you in confidence. You know it is not something I say lightly to the representative of a foreign government about a Minister in the Kutaban government, especially when I am leader of the political opposition: You must not trust Minister Gabi. He is a dangerous man of no conviction."

Bartley had no time to react before Ballo stood up, his hand no longer leaning on the desk but rather proffered in conclusion of their discussion. They exchanged no more than a few further platitudes as Bartley escorted him out of the building.

Standing at the door, watching the front gate being opened to allow Ballo out, Bartley was reminded of watching the unfortunate Andersen on an earlier occasion. The moment ended abruptly as Fiona came barging through the gate and waved.

"Hi Bartley, how are you?" She was quite breathless as she reached him. "Who was that? Was it, you know, your man the politician?" She was looking back at the gate. "The guy Okeke is always giving out about? What's his name?"

"Professor Ballo, Chairman of PDAK. Yes, it was. What are you up to Fiona, no school today?"

Fiona grinned. "No, I have the day off. We closed to pack off all our male teachers to a gender training workshop. A day listening to why they shouldn't be forcing the girls to fuck them in return for higher grades might do some good. Or at least it might encourage them to use condoms. So, what are you up to? Since your boss is still away, I was wondering whether we could go somewhere for lunch – I feel in the mood for something long and liquid, preferably alcoholic."

Bartley shook his head, as much to clear it as to say no.

"Sorry, no can do. I have to represent our nation at the Botswana National Day reception at lunchtime. After that, I have to come back here and do some work before I head off. You know I'm driving down to Bakooli early tomorrow morning."

"God, you're all business aren't you, Mr. Chargé-of-the-Fairies-While-Your-Ambassador-is-Away! How do you expect me get into the National Club if you're not going to sign me in?"

"I very much doubt that my absence would prevent you getting into the Club. It never has before."

"Ha, ha! I think I might instead just go down to Blessings',"

The problem, as Bartley knew, was not Fiona being denied entry into the Club, but rather her ability to purchase anything once admitted. The bar staff were rigorous in applying the rule of accepting payment from members only. Blessings' Bar, on the other hand, was a shebeen of somewhat dubious reputation backing onto the Bamgboshe River that served passable fish and chips or barbecued skewers of meat. More interestingly, it somehow managed occasionally to procure a stock of cold South African Castle beer or even Heineken.

"If you change your mind, you know where to find me," she called hopefully as she walked back to her decrepit Suzuki. He watched her go but already his mind was back on Ballo and Minister Gabi.

EIGHT

There was a long line of cars queuing up in front of the Botswana Ambassador's residence. It seemed there was always a massive turnout of government ministers, local dignitaries and diplomats for any African or Arab national day reception. The Chinese and Indians, for reasons relating to their growing investments, could also count on a healthy turnout. The European Embassies, by contrast, fared much less well despite their being the major donors of development assistance. Ireland's St. Patrick's Day receptions generally drew a good crowd attracted by the prospect of plenty of drink and "craic", but even they drew only a fraction of the numbers attending what Otto had once quite undiplomatically described as "Goat Stew or Towel-Head O.J. parties".

Bartley sat in the rear of the new Mercedes with Fumbe up front and the Irish tricolor hanging limply from its new and splendidly erect pole on the front wing. When it was their turn to stop in front of the steps leading up to the impressive white pillared entranceway to the house, a steward in a white jacket came forward to open Bartley's door, giving him a salute and, mistaking him for the Ambassador, offering him a "Welcome, Your Excellency."

Bartley mounted the steps and entered a vast marbled hallway joining a line of other 'Excellencies' and dignitaries being greeted individually by the Ambassador and half a dozen of his staff standing stiffly along the wall to his left. After shaking hands with each of these, Bartley followed the guests through to the rear of the house and out into the garden. A number of rather worn looking marquees had been erected offering some limited protection in the event of rain. A drinks bar had been set up under the nearest and he started toward it, but a waiter with a tray generously laden with various drinks stopped him halfway. He lifted a glass and sniffed the distinctive, perfumed scent of gin. He guessed there was little tonic diluting the alcohol. Since he had to work later in the afternoon, he would limit himself to two drinks - or perhaps three. Pausing and looking over his shoulder at the departing waiter, he used two fingers to fish out the ice cubes floating in the glass and had let them drop on the ground when he heard a familiar voice from his other side.

"Trying to poison the lawn are you?" It was Otto.
Bartley looked down at the bare dirt that covered most of the garden and grinned.
"No, I'm trying to water it. Anyway, better to poison the lawn than myself. I don't suppose they bother to boil the water here before freezing it. It's probably a lethal bacterial cocktail. For that matter, I don't see any ice in your glass either."

"Hell, no, I wouldn't even let it touch my gin. Went to the bar and got filled up straight from the gin pump with a splash of tonic. You can't beat a splash of tonic against malaria, definitely much healthier than drugs. Which reminds me, is your Ambassador still on that funny anti-malaria stuff, what's it called – Larium? They say it's a real mind bender. Could be that's what makes him the jerk you say he is.
"Speaking of Ambassadors, I've been told my new boss arrives Friday. Guess I lucked out. I thought my independence would last much longer, but The Hague apparently can't wait to send out the new man, although I can't figure out why. I was thinking I should make the most of the few days I have left, so how about heading down to the Club after this? I could do with getting steamed."
"Sorry Otto. I can't manage it today. I'm off to Bakooli in the morning and have to finish something before I leave. Fiona's already had a go at me,

wanting to rack up a few with her. She's got the day off and was a bit miffed I wouldn't oblige. Said she was going to go down to Blessings' Bar. So she's probably there now, getting pissed on her own."

"I was rather thinking of the Club. Blessings' is not really my scene." Otto sighed. Local shebeens were indeed not his style. He then looked expectantly past Bartley's shoulder toward the house.

"I see our illustrious US Ambassador has arrived. I think I'll go and have a quick word with him before he's surrounded by other suitors. I'd like to know what he thinks about these new import tariffs that P.M. Okeke is planning."

"Well, good luck with that!"

Bartley doubted that even Otto would get much from the tight-lipped American, but he had to admire his friend's pluck as he sped off to intercept the Ambassador before he was spotted by other guests. Looking around, Bartley noticed the British, Italian and Czech Ambassadors talking together off to his left. For the moment he could see no one else he immediately recognized among the predominantly African guests. He headed over to join the three Europeans.

They greeted him politely and shook hands before resuming their conversation, which seemed to be exclusively between the British and Italian, about the possible consequences of the new tariffs that had also been on Otto's mind. Bartley listened politely, feigning interest. He looked at the Czech, as round as he was short, with a wrinkled brown nut of a head. He was evidently having difficulty following the conversation in English but nodded enthusiastic agreement when either of the other two looked at him.

After several minutes the British Ambassador turned toward Bartley.

"I guess this doesn't concern you chaps too much, does it? You Irish don't have an interest in selling road plant and heavy machinery to Kutaba, do you? I guess that's quite a help and lets you concentrate on just getting on with the job of helping out on the development side wherever you can. I hear you're doing something with water for Bakooli city, aren't you? Good for you. I'd say it was a timely intervention given the latest plans for a wildlife park to build up tourism in the Region"

Bartley was not quite sure how to take this. He didn't know the British Ambassador that well and, on the few occasions they had met, he had always been struck by the Ambassador's unnerving similarity to a more youthful Tony Blair both in his physical appearance and constant air of enthusiasm. He could not quite make out whether the Ambassador was being his usual animated self or rather perhaps, plain patronizing.

"Yes, we are trying to help," he agreed. "We do have some hope of building up a wider development programme, but we may have to wait for some time until we see how our budgets work out at home. Meanwhile, the Bakooli canal is really our first toe in the water in Kutaba, if you pardon the pun."

His attempt at humour was received with a blank stare and silence. Unnerved, he continued unthinkingly, "But since you mention the wildlife park plan, is there not some reason for concern the effect it will have on the Guseni people and their way of life? Professor Ballo from PDAK called on me this morning and had some serious reservations."
"Oh Ballo, I wouldn't take him too seriously," the British Ambassador replied. "He's at a bit of a loss. He's got next to no party and he's peeved he can't make any impression as a leader of a half credible opposition. He's rather prone to exaggeration and hopes his wild stories of apocalypse will get him some attention. All he achieves is to annoy the Prime Minister.

Then, no wonder, Okeke comes down hard on him. Frankly, I don't think we should encourage Ballo. Between us, and I say this in confidence, if Ballo has an agenda it's no more than to get his own hands on a share of the development funding we all give Kutaba."

The Ambassador looked at the Italian, expecting confirmation.

"Yes, one must be careful with this Ballo," the Italian agreed in studiously enunciated English, "One can suspect his personal motivation; after all he is a politician. But as a politician he is perhaps too hasty, too much in a hurry to make a point before he is sure of his facts? He says things to make people excited but we for our part should be very careful before we accept what he says. We have a delicate relationship with Prime Minister Okeke and we must avoid any possibility that we appear partisan to the opposition by repeating any of these claims of Ballo, especially if, as my colleague suggests, he has some personal axe to grind."

The Czech Ambassador looked suitably serious and gave an emphatic nod of agreement. He was wondering what Ballo sharpening a hatchet might have to do with anything?

Feeling foolish for having raised the matter in the first place, Bartley sought to justify himself. "What do you make of claims that the Prime Minister and the KNP use a combination of intimidation and fear to control Bakooli? I keep hearing that anyone who wants even the lowest of public sector jobs has first to become a member of the KNP. And you know, the law says once you have joined one party that you are never allowed to join another. Surely that prevents PDAK recruiting members from even those who support it? Then also, in the villages where people only survive because they get regular handouts of grain, the distribution is controlled by KNP officials who look after their own. It's just another way for the party to keep the people in line and weaken support for PDAK."

He wondered why on earth he was mouthing this stuff. He should really be more careful before sounding off and repeating street gossip in front of such senior Ambassadors as the British and Italian.

"Well, that is an accusation that Ballo might certainly throw about," the British Ambassador conceded, "but there's a good deal that Ballo says that he fails to substantiate. He claims, for example, that his party has been evicted from a number of local offices by landlords who have been warned off by KNP activists, but I see no real evidence of that, although I do know his PDAK is severely short of funds and is obviously finding it difficult to pay whatever rents it owes. - Ah, Minister Gabi, how are you? Good to see you!" He broke off with an excited smile upon their being joined by a trim figure dressed in an immaculate white suit.

Taken by surprise, Bartley took in the newcomer perhaps a little too closely causing Gabi to return the look quizzically before replying. Now that he saw him up close for the first time, Bartley was struck how much younger he appeared than the sixty years he knew him to be. He had a boyish face, so dark black as to be almost blue. Tribal scars incised into each cheek did nothing to take from his good looks. Despite this, the rectangular, dark-green tinted sunglasses hiding his eyes contrived to make him appear somehow menacing.

"My dear Ambassadors how are you?" the Minister shook hands with the British, Italian and the Czech before hesitating as he came to Bartley.

The Italian Ambassador stepped in smoothly, "Minister, have you met the acting Irish Chargé d'Affaires, Mr. Ryan?"

Bartley made to offer his hand, but the Minister's face had clouded and he seemed to hesitate. Unsettled, Bartley half-dropped his hand and left it hanging uncertainly as the eyes behind the green lenses seemed to drill into him. The brief moment was broken as the US Ambassador stepped into their circle and Gabi wheeled around, his face switching instantly to a look of smiling, but somehow knowingly restrained, welcome. The two shook hands and Bartley, without thinking, took a step back allowing the others greet the new arrival before it was his turn.

"Good to see you again." The Ambassador failed to hide a visible effort to recognise Bartley, but probably felt they must have met before.

"I was just about to ask Minister Gabi," it was the British Ambassador's turn to fill an awkward pause, "for his view on the new, proposed trade tariffs. Surely, Minister, they could have a negative impact on investment in your area of natural resources exploitation?"

"Ah yes, the Prime Minister has indeed suggested that tariffs may be raised. The head of our government is an excellent *administrator*," he emphasized the word as if the concept of administration was beneath him, "but sometimes even he may fail to take all the different factors into account. Let me just say that we in government have not finished our discussions. Meanwhile, it would not be appropriate for me to say more."

"I do hope, Minister, that the Prime Minister is fully aware of our concerns," the British Ambassador nodded toward the American to include him in this.

"Yes, yes, of course," Gabi looked around the group, his fixed smile seeming to disappear once more as he came to Bartley, "but this is something we can take up between us when we meet." He nodded at the British and American before turning to the Italian. "Ah, my dear

Ambassador, I understand that you soon have some operatic entertainment in store for us?" The smile had returned.

The Italian inclined forward in acknowledgement and the conversation moved on to the imminent visit of two reasonably known, young Italian tenors. Bartley took the opportunity to make himself scarce.

Bloody wankers, annoyed both by allowing Gabi to unnerve him and by his earlier uncontrolled attempt at small talk with the Ambassadors, he sought to justify himself. *Don't give a damn about anything except not rocking the boat to keep their trade flows running and schmoozing the likes of Gabi.*

He headed off to hunt down another gin. At least he would be getting out of town tomorrow. Maybe even, when he was down in Bakooli, he could pick Fr. O'Driscoll's brain about the local situation. Why not? The Irish clergy in Africa could often offer a depth of local knowledge to which the British and even Americans with all their resources could never aspire. Then he remembered Gabi saying something about seeing the Ambassadors and wondered whether there was some particular meeting he was missing?

He wandered around quite aimlessly with a final gin for a quarter of an hour and exchanged a few short pleasantries with a number of later arrivals. Then, there was a loud announcement, calling for silence and the guests stood to attention for the national anthems of Kutaba and Botswana. Not for the first time, he was struck by the similarity between the Kutaban anthem and a rhyme from his childhood. As the amplified sound system blared out the anthem, he could remember the words:

Itsy bitsy spider climbed up the waterspout
Down came the rain and washed the spider out

Out came the sun and dried out all the rain
And the itsy bitsy spider climbed up the spout again.

Following the anthems, he decided he had better return to the Embassy and he began to make toward the exit. Just as he reached the house, Otto caught up with him.

"Heading back to the office, Bartley?" he asked. "I'm definitely off for a few leisurely beers, there's not much happening here. I was hoping I might catch up with our American friend again, but no such luck, so I might as well clear out. What about you? Are you sure you don't want to join me? I was thinking, after all, that I might slum it by going down to see how our dear friend Fiona is doing in Blessings'."

"Well, that will be a treat for her to see you in Blessings! But, I rather guessed you got nothing out of the American. It didn't seem to take him long to get shot of you."

"No, he did give me the slip pretty pronto and I'll swear he has been high-tailing it since then every time he sees me come within shouting distance. But how did you get on? I saw you were mixing it with the illustrious Minister Gabi."

"Oh, I'd hardly say that. I didn't even get to speak to him."

"That's a pity. He is an interesting guy - wealthy although no-one seems to know where the dough comes from. However, he can only go up from now on and that has to be good."

"I seem to remember you saying something like that about him before. How come? I can't see why anyone would want him running the show." Bartley looked at his friend questioningly.

Otto tapped the side of his nose, "Can't say anything that might compromise our interests. But, you know Environment and Natural Resources..." He left his thoughts unfinished.

They had arrived by the front door and already their drivers had spotted them and were hurrying back to retrieve their cars. Bartley made to follow after Fumbe to avoid his having to manouevre the car through the crush of traffic clogging the entrance.

"Give Fiona my best. I'll give you a call when I get back from Bakooli," he shouted to Otto over his shoulder.

NINE

It was some way past six-thirty by the time Bartley felt he had sufficiently revised the Embassy's SMaP report. He was pleased with the result of his efforts, which had consisted largely of cut and pasting from a series of earlier documents and reports that he believed were couched in appropriate sounding jargon. It could hardly be classed as an outstanding effort, but it did a reasonable job of ticking the obligatory boxes. The rest of the Embassy staff, including Michelle, had left sometime earlier but Fumbe had stayed on, volunteering to drive him home. He had some difficulty balancing a bundle of files under his arm as he tried to set the alarm before leaving the building. He was still fiddling with the keypad when Fumbe hurried up to relieve him of his papers – documents he wanted to look at before traveling that gave details of the Bakooli water project and names of various officials he might meet.

It had started raining again and a steady torrent of oversized raindrops was washing off the umbrella that Fumbe held over him as they hurried to the car. It was a foul night that fueled the feeling of depression he had felt since his conversation with the British and Italian Ambassadors and their offhand dismissal of Ballo. Then there was the peculiar encounter with Minister Gabi. Did Gabi know something about him? Could Gabi possibly know that Ballo had been to the Embassy that very day and warned Bartley off becoming involved with plans for a national park in Guseni? Surely he was just being unnecessarily paranoid and really just in need of some cheerful company? But, given the evening that was in it, he was glad he had not joined Fiona and Otto at Blessings'. It would be miserably wet and muddy down by the river where Blessings was situated. He could imagine the pair of them huddled with their Hippos watching the water sluice off the crude plastic awning that served as Blessings' only shelter.

As they drew up in front of the gate to his house, Fumbe blew the horn several times. The watchman in his little hut sheltering from the battering downpour was being slow to react. He emerged reluctantly with a blanket draped over his shoulders and a thin blue plastic bag tied round his head. The car pulled into the already thoroughly flooded parking area next to the house. Fumbe got out and opened the rear door for Bartley before scuttling round to retrieve the umbrella from the boot. Some of Bartley's papers had slipped off his seat and he was reaching down to gather them up.

The rain had finally driven Fiona and Otto out of Blessings, but not until they were both well tanked. For some reason she would never quite recall it was imperative that she should see Bartley before he left on his trip. She had just seen the Mercedes turning off the road in front and congratulated herself on her timing, arriving just as he got home. With the gate still open and the watchman about to close it, she blew her horn, floored the accelerator and barreled through.

Fumbe was about to open the umbrella when he heard the car horn behind him. He turned to see the watchman jumping back as a muddy Suzuki swerved through the gateway and sloughed headlong into a massive trough of water. A murky, blinding bow-wave shot up cascading over the windshield. Then, as the driver obviously panicked and stamped on the brakes, the little car went into a sideways skid. The rear end slewed to the left and then careened with an almighty wallop into the open rear door of the Mercedes.

Bartley had just picked up the last of his papers and was tucking them into a folder when his heart seemed to stop.
Despite the drumming thunder of rain, everything seemed suddenly quiet. Fumbe was rooted to the spot, oblivious to the water pouring down his

neck. The still unopened umbrella had fallen from his hand back into the boot.

Bartley was looking at the door in terror. It was hanging atilt, sagging on its hinges.

Then, as if to break the spell, the door of the Suzuki opened hesitantly and a wild eyed Fiona leaned out, one hand gripping the door frame, the other supporting her not inconsiderable weight on the door itself. She hauled herself upright and turned to peer at the Mercedes.

"Jesus! Fuck! Fuck, fuck, fuck," was all she could say.

TEN

Wednesday, 1 October.

The early morning sun was already blazing down and burning off the remains of last night's rainfall to a muggy haze as Fumbe drove the Landcruiser through the gates of Bartley's house. The damp steamed off the green tarpaulin that had been stretched hastily over the roof of the Mercedes to keep water from flowing through the gap left after Fumbe and the watchman had forced the buckled rear door closed. It had grated angrily against its hinges as they strained to push it into place, but the top rear corner still jutted outside the confines of its frame.

The shock of the collision had sobered Fiona. She had been pathetically contrite, but Bartley had been too preoccupied by the consequences and what Adrian Clendenning might do to him when he saw his car than be angry with her. He had decided immediately to keep the accident secret for as long as possible. The car was meanwhile to remain at his house, out of sight of other staff in the Embassy. He hoped, rather forlornly against all the odds that it might be possible to carry out some sort of repair before Clendenning's return. In this matter he was placing all his trust in Fumbe's network of contacts and local wide-boy reputation.

When he collected the Landcruiser from the Embassy that morning, Fumbe had already broadcast that Bartley had instructed that the Mercedes be left for safekeeping at his house until his return. He had also spoken to a 'friend', a mechanic at the Mercedes dealership, and explained the situation. Both had concluded that the door was damaged beyond repair and Fumbe reported to Bartley that the mechanic thought it unlikely a replacement door could be ordered, delivered and fitted in much less than six months. Nevertheless, convinced by Fumbe of the desperate nature of Bartley's predicament and the offer of a case of Black Label in addition to a large sum of US dollars in cash, the mechanic had promised to see if there was any way he could come up with some solution before Ambassador Clendenning arrived back.

Viewed realistically, his future prospects did little to lighten Bartley's mood as he came out of the house and dropped his overnight bag in the back of the Landcruiser before climbing in up front. He was of two minds about his trip. Part of him would have preferred to remain in Bamgboshe in the hope of getting the car repaired even though this would necessarily mean his having to sit around brooding and waiting, doubtlessly in vain, for Fumbe to conjure some solution. The other part of him argued since there was nothing to be gained by hanging around, that he was better out of town where he would not have to account for the Mercedes' absence from the Embassy's parking lot.

He slipped on his seatbelt and fiddled with the car radio, tuning into the remainder of the hourly news on the BBC World Service. Fumbe headed out into the morning traffic and turned right in the direction of the airport and the main road south toward Bakooli.

The road was lined on either side by rickety shops and streams of people heading about their morning business as they skirted around the pools of water still lying on the ground. Unusually for this hour, few of the roadside shops had yet opened, but Bartley's mind was too far away to take much notice.

Soon they reached the outskirts of the city, almost halfway to the airport turn-off. Traffic was strangely almost non-existent, but the roadside was crowded with people standing around aimlessly, not seeming to be going anywhere. It was not the usual bustle. A couple of slow moving trucks and a bus were in the lane in front of the Landcruiser. Without warning they drove off into a slip road to the right. Fumbe slowed as he saw that they had been directed to do so by half a dozen policemen blocking the road. As the Landcruiser approached, one of the policemen scanned its number plate. Recognising it as a diplomatic plate, he signalled to his colleagues to clear the way and he motioned Fumbe to continue straight through.

No sooner past the police, but it was noticeable there were no other cars on the road. There was none following them out of town, nor was there any traffic coming in. The crowds standing on either side were even more numerous. They were also beginning to jeer and look hostile. They jostled and pushed angrily against protective metal railings that had been erected to close off this normally busy part of the road. Behind them lay the rubble of shops and houses that had been demolished wholesale the previous month when the city authorities had sent in bulldozers to clear space to allow doubling the road width. It was intended that a suitably impressive four lane highway should be constructed to serve Bamgboshe International Airport.

Bartley had barely been aware of what was happening outside the car until they had been waved on by the policeman, but he sensed the tension in the crowd. He caught sight of scattered rubble and stones littering the road ahead of them. He was about to say something to Fumbe when the latter, reaching his own conclusion instants before him, stamped down hard on the accelerator. It took a moment before the car reacted, but already half a dozen stones came arcing toward them from out of the crowd. Several bounced off the road in front. One hit against a front wheel with a loud crash and then ricocheted back out to the side. The car was all too slowly picking up speed as Fumbe leaned forward to crouch behind the steering wheel. They could hear taunting whistles as more stones rose in the air around them. There was a cracking thump as one better aimed rock hit the A-frame right in front of Bartley. The impact sent him jerking in shock over toward Fumbe who was crouched so low as barely to be able to see where he was going. He was aiming the car straight down the centre of the road and still accelerating as more stones and rocks continued to rain down around. The car was belting along at 130kph before the crowd thinned out and the barrage of missiles ceased.

They were well past the airport turn-off and into the surrounding flat country when they encountered the first traffic heading toward them back into the city. Fumbe gently eased off the accelerator, but Bartley's heart was still racing. He had to admire Fumbe for charging through the gauntlet of rocks and keeping them safe. If he had been driving he guessed he would probably have stopped dead in fright and left them sitting targets at the mercy of the crowd. At the same time he was annoyed that neither of them had given any thought to the announcement that a second phase of roadside demolition was scheduled for today. They should have anticipated that those who were about to lose their homes and businesses were likely to riot. Now that he thought about it, he was also angry and incredulous that the police at the other end of the road had waved them through knowing full well that they were heading into danger. There was of course nothing he could do about this. It would be pointless to write a strong protest to the Foreign Ministry condemning the police for their failure to take action to protect a member of the diplomatic corps from an obvious threat. If it happened in any other country there might be at least an apologetic reply – but here in Kutaba the Foreign Ministry would be unlikely as much as even to acknowledge receipt.

On the other hand, he probably had very little to complain about compared to those poor sods who had been throwing the rocks. Their homes, their livelihoods were about to be taken away from them as soon as the bulldozers arrived. Their houses and shops would be levelled and anything they did not succeed in rescuing from within would be buried in the rubble. There would be no compensation, no offer of alternative accommodation. They would be told that their properties had been put up illegally in the first place and that the authorities owed them nothing. And what purpose did all this demolition serve? Well, it would allow for a wider, faster, more comfortable road for Bartley and his kind to drive back and forth to the airport. And yes, it would impress visitors to the capital.

He could not really blame the crowd for throwing stones at him in his big car. In their place he would probably want to do the same.

Wrapped up in their thoughts, neither he nor Fumbe spoke much for the next hour until they pulled into a roadside restaurant. Bartley ordered a Coke and Fumbe a coffee and a plate of samosas that arrived marooned in a puddle of grease. Even across the table Bartley could smell the rancid cooking oil. Fumbe pulled the plate toward him and scowled.

"These Kutabans, they do not care how to make food. They make bad food, they eat bad food. They think everyone will eat the same."

Having delivered this further observation on the nature of his fellow countrymen, he smothered the soggy parcels in a lurid red chilli sauce from a plastic bottle snatched from a neighbouring table. He started to eat with a degree of satisfaction that belied his earlier proclaimed disgust. The chilli sauce must have helped.

Bartley carefully wiped the neck of his Coke bottle with a napkin before putting it to his lips. He was constantly intrigued by Fumbe's ability to speak of Kutabans in the third person, as if he were not one of them and how one moment he could be disparagingly critical, the next intensely proud.

They were sitting on a small terrace to the front of the restaurant under shelter from the sun and away from the swarm of flies in the dark interior. Still, a goodly number of bluebottles buzzed around their table, settling on the damp stains on the plastic cloth and hovering above Fumbe's plate. Every few moments he tried swatting them away. Bartley looked over to where the Landcruiser was parked. He could clearly see a good-sized dent in the front window pillar on the passenger side. It offered an odd symmetry to the already baboon-dented bonnet. It must have been quite a large rock to cause such damage and he realized it was the pillar that had protected him. Another few centimetres to either side the rock could have lifted off his head. He put his Coke back on the table and carefully placed the cap on top as Fumbe swiped out again.

As he finished off his last samosa, Fumbe followed Bartley's gaze at the car. He wiped his fingers on the small quarter of paper napkin that had been provided. It looked for a moment that he was about to offer some comment. Instead, he proceeded to pour three spoons of sugar into his already sweetened coffee.

"How long will it take to reach Lion Rock?" Bartley asked.

Lion Rock Lodge was where they had arranged to stay the night. It was only a short drive of perhaps half an hour from there to Bakooli and Bartley had chosen the Lodge rather than stay in one of the few hotels in town that offered much cheaper accommodation - $15 a night for "non-residents" and $3 for citizens such as Fumbe. It was run by a Dutchman whom Otto had briefly met at his Embassy. It was he who suggested the place. The accommodation, he claimed, was top class with no fear of mosquitoes hiding in dark corners – much better than the rooms in town with their threadbare sheets and shadowy interiors that promised a night of slow tortured itching and countless sudden awakenings to the buzzing of a kamikaze mosquito in the ear. Otto had even volunteered to phone to make sure that an extra effort was made for Bartley's visit. Bartley was looking forward to the evening.

"I think three o'clock," Fumbe replied. "The road is straight. Soon it becomes a dirt road and that will make us slow. Here there has been no rain, so there should be no problems with mud."

Bartley laid some notes on the table to pay and rose, leaving Fumbe to finish his coffee and call for the bill. Rather than finish his Coke, he thought he should take the opportunity to empty his bladder in the privacy of the restaurant's toilet. The alternative was to risk being taken short and having to stop to get out of the car en route. He knew from past experience that no matter how apparently isolated the location might be, a white man pissing on the roadside would magically draw a crowd. It was not necessary to understand the words the onlookers shouted one to another - it was obvious they would be speculating as to whether a white man pissed the same way and whether his penis really was as tiny as they suspected. There would invariably be much pushing and shoving to get a proper view. Better then, to drink as little as possible before a day's travel and to avail of every single opportunity that presented itself to empty the tank.

By the time he came back to the car, still drying his hands on a tissue from his pocket, Fumbe had already started the engine and was waiting for him. He marvelled at Fumbe's capacity to drink coffee and then drive for hours without needing to relieve himself.

As Fumbe predicted, they soon ran out of tarred road. They were driving on dirt for half an hour when they came upon a massive road works operation. Huge yellow earthmoving machines raised a dense cloud of red dust that they saw in the distance long before they reached the point where the road was closed and the little traffic that passed along was diverted off to the side onto a boulder strewn, makeshift track. The dust trails from their Landcruiser and a bus in front were as nothing as they entered the heavy, red storm heaved up by the bulldozers and giant-wheeled trucks. It completely enveloped them, forcing them to close their windows and air vents until they felt they were suffocating in the oppressively hot and humid interior. Bartley felt the beginnings of a headache, as always when starved of fresh air. Layers of dirt descended on the windscreen, completely obscuring any view of the way ahead. Fumbe repeatedly squirted water over it, the wipers leaving greasy gravelled streaks where they failed to sweep clean. Trying to peer out, Bartley caught a brief glimpse of a road worker holding vertically upright a long marked pole while a cluster of Chinese engineers in high visibility vests stood alongside a tripod as one of them peered through a theodolite lens. The Landcruiser drove forward at little more than walking pace.

The diversion seemed to go on for ever, but eventually they passed the last of the bulldozers. Still, the road remained closed and they were forced to continue on the rough track, making only slightly faster progress. The thick curtain of dirt hanging in the air closed down behind them, but they were still breathing in the dust from the bus in front. Like many buses in Kutaba that were colourfully painted with giant pictures of famous footballers or other popular heroes, this one bore on its rear an outsize portrait of Queen Elizabeth II wearing a funny little hat. She seemed to be exercising some royal prerogative by refusing to allow her vehicle pull into the side to let them overtake. They were unable to speed up, forced to drive only as fast as the bus could go. There was little other traffic using this stretch and they were passed only by an occasional overloaded bus or truck coming in the opposite direction. Considering the paucity of traffic, Bartley was at a loss to understand why a Chinese construction company should decide to go to so much effort and expense to upgrade it.

"It's for the Prime Minister," Fumbe explained. "When you see a new road you know it is always for the house of a minister. The Prime Minister is building himself a big house near here. You see over there, far away in the mountains? The house will be in the hills there. It will be very beautiful, very cool. But he needs a fine road also to this house."

Bartley had indeed noticed and commented on several occasions that the only places in Bamgboshe where the roads were not badly potholed or prone to frequent flooding seemed to be in those areas where it happened that some minister might be living. The ideal location for a foreigner to lease a house - usually at some ridiculous rent that would easily rival New York, Paris or Rome - was on a street or road in which a minister was known to reside. Not only did this guarantee a good road surface, but also the certainty of a virtually uninterrupted supply of electricity. One could be sure that there would be a local electrical sub-station prioritised to continue to provide power to prevent any minister being inconvenienced by the almost daily blackouts that afflicted the rest of the capital.

It seemed that Fumbe was right, for soon they passed a junction with another road that branched off eastward toward the hills. The branch road bore evidence of having been marked out for future upgrading, while the main road, toward Bakooli, remained a compacted dirt road.

ELEVEN

They had lost considerable time, but they were now back on the main road and at last able to overtake Queen Elizabeth and her train of suffocating dust. Fumbe began to speed, steering frantically to avoid boulders and dried wheel ruts. Still, it was well after four by the time they saw in front of them the low hills of Lion's Rock creeping in closer to the road. The flat, barren landscape along which they had been travelling for hours began to give way to an undulating, acacia covered scrub. A wooden post appeared at the side of the road with a sign "Lion's Rock Lodge – 6 Km" pointing off to the left. They followed this along a track that climbed gently in long sweeping curves up toward hills where acacia mixed with denser, luxuriant bushes and trees. A wooden barrier across the road marked the entrance to the Lodge. They stopped as an ancient security guard carrying what looked like an even more ancient rifle came forward. He checked their names on a sheet of paper attached to a clipboard and made a show of marking a tick on the paper with a short pencil stub before raising the barrier.

Bartley was greeted as he stepped out of the car by Luuk, the owner and Otto's fellow-countryman – tall and lean where Otto was well filled. Taking in the dust-caked appearance of the Landcruiser and of Bartley himself, he suggested that Bartley might first want to go to his cabin to have a shower. They could then meet up for a drink in the bar area before dinner. There were apparently no other guests and Luuk evidently welcomed company.

Fumbe retrieved their bags from the rear of the car and handed Bartley's over to a waiting porter. There was usually a separate area of accommodation for drivers in this type of up-market lodge. Fumbe would always claim to have met a *good friend* after staying somewhere like this. No matter where he travelled, he seemed invariably to make fast friends among the other drivers or staff. His habit was to take himself off to the staff quarters on arrival and reappear the next morning with a satisfied and contented look. He would later regale Bartley with at least one outrageous anecdote involving one or more of his *good friends* from the previous evening. Bartley suspected that Fumbe might also charm a female or two in the kitchen and be rewarded with some extra treats or delicacies not necessarily offered other drivers.

Bartley's cabin was built on stilts safely above any night-time wildlife and affording a view of the distant plain. There was a small deck by the door that was just large enough to accommodate two canvas chairs and a low table. An aluminium bucket stood on the table filled with ice water in which two large sized bottles of Hippo beer lay cooling. There were also two inverted drinking glasses and a bottle opener. Bartley eyed the bucket thirstily as the porter unlocked the door and carried his bag inside.

The cabin was thatched, with walls of smoothly plastered mud painted a cool vanilla. Inside it was dominated by a larger than life king-sized bed with four high corner posts that supported a veil of mosquito netting. A heavy carved wooden chest stood at the end of the bed and the porter laid Bartley's bag on this before starting into his routine in broken English of pointing out the room's features.

As soon as he was left to himself, Bartley peeled off his damp shirt, hesitantly sniffing the armpits and conceding that he better not wear it again. He threw it down over one of a second pair of canvas chairs that flanked the door. He remembered the beer outside and stepped out, lifting a bottle of Hippo from the bucket. He flicked off the cap and took a long, grateful mouthful then carried it inside where he placed it on top of the three-quarter height wall separating the bathroom off at the back of the cabin.

He felt sufficiently better after his shower and change of clothes, sitting outside on his porch and finishing off the remains of the warmish Hippo, to look over some papers he had brought with him. He reckoned he should brief himself and not go off half-cocked, talking from the top of his head as he had at the reception yesterday. For once, he told himself, he should be sure to ask the right questions and cover all the angles for the Minister's visit. He had just about finished reading when he heard a roar of two or more vehicles driving up to the main reception area. The engines died, followed by the sounds of doors opening and slamming shut, loud laughter and shouting. He looked at his watch, it was almost seven and time to meet up with Luuk for that promised drink before dinner.

As he made his way to reception, he found a gold coloured and obviously very new Landcruiser blocking the entrance. Beyond it were parked a couple of other cars, one an older Nissan 4X4 painted a dark military green, together with two pick-up trucks around which stood more than half a dozen armed men smoking and quietly joking with each other. They were dressed in green uniforms, except for a couple wearing camouflage fatigues. They gave him barely a glance, even as he stumbled while trying to edge past the Landcruiser into reception. Beyond reception lay the dining area from which he could hear sounds of a raucous party. He rather tentatively made his way in.

The dining lounge ran the length of the building. It sat cantilevered out over the slope, looking down past the canopy of trees toward the flat plain that stretched far into the horizon. As he entered, he saw five men standing in front of a small bar counter at the far end. He was astonished to recognise the figure in the centre of the group, again dressed in a form-fitting white suit. Minister Emmanuel Gabi was apparently finishing off some hilarious story and his companions burst into deafening laughter. There was no mistaking his being the alpha male of the group. Bartley's entrance to the lounge caught Gabi's attention just long enough to offer a careless salute to the new arrival. He half raised a hand that clutched both a beer glass and an even larger cigar before turning back to his companions. Bartley stifled a groan and made his way as unobtrusively as possible toward the table furthest from the bar.

A waiter appeared and he ordered a gin and tonic, watching out of the corner of his eye as the waiter headed down toward the bar where Bartley saw that Luuk, previously part-obscured by the visitors, was serving behind the counter. Receiving the order, Luuk gazed down in his direction and, in a brief moment of eye contact, gave an almost imperceptible shake of his head.

The waiter returned with the drink.

"Mr Luuk, he say sorry he cannot have drink now. Maybe he comes later. Now you want order dinner?" He laid a menu on the table beside the drink.

Gabi and his entourage continued drinking while Bartley was served. He was finishing off a large skewer of charcoal-grilled beef served with sweet potato when the group left the bar and headed toward a table across from him. They must have ordered earlier because the waiter was already standing by, holding plates of food. A second waiter was placing three Hippos and a couple of bottles of wine on the table.

Gabi took a seat at one end, motioning one of his companions to sit to his right, while allowing the others to choose seats at will. Unlike his companions in civilian clothes, the one receiving special treatment was dressed in a neatly pressed, green military uniform. The waiter poured a little wine into a glass in front of the Minister and stood back. Bartley stole a look over as the soldier leaned forward and whispered confidentially into Gabi's ear. As he did so, Bartley caught sight of a long, ugly scar running from his left temple down to his jaw. It cut across the corner of his eye leaving a gouge of angry-looking reddish-blue skin. Bartley drew in a breath shocked not only to see Gabi again, but Gabi apparently in the company of the shadowy Major Mbuta.

Gabi nodded emphatically. He looked down at the beer bottle in front of him, raised it and took a large mouthful before banging it roughly back on the table. Laughing, he patted the soldier on the shoulder before turning his attention to the wine in front of him. He reached for the glass, lifted it and knocked back its contents, waving the empty glass carelessly at the waiter to pour wine all round. He looked across just in time to catch Bartley's gaze. Bartley immediately dropped his eyes back to concentrate on removing a last chunk of meat from his skewer, but the Minister's eyes remained fixed on him, a look of slight puzzlement beginning to show on his face.

A moment later, however, he was again fully engrossed in his companions and the food in front of him. He did not seem to notice when Luuk appeared and slipped into the seat beside Bartley. He carried a glass of wine in his hand and signalled the waiter to bring another for Bartley.

"I am sorry I could not join you earlier. That's Emmanuel Gabi, the Minister for Environment and Natural Resources." He tilted his head discreetly in the direction of Gabi's table.

"Yes, I recognise him. In fact, I met him briefly at a reception only yesterday, but I can't say I know him."

"Ah, if I were to be indiscreet, I would say you are better not to know him." There was a bitter tone to Luuk's voice.

"He arrived just after you," he continued. "I wasn't expecting him, but that is how he and other Ministers always come. Always without notice and always with friends, expecting that I feed them and their guests. I have to give them rooms and also as much as they want to drink. Unfortunately the Minister knows that we have only one guest this evening so I cannot use the excuse of our being full to refuse rooms tonight. Worse, it means also I will have to stay up to look after them until they decide to go to bed, whenever that will be."

Bartley stole a discreet look at Gabi in his white suit. Despite the dim light he still wore his tinted green glasses. Apart from the day before, Bartley had only seen him from a distance, speaking in Parliament. In a setting such as here there was no doubting his aura of power and haughty self-confidence, but there was something also compelling about his closest companion.

"That soldier with the Minister, do you know him? He's Major Mbuta, isn't he?"

"Yes, indeed. You know him too?" Luuk was surprised. "He is a frequent visitor and seems to spend a lot of time passing through to Bakooli. Whenever Gabi visits also, he is always with him. At least he pays his bill when he comes alone."

"You mean the Minister doesn't?"

"Certainly not," Luuk's voice could not hide more than a hint of his frustration. "As Minister for Environment and Natural Resources, he is personally responsible for renewing my operator's licence every year. He has told me he needs to visit to assure himself that everything is up to standard. Unfortunately I need his approval and permission for other things too, and he knows it. For example, I have security problems here. Look at all the other lodges in Kutaba and you will see they all have properly armed guards to protect their premises and guests. You know we all need guards not only to protect our guests in case some dangerous animal wanders into camp, but also because there are gangs of armed robbers that target tourist hotels and lodges. We are quite isolated here and have a greater need for protection than most, but, this is the only lodge or camp I know that has not yet been allowed to bring in a couple of guards with proper guns. All I have is a very old rifle that is shared by the guards at the entrance gate. Perhaps you noticed it on your way in? It's so ancient it doesn't need a licence. It is a copy of a Martini-Henry. It is what the British used in Africa in the old days. It is so old they used it even during the Zulu Wars in South Africa. Now it is probably more dangerous to the person holding it than to anyone else."

"Why is it so difficult for you to get a gun licence?" Bartley was interested.

"There are so many reasons. As long as I am looking for a licence it keeps me in my place and dependent on keeping the Minister happy. But there are also problems with the law that make it difficult for a foreigner to own a gun. I lease this land from the government, but everything else here I own: the buildings and cabins and everything inside them. I have brought it all here and paid for it out of my savings. But the government, or rather Minister Gabi, would like me to bring in a Kutaban partner to share ownership. Then they would allow me a licence. But a Kutaban partner would also need to own fifty-one per cent for the Lodge to qualify as a non-foreign operation. Naturally, I wouldn't be paid as much as a single dollar for handing over that fifty-one per cent.. My Kutaban partner would also no doubt have to be a personal friend or relative of the Minister. You can easily imagine that in a few years he could decide to throw me out and then I would be left with nothing."

Luuk went quiet, realising the danger of expressing himself too openly and afraid that anything he might say could be overheard.

"Next time you come," he promised, "we will share a decent bottle of my own French wine - not one you will find on our menu. Let me know when you are coming and I will take some good steaks out of the freezer. I have some T-bones here that you will not find elsewhere in Kutaba. But now, I am sorry, I had better get back to make sure the Minister has everything he needs."

Bartley finished his wine and had just ordered a coffee when Gabi stood up and headed out toward the reception area. He looked briefly at Bartley as he passed, again looking somewhat puzzled. Bartley returned the look with a nervous nod. His coffee arrived lukewarm and he drank it quickly, intending to make his exit before the Minister might come back. In his hurry a few last dregs from the cup spilt down the front of his shirt. He was still dabbing at it as left the table and headed toward the exit where he abruptly collided with the returning Minister.

"I know you, I think, don't I?" The Minister deftly shunted him off and looked at him suspiciously, taking in the dribble of coffee down his shirt.

"Er, yes. We were introduced at the Botswana reception yesterday, Minister - the Irish Chargé d'Affaires, Bartley Ryan."

"Of course, well done! And what are you doing down in this part of the country?" the Minister was staring at the stain.

"My Minister, the Irish Minister for Foreign Affairs, is coming to visit Kutaba in November. We are thinking we might bring him to Bakooli to see a canal project that Ireland is supporting here and I have come down to see what can be arranged and what else the Minister might see or visit in the area."

"The Irish Foreign Minister is coming? I was not told. My Ministry will need to be involved. I hope at least that our Regional Governor, Mr Awale, is aware of the visit and will make some preliminary arrangements. I will tell him to keep me informed." Gabi nodded, as if to agree with himself.

"Yes, I expect the Governor will help with some of the arrangements. I have an appointment to meet him first thing in the morning. But, of course, the

Embassy will take care of most of whatever can be organised. We also have an Irish priest locally that I will be meeting and I'll see whether he has any advice."

"An Irish priest?" Gabi craned forward, his green glasses threateningly close to Bartley's own grimy spectacles. There was no mistaking the sudden animosity in his voice. "Would that be Fr. O'Driscoll from Shole?" he practically spat out the name.

"Yes," Bartley flinched, "Do you know him?"

"Yes, I know him. I do not see how he would be of any help. It is the people of Kutaba that will give you proper advice. It seems I shall have to inform myself more of this visit. Well, it was good to meet you again Mr....." he hesitated.

"Ryan."

"Yes, Ryan." The Minister turned brusquely away. As he walked toward his table, Mbuta glanced over at Bartley. Their eyes met briefly and Bartley nodded. The soldier returned the gesture before looking up at Gabi who had pulled out his chair to sit down.

Sitting a half-hour later on the deck of his cabin, Bartley rewound his encounter with Gabi. The embarrassment of the coffee stain on his shirt and colliding with the Minister was replaced by apprehension over Mbuta's presence. Then again, why was it Gabi seemed so hostile at the mention of Fr. O'Driscoll? Was there some bad blood between the priest and the Minister?

Gabi and Mbuta's arrival had certainly lent an edge to what otherwise should have been an enjoyable and stress free evening. The Minister alone was certainly an intimidating individual and Bartley sympathised with Luuk having to pander to his demands. He wondered how the Dutchman had ended up here. He would guess him to be in his fifties. Did he have a family somewhere? Certainly he had not picked an easy place to begin a business, but as Bartley sat looking out into the distant dark, he felt a certain jealousy that Luuk should have found such a wild, beautiful place to live, well away from the mundane, everyday bureaucracy of his own life.

He could no longer hear the noisy chatter that had earlier reached his cabin from the dining room. They must have adjourned back down the dining room toward the bar. The cooling evening breeze that had met him when he had first come out on the deck had died down and the air had grown heavy. The leaves in the trees below had ceased to rustle and were now completely still. Even the cicadas had all at once fallen silent. In the distance a black bank of cloud moved in over the plain. Then he saw the lightening, successive sheets of it coming from first one side and then another while, underneath, the plain lit up and became a vast and wild stage for a firework spectacular. A first low rumble of thunder was followed by another and then one more until it rolled into one long endless crash. Bartley sat mesmerised until eventually there was a hint of a breeze returning that caused the citronella candle on the table in front of him to splutter. Heavy drops of rain began to patter down and he rose to go inside just as the storm closed over him and started to drum down against the thatch.

The storm did nothing to raise his spirits. He could not shrug off an anxiety that had overtaken him. He shivered.

TWELVE

Thursday, 2 October.

Thankfully there was no sign of Gabi, his friends or his protective detail when Bartley made his way over to breakfast early the next morning. The pathway that led from his cabin was soft and muddy and the trees above still wet and dripping, but the storm of the night before had passed. The sun was promising a scorching heat with white swirls of condensation already rising from the ground.

"Good morning," Luuk greeted him as he entered the dining room. The Dutchman was distinctly bleary-eyed, but seemed in a cheerful mood.

"Good morning, Luuk. How are you? You had a late night?"

"Yes, pretty late, but it was not as late as I had expected. Minister Gabi and the Major left some time before two o'clock as soon as it stopped raining. It seems he had urgent business somewhere down south and was anxious to arrive early today. He left his other friends here, but I closed the bar as soon as he drove off. They saw I was not offering them rooms, so they also drove off soon after."

Bartley could imagine the Minister sleeping comfortably in the back seat of his gold Landcruiser while his exhausted driver and guards made sure he was delivered safely wherever he was going. It was a feature of Kutaba he found that the local bigwigs or indeed anyone who employed a maid or driver remained oblivious to the hired helps' need for rest.

He was himself anxious to make an early start and he hurried through breakfast before heading out to look for Fumbe. He found him standing by their car, supervising the Lodge's porter finish drying off the windscreen with a leather cloth. Fumbe wore a serious, glazed-eye look that Bartley recognised. It warned him not to ask if he had spent a good night. Instead he offered a "Good morning, Fumbe, ready to go?" and when Fumbe nodded he opened his door, threw his overnight bag in the back and climbed into the car. Fumbe muttered something to the porter before relieving him of the cloth. He opened the back tailgate and placed the leather in a side pocket before easing himself forward to reach over the back of the rear seat to lift up Bartley's bag and with an audible sigh transfer it into the back storage area. He slammed shut the tailgate and wordlessly got in beside Bartley and started the engine. There was no doubting it: he was not in the best of moods.

They were no more than halfway down the hill leading toward the main road than Fumbe, as Bartley knew he eventually would, made known the cause of his bad humour. The unruly guffaws from the Minister's party down his end of the Lodge, and the more subdued talking and shuffling of the police in and out the staff quarters, resulted in his not getting any sleep until well after the group had left. Additionally, the presence of the soldiers had an inhibiting effect on the unofficial hospitality that he was accustomed to wheedling out of the kitchen staff. Inevitably his complaints focussed yet again on what was wrong with Kutabans, including people who drank too much and politicians who were always on the lookout to get something for nothing or to line their own pockets.

Privately, Bartley agreed but he thought it better not to say anything for fear of encouraging Fumbe. He might keep up this rant all morning. He also needed to focus on the day ahead, beginning first with his meeting with Regional Governor Awale.

He was still mulling over whether he could raise with Awale some questions as regards the accountability of funding for the canal, or perhaps ask the Governor's reaction to the Danish hydrologist's critique of the project, when they arrived on the outskirts of the city. From a distance it appeared dull and featureless, stretched out over a dusty plain. The hills stepping up behind perhaps saved it from total anonymity. Water flowing down the hills had obviously first prompted the building of a settlement in this otherwise inhospitable location, but as the population continued to grow water itself had become the problem. The small town it had once been had developed and grown into a low-lying sprawl. It spread across the flat plain and encroached into the nearer foothills. There, on the greener, higher ground, the houses appeared to be generously proportioned but drab looking mansions insulated behind high walls. Bartley wondered what kind of people could afford such expensive homes.

The road into the city was lined mostly with simple wooden stalls. As they got closer to the centre, the stalls gradually gave way to more substantial shops and offices built on high concrete foundations, their plastered fronts painted fading whites and blues. A river of rubbish, rotting vegetation, plastic bags and bits of broken stone lay on either side of the road washing up against the raised fronts of buildings. A couple of dirty-white goats were chewing the remnants of a discarded woven basket.

The centre of town, when they reached it, was not much more impressive. An attempt had been made to plant trees along a central reservation, but these were stunted in the sun, their sparse, pitiful leaves choking in a thick coating of dust and diesel fumes. There was a hotel, oddly named the New York Palace, probably owned or financed, Bartley guessed, by some Kutaban exile returned from the USA. It stood four stories high with perhaps a half a dozen flimsy iron balconies hanging precariously and with no obvious sense of order from its front facade. It was partially whitewashed, but at least half remained a dull concrete colour as if the owner had run out of paint. Primitive wooden scaffolding rose up along the far end where it appeared the building of an extension had also been abandoned some time previously. Beyond the hotel an older building, colonial in style and gleaming white with tall arched windows, stood somewhat lower than the hotel, but there was no mistaking the dominance of these two buildings over the ramshackle one or two storey buildings surrounding them. When Fumbe pulled up in front of the older building, Bartley had already slipped into the seersucker jacket that he had carefully left hanging from a hook in the back of the car. It looked no less crumpled for all that than if he had balled it into a corner of his bag. He fetched a small, hard-backed notebook from the glove compartment. Fumbe jumped out of his seat and made his way round to the passenger door which he held open in an uncustomary show of respect.

Several steps fronted the building that housed the offices of the Regional Administration and Regional Governor. The entrance led into an open area reaching to the rafters above. To the far left was a wide staircase that led to two timber balconies, one above the other that ran along the back and both sides of the building. Apparently the main offices were all at first or second floor level with access via the balconies. Bartley paused, looking up at the odd and precarious design. Back at ground level, twenty or more people were standing around or sitting on rough benches lining the wall to his right. They were a mix of women with young children who stared at him with open curiosity and men, some in western style shirts, others in traditional flowing robes who shuffled around aimlessly, several of them unselfconsciously scratching their crotches.

It was just gone nine o'clock, but although he had arrived exactly on time for his scheduled appointment, there seemed to be no-one here to greet him. He made his way toward a desk by the back that guarded the entrance to a corridor beyond. A woman official sitting behind the desk seemed to be only half paying attention to several men who stood in front of her talking loudly. They fell silent and turned to take in Bartley as he approached. The official looked up when he asked for the Regional Governor's office, saying he had an appointment. She wearily pointed him toward the bottom of the staircase and muttered, "You go on up top storey".

Arriving at the top of the second flight of stairs that led to the upper of the two balconies, Bartley could feel perspiration seeping from his shirt and through to his jacket. He was breathless and a little dizzy from the climb and it did not help that he found himself standing on what was really no more than a rickety platform. He was able to see the ground far below through cracks that the years had opened in the ancient boards. Half a dozen men stood around, all but one in shirtsleeves and most of them carrying notepads or files. Seeing his arrival, the only one in a jacket, a neat, bald-headed man, stepped forward and greeted Bartley, introducing himself as Colonel Uba, the RS – the Regional Superintendent. The others stood back silent and respectful. As the RS led Bartley to the Regional Governor's private office, they fell in behind. Horrified to see that the balcony ahead sagged precariously outwards, Bartley kept well away from the rail, hugging the wall to his left until he unexpectedly collided with an extremely corpulent figure that had emerged from the open doorway of one of the offices. He staggered outwards, his knees weak as Uba reached out to steady him. The overweight official began to apologise, but a glare from the RS sent him scurrying back through his door. Bartley attempted a grim smile and tightened the grip on his notebook as Uba invited him on. Where the balcony turned right there was a low latched gate that the RS opened. He stood aside, ushering Bartley into the Regional Governor's private corridor. He walked through the first door into an anteroom where three women were sitting behind cramped desks. The RS knocked on an inner door and Bartley heard his name announced before he was ushered in.

Governor Awale advanced to welcome Bartley. He was tall and fit looking for a man in his sixties, with cropped grey hair and matching moustache. He was light skinned, creamy brown rather than black. He gave the impression of a man conscious of his superior importance and dignity.

A long conference table abutted the front of the Governor's own massive dark desk on which sat two large, but rather dated looking white telephones, a couple of small flags – that of Kutaba and the other of Bakooli Region - and a gold lettered plaque reading, "Hon. Regional Governor Francis Awale". The Governor took his seat behind the otherwise clear desk and motioned Bartley to the chair closest to him to the end of the conference table. The light coming in from a large arched window behind cast Awale in silhouette from where Bartley viewed him. The RS and the group of shirt-sleeved officials who had trailed them filed in and took seats on the opposite side of the table, facing Bartley. They were followed by two of the women from the ante-room, one of whom went around turning up gaudily decorated, rose pattern teacups that sat inverted on their saucers. The second placed a couple of thermos jugs of hot water on the table, one directly in front of Bartley. She positioned a can of powdered coffee and a sugar bowl beside it.

Awale leaned back in his chair, gesturing to Bartley to help himself to hot water and coffee. The first woman had left the room and returned with a tray laden with soft drinks which she placed down on the table. She opened a bottle of Sprite and, without asking, set it on the Governor's desk. Bartley finished spooning coffee into his cup and pushed the can and the sugar across to Uba opposite. The RS helped himself before passing them down the table toward the other officials. The tray of soft drinks was also passed in a slow circuit with the first woman stopping to uncap each bottle laboriously with a flimsy, misshapen bottle opener.

It was not until this ritual was complete and the women had left, that the Governor broke the silence. "Welcome Mr Bartley Ryan, First Secretary of the Republic of Ireland Embassy, to Bakooli. We are happy that you have come to see us and that your Honourable Foreign Minister is soon to visit also. He will be most welcome. But before we start, please can we have my officials introduce themselves?"

Awale leaned back, waiting while first the RS, then each man in turn, introduced himself by name and title. It was a ritual that always took place.

"Well, Mr Ryan," the Governor resumed when they had finished, "Again I welcome you to Bakooli and thank you for your visiting us. I am happy that someone from the Irish Embassy has come, as I wish to express my gratitude for your assistance in helping us to ensure that the City of Bakooli will soon have a sustainable supply of water.

"I should particularly wish to express my appreciation for the manner in which your Embassy has cooperated with my officials in the matter. It has been a very effective cooperation that has encouraged a full sense of ownership of the project by the people of Bakooli.

"I will not say much about the future potential of our Region, in particular of the Guseni National Park and of our hopes that it will draw great numbers of tourists. I think you are already well acquainted with this. However, I will say that we look very much forward to the visit of your Foreign Minister and believe it can only contribute to unlocking our potential..." He continued in similar vein for some minutes but, while he hit all the right notes and made all the right points, Bartley was struck by how he still managed to convey the impression of a man reluctantly going through the motions out of courtesy when really he felt he had other more important business to which he should be attending.

The Governor finished and smiled, inviting Bartley to respond. He leaned forward, aware of the trickles of sweat running down from his armpits. Unconsciously he flapped his elbows, stopping when he saw the Governor observing him curiously.

"Thank you, Mr Governor, for your welcome and your kind words. I appreciate that you and your officials have taken time to meet with me today and I take that as a reflection of the good relationship that has developed between the Irish Embassy and the Bakooli Region since the beginning of our involvement in your water project.

"Of course, the purpose of my visit today is to work out with you a programme for my Minister's visit that will be of interest to him, but also importantly, show him the potential of Bakooli of which you spoke and perhaps allow him to see some areas where we could develop new forms of cooperation…"

"Ah, yes, yes," Awale interrupted. There is much detail that we must look into to ensure a successful and useful visit by the Honourable Minister. That is why I have asked the RS personally to accompany you today and to consider all these details. Tonight we will have dinner and we will review all these matters.

"Now, as this is your first visit to Bakooli and to our city, I propose before you leave with the RS that it would be most useful if my officials could give you a short briefing on their work and our plans to raise the economy of our Region." And, before Bartley could get in another word, the Governor looked down the table. "Mr Atoyo, Regional Planning Officer, please will you begin?"

Bartley sat, growing increasingly numb both in his buttocks and brain, as the officials each took their turn to offer a presentation. Some spoke quite fluently but others were faltering, their English difficult to follow. They all seemed most comfortable whenever quoting from sheets of incomprehensible statistics: kilos of grain yields per hectare over the last six months and projected yields for the future; the number of children attending school and the number of classrooms needing to be built to offer primary education to all; the ratio of population to health clinics, doctors and hospital services, including estimates of malaria and HIV infection rates for the next five years. Each official also ended his presentation with a plea for future funding from the "Republic of Ireland Embassy". As they spoke, the Governor studied his iPhone, pressing buttons. Bartley wondered if he could possibly have internet access.

When the presentations finished, Awale finally placed his phone on his desk and briefly summarised that there many areas in which help was needed and where he had confidence that Ireland would "step up to the mark".

Bartley's head was swimming. He was dehydrated from the heat of the crowded office and after the coffee he needed to pee. It was gone eleven o'clock and he was irritated that so much of his day was already lost by this totally unnecessary and useless briefing. He had sat through two hours of these men droning endlessly on about every conceivable sector: education; water and sanitation; health; transport and roads; agriculture; good governance; tourism and the environment and God knew what else. He had however, noted that there was not a single woman present and wondered what Michelle would have made of it. He felt strongly an urge to offer a presentation on 'gender issues'. It would be a tempting revenge on their lengthy expositions if he were to regurgitate a litany of accepted principles on the role of women. He reckoned he could recall much of the detail with which Michelle had once bombarded him. Her effort to educate him must, after all, have made an impression.

He decided against this, not out of any sense of tact or prudence, but rather because he knew well that it would result in more endless talk as each official sought to demonstrate that gender issues were indeed an existing, built-in part of his sector. However, he did feel sufficiently provoked to raise a couple of matters of direct interest to him – matters that might engage even Regional Governor Awale's full attention.

"Well, thank you Governor Awale for organising this most interesting and useful briefing." He was finding it difficult to sound sincere. "I have taken note of what you are trying to achieve and commend you on your efforts. I note also that Bakooli needs all kinds of assistance to advance your plans and I certainly will report all this to my authorities in Dublin.

"Meanwhile, if I could raise one issue about our present project here in Bakooli. I understand that there has been some delay in completing the canal due perhaps to some difficulty with suppliers. There has also been some suggestion of cost over-runs that have not been fully explained. If you...."

Leaning back casually in his chair and picking up his iPhone again, Awale interrupted. "Mr Ryan, I can assure you that there will be no more delay than is necessary to achieve proper and cost effective completion. Some minor issues might appear to be progressing more slowly than we would have hoped, but I have personally looked at these and I am confident that at the end of the day we will make up for any lost time. As for cost over-runs, I can assure you that everything will be accounted for according to the best practice. In this matter I would like to say we welcome that Irish assistance has been given in such a way that allows us full control. So, we can work out any problems for ourselves. This is as it should be, you will agree. Some donors interfere too much. But when we manage a project ourselves our people develop a sense of ownership that makes them more appreciative of the result."

He smiled and tapped his phone gently on the desk as if to signal the end of discussion.

Bartley could see that Awale was not to be drawn into detail about delays or costs. Also reference to donor interference and that old cliché about the need to feel *ownership* was a clear signal to back off.

"Thank you, Mr Regional Governor. That is a helpful reassurance." He paused, thinking, *Shut the fuck up, Bartley,* before hearing himself continue. "I agree completely that the people of Bakooli should have ownership of the project. I hope too that they will all benefit from it. However, if our Minister is to visit the project, we must be completely sure that there are no difficulties or problems that might subsequently come to light and cause embarrassment. If that were to happen it could put into question the possibility of Ireland extending its programme of development assistance to Kutaba. This is something that our Minister is already looking at and that he may be raising with Prime Minister Okeke. I think we would have to insist on a full, audited report before the Minister's visit." *Fuck, now I've gone too far.*

Awale did not try to hide his annoyance. He dropped his phone on the desk and turned to his right, "RS please see to it that the Embassy gets what it needs."

His gaze returned to Bartley, "So, if that is all, Mr Ryan?"

"Well, no. I did want to ask about something else." *Might as well get hung for a sheep as a lamb. Clendenning will probably kill me anyway.*

"You mentioned Guseni National Park. We hear reports that this could result in great hardship for the people of Guseni and threaten an end to their traditional way of life. Perhaps you could comment on this?"

Awale glared at the RS, as if holding him personally responsible for allowing such an outrageous suggestion to be made. He grabbed hold of his iPhone once more and mangled it between his hands.

"My dear Mr Ryan, I cannot imagine where you have heard such reports. It is true that some people are moving from one place to another but that is natural because these people are nomadic pastoralists who traditionally move with their cattle to wherever they find fresh grazing. As you know, there has been much drought and the grazing is now very poor. I do not hide that it is a problem and that there may be more movement of people as a result of the poor rains. But the Guseni is large enough to accommodate a national park and to allow pastoralists continue their traditional way of life. In fact the park should encourage them to continue with their customs and at the same time provide a sanctuary for wildlife.

"Now, I see it is after eleven and I am afraid we have delayed you too long already. You will be anxious to be on your way and I look forward to our having dinner together this evening." Awale paused and then looked over at the RS, "Colonel Uba, you are accompanying Mr Ryan today...."

With that the Governor stood up and with as much good grace as he could muster stretched across to shake Bartley's hand. His officials rose and with evident relief written on their faces quickly filed out of the room. Bartley smiled back at Awale, hiding his thoughts – *Funny how touchy and defensive you and everyone else becomes whenever I ask about the national park idea and what's happening to the locals.*

Uba was waiting at the door.

THIRTEEN

Despite the inauspicious start, Bartley was well satisfied with the outline of a programme for the Minister's visit that he and Colonel Uba had agreed upon by the time he returned to town that evening. During the course of the day the RS had quizzed Bartley on his family background and the various countries in which he had served before coming to Kutaba. For his part, however, Bartley had succeeded in learning almost nothing about the RS, not even how he had come by the title of Colonel.

They had been sitting throughout much of the day together in the back seat of the Landcruiser. Bartley felt exhausted from the constant conversation as they got out in front of the New York Palace. The RS was looking at his watch. There was time enough, he said, before the Regional Governor's dinner for Bartley to freshen up and have a shower. Fumbe had checked them into the hotel that morning and the dinner was to be hosted in its restaurant.

Bartley entered the lobby and was immediately accosted by a white man in jeans and open neck shirt who came striding toward him, both arms outstretched.

"Mr Ryan, I'm guessing. Welcome to Bakooli and to the splendour of the New York Palace. I'm Frank O'Driscoll. I got the word you were coming and I've damned well been waiting for you here for half the day."

"Ah, Father O'Driscoll..." Bartley's hand was crushed in a giant fist.

"Fuck that, Frank will do. And you're Bart?"

"Uh, Bartley."

"Whatever you want, Bartley's fine by me."

O'Driscoll was tall, red-faced, his hair shaved close to his scalp. Bartley warmed to him immediately, despite the bruising inflicted on his finally freed right hand. He could also however, now understand Clendenning's apparent dislike. This priest certainly was not the Ambassador's sort of guy.

O'Driscoll steered Bartley over to a low table where a half-full glass and empty bottle of Hippo were sitting.

"Waiter, garçon, come here. Another Hippo for me, and one quickly for my friend who is an important person from the Embassy of Ireland in Bamgboshe."

A boy had approached the table to lift the empty bottle.

"Lovemore, say hello to Mr Ryan. You must take good care of Mr Ryan because he is a friend of mine, from my country, and he is very, very important.

"Lovemore, do you know what a garçon is? It's a posh way of saying waiter in America, so here in the New York Palace you should be called *garçon* because this is a very posh American hotel."

He turned to Bartley as the young waiter hurried off beaming under the priest's jovial flattery. "Lovemore is one of mine." He hesitated seeing the look on Bartley's face, then laughed. "I mean he is one of my flock - I baptised him. I was going to christen him Francis but his mother insisted at the last moment on Lovemore. I never found out why. Anyway, I have so few opportunities of baptising anyone that I really wasn't in a position to argue with her."

Lovemore returned swiftly with their beers and they began to chat. O'Driscoll talked fondly of the Waterford village where he had grown up.

He was the only boy in his family and his mother believed her prayers had been answered when her son decided to enter the priesthood.

"It was either that or I take over running the family farm; if you could call just the few acres we had a farm. It wasn't a difficult choice and, to tell the truth, being a priest is a grand life."

Bartley smiled, O'Driscoll was an easy and relaxed companion. He had little hesitancy in answering the priest's questions about his own background - his middle class family and the expectation of his going to university in Dublin where to his own surprise he had earned a First in History.

"I suppose I wasn't sure what to do with my degree. There wasn't much chance of my getting a university job and in any case I had enough of university life when I finished my degree. Teaching in school was also the last thing I wanted to do, so I applied for a few civil service jobs, including Foreign Affairs and was offered a place as Third Secretary. After a couple of years, when I got my first posting, I found I enjoyed it even though, at times, it can be frustrating working closely with some of the odd characters Foreign Affairs has employed over the years."

"And Ambassador Clendenning might perhaps be one of those?" O'Driscoll looked him in the eye.

"No, no, I didn't say that." He answered rather too quickly and the other laughed.

Bartley had not realised that they had been chatting for quite so long until he saw that several of the officials from this morning's meeting in the Regional Governor's office had arrived in the lobby and were standing, whispering discreetly together near the door.

He and O'Driscoll talked a few minutes longer and agreed to meet the following morning to visit an orphanage in which the priest took an interest. In fact, O'Driscoll had succeeded in obtaining a small grant to build latrines for it from the Irish government's Missionary Grant Scheme. He assured Bartley that the visit would not take him too far out of his way and would not prevent him arriving back in Bamgboshe before dark tomorrow night.

"I'm looking forward to tomorrow." Bartley glanced over to make sure the officials were out of earshot. Even so, he lowered his voice. "Perhaps then you could also fill me in about local politics. I have heard some stories about, well I don't know, about some nasty goings on in the area of this new wildlife park."

O'Driscoll's smile faded and for the first time he looked serious. "I'd be only too happy."

"There was something else. I met the Minister for Environment and Natural Resources, Emmanuel Gabi, where I was staying last night. He seemed to know you?"

"Really, what did he have to say?"

"Nothing, but somehow he didn't seem too pleased when I said I would be meeting you."

"I'm sure he wasn't."

"I take it then, that you're not the best of friends?" Bartley pressed.

Before O'Driscoll could reply, Uba arrived at the door. The officials by the entrance broke apart and formed up in a line to greet him and shake hands. The little RS beamed. He looked fresh, although his suit remained crumpled and dusty from his travels with Bartley during the day. Bartley became conscious of his own dishevelled state. He had neglected to shower or change because of meeting the priest. Uba did not seem to have noticed them until one of the officials drew his attention to the pair. The RS turned in Bartley's direction but his broad smile died immediately on taking in his companion.

He approached their table as the two stood up.

"Mr Ryan good evening," he said. "Fr. O'Driscoll, how are you? We do not often see you in town." Somehow the tone in which he said this implied that the infrequency of the priest's visits to town was a matter of little regret.

He continued rather formally before O'Driscoll could respond, "Mr Ryan I am afraid that the Regional Governor has been detained by some unexpected business and will not be able to join us this evening. He has asked me to offer his apologies and to represent him."

"Well that's a surprise. I hope you didn't say anything to upset him," the priest muttered so that only Bartley caught it.

The RS realized he must have missed something and paused, about to ask, but then obviously decided the better of it.

"I think it is already quite late and you have a long drive back to Bamgboshe tomorrow. Perhaps we should go straight into the restaurant. I know they will be waiting for us.

"It was good to see you again Fr. O'Driscoll. You should spend more time with us here in Bakooli rather than out in the bush. It cannot be easy for a European to live always in such primitive conditions."

Bartley was on the point of suggesting that O'Driscoll join them for dinner, but it was evident that Uba had sought to dismiss the priest and he guessed somehow that O'Driscoll in turn was not particularly anxious to join the company. Instead, he bade him farewell, promising to meet him in the morning. The RS looked quizzical at this, but then again made as if he had heard nothing. With barely a glance back at the priest, he led Bartley to the restaurant.

The officials followed them cheerfully chatting. They were apparently dining with them and seemed happy at the prospect of a free meal in the best hotel in town.

Uba's manner had changed markedly since the meeting with O'Driscoll and suggested to Bartley that dinner with him and the officials might turn out to be hard going. Trying to make polite conversation, he had started talking about his stay the previous night at Lion Rock Lodge.

"It's a wonderful location. I can see it must be already popular, but it should become even more so as an overnight stop-over when foreign tourists start coming and drive down to visit the new wildlife park in Guseni when it opens. I presume the Regional administration in Bakooli is heavily involved in drawing up plans for running the park and setting up the infrastructure?"

"No, that is a matter for central government and the Ministry of Environment and Natural Resources." Uba's reply surprised him and when the RS failed to elaborate, Bartley tried again.

"But, surely there is huge economic potential for the Bakooli Region? You must be consulted and asked for input. It would make no sense to go ahead without having the Governor and his staff helping to guide the project. Who otherwise is going to be able to ensure it is a success?"

"It is in the hands of the Minister of Environment and Natural Resources. He is the one who has responsibility."

"Minister Gabi?"

"Yes."

"I met him last night. He was at Lion Rock for dinner, but he left early this morning for business down south, I presume in Bakooli."

"Last night? And you say he was travelling south?" Until now the RS seemed distracted, but of a sudden he looked interested.

"Yes, you didn't know? Where else would he be going south if not here to Bakooli? I gather whatever business he had was urgent as he left Lion Rock around two this morning with his army guard."

"As I said, the Minister has responsibility for the wildlife park. He must have some business in that connection out of town. But, you say he had an army guard. I think you must have mistaken – it is the police militia that provides protection for government ministers, not army."

"No, these were soldiers. They were wearing green uniforms. Isn't it black that the police militia wear?"

"Yes, yes, of course you are right," but Uba's surprise was clear. "However, it is of little consequence. But, please excuse me, Mr Ryan, I remember that I have to make a brief telephone call." He stood up abruptly and hurried off, digging his mobile phone out of his pocket.

He stopped at the far end of the room speaking into his phone and then listening silently as his gaze moved briefly back over Bartley. He appeared to say only a few more words and then hung up. Bartley could only think that the call somehow concerned him. But why, and was it something to do with Gabi?

"My apologies, Mr Ryan, it was a matter I had forgotten to attend to earlier." Bartley noticed that, for the second time within minutes, he was again *Mr. Ryan* and no longer the familiar *Bartley* that Uba had agreed to call him earlier in the day. He could not explain why, but he found the RS' apology rang false, making him more than ever convinced that the call did indeed have something to do with Gabi. He was intrigued and wondered what could be going on between the RS and the Minister - and for that matter between the pair of them and Frank O'Driscoll?

"We were talking about Minister Gabi," he decided to probe. "When I was talking to him last night, I told him I would be meeting Fr. O'Driscoll whom you seem to know quite well. I was surprised that the Minister also knew him. Would they have much to do with each other?" He waited to see Uba's reaction.

"Fr. O'Driscoll is well known... perhaps too well known. He would perhaps be better to concentrate more on his praying than..." Uba stopped, immediately seeming to regret his words.

"He should concentrate more on his praying than what?" Bartley attempted to get him to finish.

"Nothing, he seems to have too much time on his hands and should perhaps spend it in prayer. Is that not what priests should do? Ah, at last here comes our food." Uba signalled the discussion was closed.

The meal itself was entirely without flavour, but bland food was preferable to the fiery, and to Bartley's taste buds, often disgusting mix of spices that frequently swamped Kutaban national cuisine. A bowl of insipidly seasoned, lukewarm soup, billed as consommé, had been followed by stringy chicken with overcooked green beans and cold potatoes sheltering under a layer of brown doughy sauce. His knife proved unequal to the task of sawing through the rubbery meat that clung stubbornly onto unidentifiable pieces of carcass. His problem, of course, was that he was trying to use his knife and fork, whereas his dining companions, unfettered by western inhibition, happily used their hands and ripped off the flesh with their teeth. But when he tried to follow suit he soon realised that there was little more than bone and gristle to gnaw on and he quickly abandoned the effort.

The Bakooli officials proved determined to get full value from their free meal and ate copious amounts of bread with each course. Bartley noticed one rather baby-faced individual continuing to eat bread with his ice-cream, dunking his crusts in the melting ice. They each also demolished several bottles of Hippo.

Uba showed no interest in pursuing further conversation and his demeanour continued markedly reserved – a stark contrast to the friendly, talkative individual of earlier in the day. He drank water and spoke occasionally in Bamgboshe dialect with certain of the others, addressing Bartley no more than a couple of times to enquire politely if the food was to his liking. He made little effort to pretend he was enjoying acting the host. Bartley, for his part, could only conclude that the change in mood was all down to Minister Gabi – or perhaps Fr. O'Driscoll? He tried several times to re-engage, but after the first few unsuccessful attempts he resigned himself to finishing dinner in silence.

He was relieved therefore when the RS finally indicated an end to the evening, pushing away from the table and standing up. They said goodnight with a shake of hands all round between Bartley, the RS and each of the officials with whom he had not exchanged a single word throughout the whole evening. He picked up his room key at reception and headed off to bed.

Entering his room for the first time, it came as a pleasant surprise to find it looked recently refurbished. Even the bed came supplied with a duvet rather than the tired, stained blankets he was expecting. However, when he crawled gratefully into bed, he found that the sheet beneath him reached no more than three quarters way down the length of the mattress. He got up to investigate and found that it had been over-generously tucked in at the top leaving insufficient length to cover the bottom end. He started to strip the sheet off the bed only to discover that the lengthy fold-over was in fact concealing a foot long, lateral tear. He folded it back as he had found it. Then, feeling queasy at the sight of the rather intimate staining on that part of the mattress that remained uncovered, he took a towel from the bathroom to place over it. He felt exhausted as he went to pick up the duvet and throw it over his makeshift patchwork. It was at this point that he realised the duvet had no cover.

Exhausted and wanting nothing more than sleep, he felt compelled to make his way down to the lobby to complain. A drowsy-eyed receptionist behind the counter failed to understand what he wanted, but phoned the manager who appeared some ten minutes later. This latter spoke good English and was most sympathetic. Unfortunately he was unable to help. He was already aware that there was no duvet cover. The duvets had been imported directly from the US, he explained, but the covers that had been ordered with them had unfortunately not yet arrived. He hoped they would be delivered within the month but meanwhile, he shrugged, one just had to make do.

There was no point, Bartley conceded, disputing the logic: there were duvets, but no duvet covers. *Making do* was a Kutaban tradition. He was too beaten by tiredness and Kutaban logic to mention the torn sheet.

Despite, or perhaps because of his exhaustion, he lay awake for what felt like hours. His mind refused to shut down and confused thoughts involving those he had met during the last twenty-four hours - Gabi, Uba and O'Driscoll - raced endlessly round in his head. Eventually, he dozed fitfully, but sleep turned into a long series of broken dreams in which he imagined various exotic bugs crawling out from the crevices of Clendenning's desk. But for some reason it was Minister Gabi, not the Ambassador, who was sitting behind the desk. Between snatches of sleep he struggled to free his feet from the towel that kept knotting itself around his ankles.

FOURTEEN

Friday, 3 October.

As they left the New York Palace, it was Bartley's turn today to be in poor temper. Fumbe had taken one look at him as he placed his bag in the back of the Landcruiser and, mirroring Bartley the previous morning, said nothing. He himself had slept well, unconcerned by the absence of a duvet cover in his identical bedroom for which he, as a Kutaban national, had paid a fraction of what Bartley had been charged.

Bartley's mood did not improve when, upon reaching the outskirts, Fumbe turned left southwards rather than north back in the direction of Bamgboshe. When he had agreed to visit Fr. O'Driscoll's orphanage, he assumed that it lay somewhere off the road on his way home. He had not realized that it would involve a detour south again. However, since he had promised to show up he had no option but follow the directions O'Driscoll had given Fumbe while he had been in at dinner with Uba.

The orphanage took a good hour's fast driving to reach, but it turned out to be very close to the landing strip that he and the RS had visited the day before and that they hoped could be used for the Minister's visit. O'Driscoll was waiting for them with an elderly local couple, standing in front of a collection of four rather run-down buildings roofed with a combination of corrugated tin sheeting and lengths of blue plastic weighted down with stones. The buildings were no more than one or two room huts with mud plaster peeling off the walls, exposing the wood and stick frame underneath. A group of around twenty children of various ages, one no more than a baby, and several girls who could have passed for being in their early twenties but were more likely at most in their mid-teens, were lined up on a dusty playground of sorts in front of the foremost building.

O'Driscoll introduced the couple, Mr and Mrs Malinga - whom Bartley realized were also probably much younger than they first appeared - as the owners and "managers" of the orphanage. All four then stood aside, quiet as the children began singing, first in low, almost whispering voices that gradually swelled in volume. They took up a dance to the rhythm they had set, shuffling back and forward, their feet scraping the ground and raising a cloud of dust around them.

The song, O'Driscoll translated, was a welcome for Bartley and a thank you for the money that had helped build latrines for the orphanage. After some minutes of singing and dancing, the children turned sideways from the guests and raised their right hands to point in the direction of the buildings behind them. The singing stopped and in its place a childish chant rose up.

"They're saying how great it is to have new latrines, but look now at the state of the house we are living in. The roof has holes that let in the rain, the walls are crumbling and there are no proper doors or windows. They're asking if you can help with these now." The priest grinned at Bartley's discomfort and, as the children fell silent, suggested a quick tour.

"A relieving pee or just a peek at the latrines and then we can send you off back to the big city," as he put it.

Followed by the mute Malingas, he first led Bartley into the nearest of the buildings. The children stood respectfully aside although one little girl, perhaps about three, with a round face and a full head of curly hair and a huge smile seemed unable to resist the sight of the strange looking white man and rushed up suddenly to grab hold of Bartley's trouser leg. He eyed her suspiciously, taking in the sticky snot smeared over her cheeks and the clammy little fingers clutching at his knee. He was embarrassed, not sure how to react, but the huge smile she offered made him quickly forget any sense of reticence he might feel. He stopped and reached down to take her hand in his own.

"OK, you show me around." he said in English smiling back at her. He could not help wondering whether if he had initially been put off by her snot-covered face that she for her part might similarly have been repelled by his own scrofulous appearance? As he walked inside with her, self-consciously hand in hand, he hoped not. But yes, it was time he did something about his appearance.

Inside, the building was divided by a thin partition into two rooms. In the first flimsy bunk beds were ranged along the walls with several more standing in the centre of the room. He could see well worn, greyish green mattresses partly covered by a motley mix of threadbare blankets. As O'Driscoll led the way around the beds he stopped at a plastic basin on the floor. It was one of several and the beds seemed to have been moved aside to accommodate them.

"For the rain," O'Driscoll nodded toward the ceiling and Bartley followed his gaze to where the blue filtered light from the plastic above was generously punctured by spots of clear sunshine.

O'Driscoll translated as Mrs Malinga began to talk, saying that eighteen children slept in this room. They were the older ones, up to sixteen years of age, but most of them were not yet in their teens. Many of them had been here for years, some handed in as orphans, others babies silently abandoned at the door by mothers unable to care for them. She and her husband had no children of their own and had taken in first one, then two unwanted children. Over the years the number had grown and at present they had twenty-six. There were not enough beds for all and the older ones, from ten upwards, took turns at sleeping on the floor. In the last year the number of children needing a home, she said, had risen sharply. As O'Driscoll translated she glanced nervously at her husband before whispering a further comment. Bartley looked at the priest who seemed to hesitate.

"She says she is afraid there will soon be many more orphans. I'll tell you later." O'Driscoll raised an arm as much, it seemed, to change the subject as to usher Bartley forward into the second room.

Here, the little girl who until then had kept a steady grip on Bartley's hand let go and ran over to a small bed, evidently her own, in the corner. There were four more similarly sized beds in this room and alongside the central partition there were two small baby cots. The girl shouted something to Bartley and giggled loudly, throwing herself onto the mattress.

"Charity has taken a shine to you." O'Driscoll turned to Bartley, but his gaze did not reflect the happiness of the girl's face. He looked suddenly tired and paused for a moment before sighing.

"Alright, just so you know. I brought Charity here earlier this year. She is from the south, from the far side of my parish. I heard her crying and found her hiding behind some rocks on a hill just above her home...." He halted again, seeming unsure how to continue.

"I'm sure you have heard stories, the rumours. Well they are true. I spend much of my time in the centre of the area that is being cleared for the so-called wildlife park. I see what is really happening.

"The official story is about the park, but it's very far from the truth. Alright, so your friend Minister Gabi says he wants to relocate pastoralists to set aside land for a wildlife reserve. But why is there a drilling team from AMADO, you know American-Anglo-Dutch Oil, in Guseni? A wildlife park bringing in tourists would need more water supplies and that would mean digging wells. But AMADO is an oil company, not a water company. So what is going on? I believe the whole story about setting up a wildlife park is no more than a cover to get people off the land before they find oil. Then when they find it, Gabi will forget about any wildlife and start exploiting the oil, no doubt creaming off a handsome dividend for himself and his cronies. Meanwhile, the people who have been cleared off the land won't get a dollar of the revenue."

Bartley was shocked. So Andersen had been right that Gabi must have another agenda and this was it – oil. Even Professor Ballo did not seem to have known.

"The drilling team has an army escort and other army units move around to clear different areas before it arrives." O'Driscoll continued. "That's how I found Charity. I heard an army unit had been in an area and went down to take a look. I saw smoke from where I knew her family lived. When I arrived her family's huts had been burnt and were still smouldering. The carcasses of their cows were lying on the ground beside them. There was no sign of the family or any of the other families that used to live nearby. There were empty army ration cans strewn all around and truck tyre tracks, so I know it was soldiers who had been there. Then I heard Charity crying just above me. I still don't know how long she had been hiding on that hill. I tried for weeks to find some trace of her family, but I came up blank. I guess they are all dead and that their bodies have been hidden or dumped somewhere remote."

So much then, Bartley thought, for the British Ambassador and his superior sources of intelligence. This was worse than anyone could imagine.

"Are you sure it was the army that set fire to the houses and took people away? How can they murder or kill and hope to cover it up?" Despite all the evidence, he still did not want to believe it. This was way outside the world he lived in. Dammit, he was a civil servant, supposed to be writing SMaP reports, not investigating alleged army massacres.

"Yes, it had to be the army, though I can't be sure as I sometimes see police militia around. But it seems to be the army that terrorises people in the villages. The police militia mostly patrol around Bakooli city and seldom in the rural areas. When they do, the people appear less frightened of them.

"Bringing Charity here was a real risk for the Malingas. She may be a small child, but she must have seen what happened to her family. If it was suspected that there was a surviving witness living here, the orphanage itself could be in danger. Whenever anyone is killed, whenever a homestead is destroyed or a village razed, the army is careful not to leave any witnesses. Even a little girl like Charity would count as a threat and would have to be dealt with. That in turn would mean getting rid of the Malingas."

Bartley drew a deep breath. Maybe coming here had been a bad idea. It was difficult to take this all in.

"You can't be serious. How could the army and Gabi, as you say, do this? Surely Governor Awale and Regional administration as well as the government in Bamgboshe know what's happening?"
"Ah yes, Gabi's the key. He's a very powerful figure. It's hard to say who knows what he is up to or who else is involved with him apart from an army officer called Mbuta..."

"Major Mbuta!" Bartley exclaimed. "I've come across him."

"Yes, well he seems to be Gabi's local enforcer. But as for the Prime Minister, I would guess if he knows anything about the army killing people in Guseni he subscribes to the fiction that the army is dealing with armed rebels. The same could possibly be true for Regional Governor, Awale, but I suspect..."

O'Driscoll was interrupted by the sound of vehicles driving abruptly into the orphanage compound. He looked up and without a further word, followed by Bartley and the others, stepped outside to see a Landcruiser and a Nissan pick-up drawing up to a halt alongside Bartley's car. There were half a dozen police militia squeezed together on the back of the pick-up, their black uniforms streaked and faded with dust. Bartley saw the RS get out of the Landcruiser and come toward them.

"Mr Bartley, it's good to see you again. I thought you had left this morning for Bamgboshe, but I just saw your car here and thought I should stop to greet you and ask is everything well? And Fr. O'Driscoll, how are you today?"

"Fine, fine, couldn't be better. I was just showing Mr Ryan around the orphanage. You know that the Irish Embassy gave us a grant here and naturally I invited him to come and see what we've done with the money." Bartley noticed uneasiness in O'Driscoll's voice.

"Is that so? I must compliment you, Mr Ryan, on your Embassy's generosity. I was not aware of this. I would be very interested in seeing what you have donated."

"Yes, well let's have a look down the back here." O'Driscoll hurried off leaving Bartley wondering why he should be in such a sudden rush to show Uba around. But Mrs Malinga had slipped up and removed Charity's hand from his and was quietly leading the girl away. The Colonel fell in step to follow O'Driscoll. They halted at the far end of the compound in front of four boxlike outhouses each with a sloping tin roof from which a plastic pipe jutted at the rear.

"VIP latrines," said O'Driscoll and, seeing Bartley's blank look, explained. "Not for use by VIPs, but you can if you want. Ventilated Integrated Pit: it's a simple idea. There is a deep hole for waste and the pipe goes down into it to allow the smell to escape out above the roof."

He opened the door of one outhouse. At once Bartley was hit by a sickeningly pungent odour: evidently not all smells successfully escaped out through the pipe. Too late to take a deep breath, he wanted to back away, but he felt it somehow incumbent on him to look more closely. Keeping his mouth closed and trying to inhale as little as possible, he peered into the gloomy interior just long enough to make out a crude wooden toilet seat. Hastily withdrawing, he gulped for air but the whole site seemed to be reeking. He leaned forward to cough and O'Driscoll could not help but smile.

"Mr Bartley, please!" It was Fumbe.

Bartley and O'Driscoll turned in surprise as Fumbe with the broadest of grins captured them both with his cell phone camera.

"Mr Bartley and the VIP latrines. It is good to have a photograph to show where you visit!" Fumbe chuckled.

Bartley smiled. This was pure Fumbe. At the same time he noticed that as soon as Uba had seen Fumbe was about to take a picture, the RS had moved off to the side, out of shot. Now he walked off alone back to where the cars were parked.

O'Driscoll leaned toward Bartley and whispered, "I get the feeling that the Colonel would be happier if you were not to delay much longer in heading back to Bamgboshe. Perhaps you should humour him."

"Yes, I think you're right. But, we must talk again. I want you to finish telling me what's happening here." Bartley looked at the priest, who in turn, nodded silently.

They followed just behind Uba, the priest pointing out as they passed what Bartley had not seen: the kitchen area, a second dormitory and another hut that served both as dining and study room.

Uba came to a halt pointedly beside Bartley's Landcruiser and waited for him to say his goodbyes to the priest and the Malingas. O'Driscoll was suggesting that perhaps the Irish Minister might visit the orphanage as part of his trip to Bakooli and Bartley promised to put the idea forward. When he was finished, he shook hands finally with the RS and climbed into the car, allowing Uba to shut the door for him. Inside he wound down the window and waved at the children standing in a line just as they had when he arrived. Several waved back with shy smiles while others stole nervous glances at each other and at Uba's militia escort.

He could see no sign of Charity.

FIFTEEN

Sunday, 12 October.

Fiona's smashed-up Suzuki was still just about driveable as she parked warily beside Bartley's Rav. She skirted guiltily around the tarpaulin of the damaged Mercedes to knock on his door. When he called out she entered sheepishly aware that he would notice that she never bothered to knock before.

"Hi, how are you? How was your trip? Oh, Bartley, I don't know what to say. I'm so sorry about the car." It came out in a rush.

"Nothing we can do about it now. Forget it, what's done is done and, to tell the truth, I haven't had time to think about it since I got back." He managed a weak smile. The Mercedes had in fact been very much on his mind, but so also had been Fr. O'Driscoll's revelations – unsubstantiated revelations - about army atrocities in Guseni. Concentrating on the mundane details of the Minister's visit had proved nigh on impossible while he grappled within himself as to what he could, or should, do about either. "I've been working all day on the programme for the Minister's trip and some of the items he might discuss at meetings, but at last I seem to have something I can send home. If I get it sent off to Dublin tomorrow it should keep Clendenning off my case when he comes back. Anyway, sit down. I need a Hippo, want one?"

"Yes, that'd be good. Thanks"

Bartley wandered off to the refrigerator in the kitchen and she sat down on the sofa, moving aside some papers that were lying there. She glanced at the top sheet and saw it was his draft of the programme. She was still holding it when he came back.

"Sorry," she said, "I was just moving these papers out of the way..."

"No problem, they're hardly top secret," he set the beer down and pulled off the cap, "You can read them if you want. It might help to get a second opinion."

The sofa wobbled slightly when Bartley sat down and he leaned forward to adjust the books propping up the end. He sipped at his beer while she read. Despite the length of time it took him to write the programme, she needed only a few minutes to read it through.

"It's not terribly exciting, is it?" was her verdict when she had finished. "In fact, it sounds rather downright bloody boring, apart from the trip down to Bakooli."

"Good, I'm glad you see it that way. It's just what I want."

"What? Why on earth would you want that?"

"Trust me, I've been through Minister's visits before from both the HQ and Embassy side and I know what happens. Foreign Affairs will always want a smooth, non-controversial visit that avoids incurring any criticism, yet offers the Minister some publicity back home. The trouble is that avoiding criticism and courting publicity are often two conflicting ends."

Indeed, he thought to himself, *court undue press coverage and the whole human rights thing could blow open especially if allegations of sanctioned killings in Guseni became known. That would put paid to any prospect of an aid programme for Kutaba and seriously sour relations between the two countries.* That was not something for which he would want to take credit.

He took a long pull of his beer, then another. "Fuck it, at the end of the day it's best to keep a low profile and hope at most for a few good photographs of the Minister surrounded by grateful little African orphans. It doesn't leave much scope for planning anything remotely exciting. I reckon the most daring part of the visit could be that the Minister might just suggest starting a full aid programme here and, in return, ask for Kutaban support for the Irish candidate for the job of Under-Secretary General for Legal Affairs in New York."

Fiona seemed to sense his tension and was in turn unsettled by it. She had already finished her beer, but hesitated before raising the empty bottle with uncharacteristic timidity. Bartley took it and stood up to go to the kitchen for another.

"So I guess the visit you're planning to an orphanage might be the only good publicity your Minister will get?"

"Yes, with a bit of luck. Here..." He proffered a fresh beer.

"God, what a waste of time." She took a long swig, paused for a moment and then took another. She looked at the bottle then peered at him sideways. "I say, do you still have those wraps I left here the other night?"

Bartley ran a hand over the side of his face as he walked over to the bookshelf and rummaged around for a minute.

"I think I left them here, but don't see them. They must be around somewhere, but listen. I'd better not take any of that stuff tonight anyway. Do you mind? I'll look for them later and we can smoke them another time."

She felt embarrassed. She should have known he would not want to get stoned tonight. She was beginning to see something she had always suspected - that under the boozy camaraderie Bartley really did take his work seriously. But somehow it seemed that there was something else distracting him and that she was intruding. She set down her unfinished beer and quietly gathered her things to leave. He seemed barely to notice as she said goodnight and slipped out. She did not attempt to offer her usual, token air kiss.

SIXTEEN

Monday, 13 October.

When he suggested they get together, Michelle objected that she should instead be heading off to her monthly meeting of EU Consular Officers, but Bartley insisted. He needed to discuss the Minister's visit and, in particular, confirm that the Hilton had been booked. She appeared in his office holding a collection of papers. She had confirmation from the Hilton of a block booking of rooms including the hotel's sole suite for the Minister. Additionally, she had drawn up all the details for a reception the Minister might host including a list of guests that might be invited. Bartley looked at the papers and had to admit that when Michelle committed to a task, she was particularly efficient.

But then, when he tried to discuss what he felt they should do over the coming days, she quickly interrupted to drop her bombshell. She had put her name forward for an upcoming promotion competition and would be returning to Dublin for interview. HQ had already approved her travel and also her participation in a preliminary three day interview training course at Cunningham Communications and Media in Rathmines. The dates were such that she would be absent for the duration of the Minister's visit.

"I know that I'm at an early point in my career and that I can't expect to be successful at this stage, but the sooner I start to gain experience at this level of competition, the better." She volunteered this last with an unaccustomed show of modesty and air of sincerity which, if meant to be disarming, totally missed Bartley.

"Christ, Michelle! Clendenning will blow a gasket when he hears you've gone for two weeks and won't be here to help with the Minister." He could already see Clendenning accusing him of having mishandled the situation and of having failed to exercise sufficient tact to persuade her to volunteer to withdraw from the competition for the greater good of the Embassy.

Michelle was standing by the door, "Look, I have to run for my meeting. I'm really sorry if I'm letting you down, but this is important to me and it's no more than I'm entitled to."

She was right of course and there was little he could say. *Christ, I'm well and truly fucked now!* He felt a premonition of disaster as he watched her disappear quietly down the corridor.

Trying to calm himself he reached for a folder of papers, but there was a tap at his door. It was Fumbe. He bore a huge self-satisfied grin, coming as the bearer of unexpected but very welcome news. Quite incredibly and against all the odds, his mechanic contact had tracked down a spare replacement rear door for the Mercedes. Fumbe wanted to bring the car to his friend as soon as possible to have it fitted, but he first needed Bartley's approval for paying the mechanic who wanted his cash up front together with the promised case of Johnny Walker Black Label.

Bartley would pay anything to cover up the car accident. The cash sum demanded was no problem. Because the Kutaban banking system was so chaotic he had no local bank account so he kept a large personal stash of imported dollars and euros in an oversized padded envelope locked in the office safe. The cost of the door would make more than a sizeable hole in what was to last him at least another 5 months, but every cent spent to hide the damage from Clendenning would be money well spent. It was thus with a comparatively light heart, that he handed over to Fumbe the bulk of his remaining funds and sent him on his way.

The car problem had been resolved. That was one problem out of the way. Now there was the Minister's trip. He would concentrate on that. However that meant putting Guseni out of his head. He should not allow Guseni get in the way of a successful visit.

No sooner had he resolved on this than there was another knock on his door. He looked up to see Goodness, reaching out holding his coffee mug. Surprised because she usually walked straight in and wordlessly plonked it on his desk, he could see immediately something was up.

"Good morning, Goodness?" It was a question.

She placed the coffee with unaccustomed care, her hands were shaking.

"Mr Bartley, Mr Bartley, can you help please? It is my brother. It is big trouble." She seemed on the verge of tears.

"Sure, Goodness. Look, sit down. What's wrong? You can tell me."

"My brother, Mr Bartley, they done arrest my brother Ngule. The police put him in jail Friday and now I am very afraid. You must please help him."

"Sure, but I'm not sure what I can do until you tell me what happened? Why is he in jail? Has he been arrested for something bad?"

"Oh no, Ngule is a good man! He is elder from our village. He comes to Bamgboshe with other two elders to ask for help. Our village is in Guseni, but all people have now moved. They have no water, no food for cattle in new village. They want to go back to old village and they come ask Minister allow them go home. But Minister Gabi he say they bad people, make trouble in his office and the police they come take them. Now they are in jail. They stay in jail from Friday."

Goodness did not know if her brother and the two other elders had been formally arrested or charged with anything. All she knew was the police station in which they were being held and that Ngule was old and would find it difficult to endure conditions in the jail. An intervention by someone like Bartley at an early stage might secure his release.

Thus it was that Bartley found himself that morning in a police station negotiating with an Inspector of Police.

"No, this man has not been charged," the policeman was saying, "the case is still under investigation."

"How long will that take?"

"I cannot say. Sometimes it is soon finished, other times not. First we can interrogate him and when he confesses, we can charge him."

"But I understand all he did was to ask to see the Minister and that then he was immediately taken into detention. Surely he did nothing wrong?"

"Maybe, but a case has been opened and when it is open it is not always easy to close – or to forget...It is unfortunate that an old man should be left in this position."

Bartley guessed where this was very well leading. He had loaded his jacket pocket with a bundle of greasy Bamgboshe banknotes against the possibility.

"Can I see the prisoner?" he asked.

The Inspector nodded and led him behind the counter at which they had been talking and into the back of the building down a dark corridor at the end of which there was a barred cell door. It was probably no more than a metre and a half wide. It was lined with dark faces and hands holding onto the bars. Coming closer, Bartley could see the room beyond packed with so many bodies as to leave standing room only. A small barred window was just about visible off to the right. Any daylight it may have offered was all but obscured by more bodies pushing forward gasping for air. An acrid animal smell wafted into the corridor from the obviously suffocatingly hot interior.

The inspector called Ngule's name and the crowd at the door parted grudgingly to allow a feeble looking old man to come forward. A second policeman unlocked to allow him shuffle out. He had taken off his shirt and wrapped it tightly under one arm. His hairless chest and shaven head contrived to make him look all the more vulnerable. Bartley noticed also he was wearing his trousers inside out. He had heard this was an old trick used to keep trousers clean until an eventual court appearance, but this was the first time he had seen it in practice. No doubt Ngule had come to Bamgboshe in his very best trousers and wished to protect them.

They followed the inspector into an interview room that was probably no smaller than the cell into which dozens were sandwiched. Taking up most of the available space was a large table from which the inspector lifted a cane. It was a metre length and the width of a man's thumb. He thwacked it on the table and pointed Ngule to a chair in the far corner. He invited Bartley to sit beside him at the near end. He opened his hands, palms up toward Bartley.

"Well, there is no case until I prepare some papers, so perhaps I can help you?"

Bartley took an envelope out of his pocket and placed it on the table. The inspector leaned forward, his back blocking it from Ngule's view. His index finger pried open the flap and he peered inside.

"Yes, I think it would be very troublesome to open a case and I can see this man has done nothing wrong. I would like to see him go, but unfortunately there might be some trouble for me. You see it is Honourable Minister Gabi who has had these men arrested. He will expect to see three prisoners under charge and what will I tell him if there are only two?"

Bartley reached into a second pocket and took out a further thin bundle of banknotes. He placed it over the envelope, his hand resting on top. He looked to the corner where the slight figure of Ngule was hesitantly pulling on his shirt, a pale threadbare piece of material. A memory of Emmanuel Gabi's pristine white suit sailed through Bartley's mind.

"You can tell Minister Gabi that Mr Ryan from the Irish Embassy has given a guarantee that this man will make no more trouble. I think the Minister knows me."

The inspector smiled and slid the money and envelope off the table and into his pocket in a single movement. He spoke over Bartley's shoulder to Ngule and the old man got up, bowing low to each of them.

"You can take him. I have told him he can go. If he asks, I will be sure to tell the Minister that the Irish Embassy has given a guarantee for this man."

SEVENTEEN

Tuesday, 21 October.

It had been raining again in the late afternoon and although it was considerably cooler than usual, Fumbe had again turned on the air conditioning to stop the windows fogging up as they drove to the airport in the newly repaired Mercedes. Bartley shivered in the back seat. Normally he would have been happy to sit up front with the driver, however on this occasion he wanted to sit in the seat normally occupied by the Ambassador. He studied the door one more time to assure himself that there was nothing to show that the original had been wrenched off and that this was a replacement. The upholstery that had been cleaned of the watchman's greasy pant stains and rice supper matched perfectly that of the new door. He was sure it was impossible to spot anything amiss from the inside. From the outside too, it looked a perfect fit. The only problem, as Fumbe had pointed out when he had first returned with the car from his mechanic friend, was that the seating for the hinges in the doorframe had buckled. Despite the mechanic's best efforts, the new hinges would not sit entirely flush. The result was that while the door looked a perfectly snug fit, it did not glide smoothly home with the usual satisfying Mercedes clunk. As Fumbe had demonstrated, it required a hefty shove to engage it in place. Happily, this should be no problem as it was Fumbe's habit always to open the door for the Ambassador and to close it once he was safely seated. Clendenning might wonder why his driver had taken to slamming the door shut so violently every time he sat in, but he would probably put it down to the endemic wilfulness of Kutabans.

Faced with the prospect of reuniting with the Clendennings, the chill of the car did little to raise his spirits. After considerable effort, Grace had succeeded in phoning the airport and learnt that the London flight's arrival was delayed by almost two hours. It was therefore already quite dark outside with the only lights, apart from those of other traffic, being of kerosene lamps and wood cooking fires burning in front of the bars and shops on either side of the road. The campaign to demolish buildings as part of the road widening project had not yet reached this far, but the road itself had deteriorated rapidly in the course of the wet season as overloaded trucks had punched holes in the tarmac. Each time it rained these filled with water that eroded the surrounding foundation of rubble and clay and opened up huge craters resembling small lakes. Fumbe slowed and changed down gear as the car entered the virtual flood plain ahead of them. Muddy water slewed up against the side of the car as a dilapidated truck coming in the opposite direction ploughed through the water, heedless of the danger and making no attempt to slow down. At this rate by the time they reached the airport, Bartley mused, the car would be a uniform grey, not easy to tell what colour it was underneath; far less that one door had been removed and replaced by another.

There were several vehicles blocking the entrance to the VIP lounge, a large Mercedes S Class, much bigger than the Embassy's Mercedes E and seemingly just as new. An older green Nissan Pathfinder was parked behind it together with a military pick-up. Two soldiers were sitting in its rear, smoking. Fumbe thus had to drop him some distance from the door and Bartley had no alternative but to step out into a muddy morass that instantly coated his shoes and the bottoms of his trouser legs. He squelched up to show his airport pass and diplomatic ID to an officious lady sitting behind a reception desk by the door.

The lounge was no more than a large sized room with half a dozen sofas and matching armchairs in bright red leather. The sofas and chairs were all of massive proportions as if their size was to testify to the importance of the personages whose bottoms might grace them. This evening the only *personages* present comprised a tall heavily built Kutaban wearing a long traditional white robe and matching Smurf-like cap, together with his wife and three children, the eldest of whom might not be more than ten. The wife also wore traditional dress, in her case a bright green floral pattern that billowed in wide folds around her already ample frame. She was engrossed reading a copy of *Hello!* Her two younger children were taking turns climbing up and jumping off the arm of one of the sofas, shrieking loudly as they did so. The eldest child was playing with a handheld electronic device, working his mouth from side to side as he feverishly pressed buttons to the accompaniment of simulated automatic gunfire. The father was reclining fully back in an armchair with a large gin and tonic in one hand while the other waved from side to side in the direction of a half-bowed steward to whom he appeared to be delivering a lecture on, of all things, the weather in London at this time of year.

They ignored Bartley as he walked sodden-footed into the room and looked around for a quiet seat. Off to the far end were two further sofas and armchairs. These were in white leather with massive and incredibly ugly carved mahogany arms and front panels. He recalled the first occasion he had entered the lounge and attempted to sit on one of them. The steward had immediately remonstrated with him and the officious lady at the reception desk had left her station and loudly ordered him to move. The white suite, it transpired, was for the sole use of His Excellency the Prime Minister, the Honourable Anthony Okeke, whenever he happened to pass briefly through. Bartley chose a sofa on the far side of the gesticulating Kutaban, keeping the man between himself and the children. He regretted not having brought a newspaper or some other reading material that would offer him an excuse to avoid eye contact with any of this family.

Luckily he did not have long to wait. Grace's informant had been unduly pessimistic and the plane had in fact already landed. He had been sitting for little more than five minutes when to his surprise the Clendennings arrived in through a rear door from behind the white suite. A wealthy looking Kutaban in a western business suit followed them. Bartley rose and moved forward to greet the Ambassador and his wife. He guessed that the Kutaban was a business class passenger and yet the Clendennings had arrived in the lounge just ahead of him. This probably meant that the Ambassador had somehow wheedled a free upgrade from economy for himself and Brigid. His impression was confirmed when Clendenning shook his hand with unaccustomed friendliness. His breath smelt strongly of business class Cognac. Even Brigid seemed quite jolly.

Bartley barely noticed a further arrival into the lounge until the father of the waiting family jumped to his feet and loudly shushed his children. His previously flamboyant demeanour had changed and he seemed to have shrunk into his flowing garb as he rushed forward bowing to the new arrival. Bartley froze mid-way through the act of ushering the Clendennings to a sofa, taken aback to recognise the newcomer as Major Mbuta. The Major carelessly waved off the bow and turned around to take in the others in the room. As his gaze lighted on Bartley, his head seemed to jerk back, also in surprise but he did nothing otherwise to acknowledge recognition.

Bartley tried to regain his composure. Sitting down beside Brigid he enquired politely about the flight. It was the Ambassador who replied. He was obviously in a mellow and expansive mood, but Bartley was not really listening, finding he was ill at ease at the coincidence of seeing Mbuta again.

"Excellent flight, thank you, managed a decent sleep. They've just put in these new extra-long flat beds that make all the difference. The food was quite good for a change, wasn't it?" He looked at his wife for confirmation, but continued without waiting. "They also served a pretty acceptable Spanish Navarra."

Bartley tried to focus on the Ambassador once more – indeed, he must have had quite a skinful as he was still apparently slightly under the influence.

"We had a good break which was much needed after six months here, eh Brigid? The weather back at home was unusually mild and clement for this time of year so we quite enjoyed ourselves. But, I'm ready for work again and I must admit I'm looking forward to Canavan's visit. I had planned to meet the Minister and discuss some of my ideas for his trip, but unfortunately he was called away on urgent business. I understand he was disappointed that he wasn't able to see me. Still, I'm sure everything will be fine. When we get back to the Residence we should sit down for a few minutes and you can bring me up to speed on how arrangements are progressing."

An immigration official came in and collected their passports which he took over to the reception desk to process. He had just finished stamping them and was holding them up to be taken back when a porter arrived with a couple of suitcases. Mbuta pointed to one of the cases, ordering it to be taken outside and went over to collect his passport just as Bartley at the same moment was taking back possession of the Clendennings'. The two made immediate eye contact.

"Mr Ryan, I believe?"

"Yes." Bartley was taken off-guard.

"I think we came across each other before? At Lion Rock Lodge was it? I was with Minister Gabi's group."

"Yes, I remember."

"And since then you have been to Bakooli and met the famous Fr O'Driscoll. But I also hear very recently that you have been visiting a jail here in Bamgboshe in connection with some possible terrorist from Guseni who was threatening the Minister's life. I should warn you Mr Ryan that there are some very dangerous and criminal people in Guseni and you should in future keep away from them."

Mbuta plucked his passport from the official's outstretched hand, before leaning in close.

"Take care, take great care. You do not want Minister Gabi as an enemy."

Bartley had no time to react before Mbuta strode out, leaving him to return shaken to the Clendennings. The Ambassador appeared to have run out of steam and the three sat without speaking as the lounge gradually emptied, the businessman having left with the second bag and the family having been called out to board. Bartley began to cast glances in the direction of the rear door hoping that at any minute another porter would appear with luggage.

Eventually Clendenning wondered aloud what might be causing the delay and Bartley took the hint and approached the reception desk to enquire. A phone call was made and the receptionist confirmed that there was no further luggage to be delivered from the flight. She shuffled through a tray of papers and proffered a lost luggage claim form.

"Come on Brigid, let's go." Clendenning stood up abruptly and snatched the form from Bartley's grasp. He briefly glared at it before balling it up and giving it back. "You can get Grace to fill that out in the morning." He glowered angrily at the receptionist standing by the door.

"Welcome back to Kutaba, my dear. It's not as if the plane was even half full, which is no surprise since you would wonder who in their right minds would want to come here anyway, and yet they still manage to lose our bags."

Outside, the large Mercedes, the Nissan and the pick-up had all disappeared and Fumbe had been able to drive up closer to the door. Even so, to get into the car meant walking through a length of churned up, muddy ground that did nothing to improve the Ambassador's mood. He remained dangerously silent as he settled into the back seat while, with a groan of relief, Brigid, kicked her soiled high heels off a pair of feet swollen badly after the long flight. Fumbe slammed the Ambassador's door hard shut.

Clendenning's temper peaked upon arrival at the Residence. He insisted that Bartley brief him immediately on everything that had taken place in his absence and, in particular, on the arrangements for the Minister's imminent visit. He sat down behind a huge desk in his otherwise rather small private study. Across from him Bartley faced a row of photographs. Central prominence had been given to a picture of Clendenning presenting his credentials in tails and top hat to the President of Portugal. A stuffed Thompson's gazelle stood squeezed between the desk and the wall and offered Bartley an alarmingly glass-eyed stare. It was a trophy from a hunting trip taken shortly after the Ambassador arrived in Kutaba. He had let it be known that the gazelle was just the first in what he hoped would eventually become a sizeable collection. Bartley edged to the left in his seat, trying to angle out from its gaze.

As feared, the Ambassador was apoplectic when he learnt that the Third Secretary would be absent at the critical time leading up to, and then during, the Minister's visit. In his mind it was obvious (as Bartley had predicted) that the First Secretary whom he had left in charge had mishandled the matter. He was even less pleased upon reading a copy of the Minister's programme and other related papers which Dublin had by now essentially approved.

"It's insulting that the Kutabans are offering so little. These damned Foreign Ministry officials are just too offhand. They're not taking this visit half-seriously enough, are they? Is this all they came up with? Did you go back to try to get something more from them?"

"Well, Ambassador, HQ was pressing me to let it have whatever I had to hand on what the Kutabans have in mind. I had only that paper you're looking at now. There was no time to go into the Ministry before I sent it off," Bartley replied truthfully, if quite disingenuously.

"Well, I suppose there's nothing we can do about it now," Clendenning tossed the paper aside.

"I see also Minister Canavan has ruled out my proposal for a wildlife drive. That's disappointing. It's a pity I didn't get in to see the Minister to tell him about it."

In fact, the reason that Clendenning had failed to secure an appointment with the Minister was precisely because the Secretary General suspected that he might suggest something of the kind to Canavan. McNamara viewed a game drive as nothing more than a frivolous diversion. Had Clendenning succeeded in putting forward his proposal, the Secretary General would have been obliged to invite the Minister to consider the consequences - at this time of austerity - if the Sunday Independent or Evening Herald were to learn of a government Minister going on a taxpayer-funded safari.

But what especially infuriated Clendenning was that the safari had been supplanted of all things by a visit to an orphanage patronised by the foul-mouthed Fr. O'Driscoll.

"I know I told you to sound out Fr. O'Driscoll, but giving him a lead role is simply outrageous. The man's a law onto himself and can't be trusted. I knew we couldn't keep him entirely out of the picture, but really this is unacceptable. We will need all hands on deck to keep him under control, but there again you've fucked it up, telling Michelle she could head off home for the duration".

"About Michelle," there was no point trying to explain that she had left him no option, but he needed somehow to appease the Ambassador, "I know it's a problem, but I had been considering that we ask Fiona Scott, you know - the Irish volunteer teacher here in Bamgboshe – if she might help us out." This notion had, in fact, just occurred to him "She knows her way around and understands how to deal with Kutaban bureaucracy."

He had no idea whether this was true, but he hoped it sounded positive.

"Hmm, well I suppose that would be better than nothing," Clendenning grudgingly conceded.

Bartley drew in breath and noticed for the first time that there was a definite, if slight, pong coming from the gazelle. It reminded him of the sour earthy smell of the *knocked* goat. Recalling that incident brought back to mind his most recent encounter with Mbuta and his warning not to make an enemy in Minister Gabi. Mbuta was linked to Gabi, but also to Ballo and O'Driscoll. What they had in common, what connected them all, was Guseni. He wondered again whether he should say anything to Clendenning. But where would he begin? There were too many too many possible starting points – Gabi, Mbuta, Ballo, O'Driscoll and even Ngule, hopefully now back in his new village? No again, he decided, it was best to keep his counsel. There was no point risking further ire. He could not help a wistful glance at the gazelle, and this not without a tinge of jealousy. The beast's suffering had been comparatively short - finished off with a single shot. It never occurred that someday someone might want do the same to him.

EIGHTEEN

Saturday, 1 November.

The Ambassador was balancing a briefcase on his bony knees and muttering in irritation as he shuffled through the various papers that made up the Minister's brief. Bartley sat alongside in the rear of the Mercedes looking out the window and hoping Clendenning would ignore him. The brief had been e-mailed from HQ late in the afternoon leaving little time to go through it before they headed out to the airport for Canavan's actual arrival. While it had been painstakingly collated in Dublin with contributions from a number of different sections, Bartley knew well that it would be a source of annoyance to the Ambassador that he had not been allowed an opportunity to vet it before the Minister was given a copy. He also saw HQ's logic in holding on to it to the last minute. If finalisation of the brief were put off until Clendenning declared himself satisfied it would never be finished.

As usual, the brief contained the detailed programme for the visit together with any possibly useful addresses and phone numbers beginning with the Embassy, its staff and the hotel in Bamgboshe. It also offered background political, economic and historical profiles of Kutaba, notes on the personalities the Minister might meet and suggestions for *speaking points* – what he might actually say during his various meetings. There were further *steering notes* to guide him through any issues that might possibly come up and a full set of separate documents relating to Ireland's overseas aid programme both globally and with particular reference to Kutaba. Overall, there were more than one hundred pages of notes and information, significantly more than any Minister would need or could conceivably be bothered to read. From his muttering it was clear this was still not enough for Clendenning.

He groaned aloud and then, as if only now conscious of Bartley beside him, snorted.

"This is simply intolerable. Even the introductory note on weather conditions is wrong. Yes, it is officially the dry season, but the Minister should have been warned that what with El Nino, he might expect some rain. The more I look at this brief the more mistakes and omissions there are. Did you see this?" He thrust a page accusingly under Bartley's nose. "This note on international arms issues makes no mention of the announcement that Kutaba is about to destroy its remaining stock of landmines. I told Dublin about this last week and given our position on landmines pointed out how important it is that the Minister congratulates Prime Minister Okeke. The *speaking points* and *steering notes* will simply have to be rewritten."

Bartley muttered non-committedly. He could never read in a car without feeling queasy and he was already quite nauseous from glancing at the page in front of him. Personally, he very much doubted that any changes the Ambassador might introduce would make the blindest bit of difference to the Minister.

It was with considerable relief that he stepped out of the car by the door to the VIP lounge. At least this time Fumbe had been able to drive right up to the entrance. The Kutaban Chief of Protocol and several other officials were waiting to greet them. Clendenning was ushered in first to sit on one of the oversized sofas beside the Chief who informed him that the Minister's aircraft had already entered Kutaban airspace some half an hour earlier and could thus be expected to land any moment now.

It might have seemed quite straightforward, but Bartley had expended an inordinate amount of time in getting clearance for the government's Gulfstream IV to fly Minister Canavan into Bamgboshe. Unfortunately for the Minister however, the jet would be unable to stay for the duration of his visit as it was needed back home in Dublin the following Monday to fly the President to the United States where she was invited to address a symposium at Notre Dame University on the Irish contribution to the world of arts and literature. The symposium was more than a little ambitiously titled "Irish Literature from Jonathan Swift to the Present Day". It would not normally have merited the attendance of the President had it not been for the suggestion that she might wish to offer some of her own poetry for discussion. Stung by some recent criticism of her literary endeavours, the President had gamely accepted the invitation as an opportunity to defend her reputation. A programme had been arranged that included her attendance at a trade promotion event in Chicago which offered sufficient cover to justify the cost of the trip. All this meant that Minister Canavan would be abandoned by the Gulfstream in Bamgboshe and forced to use a local commercial airline to fly on to Kampala, the next stop on his tour.

Bartley hovered in the background as Clendenning and the Chief of Protocol engaged in inconsequential small talk until the receptionist, the same one that had been on duty on the occasion of his last visit to the lounge, walked over to say the Minister's plane was about to land. She escorted the group, the Ambassador, Chief of Protocol, Bartley and the accompanying officials, out through the rear door and across the baggage claim area where a clutch of passengers from the Lufthansa flight that had landed more than an hour earlier stood forlornly beside a stationary carousel waiting for their bags. At the far end of the baggage hall an armed guard opened a door and let them through to the apron.

Within minutes they saw the landing lights of the small aircraft as it made its approach. Moments later it touched down at the very end of the airfield, its engine screaming as the pilot braked until the plane had almost come to a stop halfway along the runway, where it turned sharply in toward the terminal and taxied gently toward them. Despite the muggy warmth of the evening, Bartley felt a patriotic shiver when he saw the white jet with the national symbol of a harp adorning the tail-plane and the discreet tricolour flag painted above.

Canavan was first to descend from the aircraft and was greeted by the Ambassador and the Chief of Protocol. He gave Bartley barely a glance as he strode off toward the terminal flanked by his two principal greeters - Clendenning had made no effort to introduce his First Secretary. Bartley lingered to greet Eddie, the Minister's Private Secretary whom he vaguely knew, as well as the Director for Africa in the Overseas Aid Division, Andrew Smith. He introduced himself to the two others, the Minister's Programme Adviser, Charlie Fields, and Press Officer, Frank Mitchell. An elderly, somewhat dishevelled individual, his torso crisscrossed with camera bags, introduced himself as Sean, the photographer employed to record the Minister's trip and to ensure a steady supply of images for the press back home.

They trooped back into the VIP lounge where one of the minor Kutaban officials went round to collect the newcomers' passports. Frank, the Press Officer, slung the rucksack from his shoulder onto a white Prime Ministerial sofa and was about to plonk himself down alongside it when the receptionist darted forward and snatched up the bag by its straps. She also took hold of Frank by the arm and unceremoniously directed him toward one of the vacant red armchairs beside which she dumped his bag. Frank looked askance until Bartley quietly stepped forward to explain. Frank fished his passport out of the bag and handed it over to the official who had already collected all the other arrivals' passports, then turned back to Bartley.

"Bart was it? Yes Bart," He did not wait to be corrected as he was already delving inside his rucksack on the floor and pulling out his iPad.

"What's the wireless internet code? I guess they have one here in VIP? The Minister's been in the air all day and I need to update his Twitter account. You know Minister Canavan was the first Minister to have his own Twitter account? He has a good few hundred followers. He's also on Facebook, but I guess we can wait to the morning before we update that."

There were some people, Bartley guessed, to whom even the most comprehensive of briefs could not convey the reality that not everything worked in Africa as it did at home.

"Sorry, Frank, but this is Kutaba. There is no internet here in the airport. I'm afraid you'll have to wait until you get to your room in the Hilton to use the internet. But even there, like the rest of Bamgboshe you'll probably find it erratic to non-existent."

Frank viewed his iPhone, "In that case I'll text the Constituency Office and have them issue an update."

"Eh, no," Bartley saw no reason to sugar-coat further bad news. "They do use mobile phones in Kutaba, in fact they're very common here, but there are no facilities for texting. Prime Minister Okeke doesn't like it. He won't allow phone companies to offer texting facilities in case they might be used to disseminate anti-government propaganda and encourage terrorists."

The Press Officer tilted his head backwards and looked him sceptically in the eye.

"You're kidding, right?"

"Not at all," Bartley managed to suppress a smile.

Meanwhile, Ambassador Clendenning had intercepted the official collecting passports and was insisting, for reasons unknown, on examining each one until he found the Minister's. Canavan was at that moment talking to the Chief of Protocol and appearing to be having some trouble in making himself understood. The Minister, despite his patrician bearing and years of Cabinet seniority, had done little to lose his Kerry accent, indeed it could be said that he depended on it for a sizeable proportion of his local vote.

Bartley excused himself to Frank and hastened over in time to hear a puzzled Chief of Protocol intone, "Mushroom? You need a mushroom?" There was a look of confused incredulity on his face. The Minister was repeating himself and truth be told, Bartley too was having some difficulty understanding him.

"Washroom, where's the washroom?" Eddie, the Private Secretary, came up behind them and interpreted helpfully.

A much relieved looking Chief of Protocol led the way to a door beside the rear exit, off behind the white sofa ensemble. Bartley shrugged. He too had thought Canavan had said "mushroom". He wandered off to stand behind one of the sofas alongside Eddie, who was keeping a discreet distance between himself and the rest of the group.

It took very little time for the official to return with the passports and Bartley stepped forward to help distribute them. While he was doing so, Clendenning suggested that they would all leave immediately for their hotel. Although the luggage had not yet arrived, he announced, there was no need to worry: Bartley would be staying behind to attend to its collection and safe delivery to the Hilton.

This took Bartley by surprise. It would mean he would have to arrange to squeeze what he expected would be a formidable amount of luggage into the Landcruiser with only Fumbe's cousin to help – the latter having been hired as a second driver for the duration of the Minister's visit.

It took in fact only about a further five minutes after the Minister had left in a convoy of flashing blue lights for Bartley to collect the luggage and supervise its loading. Feeling pleased to have accomplished this so speedily, he was therefore disappointed to find the Ambassador in a heightened state of agitation when he arrived at the Hilton. Despite the last minute cancellation of the World Bank visit, it transpired that there had been a double booking of the suite intended for the Minister and another guest was already checked into it. Until some solution could be found, Canavan had retired temporarily to his Private Secretary's room. Clendenning stood in the middle of the lobby remonstrating loudly with the duty manager. Grace, who had been assigned the task of attending at the hotel and facilitating the check-in process, stood to one side, close to tears after coming under fire from the Ambassador and receiving a major portion of the blame for the mix-up.

Clendenning scowled upon seeing Bartley arrive but remained intent in his attack on the manager which allowed Bartley to catch Grace's eye. He drew her aside over to the reception desk to find out what was happening.

It was at that moment that an Indian gentleman approached the desk to ask whether a fax message he had been expecting had yet arrived. As the receptionist went off with a set of keys to check the fax machine in the hotel's now locked business bureau, he was left standing beside Bartley and Grace who was doing her best to overcome the tearful choking in her voice to bring Bartley up to speed on the latest mishap.

"Adrian, the Ambassador", she corrected herself, "threw a fit when he arrived with Minister Canavan and found out that some Indian businessman has been given the Presidential Suite and that the Minister was going to have to stay in an ordinary room. He was very angry and shouted at me in front of everyone. He said it is my fault that the Minister does not have a suite. He said I should have checked earlier. He said it is a complete disaster." She lowered her voice before continuing in embarrassment, "He said it is a *fucking cock-up* and wants to know why I am trying to ruin the Minister's visit." Grace's eyes welled up with tears and she was finally unable to continue.

The Indian had listened with increasing interest. Now that she had finished he leaned forward.

"Madam, sir, I am so sorry to intrude but I fear I am this businessman of whom you are speaking. My name is Ramachandran Ansari, textile manufacturer."

He fished into a small handbag he was holding and drew out two business cards.

"Please my business card. I think I can help you. I am the very person staying in this room suite that you require for an Irish Minister. I am very fond of Ireland. I have visited your Dublin where my son is now working in computing consultancy capacity. He is very happy there and soon his wife will join him. It would make me very happy to offer my suite to your honourable minister. The hotel can put me somewhere else. It is no problem for me."

It took Bartley several minutes before he could interrupt Clendenning long enough to convey this most unexpected and generous offer. The cowed duty manager was unable to hide his joy to be offered a reprieve from the dire retribution the Ambassador had been threatening to visit on him and his hotel. He undertook immediately to see to the necessary arrangements for the changeover of rooms. For his part, Clendenning appeared somewhat ungrateful, due mostly to his annoyance that the wretched Duty Manager (and why had the *General Manager* not attended for the Minister's arrival?) should be so easily let off the hook. With some difficulty and a distinct lack of grace, he assumed a rictus-like smile when he went over to thank the Indian businessman. Bartley slipped outside to supervise the offloading of the luggage and its assignment to the appropriate room numbers.

Happily it turned out that the generous Ansari, who had just arrived on the earlier flight from Frankfurt, had not yet unpacked and the manager was able to inform the Minister that he could move straight into his suite.

Coming back into the hotel, Bartley found that the Indian had disappeared but his place at reception had been taken by Clendenning who was insisting that the business centre be reopened to allow him and Grace to enter to do some typing and photocopying. He was determined to finalise and assemble those sections of the brief that he believed required revision. He saw Bartley with the bags, nodded in approval and commanded that he join them in the business centre as soon as he was done.

A porter took charge and loaded the luggage onto a flat trolley that he wheeled into the lift. Bartley went outside again to give Fumbe's cousin his final instructions for the next morning. When he finished he came back to join the Ambassador, but then noticed the Press Officer's distinctive rucksack sitting abandoned on the floor in front of reception. He picked it up and excused himself saying he had better deliver it upstairs.

Frank was already having conniptions when Bartley knocked on his bedroom door. He was convinced that his bag had been stolen and seeing it in Bartley's hand he snatched it immediately to check inside for his precious iPad. Seeing that it was indeed safe, he then thanked Bartley somewhat peremptorily before rather rudely closing the door in his face.

A bemused Bartley headed back toward the lift but found he was obliged to squeeze past the porter and the luggage trolley obstructing the corridor in front of the door to the Presidential Suite. It was precisely at that moment that Canavan opened the door to the porter's knock and caught sight of the rather unprepossessing official he had scarcely noticed when he had stepped off his plane and then again later in the VIP lounge. The Minister pointed a finger at him.

"You, you're with the Embassy aren't you?"

Bartley confirmed this was so.

"Well come in here. I've got all these damn papers – absolute waste of time trying to read through them to find out what the story is here. You can fill me in."

They were both inside the room, Canavan already sitting down in an armchair and motioning Bartley to a sofa. The porter placed a suitcase on a stand near the door and looked expectantly over at Canavan. The Minister ignored him. Realising there was no prospect of a tip he left, wordlessly closing the door behind him.

Canavan looked across at Bartley.

"And your name is?

"Ryan, Bartley Ryan"

"Good. Well then, Bartley Ryan, tell me about this Prime Minister Okeke. Is he any good?   I guess he wants more money from our aid budget. How do we know that he won't keep the money for himself?"

Bartley was straining to tune into the Minister's accent and did his best to offer brief, accurate answers to this and a follow-up barrage of unexpectedly probing questions over the course of the ensuing half hour.

"Right then, is there anything else I should know?" the Minister was finishing.

Bartley hesitated, "Well, there is something...actually it's not something that's actually proven, but there are certain allegations..." He knew he should shut up but it was as if someone else had taken control of his body and was speaking on his behalf. "There is an area in the south of the country called Guseni. It's part of Bakooli Region that you're visiting tomorrow. The people are traditional nomads who move village from time to time to follow the grazing, but they are being relocated to make way for a wildlife park. There are certain allegations, I must say unsubstantiated allegations, that the Kutaban army has killed a number of people as part of the process. I've also heard it suggested that the real reason for clearing the area is not in fact to create a wildlife preserve but to exploit its possible oil potential..." The voice which had taken control of him faltered and tailed off.

"But nothing is really known or proven?" The Minister was unhesitatingly sanguine. "I don't think in that case that there is anything that I should say to our Kutaban hosts about this. Sure, I can't accuse them of murder on the basis of some rumour spread by some opposition fellas. God almighty, if even a fraction of what the opposition accuses the Taoiseach of were true he'd have been dragged over to The International Court in The Hague years ago." Bartley did not know whether he should be relieved or disappointed with the Minister's dismissive conclusion. "Right you are then, that should do it. Thank you, Mr Ryan. Goodnight"

The Minister remained seated but glanced at the door indicating that he should leave. He got up and was almost at the door when he heard Canavan's drawl.

"Your Ambassador, a bit highly strung isn't he? Don't need that. You keep me informed of anything I need to know, Ryan."

Back downstairs, Bartley found Clendenning and Grace had succeeded in gaining access to the business centre, where the former was down on his knees with sheets of paper in a line of small stacks on the floor in front of him. He was picking a page from the top of each stack and, when he reached the end of the line, handing them to Grace who stapled them together. He paused upon seeing Bartley and stood up, stretched and ran his hands back through his long, lank locks.

"Where the fuck were you? I thought I told you to get right back down here. You know we have to put together eight new copies of the brief. Don't you ever listen to your Ambassador?"

Bartley hesitated, afraid to tell the truth, but realised he had no choice.

"I'm sorry. I was upstairs passing the Minister's door when he came out. When he saw me, he said he wanted a word and asked me into his room."

"What? What did he want?"

"Well, he had a few questions about Okeke and about Kutaba in general."

"Are you telling me that you went in to brief the Minister in private without letting me know? Have you forgotten that I am the Ambassador and that I do any briefing that the Minister wants? Why didn't you call me?"

"I couldn't. I was in the Minister's room. I could hardly say *'Hold on, I'll just get the Ambassador*, could I?"

"Don't you dare speak to your Ambassador in that tone! It seems that you are not only incompetent, but also disloyal - if not damned treacherous."

The ensuing silence as Clendenning glared at him was broken only when Grace, who had just lifted several sheaves of stapled papers off the floor, tapped them loudly together on the table, her head down and eyes averted. Clendenning turned at the sudden sound.

"Well, at least help me get this fucking brief together now." He returned to the papers on the floor, gesturing impatiently for Bartley to join him.

'*Highly strung*'? Bartley shivered, wondering how Clendenning would react if he knew what he had told the Minister about Guseni.

NINETEEN

Sunday, 2 November.

The air was already wavering in the heat that rose from the tarmac under an early morning sun. It promised to be a blisteringly hot day as the Minister's group headed out toward the small plane that had been chartered to fly them up to Bakooli. The Irish Gulfstream was still parked down near the VIP lounge. Its crew remained at the Hilton, resting before being allowed to fly back to Dublin. Minister Canavan, appropriately dressed in beige slacks and an off-white safari shirt, strode forward with all the confidence of an early Victorian explorer first setting off in eager anticipation of the undiscovered mysteries of darkest Africa. The fact that the boxy, single propeller plane in front of him looked puny and primitive when compared to the sleek lines of the Gulfstream only heightened his sense of adventure. Ambassador Clendenning for his part shared no such sentiment. He had asked Bartley to find a twin engine charter in the belief that should one engine fail the second would save them from disaster. When it turned out no such plane was available, Bartley had attempted to mollify him by explaining that a single propeller was actually safer than two. If the engine were to cut out, the aircraft could glide gently and, hopefully safely, to ground. Whereas with a twin engine, should one fail, the pilot would have extreme difficulty maintaining a straight course as the remaining engine would force the plane into a tight circle risking a sudden stall that would send it plummeting to earth. Bartley was unsure whether this was in fact true. It was what the agent, who happened also to be the pilot, had told him. Personally, he had gained some comfort from the claim.

Today however, it seemed no assurance of this or any other sort could possibly offer Frank, Canavan's Press Adviser, the slightest comfort. He was sweating under the weight of his rucksack as he trudged behind the rest of the party. Inexplicably, he was wearing a tweed jacket more suited to a summer walkabout in Kerry than the hot (but, according to Clendenning's revised brief, no longer reliably dry) season in Kutaba. He was inconsolable that he had not yet succeeded in updating either of the Minister's Facebook or Twitter accounts. He was in some considerable discomfort also from a rash of mosquito bites suffered the previous evening when he had unwisely taken a brief exploratory stroll in rolled-up shirtsleeves through the streets surrounding the Hilton. Perhaps it was a belated urge to protect his already itching arms that went some way to explain this morning's tweed jacket. But worst of all, Frank was terrified of flying - whether in the largest Airbus or Boeing, never mind anything smaller. Flying in the Gulfstream would always be an ordeal for him, so the sight of this little aluminium toy plane filled him with the utmost dread. His legs felt leaden and it was only his dedication to Canavan and the Minister's political career (plus an Adviser's salary some €20,000 above the recommended maximum of the scale) that kept him moving forward.

At the head of the group Bartley paused and waited for him to catch up.

"Alright Frank?" he asked.

"No, I'm not bloody alright. I was dinner for a whole flock of mosquitos last night."

"You mean a swarm," Bartley corrected him.

"Warm? I'd call it fucking bloody hot." Frank misheard him. "Then to make it worse some tart woke me up at two o'clock, knocking on my door offering me a blowjob. And now you want me to get into this tin can. I hate fucking flying."

They had arrived at the plane and he looked at it fearfully. Canavan and the others had started to climb in.

"Look, just make sure I get a seat at the back Bart, ok? I don't want to see out in front and know what's happening outside."

Bartley had been in similar small planes before and knew that the back seat was probably the worst place to sit. You felt every bump and jiggle. Worse, your line of vision along the cabin and out front past the pilot gave the impression of the plane pointing in one direction while you at the back appeared to be travelling in another. He decided to say nothing. It would mean that there should be at least one seat for him somewhere nearer the front.

"Jeez, look at that!"

Frank was pointing at a panel in the fuselage where it looked like a hairline crack had been tacked together with a line of rivets. He hiked his bag higher on his shoulder before bending his back and reluctantly climbing aboard where he squeezed into the single rear seat behind the door. The cabin roof sloped down sharply to the tail end of the plane and when he sat down the lack of headroom forced him to bow his head. Bartley entered last and found an empty forward seat directly behind the Minister who was in the front row across the aisle from Clendenning.

The pilot was already in his seat wearing an outsize pair of earphones. One side was pushed to the back of his head leaving an ear uncovered so he could hear his passengers.

"Everybody aboard then?" he asked counting, "Six, seven, eight. That's it. OK then, whoever is nearest, can you shut the door? "

Frank was the closest, but had wedged himself in position with his seatbelt already fastened as tightly as it would go and was showing no intention of moving. Andrew, the Africa Director, was right in front of the door and got out of his seat, crouching to heave it closed.

"Just make sure it's locked. Turn the handle down full to the left," the pilot called cheerfully.

Frank peered nervously at the red handle when Andrew finished. He would continue to keep it under close observation throughout the flight, fearing that it could at any minute bump out of position allowing the door to swing open either causing the plane to crash or him to be sucked out like some guy he had seen in a movie. He wasn't sure which he dreaded more: sitting in his seat alongside his fellow passengers as the plane hurtled downward, spinning out of control, or finding himself alone in space, accelerating earthward in free-fall.

The take-off was smooth. Bartley was always pleasantly surprised in these small planes as they sped down the runway. He liked to think of it as a fast car magically sprouting wings to rise gently off the ground. There was none of the sudden heave upwards that unnerved him in large jets. It was just after 8.00am and the air was still untroubled by the thermals that would build up with the heat of the day. Their continuing ascent met with only the slightest of bumps. He knew the effect of even the slightest jerk or sudden loss of altitude would be greatly exaggerated in the rear and chuckled to himself at the thought of Frank huddled back in the tail section. He looked out the window in the direction of the city off to the left. He could just about make out the Hilton in the centre, while below the patchwork of rusting tin roofs of the sprawling shacks soon gave way to open countryside that was predominantly brown save for isolated patches turned briefly green by the recent rains.

The flight lasted less than an hour and soon they were circling over the hills that backed Bakooli and coming in low toward the landing strip that Bartley had reconnoitred with Colonel Uba. The engine noise had all but ruled out conversation, but now as he felt the plane making its descent, the Minister inclined toward Clendenning.

"About this human rights thing down here, these locals allegedly being killed, should I raise it with these people down here today?"

Clendenning looked at him, nonplussed. "Locals being killed? I'm sorry, what do you mean?"

"What your man Ryan was telling me about – that the army may be responsible for killing people down here. It might clear the air to raise it now, rather than be embarrassed by something coming out later on. On the other hand, I'd rather not get into anything like that - just let you follow up sometime if we need..."

Before the Ambassador could reply, the plane tipped abruptly to the left affording an instantly disquieting view of treetops practically brushing the wingtip. The pilot adjusted quickly, over-correcting slightly so that the plane first lurched to the right before it levelled off to swoop along the length of the landing strip. Then, with a piercing whine of the engine, it shot skyward again in a precipitous banking turn back in the direction it had come.

Having been thrown left and right, then pinned back in their seats, the passengers let out a collective groan. Bartley dared to peek out the window and caught a glimpse of a pickup truck chasing off several startled antelope and zebra grazing on the landing strip below. The plane continued its turn until it had circled back over the hills and then started a second descent, heading toward the line of trees standing sentinel at the near end of the runway. The pilot again dropped to fly no more than a few metres above the line and race the length of the grass strip checking it was now clear. At the last minute he throttled up and the plane's nose rose sharply. Half a dozen stomachs heaved.

Across the aisle from Bartley, Canavan's Private Secretary was moaning softly. He was pushed back into his seat, his eyes closed and his hands clenched white on flimsy armrests. For his part, Canavan seemed as startled by his Private Secretary's whimpering as by what he believed were two failed landings.

"What's happening? Why didn't we land?" he shouted across to Clendenning, who at that moment was focussed rigidly on some distant spot past the blur of the propeller in front of the pilot. He appeared not to hear. Canavan leaned back to look enquiringly at Bartley behind him.

"Normal procedure, Minister, we have to give way for a zebra crossing."

The Minister first did a double take, twisted fully round in his seat and glared at him. Bartley realised it was not the best time for flippancy.

Relief in the cabin was as palpable as the earlier drop in air pressure as the plane at last touched down and pulled to a halt near a line of waiting cars. Andrew levered open the door and was first to step out. He was followed slowly by Frank who seemed to have some difficulty unlocking his limbs to wriggle out of his tight cubby-hole. The others stayed in their seats to allow the Minister and Ambassador to disembark.

The welcoming party was led by Regional Governor Awale wearing a traditional white jellaba. Beside him stood the RS, Colonel Uba. Awale greeted the Minister first with a handshake and then, to Canavan's surprise, a hug and kiss on both cheeks. Clendenning stiffened in anticipation. Although accustomed to the familiarity of a Kutaban greeting he remained more than uncomfortable with any ritual that involved the physical embrace of another male. Awale introduced the rest of the welcoming party who were at least content to offer a simple handshake. The Minister, apart from introducing the Ambassador, was happy to allow the rest of the Irish entourage make their own introductions as they wished.

At the end of the receiving line stood Fr. O'Driscoll in a faded green tee-shirt and well-worn chinos, a battered Olympus camera strung over one shoulder. Fiona was beside him with a broad beam of a smile covering her face. Clendenning introduced them to Canavan, explaining that Fiona was a teacher in Bamgboshe who had volunteered to help out over the next few days. Fiona's smile widened even further as the Minister showed interest and asked where she was from. Her involvement with the visit offered her not only an opportunity to meet the Irish Foreign Minister, but also to take a few days off school. Bartley had even arranged that she would be able to fly back from Bakooli to Bamgboshe in the private plane with the ministerial group. She would certainly have a good story to tell back home.

Awale suggested their immediate departure in view of the very full schedule ahead. The Bakooli programme had expanded since Bartley had first explored the possibilities.

Indeed it was destined to turn into quite a marathon.

TWENTY

The first stop was the canal that Ireland was helping to finance. However, if the Minister was expecting some impressive excavation reminiscent of the Grand Canal in Dublin, he would have been disappointed with what he saw to be no more than a deep V-shaped culvert so far devoid of water. The equally dry statistical account of the history of its construction by the Regional Water Officer, Bartley observed, added little to fire his enthusiasm. Alone of the visitors, Fr O'Driscoll appeared in his element happily clicking away with his trusty Olympus.

A short drive brought them to their next stop-off, again an Irish related project to supply milking cows to local peasants. A planeload of cows had been delivered to Kutaba a year earlier and distributed throughout the country. The Minister's Department had assisted with funding.

Waiting for the convoy to arrive were a group of police militia and a very large woman surrounded by half a dozen children of varying ages. She was introduced as the beneficiary of one of the cows and she led the visitors round the back of her home to where a small stockade fenced in what indeed appeared to be a very Irish looking cow. The enclosure was scarcely longer than the animal itself and not much wider, with not even enough room for it to turn round. Still, it looked content under the rough thatch shading with a trough full of fresh grasses in front of it.

"It sounds rather costly to fly cows all the way to Africa." The Minister commented quietly aside to Clendenning. "Surely cows pollute the atmosphere sufficiently already without adding a good few tons of jet fuel to fly them thousands of miles? Does Kutaba not have a supply of cows we could provide locally?"

"Yes, but apparently not the kind of cow that comes from Kerry, as did most of these." Clendenning avoided eye contact.

The Minister gave a little cough, "From Kerry, you say? Well fine cows they are indeed. Sure, they're bound to improve the local stock. But it must be a pretty tough environment for them after Ireland." He surveyed the landscape. Flat and featureless, the earth reddish clay with the occasional piece of scrub and a few acacia bushes, there could be no greater contrast to his green Kerry constituency.

The Regional Agricultural Officer offered a lengthy expose of the details of the project, concluding that at some future date it would be arranged that a bull be brought to service the cow. Any calf born would be donated to another needy family.

Standing beside him, Bartley heard Fr O'Driscoll chuckle at this last.

"What's the problem about the calf going to another needy family?"

The priest gave him a knowing smile. "It's just that the first cow hardly went to a needy family, did it? Sure your woman has always been the richest in this village, even beyond. She's a real businesswoman, always owned a pile of chickens and sold the eggs. She's also the money lender hereabouts and she charges a handsome interest. Now, with the profit from this cow and its milk, she's even richer.

"Of course the reason she was picked to be given this cow in the first place was simply that she was the only one in the village who could pay to build a place to keep and feed it. You can't give a cow to the poorest family and expect it to be able to afford to look after it. So whenever, indeed if ever, a calf comes along she will probably have to keep it herself"

Bartley looked at him. "You might tell the Minister that," he suggested.

O'Driscoll snorted again, but more loudly. "There's a lot more I would like to tell your Minister, and not just about cows, but about the army and Guseni – but not with the Governor and the RS around. Did you notice how close our friend Col. Uba is sticking to the Minister? That's not him being just friendly. He's making sure nobody says anything to your man without him knowing. "

"I know," Bartley glanced nervously over in Uba's direction. "I said something myself to the Minister about Guseni, but he's not interested. We would need some proof before he or anybody else will do anything. I don't know, but I would like to help. Maybe when this visit is all over I can come back and we can work something out?"

"Ryan!" They were interrupted by a shout from Clendenning, "We're heading off now, will you please see that everyone gets a move on and that we leave no-one behind?"

O'Driscoll nodded at Bartley. "I'd welcome that, if you could come back."

A large crowd was waiting for them in the village when they arrived for lunch. A dozen members of the police militia loitered alongside looking hot in their black uniforms and ill at ease among the villagers. The metal barrels of their semi-automatic weapons were scorching hot in the sun and they hefted them gingerly.

The village comprised no more than a scattering of mud rondavels and a recently built health post fronted by three large acacia trees offering at least some shade from the sun that was blazing down at its hottest from directly overhead. A covered porch ran the front length of the health post and in front of it, under the trees, trestle tables had been erected on which had been set out various large aluminium pots and several stacks of mismatched plates.

Awale and the Minister were offered seats under a lean-to shelter of canvas strung across wooden poles. Two large cool boxes packed with samosas were taken from the back of Colonel Uba's car and deposited on the trestle tables where Fiona took charge of arranging the contents alongside the pots. Two women emerged from the open door of the health post carrying crates of soft drinks, Pepsi and Fanta. They went around offering drinks first to the Minister and Awale, flicking bottle caps into the dust.

If Paris had fallen short, Bartley wondered what the Minister would make of this food. One pot held a dark, oily mixture he recognised as goat stew. A second contained a grainy white sauce of mashed groundnut to which some chicken bones had been added. Two further pots were piled with white, doughy cassava. He hid his amusement as he watched Canavan opt to take three of the samosas and a bread roll, arranging them so that they all but covered his plate. At Awale's urging he added a small spoonful of cassava and fished fruitlessly about for a single morsel of meat from each of the stews.

Standing a few places behind in the line that had formed, Bartley helped himself to the sauce from the pots together with a mound of cassava. He knew better than to expect to find much meat in either of the stews. He was happy to leave the Kutabans to suck any goat bones dry and to pick out shards of chicken bone to grind down to a paste between their molars. As a rule, he hated Kutaban food. However he had developed a taste for groundnut sauce and decided to take an extra spoonful with his cassava, scraping the other sauces to the side of his plate. He looked at the samosas that had been deep fried either early this morning, or perhaps even a day earlier, and gave them a miss. Unlike Fumbe, he distrusted fried food, the only exception being the occasional fish and chips in Blessings' Bar.

The villagers had meanwhile begun to chant. A group of some thirty of the younger men and girls sauntered forward and formed into two lines, men facing women. They took up a murmuring beat. A few more mischievous girls started to shout across as if to provoke those opposite. In response the men stamped the ground or began leaping in the air, strings of little bells tied to their ankles tinkling. Most had painted legs that looked like long white socks, while others had decorated their bare chests with diagonal stripes. Several were so finely featured as to be easily mistaken for any of the girls taunting them.

In contrast the girls were much less elaborately decorated except for their hair which was intricately braided and sculpted with animal fat. For the most part they wore short tunics or skimpy tee shirts.

Suddenly there was a loud whoop and the two sides charged each other. As they met in the middle, individual couples appeared to challenge or tease each other. Just as unexpectedly as they had advanced, they now withdrew, leaving just two couples momentarily alone between them - two men circling behind two girls who kept backing away until they too ran off to join the other women.

The mocking insults across the open space intensified, becoming increasingly raucous. Again, every few minutes the two sides would rush at each other before, just as suddenly, pulling apart. But now, when they separated one or more of the girls would break ranks to step forward and come skipping up along the line of men, singling one out to tease him and then running quickly back to safety when he rushed out to catch her. But, as the dance continued, more and more couples remained in the centre after others had withdrawn. They circled each other, leaping and shrieking until, laughing, they retired from the dance, sneaking off to disappear somewhere behind.

"Is there some symbolism to this dance?" Canavan was asking Awale after having spent the last while politely rearranging the cassava and stew on his plate. "I could imagine that the dance could well represent warriors and their traditional hunt. The boys are warriors and the girls mimic their prey. Am I right? "

The Regional Governor laughed.

"Yes in one way you are very right, but in fact in this dance the girls are the hunters and the boys are their prey. They dance like this for special celebrations maybe once or twice a year when the women are allowed to take control. You notice how a girl comes forward always to tease the boy? He is one she has chosen. The boy does not choose her. She may be already married to another, but in this dance she can choose a different partner. When they dance at night and a couple are finished displaying for each other, they may leave together and go off somewhere dark. It is allowed and there are no problems with husbands since they too may have a different partner for the night."

Canavan's face showed his shock and Awale laughed again.

"Do not worry, today they are dancing only as entertainment and nothing will happen. Indeed we are trying to educate the people so that they abandon these practices and dance only as a cultural spectacle."

Bartley, as unofficial timekeeper for the day, was about to announce that they should prepare to leave when O'Driscoll confidentially sidled up to him.
"So we're going to visit the orphanage next?" he whispered. "The Malingas are quite nervous about it. When I suggested your Minister visit them, they were quite happy at first, but since they realised Awale, Uba and a crowd of militia would be coming too, they have been quite upset. They've hidden Charity away, so don't go looking for her or asking after her, alright?"

As far as Bartley could see, when they arrived at the orphanage, the Malingas were well prepared. Wooden poles had been erected at the compound entrance to form a rough arch from which strips of green, white and red cloth had been strung in an approximate representation of Ireland's national colours. The children were lined up in front of the dormitory building with the blue plastic roof and the Malingas were waiting by the roadside. But he was surprised to see Professor Ballo standing beside the Malingas.

Already Fr. O'Driscoll, together with Fiona, was out of his pick-up and hurrying forward to introduce the couple to the Minister and Awale, but before he could do so Ballo stepped forward to take over the role of chief greeter. Bartley noted Awale's irritated surprise as the politician introduced himself to Canavan. The latter happily shook hands, no doubt accepting it as no more than his due that a representative of the political opposition should be on hand. Clendenning for his part showed some confusion when Ballo greeted him in turn like some dear, long absent friend. He hesitated just a little too long before responding, allowing Col. Uba to step forward and wrest control. He had until now stayed somewhat in the background although Bartley could not fail to see that he had been constantly on the alert, keeping a watchful eye on the periphery and orchestrating the movement of the militia at each location. He guided Canavan to the middle of a line of plastic chairs arranged in front of a makeshift lectern and directed Awale and Clendenning to sit on either side. Then before Ballo could move forward, Uba had adroitly placed himself and O'Driscoll in chairs on either flank. The politician stood aside for a moment looking discommoded before reluctantly taking an end seat.

Mr Malinga moved forward to the lectern on which he unfolded several creased sheets of paper on which he had written out a welcoming speech. O'Driscoll rose from his chair to interpret.

"Distinguished and Honourable Guests, Regional Governor, Honourable Mr F. Awale; His Excellency Minister of Foreign Affairs of the Republic of

Ireland, Mr D. Canavan Member of Parliament; His Excellency Ambassador of the Republic of Ireland, Mr A. Clendenning; Honourable Regional Superintendent, Colonel C. Uba; Honourable First Secretary, of the Embassy of Republic of Ireland, Mr B. Ryan; Mr A. Smith, Director for Africa of Overseas Development Assistance of the Republic of Ireland......"

It was the beginning of a long and laborious effort which described the origins of the orphanage, then went on to thank the Irish Minister for financing the new VIP latrines and concluded with a plea for more funding to help rebuild the dormitory house.

When he finished there was some gentle applause which, in Bartley's case at least, was as much in gratitude for the speech having come to an end as for its content. Malinga motioned to the children who had lined up behind him. At his signal they turned to face left, starting to move forward. They used their feet to scuff the dusty earth to set a rhythmic beat which they then echoed with clapping hands. After just a few steps first in one direction, they swung around and shuffled back in the other. Bartley recognised the movement from his earlier visit and wondered if the Minister would be as enchanted as he had been that first time he had seen the children dance.

Now one of the smaller girls stepped out in front and began to sing in an astonishingly clear, sweet voice. Bartley knew she would be giving thanks for the gift of the latrines and that she would finish with a plea for yet more help. Regional Governor Awale was whispering into the Minister's ear, translating the words of the song in which the other children joined, their singing a deeper murmuring against the single lead voice. Bartley found himself grinning as the dancing finished with the children forming two lines, one on its knees, hands held out to the Minister, the other standing, half-turned with arms raised pointing at the makeshift blue roof. Even without an interpreter, there was no missing their point.

The Minister led the enthusiastic applause and the guests stood up as Fr. O'Driscoll suggested they follow their hosts to view the latrines where the Minister was to unveil a plaque. Canavan was still applauding as he walked over to the girl who had been singing. He leaned awkwardly down and took her hand. The girl lowered her eyes and shook her shoulders as if to shrug off her embarrassment. Sean stepped in to capture the moment. Hearing the camera, the Minister turned toward it and went down on one knee still holding the girl's hand. Her embarrassment grew to panic and she started to pull away. Canavan retained a firm but gentle grip long enough to smile directly at the camera, allowing Sean to finish.

Bartley hung back as the Malingas and O'Driscoll conducted the tour that was to end with the unveiling. He was happy to see the four VIP outhouses had been cordoned off by a low mud wall and a wooden gate fixed between two shoulder height pillars. O'Driscoll and the Malingas halted where a green cloth had been pinned to one of these and the priest ushered Canavan forward.

"It is a privilege and a joy to be here today." The Minister began an impromptu speech. "I like to think there is a special bond between Ireland and African countries such as Kutaba – a bond forged from our shared experience and history. We are both young countries and have both served colonial masters. Our long links with Kutaba come not as a product of our seeking an empire, or territory or financial gain. They come from our Irish missionary priests and nuns who established themselves here to help and to educate. It is a fact that many African leaders today, including many prominent persons in Kutaba, received their first education from Irish missionaries.

"Today we have fewer Irish religious missionaries, but those who came before have left a footprint for our lay charities and development organisations to follow. I am proud that the Irish people and the Irish Government that I represent have one of the finest aid organisations in the world working within my Department bringing assistance to the very poorest countries in the world."

It struck Bartley that he might sometime ask O'Driscoll whether the sandals he wore were an appropriate *footprint*.

"Wherever we work, it seems true also that Ireland is known for having a special insight and understanding of how proper sustainable development should work." The Minister was moving forward into the next phase of his speech which Bartley could only compare to some form of *Bono-speak*. It was something with which he was all too wearily familiar. He was paying scant attention and was thus easily distracted when he thought he heard raised voices somewhere in the direction of the front of the compound. Turning toward the flag-festooned archway he could make out half a dozen police militia, bunched together, partly obscured by the corner of the dormitory. Stepping to the side to peer around, he caught sight of Professor Ballo, surrounded by militia. It looked like he was involved in some sort of altercation with Col. Uba. The latter was speaking quietly, but even without being able to make out the words, there was no mistaking their angry, menacing tone. Ballo, on the other hand, wore an untroubled-looking smile. The RS lifted a finger to point directly to him, but then shook his head as if changing his mind and turned abruptly to march away. Bartley retreated nervously behind the dormitory, but not before he saw Ballo offer a defiant laugh as a militia officer raised a restraining hand to motion him back.

The sound of cheers and applause drew Uba over as the Minister finished speaking. The RS caught sight of Bartley as he passed and their eyes locked momentarily before Bartley guiltily broke contact. Trying to remain unobtrusive, he too joined the group watching as the Minister drew aside the green cloth to reveal a wooden plaque bearing the commemorative inscription.

VIP Latrines

Gifting of Govt. Rep. of IRELAND

Opened by Foreign Minister

H.E. D. Canavan M.P.

There was no date as it appeared the sign-writer had run out of space and, indeed, the Minister's name itself appeared to have been squashed in at the bottom. There was more applause as the Minister posed for several formal photographs with the Malingas standing proudly on either side of the plaque.

The visiting party prepared to leave, but there was one final delay when Canavan's attention was drawn by a commotion where Fiona was squatting on the ground surrounded by a dozen or so children. They were either laughing wildly or giggling nervously at the pictures she had taken on her digital camera. Others were screaming that she should take their picture too and display it on her little screen. There was no doubting the Minister's intent and Sean, the official photographer, strode quickly after him as he hurried over. Within an instant he was down on one knee, interjecting himself in the centre of the children and forcing Fiona off to one side. He looked up expectantly as Sean's camera shot off a quick succession of photographs.

Bartley could envisage Frank's delight that Sean had succeeded in capturing such heart-warming images. These should surely appeal to readers of the Sunday newspapers. Indeed, he could see Frank and the other onlookers beaming happily. But scanning the group of now familiar faces, he realised one was missing. There was no longer any sign of Professor Ballo.

TWENTY-ONE

Monday, 3 November

Bartley was struck by Canavan's grey pallor as the Minister unfolded slowly out of the Ambassador's car when it drew up alongside the main entrance to Kutaba's Parliament. He had been waiting for fifteen minutes and the Minister was late and definitely not looking well. Bartley heard him let out a low gasp of pain as he straightened. It seemed he had succumbed to the same food poisoning that afflicted other members of his party as early as yesterday evening as they flew back to Bamgboshe.

It would have been a sufficiently unpleasant flight in its own right, but members of the group were already beginning to feel queasy from the samosas they had eaten for lunch. The intense heat of the afternoon had conspired to whip up a stormy sea of high pressure air currents through which the little plane had bucked and heaved. Each time the plane dropped, stomachs remained suspended somewhere above and nerves jangled with the follow-up roar of the single engine as the pilot throttled to regain altitude. By the time they landed a good part of the delegation felt seriously ill and nauseous.

Canavan groaned a second time as he waited by the Parliament steps for the Ambassador to join him from the far side of the car. Clendenning looked little better. The pair hesitated at the bottom of the steps, waiting for the rest of the party to catch up.

It was obvious as they trudged up the steps that to varying degrees most of the others were also very much under the weather. There being no sign of Frank, Bartley stopped to ask Andrew what had become of him.

"Frank, oh, he surfaced briefly at breakfast." The Africa Director chuckled. "As soon as he got the first whiff of my bacon – you know that Muslim-friendly beef stuff – he went green about the gills. Then, when I asked how he'd like his eggs, scrambled or fried, he just sort of ran off. He phoned Eddie before we left the hotel to say he was in bed and would join us later, if he didn't die first."

Hearing of Frank's suffering somehow helped lessen the usual feeling of dread Bartley experienced whenever confronted with the ordeal that was Prime Minister's Questions in the Kutaban Parliament. He could even feel some anticipatory sympathy for Canavan who had been invited to attend this twice yearly event. The idea of PM's questions was a novel concept in many an African country. Okeke took full advantage to present it as a show of gratuitous generosity toward the Opposition and to demonstrate to the world the flawless nature of the democracy that he had nurtured for more than two decades.

The Chief of Protocol was waiting to escort the group into the building and down a short corridor, past a pair of tall wooden doors through which MPs were already filing, and then to the right up a flight of stairs that opened onto a gallery overlooking the parliamentary chamber. If anything, the chamber resembled the interior of a church with a vaulted ceiling and rows of seats facing forward to an elevated dais at the far end on which stood the long bench-like desk of the Speaker and his officials. An imposing lectern had been mounted in front of the Speaker who was already in his seat with only the top of his head visible as he sorted through his papers.

Since Bartley was familiar with the lay-out of the gallery, he took over leading the way down the central gangway of the balcony to the end of the front row that he knew was reserved for very special VIPs. He halted at the bottom to allow the Minister pass him, but the Minister stopped and turned around motioning Clendenning who was directly behind to go first. This involved a complicated manoeuvre, with Bartley having to lean up against the balcony rail with the Minister squeezed on top of him while the Ambassador edged past in the constricted space. Canavan appeared to recognise the awkwardness of having Bartley standing half-blocking the passage and impatiently signalled that he should go next. Whether by accident or design, this resulted in Bartley ending up seated between the Minister and the Ambassador.

The US and British Ambassadors were already sitting in their usual places in the second row, engaged in quiet conversation which they broke off briefly to acknowledge Clendenning and nod politely to the Irish Minister as he passed. They stood up to allow the diminutive French Ambassador squeeze past to a seat beyond them. Other Ambassadors or their representatives were arriving, taking their places on the hard wooden seats and greeting each other with the bonhomie reserved to an elite group well used to the intimacy of each other's company. Theirs' was a peripatetic club that met at a   succession of national day cocktail receptions and dinner parties. Their accustomed exchange of greetings and jovial asides affirmed a common bond that helped alleviate the deadly tedium of official occasions such as this.

The rows of benches in the chamber below quickly filled with Members, followed lastly by senior Ministers who took their places in the front row on the right. But even when the last of these was seated and the doors to the chamber had been closed, there was still no sign of Prime Minister Okeke. Bartley picked out Foreign Minister Roble below in the front row leaning over to speak confidentially to the Finance Minister. He thought he recognised two of the other Ministers sitting alongside them, but could not be sure.

"What's the delay? Is there a problem?" Canavan asked after ten minutes of listening to the muted coughing and shuffling of papers below.

"No Minister. The Prime Minister usually waits for about fifteen minutes or so after everyone is in the Chamber before he comes in." Bartley was conscious of Clendenning's annoyance that he had lost his place beside the Minister and that his junior might end up fielding Canavan's questions. On the other hand, this was his first occasion to attend Prime Minister's Questions, so perhaps it was better that Bartley sit where he was rather than that he should risk exposing his ignorance of how the session was conducted.

"And nobody complains?"

"I don't think anyone would dare."

"Extraordinary, there would be uproar in the Dáil if An Taoiseach tried that. So what exactly happens when the Prime Minister finally arrives? Is it the usual rough-house that we have? How many questions are there? I imagine quite a few, if he only takes questions twice a year."

"No Minister. Normally, he answers perhaps two questions, but sometimes, if it is a long answer, only one."

Canavan was nonplussed.

"What do you mean? Are you saying that Prime Minister's Questions only take place for a morning session twice a year and yet he manages to answer no more than perhaps two questions each time? How the hell can that be? Are the Opposition so long-winded in asking questions or what? Can the Speaker not control them?" He frowned, recalling how at home, despite his testy control of proceedings, the Ceann Comhairle, the Dáil's equivalent of Speaker, frequently failed to rein in the verbal acrobatics of some of the Government's more outspoken critics.

"Actually Minister, the Opposition hardly speaks at all. The Member tabling a question does not get a chance to stand up to ask it in person. Instead, the Prime Minister simply reads out the gist of it and then gives an answer. Okeke might take up to an hour to reply and it isn't until he has finished that the Member who has put the question can speak."

"Really, the Prime Minister reads out the questions? Why can't the Member asking the question put it to him across the floor?"

"That wouldn't be possible. The protocol is that no Member is allowed to speak in the House before the Prime Minister has spoken. So you see, you can't technically ask a question until the Prime Minister has already answered it."

Clendenning shifted awkwardly in his seat. This was all very strange and he did not feel it helped the case for an aid programme that Bartley should be so blunt about local restrictions on the basic democratic process.

"Of course, then there is another problem," Bartley had not finished. "There is no advance notice of which questions are being taken, so even if the Opposition were allowed to speak first, they wouldn't know which question to ask. They will only find out which questions are being answered today when the Prime Minister reads them out and gives his answers."

"Good God, but I expect the real donnybrook starts after that, when the Opposition gets stuck into supplementary questions, eh?" Canavan persisted.

"Not as such. The Member whose name is on the question is allowed five or two minutes, according to the size of his party, to offer a view on the PM's reply, but he is not allowed to ask a further question as such. When his two or five minutes are up, the PM usually takes about half an hour to summarise the debate."

"*Debate*, I wouldn't call that a debate. By god, it's completely one-sided. We wouldn't get away with that for a moment in the Dáil. But, about there being no more than a couple of questions answered each time, what about the other questions he doesn't get round to? There must be hundreds. Do they get written replies?"

"Not as I understand it, Minister. I mean there aren't that many questions. I did on one occasion ask one of the officials in the Speaker's Office about that and he said the Prime Minister normally receives no more than three or four questions for each Question Time. The Speaker's Office is apparently of the view, therefore, that having replied orally to perhaps 75% of all questions that have been submitted, the Prime Minister should not really have to offer written replies to the tiny proportion that is left."

"So why don't the Members submit more questions?"

"Because they don't see any point, Minister."

Canavan felt a return of his nausea. He was finding this upside-down version of the natural order was making him dizzy.

The Prime Minister chose this moment to make his entrance through a door to the side of the Speaker's dais. He strode over to his seat in the front row alongside his most senior Ministers. He was short and looked trim and fit for his years. His light skin accentuated a wispy, horizontal line of dark hair growing just above the forehead of an otherwise bald head. From a distance it resembled a fake moustache that had been glued onto the wrong place. The thick round lenses of his glasses might have completed a comic look in a lesser personage, but in Okeke's case they made him appear commanding, at times perhaps even sinister. The murmurs of conversation in the chamber died off with his entrance. The Speaker announced the opening of the session, proclaiming the morning would be given over to Prime Minister's questions. He invited Okeke to take the floor.

The Prime Minister took his time approaching the lectern where he slowly and deliberately tapped his thick sheaf of notes neatly together. He looked out over the rows of parliamentarians like a headmaster surveying a school assembly. An usher came forward and placed a glass of water beside him. When he spoke his voice was surprisingly deep.

"Mr Speaker, Honourable Members of the House," he began, "it is a tradition established by my Government that I, as Prime Minister, should be held fully accountable by this august House and that in fulfilment of that obligation and the democratic principles which we are sworn to uphold, that I should appear before you on a regular basis to address your legitimate concerns though the answers that I give to Questions that have been laid before the House.

"This morning I wish to reply to two Questions that have been tabled by the Leader of PDAK, the People's Democratic Alliance of Kutaba, Honourable Professor Ballo M.P."

Bartley now for the first time made out Ballo sitting in the front row to the left of the central aisle. He had been hidden behind a rather large female until he jerked attentively forward. Even at a distance he looked tired and not his usual dapper self, perhaps a consequence of his long drive back to Bamgboshe overnight. Had he driven from the Malingas' orphanage immediately following his encounter with Col. Uba?

The PM continued. "First, the Honourable member wishes that I respond to allegations that the right to free political association is being denied in the Region of Bakooli and that the PDAK party is subject to unfair discrimination."

"Mr Speaker, I can be brief. The allegations to which the Honourable Member refers are allegations made solely by himself and members of his Party. It is a well-known fact that PDAK has in recent times witnessed a significant decline in its membership while there have been considerable increases in the number of citizens seeking to join the KNP, the Kutaba National Party, the Party of Government that has for so long secured the stability of our nation while witnessing the turmoil that afflicted so many of our neighbours.

"Mr Speaker, I think it speaks for itself that so much of the KNP's recent growth has taken place in the Bakooli Region, the Region which many might have assumed was the heartland of the PDAK.

"It is a fact that the expansion of the KNP in Bakooli has been at the expense of PDAK and that the latter's leadership is much aggrieved. It has sought to excuse its own failings by pointing the finger of blame at Government.

"Mr Speaker, no-one is more concerned with the right to freedom of political association than my Government and no-one is more concerned with protecting the people of Guseni. That is the true reason why these very same people have turned to the KNP and rejected PDAK. They see their traditional way of life is under threat as successive droughts diminish their grazing areas and their young seek an education and a better life in the towns. They see the KNP as the party that will help them.

"Just one of our initiatives to help the people of Guseni is the proposal that we establish a National Wildlife Reserve that will draw in tourists from abroad. This will result in many employment opportunities and new prosperity.

"Mr Speaker, it is a matter of considerable regret to me, and to my Government, that our efforts to improve the lives and conditions of the indigenous people of Guseni should become the object of unfounded allegations by the Leadership of PDAK. I call upon PDAK to desist from baseless accusations and to lay aside their differences so that we can work together for the good of Kutaba, the Region of Bakooli and the people of Guseni.

"Thank you, Mr Speaker."

"That seems a little sharp, but overall rather reasonable." Minister Canavan leaned toward Bartley. "You told me about these human rights stories going round, but I'm impressed that the Prime Minister can tackle them head on in Parliament. It doesn't sound like there's any real substance to them."

"But no, Minister," Bartley could not help contradicting. He was appalled at the Minister's apparent naïveté. He wondered whether Canavan could possibly believe this. "Minister, I do believe that PDAK does have real grounds for accusing the Government of not just discrimination but of human rights violations in Guseni. It may well be that people have actually been murdered by the army."

Bartley was half-turned toward the Minister in his seat and felt Clendenning leaning across to interrupt. He hurried on, thinking that having already gone so far there was little more to lose.

"Also, the Prime Minister's claim that his Party is growing in the Bakooli Region at the expense of PDAK does not reflect the facts on the ground - the intimidation, the withholding of food hand-outs..."

"Minister," Clendenning had succeeded in pushing forward, pinning Bartley back in his seat, "these allegations have been thoroughly investigated by other countries with greater resources at their disposal than we have. We have discussed them at length at our meetings of Ambassadors here in Bamgboshe. We haven't seen or heard anything to suggest human rights are being abused and certainly unfounded allegations to that effect would not be something we would wish to make an issue of. I applaud Mr Ryan's sense of fair play, even if perhaps expressed with too much enthusiasm and in the absence of any evidence, but really, the Opposition's complaints are groundless."

"But Minister," Bartley burst out, "just yesterday it looked like the authorities were trying to intimidate Professor Ballo when we visited the orphanage. I saw what appeared to be the RS, the Regional Superintendent Col. Uba, and his militia threatening him."

"What? What *are* you talking about? I didn't see anything. I doubt that anything of the kind could have happened without all the rest of us seeing it. You must be mistaken and seeing only what you want to believe."

"Quite right, Minister," Clendenning jumped in, outrage telling in his raised voice. "I'm sure we would have seen something like that if it had happened."

Bartley was about to protest further when a warning cough sounded from the French Ambassador behind and Clendenning gave Bartley a steely ball-bearing eyed glare before withdrawing back in his seat. Bartley drew in a deep breath. He had seriously overstepped the line and his heart was beating that little bit faster.

While this exchange was taking place, Prime Minister Okeke had declared that he would proceed immediately to answer the second question of the day. He further proposed that, with the Speaker's consent, the Opposition could respond to both his answers after he had finished. The Speaker agreed.

"The second Question to which I must respond today asks what actions are being taken by my Government to promote employment among the youth of Kutaba. I am pleased that this question has been put forward as it shows perhaps that PDAK may in this area at least be taking a constructive approach to opposition. Youth employment is a matter of great importance to my Government and I intend therefore to offer the fullest reply.

"Before I begin, I must set the economic context, both globally and domestically, in which the Government is working...."

He proceeded to spend an inordinately long time expounding on the state of the world, covering every aspect from trade wars and political rivalries between the super-powers to the consequences of global warming and environmental degradation. He went on, in more precise detail, to explain how these impinged on Kutaba and its economy. On the plus side, he listed the different possibilities of which his Government intended to take advantage. He welcomed the growing relationship with China and promised he would seek to maximise the potential benefits of investment from that country. He regretted the faltering assistance being received from the western countries of Europe and North America. He would strive to find ways to alleviate the certain hardships that would otherwise result from cuts in the level of aid that these countries had promised, but were now failing to deliver.

Minister Canavan was well practised in the art of sitting through the lengthy droning of the Taoiseach and his fellow Ministers while at the same time maintaining the appearance of listening with keen interest even if actually asleep. This was usually achieved by offering an occasional vigorous nod or grunt of approval. But even by Irish standards this was stultifying stuff. He watched as the PM finished another page of his speech and set it to one side. The thickness of the sheaf of papers remaining to be read did not appear to have shrunk in the slightest.

The effects of food poisoning were all but gone, but had been replaced by a dull headache and a weary tiredness made all the worse by Okeke's mindless droning. He yawned, the intake of oxygen offering but temporary relief.

Bartley noted the Minister's yawn and taking it as a warning sign remained rigidly still, his gaze rigidly fixed on Okeke buttressed behind his lectern below.

Okeke signalled that he would be coming later to the matter of fiscal revenue, "But first, I should first lay out the position as regards imports and exports. A crucial underlying factor here is the ever rising cost of cement..."

Bartley wanted but did not dare close his eyes as the Prime Minister embarked on a lengthy treatise demonstrating his meticulous understanding of the macro- and micro-economic (and social) impact of rising cement prices. His head grew heavy. It was as if Okeke had conjured up a cement truck and was physically dumping its load somewhere deep inside his skull.

Finally, he stole a surreptitious glance at his watch and, to his relief, saw it was time to leave. Unfortunately, this required renewing contact with the Minister. He reached out tentatively and tapped Canavan on the shoulder. The Minister gave a start.

"Minister, it's time to go. We can leave if you're ready."

"Eh, good, fine. Can we just walk out in the middle of this?" Canavan felt groggy and was unsure whether he could trust Bartley. He squinted past him, over to Clendenning.

"Yes, we can go." The Ambassador confirmed.

As the Irish party slipped as soundlessly as possible out of their seats, the French Ambassador frowned, momentarily distracted from the PM's meandering discourse on which he was taking copious notes. The US and British Ambassadors offered indulgent smiles. The rotund Czech Ambassador appeared to be fast asleep.

TWENTY-TWO

Emerging from Parliament, Canavan was grateful that Fumbe had kept the car air conditioning running while they had been inside.

"So what's next?" he asked.

"A short drive, perhaps a half hour or less, depending on traffic, to the other side of town. It's a water sewage plant the Kutabans insisted you see. Bartley, you have all the details, perhaps you could describe it to the Minister?" Clendenning had only the haziest notion of the project and had no alternative on this occasion but to defer to his junior.

As Bartley well knew, the visit to the sewage plant had in fact been arranged at the insistence of the Minister's political advisers and not of the Kutaban authorities. An Irish engineering company was interested in winning the contract to upgrade the facility and if Canavan assisted – if necessary by offering some funding from the aid budget – a successful bid was guaranteed to boost support in the Minister's constituency.

"We are going to the city sewage plant. It was commissioned only ten years ago to serve the needs of Bamgboshe as they were then. But since then the city population has grown phenomenally so that already it is unable to cope with the amount of, err, *waste*. The government has invited bids for a contract to carry out a major upgrade. It will be a rather massive undertaking. In the event that we, or rather you, Minister, decide to designate Kutaba a new priority aid country, it might be possible to consider allocating some funding toward helping. And, um, Raeburn Engineering, err, the Irish company is hoping to put in a bid."

The Minister picked up. Raeburn was indeed a big name in his area.

When they arrived, they saw a welcoming party in wait. Standing by a gold-coloured Land Cruiser, Bartley instantly recognised Environment Minister Gabi at the front of the group. This was unexpected but could explain, it occurred to him, why he had not seen Gabi earlier in Parliament. He may well have used meeting the Irish Foreign Minister as grounds for excusing himself from the nightmare of Prime Minister's Question Time.

As they stepped out of the Mercedes, Gabi came forward and, unable to distinguish between the Irish Minister and his Ambassador, addressed Bartley.

"Mr Ryan, we meet again." He did not offer a handshake but looked expectantly in anticipation of the appropriate introductions.

"Ah..., yes, Minister." Bartley stuttered. "Can I, uh, introduce, eh, the Irish Foreign Minister, Minister Canavan," then gesturing to Clendenning, "and the, em, Ambassador, Ambassador Clendenning."

"Minister," he turned to Canavan, "the Minister for Environment and Natural Resources, Minister Emmanuel, eh, Minister Gabi."

Embarrassed, he stepped back allowing them to shake hands, but at the same time he was aware that Clendenning must be mortified in front of Canavan that Gabi failed to recognise him, but obviously knew his First Secretary.

"Minister Canavan," Gabi offered the slightest of smiles, "I am delighted to meet you. I had hoped to be able to welcome you when you visited Bakooli, but unfortunately I had urgent business elsewhere. However, today since you are visiting this site which fortuitously falls within my area of responsibility as Minister for Environment and Natural Resources, I thought I should make sure to greet you.

"Now, while we have experts here to act as your guides, please allow me to escort you on your tour of this facility. It would be useful, I think, to be able to exchange views."

"Well, thank you, Minister, err, Minister Gabi," Canavan was unused to meeting individuals of Ministerial rank without prior warning - the Embassy should really have told him that there might be a Minister on hand - but he recovered quickly with a smile as equally thin as Gabi's. "I think that would be very interesting."

"Yes, thank you. Now, here we have our Director of Waste Management who will show us around," Gabi motioned toward an exceptionally tall, lank individual in a dark green suit, shiny with age. "Mr Sumalu, please show the way."

Sumalu shuffled forward.

"Welcome Honourable Ministers to what we refer to as a sewage farm. First, we will visit our cleansing ponds."

They followed him past a series of circular gravelled areas to what he had called the cleansing ponds.

"These ponds," he began "successively filter waste water downhill to those large rectangular pools that you see below. When we arrive there, I think you will be surprised by how clear the water is. It is so clear and clean at that stage that we discharge it safely and directly into Bamgboshe River."

Minister Canavan murmured appreciatively. Beside him, Minister Gabi took up the narrative.

"Unfortunately, as you will see, while this is impressive, it no longer accounts for all the waste water we must now discharge into the river and we need to carry out extensive upgrading. It might be a project that you would consider offering some modest support since I understand you may be contemplating agreeing on a programme of development assistance to Kutaba. Of course, I should say how grateful we already are for your contribution to our canal project for Bakooli City. However, there are a good number of other areas where your support and particular expertise could prove very effective."

Canavan looked up, surprised that Gabi should be so immediately forthright. He was certainly aware that his Department was considering adding Kutaba to its list of assistance countries. He had only the haziest grasp of the detail, but he did recall reading, or perhaps being told, about some wildlife – tourist related – initiative? "Ah indeed, you know I've just come from Parliament where your Prime Minister was speaking earlier about tourism. Certainly tourism is one of our main areas of expertise. And you are working on a wildlife programme to encourage tourism? That might, for example, be an area where we could well help. You know, marketing advice, even infrastructure." Canavan was warming to his theme, vaguely remembering pieces of his brief and envisaging the opportunities that an aid programme could open up for any number of Irish companies. "Yes, I hear about your plans for a wildlife park. I would imagine that would be a major undertaking? You'll need accommodation – a hotel or hotels – and catering. You'll need roads to bring in supplies and, of course, to bring in the tourists themselves. You might also think of an airport. What you have at the moment, if you don't mind me saying, but since I have seen it for myself, is not the sort of air service or airport you would need for regular tourists. All in all, I imagine what you are talking about is a really major, even massive, programme?"

It dawned on Bartley that the Minister was quite capable to shedding his Kerry brogue and making himself perfectly intelligible whenever he chose. Gabi, for some reason, had a sudden surprised look on his face.

"You mean Guseni National Park?" he stumbled. "Yes of course, I'm sure we will need help with setting up the park – but that's a little in the future. It's not something we have as yet gone into very deeply."

Coming from an operator the calibre of Gabi, that didn't sound so convincing. Bartley could only agree with his Minister that the Guseni National Park would have to be a really big deal. Surely Gabi should be fully on top of the detail? And, also should he not be delighted with the opening offered by Canavan and wholeheartedly embrace it rather than, in effect, kick the can down the road? Could it be that Gabi wasn't that much interested in the project, or that perhaps it didn't really exist, that it might be a smokescreen for something else?

"May I ask, Minister, how far your planning has progressed?" Bartley addressed Gabi before thinking it through. "I would imagine there are considerable costs. For example, you already have a team in the area with drilling equipment? Looking for fresh water supplies that you will need?"

"Yes, there is a team working in the area, looking for possible borehole sites. But it is an independent company that we have allowed in and it is offering its preliminary services to us without any charge to our budget at this stage."

"But I have heard, Minister, that there are those in Guseni that claim the team is looking for oil, not water. Is there any truth in that?"

"No, of course not!" Gabi's face darkened. "We need to assess the water potential of the area before we proceed and that is where the drilling team is helping us. Whatever you may have heard is the same old story that uneducated people in places like Guseni always come out with whenever anyone comes to look for water: *Our land is full of oil. We should all be rich. We should not trust drilling companies. Regardless of what they say, they only want to steal our oil.* Nonsense! Absolute nonsense! I can assure you they are looking for water, not for oil."

"Yes, of course, Minister, I can see how these stories might get around." Canavan offered in a placatory tone. But Bartley was loath to stay silent.

"Some locals also claim, Minister, that they have been driven off their land and that their homes have been burnt down by security forces. There are even allegations of the army killing civilians. Is that also untrue?"

Gabi stopped and stared. For a moment it looked like he might even be ready to square up to Bartley.

"I'm sure no such thing is happening, Minister." Canavan again stepped in quickly. "I suppose it is part of the job of the diplomat in any country to pick up gossip on the ground, but that is not to say we should give it credit." His look told Bartley, *"Enough!"*

They were walking along the top of a series of low concrete walls that separated the various ponds. Mr Sumalu was explaining their features and detailing their capacities but this did little to lift the air of tension. Bartley for his part was seething, angry that he could not pursue Gabi further, but at the same time petrified of what Canavan might say to him later.

They headed back uphill and it was here that the real problems of dealing with all Bamgboshe's sewage became apparent. Nowadays only a fraction could be treated by the plant and ever increasing volumes were being diverted directly into the river. Sumalu led them off to one side in the direction of a series of filthy pools of decomposing waste oozing one to another and eventually flowing brown and thick into the river some distance downstream from where the clean, treated waste water was being discharged.

They took a different route back to their cars. It was wet and muddy, but also strewn in places with excrement so that Canavan had to stop to wipe his shoe on a small, isolated patch of dried grass before saying goodbye to Gabi. The latter offered a stiffly formal handshake, before scowling over in Bartley's direction and striding off.

TWENTY-THREE

The Bamgboshe diplomatic corps was out in force in the Hilton to attend the lunchtime reception hosted by their Irish colleague to mark the Minister's visit. Neither Canavan nor Clendenning had uttered more than a curt word or two to him since his run-in with Gabi and Bartley felt he had been somehow quarantined. A moment earlier, Canavan and Foreign Minister Roble had concluded their formal, set-piece speeches of mutual friendship and regard. The Irish and Kutaban national anthems had been played – the latter anthem again reminding Bartley of its uncanny resemblance to "*Itsy bitsy spider*". At last he could escape briefly to seek out a friendly face.

He soon found Otto in conversation with the Papal Nuncio. The Nuncio, popularly known (but not to his face) as *The Nunce*, was a good humoured, down to earth type with an unconcealed fondness for whispered gossip about the private lives of members of the Kutaban government. The Nunce probably had an insight into the secrets of Kutaban politics that far exceeded that of all the other Ambassadors. Bartley had taken a particular liking to him since the occasion the two had met on their way into a reception hosted by the Cuban Ambassador - an event that Clendenning had decided out of personal prejudice was more appropriately attended by the Embassy's number two.

The pair had been met at the door by a rather pretty waitress in a short white apron and even shorter black skirt carrying a tray laden with mojitos. The Nunce had been intrigued that the glasses appeared full of some sort of salad and was so taken by the refreshing mint flavour of what he assumed was a relatively harmless punch that he emptied his glass with unaccustomed alacrity. He had barely entered the Cuban's large living room before he had lifted a further two glasses, offering one to Bartley, urging him to finish off his still half full, first glass. The other guests at the reception, as Bartley recalled, were not the usual crowd. There was a good showing of African diplomats, and of course the Russian Ambassador was there. The US Ambassador was absent and so too were many of the Europeans. The Nunce and Bartley had kept each other company and were on their fourth mojito when the Cuban Ambassador approached offering his ludicrously expensive Cohiba cigars from a wooden box. The Nunce had immediately taken two that he then slipped into the breast pocket of Bartley's suit jacket. He patted the pocket carefully before taking a further two Cohibas and burying them in the deep folds of his cassock. He then thanked the Ambassador profusely on such unprecedented generosity and complimented him on the flavour of his excellent mint cordial. The Ambassador beamed before heading off to offer what remained in his box to a group of African Ambassadors who looked to be on the point of leaving. The Nunce gathered Bartley by the arm suggesting that they too should leave, chortling all the way to the door about what a marvellous and unusually entertaining reception this had been.

If anyone could cheer him up, Bartley reckoned therefore it would be the Nunce and Otto. The Nunce welcomed Bartley, raising his right hand in his flowing white cassock as if bestowing a benediction.

"Well, Bartley, how's the visit going?" Otto asked jovially.

"The visit's fine, but I think I have severely blotted my copybook."

"Oh, what did you do – overindulge the wine at dinner?"

"If only I had, I could live with it. No, I seemed to get into a public scrap with Minister Gabi that ended with my Minister telling me to shut up."

"What the hell have you got against Gabi? He's an important guy with a lot of influence. I don't know what you said to him, but you'd be best advised not to cross him. You don't need him as an enemy."

"It's funny you're the second one to tell me that. What is it about Gabi then that makes you think he's dangerous?"

"Hey, what's this?" Otto broke off to look at the stage as the hubbub of conversation tailed off and the guests turned toward where Fiona had assembled a line-up of her pupils. They were wearing green tee shirts and short green skirts of some shiny, synthetic material sourced from one of the local Indian shops. Fiona was readying to launch them into the mini *Riverdance* routine she had devised for the occasion.

A sound system stuttered into life with a blast of fiddle music and the girls joined hands aloft. Fiona dramatically flung her arms apart and the girls offered an introductory bow. They were of varied ages and size with the two smallest, obviously the youngest, at either end of the line. Two girls in the centre were noticeably older and more mature, one of them wearing a blonde wig. The two younger girls came forward to perform a high kicking strut from one side of the stage to the other, while the remaining dancers retreated to the back, linking arms.

Otto's eye was caught by the blonde at the rear. She was spectacularly attractive and when she took her turn to come forward to perform a somewhat provocative solo of high kicks, first facing and then with her back to the audience, he nudged Bartley and leaned over to whisper in his ear.

"Nobody does a reception like you Irish guys. Do you reckon Fiona would lend me a couple of her girls for a night or two to practice my Irish dance routines?"

"Christ Otto, if Fiona ever hears you suggest anything like that, you can bet she'll have your balls off."

Otto laughed. He turned to the Nunce who, being oblivious to the nature of this exchange, was happily tapping his ring against a glass in time with the music.

"Great show, your Grace," Otto called over.

The *show* went down very well with all the guests. Bartley was amazed that Fiona had managed to teach her students the dance steps. He could not imagine it possible that anyone of her outsize proportions could have demonstrated the routine without risking serious injury and likely heart failure. However she did it, he was impressed and more importantly so was the Minister, since Canavan applauded loudest at the end. Bartley hoped the Minister's mood had improved.

Indeed the Minister did seem to be in a much cheerier frame of mind when they trooped in later for the official meeting with Okeke in the conference room of the Prime Minister's Office. Bartley found himself sitting at one end of a long table beside the Africa Director waiting for the Prime Minister to arrive.

"Bartley, I haven't had a chance to speak to you since this morning," Smith leaned forward confidentially, keeping his voice low.

"Your little altercation with Minister Gabi in front of Minister Canavan was very ill-advised. It won't do you or anyone else any good to be seen rocking the boat. We are pretty much agreed in the Department to set up Kutaba as our new programme country. It's not just that the Minister has given approval in principle, but he's also personally committed.

"So listen, we have to be prepared for any possible criticism. We've had enough bad press recently about having several million ripped of us in two of our present countries. The taxpayers' mood could turn at any time against our keeping foreign aid running. If any hint got out that Kutaba was violating human rights, it could scupper our plans and, frankly, we need Kutaba."

"What do you mean *we need Kutaba?*" Bartley was at a loss.

"While we're keeping money back from the other countries after the scandals, we need somewhere else to invest it. Otherwise it'll look like we can't spend our budget and there'll be no excuse not to cut our subvention for next year."

"But surely human rights abuses, particularly if they involve a government murdering its own citizens should take precedence over all other considerations?"

Smith sighed wearily. "I agree, Bartley, but we don't see any real evidence of that here, do we? And it doesn't help that you embarrass Canavan by starting a fight with a Kutaban Minister over some unsubstantiated rumours."

"I'm sorry, but I really can't agree. If people are being killed by the Kutaban government we can't ignore it."

"Look, just drop it. If there was anything here, we would have heard about it long since from the Americans or the Brits."

Bartley was about to say that these would probably be the last to advise them of any such thing, when they were interrupted by the arrival of the Prime Minister, followed by Foreign Minister Roble and a line of officials, entering by a door at the far end.

The ensuing meeting followed its strictly choreographed agenda. Both sides offered their assessments of the agreed list of current bilateral, national and international issues. It was a ritualistic exchange of views, but Bartley was struck by the contrast between his Minister reading from a prepared script and the spontaneity of the Kutaban Prime Minister who spoke without reference to notes or to any of his advisers. It was a routine, friendly meeting that, unlike the encounter with Gabi, unfolded smoothly and without drama.

As they filed out of the room, with Okeke saying his farewell, the Chief of Protocol came bustling up to Bartley, urgently washing his hands in agitation.

"Mr Ryan, you should know I have only now received word from the airport of a change in the schedule for Minister Canavan's flight to Kampala. Yesterday's flight was cancelled due to some technical problems and, as a result, today's departure time has been brought forward. We have slightly less than two hours to take-off. The Minister and his party will need to return to the Hilton immediately to collect their luggage and check out. We will need to leave for the airport without delay."

Bartley broke the news to Clendenning, suggesting that while the Ambassador spoke to Canavan he would inform the others of the change in plans.

It was quite an effort to organise them to check quickly out of the Hilton and Bartley was much relieved when every last member of the delegation and piece of luggage were finally in the cars. He had to admit that they all had cooperated with a will even to the extent of the Minister packing his own bag rather than waiting for his Private Secretary to do it for him. It seemed not one of them wished to miss the flight and risk spending a further night in Bamgboshe. Inevitably, of course, the last person to be accounted for was Frank, who worried that he might have left something behind and had to be persuaded that there was no time to go back to his room to check.

They were waiting in the VIP lounge, their passports just having been returned with their exit stamps and Bartley was standing beside a relieved

Frank who had finally found his iPad at the bottom of his rucksack. Canavan and Clendenning were seated on the sofa with their backs to them.

"I just want to say that I think this visit went well, all things considered, and thank you, Ambassador, for all you've done." Bartley could just about make out what the Minister saying. "I think we should be well on track to make Kutaba our next priority country, although we will have to wait to see how our budget turns out before we make any final decision. Still, it should be possible.
"We'll need you to travel back to HQ to help with planning the programme, probably sometime in the New Year. I presume that won't be a problem?
"Something else, we don't want anything or anyone to rock the boat on this..."

Bartley stepped in a little closer. "Your man – Ryan isn't it? You need to keep him under control. The way he spoke earlier today to that Minister, what was his name?"

"Gabi, the Minister for Environment and Natural Resources."

"Yes, that's the one. It was totally inappropriate how he talked to him. You need to keep a rein on Ryan, prevent him annoying our future partners. And, for God's sake, stop him running round shooting off his mouth like he's some Holy-Mary-Full-Of-Human-Rights-Robinson."

He was interrupted by the arrival of the Chief of Protocol announcing they should head out to the aircraft. He led the way through the door at the back of the lounge while an airport official held it open until the last of them had filed through. Together they crossed the empty baggage claim area and out through the door onto the apron.

Their aircraft stood some short distance ahead of them, a 737 with the airline's logo of a maned lion's head painted on the tail. To their left a crowd of fellow passengers jostled impatiently behind a line of soldiers. The majority were laden with outsize hand baggage and pushed to get in front. The soldiers would hold them back until the Minister and his party had boarded, after which they would be released in a wild free-for-all to grab the best of the remaining *free seating* and cram the overhead storage bins to overflowing.

The crowd began to press forward more urgently as Canavan shook hands with the Chief of Protocol and then sought out the Ambassador to offer his final thanks. He started up the steps, having ignored Bartley beside Clendenning.

Frank was the last to follow him up, his rucksack reluctantly bumping from step to step. Watching him, Bartley was almost tempted to wave goodbye. But then just as Frank reached the top step, there was a deafening explosion, followed by a plume of black smoke belching out of the nearside jet engine. Frank ducked instinctively and turned with a look of panic, seemingly contemplating rushing headlong back down onto the tarmac. But what he saw below was a wild mob, now released by the army, charging toward the steps. He retreated to disappear inside. It was an innocent moment Bartley would remember later.

TWENTY-FOUR

Thursday 22 January.

Bartley found the months immediately following the Minister's visit frustratingly difficult. Clendenning had kept him fully occupied with an obsessive zeal, ensuring that he complied with the humdrum minutiae of daily embassy life. He had been denied any opportunity to escape the immediate confines of Bamgboshe much less visit Fr. O'Driscoll in Shole where he still hoped to get closer to the truth of what might be happening in Guseni.

Perhaps, he reasoned, things could be worse. News of his confrontation with Minister Gabi and Minister Canavan's displeasure had inevitably travelled around the Department. Phone calls from his few friends at HQ and elsewhere had confirmed this. If he were to salvage any prospect of future advancement within the Department of Foreign Affairs and Trade, they advised he should keep his head down and follow orders without question.

Still, it chafed that he had had no further contact with O'Driscoll and that no-one else seemed interested in Guseni.

On the plus side, his relationship with Michelle had distinctly improved. Word had come from HQ of her unexpected success in the promotion competition. She was now on a panel awaiting reassignment as First Secretary. He had congratulated her on her success. He was surprised to find he truly believed she merited such early promotion. For her part, now that they were essentially on an equal footing, she seemed less inclined to challenge him. For Bartley too it was a bonus that her imminent promotion had resulted in her becoming somewhat of a confidante to Clendenning, thereby to a certain extent relieving him of the purgatory of time he would otherwise have spent in the Ambassador's company.

The Department's aid budget had taken a further, inevitable hit in a new reallocation of resources. Kutaba would not now become one of Ireland's priority programme countries, but there was a promise to enter into funding arrangements with the Kutaban government on a limited number of new projects. Precisely which projects would be the best fit for the money and personnel resources available was the subject of an extended workshop beginning in the Aid Division at HQ that very week. Clendenning had flown back to Dublin to offer his contribution to the discussions and Brigid had travelled with him. The pair intended to take a brief vacation at home before returning. For the first time since October, Bartley found himself in charge of the Embassy and briefly free from the shackles that Clendenning had placed on him.

So it was he who was opening the letter for the Ambassador that had just been delivered from the Kutaban Foreign Ministry. It turned out to be an invitation to observe the destruction of Kutaba's stockpile of landmine ordnances. He recalled Minister Canavan, at Clendenning's urging, had congratulated Prime Minister Okeke on this very matter. Reading on, he saw the event was scheduled to take place on 3rd February and that the location was somewhere in the Bakooli Region.

He leaned back in his chair, staring at the invitation.

Well, he thought, *Clendenning is keen on landmine destruction. I'm sure he would want the Embassy to be represented.* More importantly, if he travelled down to Bakooli as an observer he would have an excuse to touch base with Frank O'Driscoll. Perhaps he could arrange to spend a day or two with him in Guseni.

His phone rang and he picked it up, his mind still assessing the possibilities.

"Yes?"

"Bartley, it's Grace. There's someone here at reception would like a word with you – a Mr Luuk. He says you know him from a hotel he owns - Lion Rock Lodge?"

He was surprised, he had almost forgotten about Luuk.

"Sure, I know him. Bring him in."

He placed the Foreign Ministry letter to one side of his desk. As soon as he was finished with Luuk, he would give some serious consideration as to how best make use of the opportunities it offered.

He stood up and held out a hand as Luuk was ushered in.

"Luuk, it's good to see you. Have a seat."

"Mr Ryan, thank you for seeing me. I am a little embarrassed to come to your Embassy."

"Please Luuk, it's Bartley."

"Thank you, Bartley. I am sorry to call on you. I don't know if you can help me, but I've already been to the Dutch Embassy and I am ashamed to say they refused to help. They scarcely listened to me."

"Really? I'm surprised. I have good contacts with the Dutch Embassy and I'm amazed that they would not want to help one of their citizens. But what's the problem?"

"It's all about Lion Rock Lodge. Maybe you remember that I have to renew my operator's licence every year and that I rely on the Minister for Environment and Natural Resources to give his approval?"

"Yes, in fact, Minister Gabi was having dinner at the Lodge the time I visited."

"Yes, that's right. So you know also how I have to entertain him and his friends to make sure I have no problems. I thought this was working well enough, although it does cost me money. But then, last December, when I applied for my licence for this year, I received a letter from the Ministry saying that I no longer qualified. It gave no reason. It just said I was "ineligible". It ordered me to leave the Lodge before the first of January and to hand over to a representative of the Ministry who would take over running it.

"I tried to contact Minister Gabi directly, but I could not get near him. Then I went to my Embassy and spoke to the Ambassador. He said questions of licences or leaseholds on properties are matters for the Kutaban government. He said that he has close relations with Minister Gabi but that the Netherlands is depending upon the Minister's goodwill to help push through some other major deal. He didn't say what, but he did let me know that he could not put relations with the Kutaban government or Minister Gabi at risk over any personal complaint I might have. I had hoped he would make some appeal on my behalf, perhaps through the Foreign Ministry, but he wouldn't even listen to the rest of my story.

"So now I've left the Lodge. Before Christmas, I was forced to pack up and move out with whatever I was able to load onto the back of my pick-up. I've been staying with a friend here in Bamgboshe, but now I am afraid my residence permit will also be taken away and I will have to leave the country without being able to appeal or even claim some compensation for what I've lost...you know I put my life savings into Lion Rock..." Luuk's voice choked, "I'm sorry. I haven't really been able to talk to anyone about this."

"That's alright, Luuk. I am sorry for your trouble. I'm shocked that this could happen and that you could be left in this position. Somehow, I'm not surprised by Minister Gabi's involvement. He's not exactly one of my favourite people since I had a run-in with him myself not so long ago. He's obviously the type of individual who doesn't take kindly to being crossed or contradicted. But tell me, what's become of the Lodge now?"

"The so-called "representative" of the Ministry arrived sometime in December and took over when I left. It turned out he was a cousin of the Minister. The first thing he did was tell all my staff that he would have to cut their wages by 50%. Before I was thrown out my cook had already left. He should find a job somewhere else, but the others had to stay - either that or end up with no jobs and no pay at all.

"They are good people and I have tried keep in touch with them. They tell me Lion Rock now serves as no more than a brothel for wealthy businessmen and officials escaping their wives in Bakooli. They use the cabins to sleep off their hangovers or have sex with the prostitutes that the Minister's cousin brings in by minibus every weekend. They say the Lodge is unrecognisable. It's run-down and filthy. I don't think I would even want it back now. I would like some compensation, at least a little to help me start somewhere else, but it looks like I will get nothing."

"Surely, you're entitled to compensation. Have you spoken to a lawyer about it?"

"Yes, but the problem is that I don't have a copy of my leasehold agreement or other papers that I would need. I got them out of the safe in my office and put them in my briefcase when I was packing my things, but they disappeared. I think someone must have taken them out of the briefcase when I left it in the office for a half an hour while I was loading my pick-up."

"Christ, Luuk, I don't know what to say. I'm not sure what I can do. You probably think it won't do much good, but I'll speak first to my friend in your Embassy. Even if he says he can do nothing – and, from what you say, I suspect his Ambassador probably won't want him to try - at least then, they will know that another Embassy is interested. That might just embarrass them enough into making representations of some sort on your behalf.

"Also, by coincidence, I am hoping I'll be travelling to Bakooli at the start of February," Bartley fingered the letter on his desk, "Maybe I can ask some questions down there. It's not much, but perhaps it's a start."

"Bartley, I am grateful. I appreciate anything you can do, no matter how little you think it is. Believe me, it's already a relief to have been able to talk to someone like you about it. Let me give you my friend's telephone number. If you have any news, perhaps you can let me know. But, I won't take up any more of your time." He got up and reached across the desk, offering both hands to shake.

Bartley's head was buzzing as he returned to his office after seeing Luuk out the front door. No matter how much he had tried over the last couple of months, he had been unable to quite get Emmanuel Gabi out of his head and here, now, his name had come up yet again. It was unfortunate that Otto had also gone off for a brief vacation, but he would be sure to speak to him as soon as he came back.

TWENTY-FIVE

Tuesday, 3 February.

Bartley and Fumbe had spent the night in the New York Palace in Bakooli city. The hotel was no more comfortable than before, but a least there had been a full-sized sheet on the bed to cover the still bare duvet. Fumbe was surprised that Bartley had chosen not to stay at Lion Rock and was outraged when he learnt why.

"These bastards are not Kutaban. They come from the devil. Someday," he hissed, "we will send them back."

Bartley did not see this happening anytime in the near future, but it was a pity, he reflected, that there were not more people like Fumbe around. However even if there were, he guessed the system would likely find a way of getting shot of them. That reminded him of Fumbe's own precarious position within the Embassy – a position of which the driver was unaware. It had only come to Bartley's attention because Michelle had confided in him after Clendenning had let it slip to her in the course of one of their increasingly frequent tête à têtes. He had said he was considering replacing Fumbe with the cousin who had worked as temporary driver during the Minister's visit and had since been employed when Fumbe was due some leave. The Ambassador was of the view that Fumbe had grown a bit too cocky and sure of himself. He was also weary of his viciously slamming the car door every time he got in the back seat. The cousin, he opined, seemed a far quieter and overall more amiable character.

"Our politicians they are all greedy." Fumbe continued. "They give my country a bad name, but my people do not care. That is why Kutabans deserve Minister Gabi and his cousin and the politicians who think only to make themselves rich. These politicians are not honest."

"I can't disagree with you Fumbe, but on the other hand, I'm not sure how many truly honest politicians I've come across anywhere else in the world – certainly very few from Ireland. They seem less interested in doing any real good than in staying in power. And with power, of course, they can pay themselves huge salaries and all sorts of other perks.

"I suppose I can think of one, or perhaps two, who might credibly claim to be in politics to serve. The others have one face for the voting public, but show another when they deal with civil servants like me. That's when you see their arrogant side. The rest of the time they are busy trying to look good to get re-elected. Being in parliament is as good as winning the lottery."

Bartley had allowed some of his recent frustration to the surface, but he pushed such feelings aside. This morning, for once, he had every reason to be in an upbeat mood. He was looking forward to the next few days even if he felt a little nervous. One way or another he was hoping he might find some closure or resolution to the conflicting emotions that had troubled him over the last few months.

It was early, not quite eight o'clock but the sun was already searing down. He could feel it burning through the few cottony strands of hair brushed across his scalp. He must remember to check that his baseball cap was somewhere in the car as he would probably need it for his travels with O'Driscoll. He had informed the Foreign Ministry that he would attend the decommissioning exercise and had received permission to travel into the Guseni region afterward to visit the priest.

The decommissioning was to take place on a dusty plain quite some distance from Bakooli City. There was a police checkpoint on the dirt road as they drew near, but Bartley's name and car registration were on a list so they were waved quickly through. They left the road and drove over rough ground toward where they could see a number of vehicles in the distance, a mix of army trucks and jeeps, white Landcruisers and a small bus parked in front of two large khaki coloured tents. As they drew up Bartley saw a number of white faces among the black soldiers and officials. They were standing under a long canvas awning looking out over the plain. Pulling on his baseball cap with the NY logo, he stepped out of the car and headed over to this group. As he came close, he was surprised to see Otto beckoning him over.

"Good morning, Bartley! I didn't know you were coming. Did you drive down?"

"Otto, I thought you were still in Uganda."

"No, I got back yesterday morning and slept the whole day. I guess I was exhausted from all that getting up at dawn to go see *gorillas in the mist*. We flew to Bakooli in a charter this morning." He motioned to the half dozen diplomats – the round Czech Ambassador, a couple of military attachés and other vaguely familiar faces standing around.

Their attention was drawn by an army captain rapping a cane on a trestle table.

"Members of the diplomatic corps, observers, thank you for your attendance today." he began. "I will explain simply what the purpose of our exercise is today. If you require any further technical information, you may wish to take copies of the documents we have prepared for you here." He gestured to the papers spread out on the table before him. "In brief, our armed forces, after independence, originally amassed a stockpile of four different types of landmines. We will be decommissioning three types today. The fourth type, the *jumping jack*, as we called it, was a device detonated by tripwire that shot upwards discharging a cascade of steel balls at groin level over a wide radius, and has already been completely disposed of. The types of mines being destroyed today include two of the more traditional type with which you would be more familiar. These are mines that are buried in the ground. One is designed to be set off when someone walks on it. The other is a heavy duty explosive used as an anti-tank device, but which of course will detonate when any other vehicle drives over it. The third type is a smaller mine, known as a butterfly type that is dropped by aircraft over an area. This type is well camouflaged so that it is difficult to notice at a distance and indeed can easily be mistaken for a rock.

"The ordnance we are destroying today has been stacked in four deep pits in the ground where they will be detonated in a series of controlled explosions. I invite you now to come forward to inspect the pits and, if you have any questions, please feel free to ask."

As they walked across the plain toward the distant pits, Bartley could not help but feel uncomfortable. He came from a country where, despite the so-called *Troubles* of the past, most people he knew had little or no contact with the army or explosives. The Irish police force generally went about its business unarmed. Guns and bombs belonged to television screens. But he knew about landmines and the horrible injuries they were designed to inflict and he was wary of getting up too close to view any such devices. He took comfort that the Kutaban soldiers appeared to know what they were doing. Otto, for his part, showed no fear as he strode forward, confidently eager to have a look down into the pits.

Bartley held back from the edge of the first. It was a square hole, about four metres along each side. He could make out stacks of black metal cans of two different sizes packed in neat rows below. From his position he could still make out what looked like Russian lettering stamped on some of the cans. Black wire, probably fuse wire, laced between them and he saw at least two sticks of dynamite - or so he guessed - nestled down between two of the stacks of cans closest to him.

The pits were spread some distance apart. Two others were identical while the third, in addition to its complement of stacked tin cans, contained an untidy pile of what looked like flat pieces of stone of a dull, sandy colour in the shape of oversized wing-nuts. These must be the butterfly mines.

At each pit the captain read out an inventory of contents that the witnesses would later be asked to verify as destroyed. At the third pit, he looked around as if to invite questions. There appeared to be none and, satisfied, he moved to lead the group away, but before he could do so Bartley cleared his throat.

"Excuse me, could you just clarify something?"

"Certainly," the captain drew to a halt and smiled.

"We can see these pits are full of mines and I presume we will see them blown up and be able to verify that they have all been destroyed. But how does it exactly work as to the number of mines destroyed? I mean how are we supposed to know how many mines are here in each pit? Looking down from above, there's no telling how far down into the ground each pit had been dug and therefore how deep each stack of mines goes.

"We can observe and verify that a number of mines have been destroyed, but I presume you don't expect us to verify any specific number. Is that correct?"

"This certainly is a huge mass of weaponry." Another voice cut in before the captain could answer. Bartley turned round and to his surprise found Major Mbuta standing behind him. He had not noticed him among the group when he had arrived.

"Major Mbuta..." He was caught off-guard.

"Of course, Mr. Ryan, we cannot expect you to climb down into each pit and start counting, but you can clearly see that there are vast amounts involved – our army's total remaining stockpile of such weapons in fact, is that not correct, Captain? And I think that is all we can reasonably ask you all, as observers, to verify."

"You mean that we verify that there is a vast amount here, but not that this is all that the army might have?" Mbuta's patronising tone annoyed Bartley.

"I assure you it is all one of the same. These amounts are all that remain. But perhaps we could now move on to the last pit?"

They clustered around to look down into the fourth pit. This last, like the first two, was filled with black metal canisters. When he felt they had seen enough, the captain called them together and led them back toward the tents. Already soldiers had started manhandling sandbags that had been stacked alongside and were positioning them into place above the explosives in the pits. When Bartley and the others arrived back under the awning that was to serve as their observation post they watched as a mechanical digger moved in and worked further on covering over the now buried ordinance. There was an amount of talking over military radios and the remaining soldiers started drifting back toward the observation area. The digger followed them. There seemed to be four or five figures still moving around out there but eventually they too started back. They stopped halfway and disappeared into the earth into a dugout behind a low wall of sandbags that Bartley had earlier missed but could now just about make out.

There was more talking on radios. The captain warned the civilians to prepare themselves for the crash of explosions. His radio crackled one more time and he spoke into it.

"Ten seconds", he announced and started counting down.

At zero there was a massive eruption from the ground followed by a huge dust cloud rising high over the plain before the first boom reached the observers. The cloud seemed to hang in the air before clearing to reveal a shower of sand, rock and molten pieces of metal cascading back down to earth.

Three further blasts followed in quick succession. Each was a loud hollow thumph but not the ear shattering boom that Bartley had expected. The earth beneath trembled with each detonation.

After the explosions there was a delay before a group of soldiers approached the blast site and started picking their way round. Some fifteen minutes later the civilians were invited out. Otto again hurried forward. Arriving at the spot where the pits had been dug, he began searching round anxiously to find some souvenir. Dust and a burnt cordite smell mingled in the air. The pulverised earth was covered in shattered rocks and stones shrouded in sand and littered with occasional pieces of twisted metal or wire. They walked around aimlessly for ten minutes or more. There was really nothing to see. Bartley spied Otto surreptitiously pocketing a small misshapen piece of metal that he took to be the remains of one of the cans.

Before the diplomats started back to their bus, the captain made a short speech thanking them again for their presence and asking them to fill in their details and sign a list that he passed round.

"Making sure that you're not signing anything you shouldn't?" Otto teased Bartley who was, in fact, checking to make sure that he was signing only to the fact that he had observed the destruction of an unspecified quantity of landmines. "Were you trying to wind up our poor Major earlier? I didn't realise you and Mbuta were so close."

"Believe me we are not and the less I see of him the happier I am. I wasn't expecting to see him down here today."

"Mbuta? I don't think you should be surprised. Between you and me there's little that happens down this neck of the woods without him being around somewhere. Anyway, tell me are you driving back to Bamgboshe? Why don't you come back with us? There are a couple of empty seats on the plane. You could be back in time for sundowners in the Club this evening."

"Thanks, but no thanks. I'm staying around for a couple of days. The Foreign Ministry has given me permission to visit Guseni to meet Fr. O'Driscoll, our Irish priest here."

"What, do you seriously want to go trailing round in the bush for the next few days bouncing your butt up and down on dirt roads when you could be having a cold beer with your buddies at home? Well, enjoy yourself, if that is possible out there." he nodded in the direction of the empty plain where some plumes of dust still hovered after the explosions.

"Uh, Otto, there was something I wanted to speak to you about. You know Luuk from Lion Rock Lodge?"

"Oh Luuk, yeah. What about him?"

"He called at my Embassy when you were away. His Lodge has been taken away from him."

"Yeah, I heard he'd lost his licence."

"No, it's not that simple. Minister Gabi had him evicted so he could give the place over to his cousin. Luuk did nothing wrong. The place has simply been stolen from him."

"Is that what he told you? I heard he just forgot to renew his licence in time."

"No, no! Gabi probably wanted it for his cousin all along."

"Hey, I don't know about that."

"So you don't know Lion Rock is now running more or less as a whorehouse? Can't you do something to help Luuk? After all, he is one of your citizens. If you can't get it back for him, surely you could help him win some compensation?"

"Look I agree it's a shame if that's what's happened to the place and that he's lost everything, but there's nothing I can do."

"Have you tried? Have you spoken to the Foreign Ministry?"

"No point. It's a domestic matter. The Embassy can't interfere."

"But surely when it involves a Dutch citizen, you have the right to express your concern?"

"Normally, yes, you could say that. But we have to look at the bigger picture and what's in our best interests..."

"Otto," they were surprised by Major Mbuta. "I am happy to see you again and that the Netherlands has also been represented here today."

"Well thanks, Major, it's good to see you too." Otto beamed.

"But I am sorry to interrupt you and Mr. Ryan, I simply wished to greet you before you leave."

Otto? Bartley was struck by the familiarity and looked at his friend, then back to Mbuta who was about to take his leave.

"Oh, you're not interrupting at all, Major. In fact we were just talking about Lion Rock Lodge. I know you are familiar with it." Bartley plunged ahead before Otto could stop him. "We were just saying how surprised we were to hear that the Dutch owner has been evicted and that management has been taken out of his hands." Otto scowled. "It seems such a shame as he obviously put so much work into it. I understand the new manager is a cousin of the Minister for Environment, Minister Gabi, that is. I wonder how he's getting on, perhaps you know?"

It was Mbuta's turn to be taken aback. The scar on his face had turned a darker red. "Yes, I have heard that the Lodge has been taken over. However..."

"I'm sorry Major. It's been a pleasure to see you, but I really must go. My colleagues are already leaving and I have to go with them." Otto removed himself adroitly from the conversation and hurried off with one last frown in Bartley's direction.

"Actually, Mr Ryan, I want a word with you now that the opportunity arises." Mbuta seemed also to have no desire to continue a conversation about Lion Rock, "I understand you will be staying in Guseni for a few days, visiting with your Fr. O'Driscoll. I understand the purpose of your visit is to offer funding for some parish project the Father may have in mind. I advise you strongly to concentrate on that and not to become involved in other matters. You should know there has been some conflict recently in certain districts because of cattle raids between villages. You should restrict your movements to the area near where the good father lives in Shole. Other parts of Guseni could prove dangerous for you."

"Well, thank you Major Mbuta, but the Foreign Ministry has given me permission to travel in Guseni and said nothing about not going where I want."

"The Foreign Ministry may know what is happening elsewhere in the world, but that does not mean it is in a position to offer advice about

Guseni. Believe me you do not want to travel beyond Shole." He paused and looked Bartley in the eye. "Goodbye, Mr. Ryan. Take care."

TWENTY-SIX

It took Bartley and Fumbe a couple of hours driving over rock strewn roads to reach O'Driscoll's house at Shole. They arrived hot and grubby. Rather than turn on the Landcruiser's air conditioner at the cost of using their limited supply of diesel, they had driven with the windows open and thus quickly become coated in dust. On arrival Bartley had immediately accepted O'Driscoll's offer of the luxury of a shower from a perforated water bucket in the bathroom at the back of the house. Fumbe meanwhile headed off to inspect his room in the *boy's quarters* as O'Driscoll called the little annex built off to one side. Afterwards they all came together again to eat a stew of some tough beef that the housekeeper had prepared earlier in the day and that O'Driscoll had reheated over a small gas burner sitting on a table in the tiny kitchen. He ladled hot stew over mounds of cassava and handed each of them a plate to carry through to the table in the main room. The two visitors found that they were extremely hungry and ate quickly, more or less in silence, allowing the priest to do most of the talking. As soon as they were finished and deposited their dishes back in the kitchen, Fumbe excused himself saying he wanted to head off for an early night. He had an extraordinary capacity to drive without a break the whole day if necessary, but was able to compensate generously with sleep at night whenever the opportunity arose.

It was hot and the other two moved outside to sit on the verandah taking advantage of the slight evening breeze that filtered through the mosquito netting. O'Driscoll carried out a paraffin lantern and set it down together with a bottle of water on a side table that stood between two homemade wooden seats vaguely resembling steamer chairs. Bartley fetched two glasses and one of the two bottles of Jameson whiskey he had brought as a gift. He proceeded to pour a generous measure into each glass, topping up his own with a splash of water.

225

"God is good," O'Driscoll settled into one of the chairs, lifting his glass, sniffing it and taking a sip of the neat spirit. "A good Jameson whiskey generously provided by the Irish Embassy; beef with fresh vegetables from my own garden, sure what else would a man want?"

He waved his glass out toward the front of the house in the direction of several straggly rows of rather desiccated cultivation. He had earlier shown off his *vegetable garden* – several rows of onions, cassava, corn maize and a few dusty cabbages - proud in succeeding to have grown something in the otherwise arid landscape.

"For all the effort I put into my vegetable garden, it's difficult to get anything out, but I'm fortunate that I've managed to grow a few things. If only the area to which I have been sent by the Lord – that is My Lord Bishop of Bakooli - for my religious labours were equally fruitful. I have very few parishioners for whose spiritual needs I have to care. In the old days there used to be a large Irish missionary presence in Guseni, based further south at Kuranata. We'll drive down tomorrow and let you see the old mission station which, I'm afraid to say, is beginning to crumble. But, even when we had quite a few priests down there, the people were always largely uninterested in Christianity and we didn't make many converts. The local nomadic lifestyle was part of the problem. You might be making some progress until, one day, you got out of bed only to find a whole village had upped sticks and disappeared off to some new grazing area. The mission's work was therefore mostly running a health clinic and a school for whatever youngsters, and often adults too, that happened to be around.

"Nowadays I spend most of my time trying to help different villages as how to better manage their water supplies. I offer little workshops on how to avoid preventable diseases and sickness. It's surprising how many people can turn up and how eager they can be to learn. I can be talking at first to perhaps no more than two or three when others will start wandering into the group. It's funny but they always walk in very quietly and seem shy at first and then, as soon as a discussion starts, become quite animated and excited. But they are always polite, to me and to each other. There is a great gentleness and courtesy in the Guseni."

As he talked Bartley sensed O'Driscoll's deep love for the people among whom he lived. He guessed too that the people most probably reciprocated those feelings.

O'Driscoll also was apparently a keen photographer and carried around his old Olympus wherever he went, taking photographs of local life. During dinner he had shown Bartley and Fumbe some of his pictures, many of them portraits in black and white.

"It's one of my joys to be able to develop these photographs myself," he had told them. "I have my own little darkroom - well, truth be told, it's really no more than a large cupboard at the back of his house. It's also one way of passing the evenings. I have to confess that they can sometimes seem long as I almost always find myself alone out here."

Bartley had been impressed. The photographs were an extraordinary collection of intimate portraits of village life that only someone who had succeeded in getting unusually close enough to win the trust of the subjects would have been able to take.

Settling down with their drinks, Bartley described the landmine decommissioning exercise he had witnessed that morning.

"Major Mbuta was also there." Bartley found he was unsettled by his latest meeting with the officer and wanted to confide in O'Driscoll. "He knows that I'm visiting you for a couple of days. He warned me about cattle raids between villages and said it could be dangerous so that I should stay here around Shole. I told him I have permission from the Foreign Ministry, but it seems every time I meet him he warns me about something or other. I get the feeling he doesn't much like me, or you for that matter."

"That's so much bullshit, if you'll pardon my French, about there being cattle raids. I haven't heard of anything like that happening for well over a year. The villages in Guseni have more than enough problems keeping the cattle they already own alive – finding them grazing or water in the areas they are still allowed to live – without wanting to steal any more. I'd say what this comes down to is that there are places and things that Mbuta does not want you to see and if he thinks you are getting close, he'll find a way to warn you off. Well, feck him. I'm going to bring you down to Kuranata tomorrow and there's nothing he can do about it. I even saw Uba, the RS, in Bakooli last week and told him we would be going down there. He didn't seem to have a problem even if he suspects I want to show you some things that he or some others would prefer I did not.

"Of course, he and the local authorities don't much care for me and that's putting it mildly. They know I travel around Guseni all the time, that I talk to people and that I see and hear things, but they can't stop me as this is still officially a Church parish and they don't want to cross the Catholic Church. I suppose that sooner or later somebody, whether it's the Governor or even Minister Gabi or Mbuta, will find a way to make me leave. Meanwhile, they're stuck with me and portray me as a crank, a nutcase, a conspiracy theorist. It's a strategy that seems to work. Even your former Ambassador, and now it seems his successor, Clendenning, seem to consider me all these things. But, don't get me wrong - that isn't to say that that is an entirely bad thing. You could say I have a fool's pardon of sorts that allows me to stay here a little longer to help the people. Also, the more I see, the more I learn so maybe someday someone will take me seriously enough to protect the Guseni."

"So what is happening?" Bartley wondered. "The first time I visited the Malinga's orphanage you were telling me about Charity and about her family. You said they had been killed. Then Uba turned up and everyone seemed to become nervous. What's his role?"

"Uba is an essential part of what is going on here in that he oversees the carrying out the Regional Governor's orders. I can't say exactly what those orders are, though I suspect Awale would say he does nothing that does not have the direct approval of Okeke and the authorities in Bamgboshe. Perhaps he is in cahoots with Minister Gabi, perhaps not. I can't say for certain, but I doubt that Awale and Uba do anything without first clearing it in Bamgboshe. Except, of course, I am sure they have kept quiet about skimming off some of the money your Embassy has kindly donated for the Bakooli canal." O'Driscoll smiled.

"So it is true then that we have been ripped off? We've had our suspicions. We keep being told costs have risen for cement and other materials beyond what was budgeted, but the figures seem to be out of proportion."

"Prices have certainly gone up alright," O'Driscoll laughed, "but anyone in Bakooli town would tell you that the extension to Awale's residence did not come entirely from his salary or the regional budget. Nor did Uba's new Landcruiser. I wouldn't be surprised that even Prime Minister Okeke suspects what they've been up to but writes it off as small change in the scheme of things."

"So what is the real *scheme of things*?"

"That depends what you mean. For Kutaba in general *the scheme of things* is a chain of corruption from petty to major that keeps the country from grinding to a halt. But if you mean Guseni, then that's something else. From what I can see, it's a plan to quietly clear out the area of as much of the population as possible. Why? Gabi claims it's to set up a new park or wildlife conservation area. That's the kind of worthy project that won't draw too much criticism from the Embassies and NGOs in Bamgboshe, even if they hear people are being forcibly moved out of their traditional grazing areas. For myself, I find that the whole concept of the park suspiciously vague. Have you seen any detailed plans or maps? Of course you haven't.

"What's really going on, I can't tell for sure. One thing I do know is that there are foreigners out there with army escorts, drilling holes in the ground. They are supposed to be looking for water that will be needed to sustain a future tourist infrastructure. The locals suspect they're prospecting for oil. Why else would an oil company like AMADO be involved? There's a rumour among the villages that there must be huge oil reserves waiting to be discovered somewhere out there in Guseni. They say the government wants to clear them out before they can claim any ownership.

"Meanwhile the government keeps to its story that it's developing a wildlife park. For my part, I'm more inclined to believe that this whole thing is about oil."

"But isn't it the case whenever anyone sends out survey teams to look for water in any part of the developing world that suffers from drought, that the locals all immediately believe that they're really looking for oil and that someday they'll all be rich?" Bartley recalled Gabi's argument.

"You're right and I can't prove otherwise. As I said, everyone knows I'm a crazy conspiracy theorist so no-one pays the slightest heed when I say anything. Still, I am sure that the army is responsible for murdering innocent people in Guseni. Maybe I can go some way to proving that to you. To begin, I want to show you where I found little Charity and what remains of her family home. I can't bring anyone else there, but you have permission from the Foreign Ministry to visit me in my parish and that includes parts of Guseni that are officially closed areas. I can also bring you to meet some people who have been evicted from their villages so you can hear their stories and see how they are now forced to live. It would count for a lot if you could later tell others what you have heard and seen. The word of a diplomat would certainly carry a lot more weight than that of the crazy priest. Sure they would just say I've been living alone too long or else too long out in the sun so that my brain is fried."

"Would the foreigners in the drilling team not see anything wrong and report it?"

"Perhaps they would, perhaps not. I don't know Bartley. For a start they have an army escort everywhere and might be shielded from seeing anything. Then again, if they really are looking for oil, they're probably the type of guys that are used to working in tough and dangerous places where security is an issue and where the local authorities tend to be heavy handed.

"I could ask you also how much certain Embassies or Ambassadors in Bamgboshe already know? Have they told you that AMADO is in Guseni? If they admit AMADO is here, does that mean they know all this talk of a national park is nothing but a plausible cover-up? It wouldn't be the first time an international oil company and some country's Embassy have turned a blind eye to murder or genocide. Look at what they allowed to happen to the Ogoni people in Nigeria and to Ken Saro Wiwa. Do you know his story? I knew him when I was a young priest in Nigeria in the nineties. He was a famous writer and poet who went on to lead a non-violent organisation to claim some compensation for the Ogoni whose land was being polluted and destroyed by oil extraction. The government arrested him on trumped up charges of murder. Witnesses were bribed or intimidated into giving false evidence against him. It was said that it was the Shell oil company that ultimately urged the government to execute him. I heard they hanged him from a rafter, kicking the stool out from under him – three times. The rope apparently wasn't short enough on the first two attempts. Meanwhile the British and Americans sat on their hands. No, I don't see the British or American Embassies in Bamgboshe standing up for the rights of a few nomadic cattle herders in a backwater like Guseni if another of their oil companies is about to strike it rich."

Despite the heat of the evening Bartley felt a cold shiver as he listened. He knocked back his whiskey and his hand trembled as he refilled the glass. He topped up O'Driscoll. He had to admit he was not completely surprised. His friend, and he now realised he did regard O'Driscoll as a friend, was only articulating what he felt he should have long suspected and which the diplomat's instinct towards caution and reserve had prevented him from pursuing.

Sitting here in Shole, removed from the stereotypical analysis of Kutaban politics that went on in Bamgboshe, it seemed incredible that Guseni was never a subject tabled for discussion at the monthly meeting of Ambassadors. Was it because certain countries did not want others to know what they were up to? The Ambassadors could talk in general terms about good governance and respect for human rights, but from his present perspective, the real problems were seldom directly addressed. How many times had he heard an insistence on the need for *quiet diplomacy* or seeing the *wider picture* being used as an excuse against debate? These seemed no more than a con to hide financial self-interest.

Whether it was the aura of the Shole night or the whiskey, Bartley determined now to find out the truth and somehow or other force it out into the open.

TWENTY-SEVEN

Wednesday, 4 February.

Heat radiated from the already seared earth as they set off early the following morning with Bartley and Fumbe sitting up front in the Landcruiser.

"This is quite some luxury. You diplomats do look after yourselves rather well, don't you?" O'Driscoll offered as he lay sprawled across the back seat. "Do you think the Embassy could make me a gift of this Landcruiser when you're finished with it? What, it must be almost three years old by now and surely, don't you diplomats change your cars at least every two or three years?"

Bartley listened, smiling as the priest teased him. He saw no need to point out that the Landcruiser was already at least ten years old. With its battered bonnet, held in place by a wire catch that Fumbe had recently substituted for rope, the car spoke for itself. But, he could hardly fault O'Driscoll's wanting a new car. His old pick-up looked pretty decrepit, with the stuffing coming out of the front seats and even the St. Christopher figurine on the dash leaning lopsided where someone had clumsily re-glued it back onto its broken base.

Coming out of the compound enclosing O'Driscoll's house, they headed down the dirt road that skirted the small settlement lying off some distance to their right. Low acacia bushes grew close to the side, their long silvery spines threatening to score deeply into the car's dusty paintwork or to rip through the flesh of any arm left carelessly leaning out an open window. Some distance beyond the hedge Bartley could make out a village of perhaps twenty small round mud-walled huts with thatched roofs. They stood out alone in the landscape surrounded by low scrub and scattered bare patches of earth pinpointed by red anthills. Beyond the huts the scrub grew higher with tall shaded acacia stretching in the direction of a distant line of low-lying mountains, hazy and indistinct.

"Slow down a minute," O'Driscoll sat forward, leaning over the front seat just as they passed a gap in the acacia.

"You see out there?" He was pointing to the outline of a track leading out onto the plain, skirting west of the village. "Sometimes I get away from it all out there. Just a kilometre, kilometre and a half, there's a hill and on the far side of it that's where I have a little hut. The people in the village built it for me. They say I can only understand them and their land if I sometimes live like they do, out in the bush under a thatch roof. It really is a magical place to spend a night. My hut is just in the shelter of the hill and looks out west to give me the most beautiful sunsets in the evening. It gets so quiet at night when the cicadas stop that the silence actually sounds loud. Some nights the stars light up the whole plain. It can be so bright it makes me wonder why cities need streetlights. Sleeping out there gives me a different perspective on things and maybe it does help me see things as the local people do. Our world is something quite alien to them. Out there, I can escape it for a while. The hut is my own special hideaway from our modern world."

Bartley turned in his seat to look back at O'Driscoll, surprised by his soft eloquence.

"But I guess you diplomatic types wouldn't last too long in a place like that without your air-conditioning, eh?" O'Driscoll grinned. His jovial self once more, he stretched out comfortably the full width of the back seat.

They soon entered a forest of thick acacia and scrub that blocked any view from the side. Looking straight ahead, the road was no more than an irregular track following the contours of the bare ground littered with bleached stones. It stretched downward to disappear into the bush only to reappear in the farthest distance as a pencil-thin line of red contrasting starkly against the green.

They drove in silence along this for almost an hour. Then the bush began noticeably to thin and the hard earth to turn to white sand before they came to a junction with a larger, more travelled road. To the right it led back north to where the army had destroyed the landmines and beyond that to the city of Bakooli. They turned left to the south.

Almost at once they saw ahead of them a white pick-up, its backboard painted TOYOTA in large red letters. It was parked in the shade of two large acacia trees and surrounded by a group of men in black militia uniforms - the first sign of life since leaving O'Driscoll's house apart from an occasional vulture flying high in the thermals. They would have seen the dust cloud thrown up by the Landcruiser long before catching sight of the vehicle itself. They appeared to be waiting for it and now two ambled forward out of the shade onto the roadway.

One of them raised an arm and swung it round, motioning they should pull in under the trees. Fumbe obeyed and drew the Landcruiser to a halt behind the Toyota. He turned off the engine and sat unmoving while Bartley and O'Driscoll got out. The militia officer introduced himself as Lt. Farka. He was wearing a neat black uniform, a matching peaked cap and round-lensed sunglasses. His ears seemed disproportionately long, reaching up in points to either side of his cap. To Bartley he looked something like Will Smith, but more serious and without the toothy grin.

There were four further men with him, wearing loose fitting fatigues. Three wore forage caps that had long flaps attached to protect their necks and the sides of their faces from the sun. They each carried some form of automatic weapon. The fourth had a beret around which he had wrapped a grey and blue scarf covering the lower half of his face. A white holster attached to a wide belt held an outsize pistol. All in all, they formed a rather intimidating group.

"Mr Ryan I am to ensure your safety during your visit," Farka explained, "My men and I are in any case to patrol south and the RS, Colonel Uba, has asked that we meet you and serve as an escort for your protection as you are going to be travelling down the same road. I understand that you are to stay at the old Catholic mission at Kuranata tonight and we will be happy to accompany you that far. We will drive ahead to make sure there are no problems on the road and that you can follow safely."

Bartley was about to thank the officer when O'Driscoll interjected. "It's good to meet you again Lt. Farka and it is very kind of you to offer to look after us, but I am sure it is quite unnecessary. You know I frequently drive myself down to the old mission and I have never had any problem. We will be driving much more slowly than the speed I imagine you would want to travel and we certainly would not wish to delay you or interfere with your patrol."

"Ah yes Fr. O'Driscoll, I understand. But Mr Bartley is the representative of an Embassy and we have a special duty to guarantee the safety of foreign diplomats at all times. On this occasion it is a happy coincidence that we are already travelling the one road so it is no hardship for us and you will find that we do not drive as fast as you perhaps think."

O'Driscoll looked distinctly uncomfortable. The priest obviously did not want any army escort, but Bartley saw no immediate way out of refusing Farka. He feared an argument might soon develop between the soldier and priest and decided he should quickly intervene.

"Lt. Farka I appreciate your concern for my safety. Although I've never had the need before of any security, it'll be a comfort that you are clearing the road ahead of us and that we can be confident that we will not meet with any difficulty. So if you would like to lead on we'll follow as soon as your dust trail settles down. We wouldn't want of course to be driving too close behind and have to breathe your dust all day!"

O'Driscoll seemed none too happy with Bartley's interruption, but Farka evidently accepted this assurance as he simply nodded before walking off to get into the front of the Toyota. The militia officer with the scarf joined him on the driver's side while the others climbed on behind. Bartley saw they would well need their flapped caps if they were going to spend the day standing in the back exposed to the full strength of the Guseni sun.

"Bugger! We need to get rid of this lot!" O'Driscoll fumed as he and Bartley got back into the Landcruiser. Bartley glanced quizzically at Fumbe who had remained quietly in his seat and uncharacteristically mute. He guessed that Fumbe was no happier with the militia's presence than was the priest

"Sorry, Frank, but I don't think we have any choice but to at least pretend to play along with this Farka guy. We can pull back some distance behind him and maybe lose him for a while if we need to."

"I don't know," the priest could not hide his frustration. "If I know Farka, he'll be watching closely and will come racing back if he thinks he's lost sight of us. I don't know how much time that will give us. There's a track down the road a piece where I wanted us to turn off. It leads to where Charity came from. Maybe there's a chance we could get there and have a look before he catches back up with us."

"Well, let's at least try. Fumbe," Bartley ordered, "drive as slowly as you can and build up as much distance as possible between us and the soldiers."

"Yes, I can do that, but I do not like this militia. He looks dangerous and we should not make him angry with us," Fumbe was understandably nervous. As a Kutaban, he had perhaps more at stake than the two foreigners.

"So what about this Farka, Frank? You know him from before?" Bartley hoped O'Driscoll could offer some reassurance.

"Yes, I have met him several times. He's quite clever and not the worst sort. In fact he probably is quite decent. I haven't heard him being mentioned in any of the stories I've been told. I know he comes from a wealthy family. He once told me his father was a senior official in the old administration who had gone to a boarding school run by Irish priests in Uganda. He's well educated and especially well disposed to us Irish. But he'll carry out to the letter any orders he has from the RS."

The road continued sandy with the Toyota throwing up a windblown cloud in front. It carried across the road, forcing them to close the Landcruiser's windows. But even then dust still seeped in, layering them a greyish white and causing Bartley to cough repeatedly. Outside he could see sparse acacia of the type that seldom grew above shoulder height. Few of the bushes were green, most were grey, stunted and covered in sunburned sand. Dust devils swirled on either side, thin and dense at their base before billowing out like smoke from a dozen scattered fires.

Fumbe drove slowly, allowing them to fall back until the Toyota's trail was well off in the distance. O'Driscoll was leaning forward over the back of the two front seats, staring through the cloudy windscreen at the road ahead.

"We want to turn off to the right soon," he said. "Look out for a track turning off to the right. It will be hard to see, but there should be tyre tracks marking it."

Fumbe pushed closer to the windscreen and almost immediately began to brake, "Here," he said, "I see tracks, is this it?"

"Yes, turn here. But drive quickly now, fast as you dare. It is almost two kilometres along here, then we stop before Farka catches us".

Bartley turned to look at O'Driscoll.

"This is where I found Charity. You will see for yourself where her home was and how it was burnt to the ground."

The Landcruiser made a low drumming sound as Fumbe raced along the broken ground, sending stones skimming out sideways while heavier rocks came crashing up against the underside. O'Driscoll was still staring out ahead while his hands pulled open his camera case and grabbed his Olympus. Abruptly he told Fumbe to stop, looked out the side and then ordered him to back up. With that, he threw open his door.

"OK Bartley. We had better be quick. Come see," and he strode off with Bartley hurrying to catch up.

They stepped around a line of dried acacia branches that had been cut to form a protective thorn barrier that had since collapsed. Scattered branches now littered the rock strewn ground. Beyond stood the skeletal, fire-blackened remains of several huts - no more than the bent and twisted branches that had formed their frames. O'Driscoll paused, raised his camera, winding quickly forward as he took a succession of photographs.

Past the huts a rectangular mud-walled cabin stood on its own. It was perhaps no more than five metres long but it must have had pride of place in the settlement as the only permanent and comparatively solid structure. Now it stood without a roof. A sheet of corrugated tin lay at an angle in what had once been the doorway, while the wall above the door had caved in to uncover the bare sticks to which mud had been plastered. To one side of the door was a window, a small square, no more than forty or fifty centimetres wide with a second piece of tin covering it. In this building it looked an extravagance to have a window cover - a single embellishment emphasising the poverty of those who had once lived here.

In front of the cabin, just off to its right was a circle of charred earth of about equal size. Bartley looked down at the burnt rocks and the remains of ash that still covered them. O'Driscoll backed away for a better angle, his camera obscuring his face as he focussed to capture the scene.

The silence with which the two had made their way over the ground was broken by a shout from Fumbe sitting in the car. He had seen a fast rising dust plume behind them. Farka was on his way.

O'Driscoll lowered his camera and motioned Bartley to examine the earth beyond the cabin and the circle of ash where a rondavel had once stood. The ground was littered with dozens of empty cans, shining silver among the rocks.

"Military rations." he said, "You can see there must have been a good size force of soldiers here and that they ate after they had finished their work. They could have taken any bodies and dumped them somewhere in the bush." He paused and let his eyes sweep over the area. "Strange, the carcasses of the animals that were here when I found Charity seem also to have disappeared."

He looked up. The sound of the army pick-up now carried clearly to them and already it was in sight.

"That's where I found Charity, up over there." He pointed in the direction of a small rise and some bushes farther off beyond the cabin. "I heard her crying. She was only half-conscious and severely dehydrated. She must have been hiding there for at least a day or two and certainly would have died if I hadn't come across her." He raised his camera once more, took two shots of the empty ration cans, and headed back wordlessly to the Landcruiser. Bartley stood alone and looked around him, suddenly feeling a cold chill. He shook to shrug it off and then hurried after O'Driscoll. But he knew there was something here that he would never forget.

Farka managed to remain polite, despite visibly seething when he caught up with Bartley by the Landcruiser. He stared hard at O'Driscoll who had opened the back door of the car and already slipped his camera inside, but he addressed himself directly to Bartley.

"Sir, I don't think you understand how dangerous it is to travel alone out here. You know that there are people here who kill each other for a few cattle. Think what they would do if they were to find a white man, especially a diplomat? They would kidnap you and demand a ransom from your Embassy and then, when it is paid, they would probably kill you. I thought you understood that I am responsible for your safety. I believed I had your word that you would keep close behind me. Please, can we now return to the road and will you now do as I ask?"

"I am sorry, Lt Farka. You're right, of course," Bartley tried to look suitably chastened. "I assure you, we will keep behind you. It was simply an innocent mistake turning off the road and, as you can see, we realised we had come the wrong way and stopped to turn back when you caught up with us."

"Yes, please be more careful in future." Farka was looking around him, his eyes widening as he took in the remains of the little compound, the scorched earth and scattered tin cans. He suddenly looked nervous. "Alright, turn the cars, let us go back quickly." he ordered.

They waited while Fumbe and the Toyota driver manoeuvred the vehicles. Strangely it was Farka, not Bartley, who now remained defensively silent. Bartley took a last look at the sorry scene around him before following O'Driscoll into the Landcruiser.

Farka and his soldiers drove off first, but after less than a hundred metres stopped and waited for the Landcruiser to catch up. Until they arrived in the late afternoon at the mission, Farka was to keep them close, so close that the Toyota's sandy wake would keep them choking for the rest of the day.

TWENTY-EIGHT

Thursday, 5 February.

Bartley slept well despite the sound of O'Driscoll's snoring before he first drifted off. They had shared a room, himself, the priest and Fumbe, sleeping on cots covered in threadbare sheets that O'Driscoll had at the last moment thrown into the car the previous morning. The mission station at Kuranata had once had three Irish priests in residence with three bedrooms, but it had been more or less abandoned for over a decade. There were three buildings in various stages of decay, each more dilapidated than the other. Their original whitewash and the blue borders that had been painted at ground level were all but completely bleached out. They were fronted by the remains of what had long since ceased to be flower beds and a vegetable garden. At the rear were four trees that O'Driscoll claimed had once been fruit bearing apple trees planted long ago by his early predecessors; they were now withered and dead.

O'Driscoll had kept one bedroom in the main residential building in use for his own visits whenever he came down. He quite evidently expected little comfort for himself and Bartley suspected that the provision of the thin bed sheets on this occasion was an unusual luxury provided in deference to his guests.

An elderly caretaker had shown up soon after their arrival and O'Driscoll had handed him a bag of rice and some mealie corn, entrusting the old man to prepare them an evening meal. It seemed for all his travels that O'Driscoll remained unable or stubbornly averse to any form of cooking for himself. They had eaten later, balancing chipped plates on their knees, sitting on old dining chairs adjacent to the room in which they were to sleep. Presumably there had once been a dining table, but it and indeed almost all the other furniture had been taken away.

This morning, O'Driscoll could not hide his disappointment over how the previous day had developed. He had hoped for a less direct route down to the mission, allowing him to lead Bartley meandering off the road to look at several other sites he had either seen for himself on previous occasions or others that he had heard of where homes had been burned. In particular, his contacts had told him of the destruction of a whole village some distance off the main road. But it was as if Farka was reading his thoughts for when they approached the junction with the road that ran toward the supposedly burned village the Toyota had stopped, waiting for the Landcruiser to draw level before starting off again. O'Driscoll worried today might turn out fruitless.

Farka and his men had set up a crude camp close by the mission compound. They had filled their water containers with the priest's permission from the almost dry well and then sat down within view of the mission to eat an early supper from plain silver cans of rations they had brought with them. The cans were identical to the empty ones Bartley had seen scattered around the remains of Charity's home. The men had settled as soon as it grew dark, lying on the ground with only a blanket to cover them, while one remained sitting upright on guard. Farka had made it clear that he would keep them within sight, ostensibly for their protection until Bartley and O'Driscoll were ready to return home.

Bartley's permission to visit the area had been ill-defined. It now appeared that he had not been given carte blanche to wander round at will and that Farka's brief was to ensure that he did not do so. But already Bartley was shocked by what he had seen. Charity's family home had evidently come under attack and set on fire. The empty silver cans pointed to either the army or militia as having been responsible. He wanted to see more. O'Driscoll had been hoping before Farka had turned up that today they would be able to visit a village twenty kilometres down the road that was crowded with refugees driven out from other villages even further to the south. This was now in doubt.

For the moment however, Bartley had a more pressing problem. He felt his belt biting into his belly, his stomach bloated and full. He had ventured into the tin hut covering the latrine pit - the mission's flush toilet had disappeared with the building's furniture leaving only an unusable circular hole in the abandoned bathroom. He took a deep breath, but heave as he might he failed to expel anything more substantial than a few farts. The stench rising from the pit as he gasped for air finally drove him out, his stomach still knotted and cramped in constipated agony.

It had been agreed they would tell Farka they wished to drive twenty kilometres south to see where Irish priests had years earlier built a dam. They did not mention that it lay next to the village O'Driscoll wanted Bartley to see. While it was doubtful that Farka would allow them enter the village, O'Driscoll reckoned they would be more than close enough to see the conditions under which the villagers and the refugees brought in from elsewhere were forced to live. The policeman had reluctantly agreed to go as far as the dam and gathered his small force together, setting off, ever careful to keep the Landcruiser tucked in tightly behind him.

The road from Kuranata was if possible more of a corrugated washboard than yesterday. Iron-hard ruts rattled their backbones even in the comfortably sprung Landcruiser. The stones littering the road were long and lethally sharp as they crunched and fired out from under the wheels.

It was one of these stones that was the Toyota's undoing. They had been underway for no more than fifteen minutes when one cruelly sharp shard embedded itself deeply into one of the pick-up's rear tyres reducing it instantly to shreds and sending the car skidding violently to the side. The three soldiers standing in the rear found themselves grabbing desperately for a handhold to avoid being thrown off.

Fumbe swerved to dodge the pick-up. Then he brought the Landcruiser to a halt a little distance further up the road. Bartley and O'Driscoll got out and walked back to join Farka and his men to inspect the damage. The tyres on the pick-up were narrow and considerably less robust than the monsters fitted on the Landcruiser; additionally they had to bear the extra weight of three soldiers mounted up back and two in front. A burst tyre could easily be predicted and indeed, the Toyota carried not one, but two spares. Normally there should be no great problem, but when it came to putting on one of the spares, Farka's driver found the wheel had overheated and welded one of the nuts to a bolt. It was going to be quite a job to remove it.

Farka was livid. He berated the driver for not having routinely checked the wheels. Then the wheel wrench they carried began to buckle and bend as they tried unsuccessfully to lever off the damaged nut. Farka checked their on-board tool kit and in desperation produced a small hacksaw. There was no option he reasoned, but to start cutting slowly through the nut.

O'Driscoll was soothingly sympathetic but persistent in pointing out that the militia's mishap should not bring Bartley's trip to a halt and that he and Bartley should be allowed to continue on. Farka was compelled to agree and proposed that he and one of his men accompany them in the Landcruiser.

It was Bartley who in no uncertain terms ruled this out. His vehicle had diplomatic plates and there was no way he would allow its immunity or neutrality to be compromised by being used as transport for weapon-carrying members of a foreign army or militia. He insisted that this was an accepted principle of international law. Although he could not be sure that this was indeed legally correct, he kept any doubts to himself and remained unrelenting in the face of Farka's protests. In the end Farka recognised he could not force them to stay or prevent them driving off. He could only hope his wheel could be replaced quickly enough to allow him to catch up.

As Bartley pulled shut the door of the Landcruiser he heard O'Driscoll behind him.

"'The fishes of the sea, the birds of the air, the beasts of the field, and every creeping thing that creepeth upon the ground, and all men that are upon the face of the earth, shall be moved at my presence: and the mountains shall be thrown down, and the hedges shall fall, and every wall shall fall to the ground': Ezekiel 38.20. *Yea and even the stones of the road shall smite their chariots: O'Driscoll, February the Fifth.*" Hidden from Farka on the far side of the Landcruiser, he wore the widest of grins and offered Bartley a high-five from the back seat.

Their mood continued upbeat until they were within halfway of their destination and saw a dust trail hanging high on the road ahead. It was rapidly approaching them.

"Looks like some-one coming our way." Bartley observed.

O'Driscoll craned forward.

"It can only be more army or maybe a drilling team. Fumbe take care. Whoever it is, army or drillers, they don't make way for civilians. You'd better slow down and keep well to one side when we get close."

"No, wait a minute." Bartley turned first to look him and then back to Fumbe. He touched the driver lightly on the shoulder. "Fumbe, stop here, just here. Don't pull into the side. Let's make it look like we have a problem."

"What are you up to?" It was O'Driscoll's turn to sound anxious as the car drew to a halt.

"OK, let's all get out. Quickly, open the bonnet and get around as if we're looking at the engine. If they think we're broken down and if we're in the middle of the road, they'll have to stop, won't they? If it's a drilling team, maybe we can find out what it's up to, whether it's looking for water or for oil."

"But what do we say is wrong with the car?" The priest remained dubious.

Bartley looked at Fumbe who was already working at the wire holding the bonnet. When he had untangled it, he propped the bonnet open.

"I don't know, Fumbe? Wait, oil - we can say the oil pressure warning light came on and we're checking the level. OK?"

They clustered round the front of the car and within moments were able to make out three vehicles coming their way. There were a couple of 4X4s, followed by a larger truck. They were travelling at considerable speed, but were forced to slow down upon catching sight of the Landcruiser, stranded with the bonnet up in the middle of the road.

They stopped as they drew level. Bartley saw that the lead vehicle was an oversize double cab pick-up of a type that he did not recognise. It looked like some American model, perhaps a Ford or Chrysler. It was not one of the Toyotas or Nissans one usually saw in Kutaba. Metal struts formed a box frame fixed to the rear and extended forward over the cab to meet with two uprights welded onto the front chassis. The frame was stacked with long metal pipes or tubes. Below these a tarpaulin covered whatever cargo had been placed on the flatbed floor at back. The 4X4 behind was a green Nissan, while the truck was a military green, open at the back with wooden sides against which several soldiers were leaning, their backs still turned in against the rush of grime and debris kicked up by the cars in front.

"A drilling team," O'Driscoll murmured, "They travel everywhere with a full military escort. The difference between their escort and ours is that theirs follows them wherever they *want* to go and does not object when they want to stop anywhere."

The front doors of the double cab opened and a tall, sunburned man with fair hair emerged from the passenger side. He was followed a moment later by the driver, who hesitated before reaching back in and pulling out a white, protective helmet that he slipped onto a bald head.

"Hi, how're y'all doin'? Got a problem here?" the fair-haired one was asking, his accent American. He stopped and looked behind at the sound of a door slamming on the Nissan. A soldier was stepping out of it.

"Hi, yes, we think we've something wrong, we're just checking. My name's Ryan, I'm from the Irish Embassy in Bamgboshe," Bartley held out a hand, at the same time peering closely. The American was somehow familiar, but not in a pleasant way. Had they met before? Dammit, was this not the American who had bullied Saleh, the Customs officer, all those months ago?

Fair Hair ignored the hand and walked past him to look under the raised bonnet.

"So what's the problem?" he asked.

Fumbe was fiddling with the dipstick. "It is the oil pressure warning light. It is coming on and I am thinking we are losing oil"

"Did you check the level?"

"Oh yes. I am checking now. I think maybe it is alright." Fumbe examined the dipstick in his hand.

"Let me have a look inside then," Fair Hair opened the driver's door and reached in without asking permission. Bartley stood back and looked at

Fair Hair's driver, his attention drawn to his hard hat. There on the front was emblazoned the distinctive lettering of the AMADO logo.

He had no sooner taken this in than the soldier joined them. Bartley took his gaze off the hat and was startled to find Major Mbuta staring at him in annoyance.

Fair Hair had turned on the ignition inside the Landcruiser and now called out, "No light on now, it seems alright." He drew himself out of the car. "I'd guess it's no more than a loose wire somewhere, nothing that should cause a problem." He looked up as one of the back doors of the double cab opened. He waved with the flat of his hand to motion whoever had opened it to stay back.

"It's ok, we're moving out," he called out. "Right, Ken," he motioned toward his driver, "let's move." Then, over his shoulder as he strode off, "Y'all take care. You coming, Major?"

Mbuta had remained silent until now.

"What are you doing here? I told you to stay in Shole. You are not allowed here."

"What am I doing here?" Bartley determined not be intimidated. "I told you I have permission from the Ministry of Foreign Affairs to visit Guseni. As for having to stay in Shole, we have in fact a militia escort looking after us down here."

"A militia escort?" Mbuta was evidently surprised. "So where is it?"

"Well, unfortunately, there was some difficulty with its pick-up a while back. There seemed to be some problem in changing a wheel, but I'm sure it will be here any moment." Bartley could not resist a smirk. "But perhaps I could ask what you are doing here, Major?"

"So, you have permission to be here." Mbuta ignored the question. "But you must wait here for your escort before you travel any further." he ordered and turned angrily to stride back to the Nissan. He paid no attention as Bartley wandered over to the American's pick-up where he peered into the back where two more white men were sitting.

"Thanks for stopping. We appreciate it." He gave a half wave and drew back, stepping further past to rise slightly on tip-toe and look over the tailboard. A tarpaulin covered its load leaving only a couple white helmets bearing the AMADO logo visible in the far corner.

The pick-up's engine started and he was forced to back off as it drove away, followed immediately by Mbuta's Nissan and the army truck. They steered to the side of the road to skirt past the Landcruiser.

"An AMADO drilling team prospecting for oil, I would say." O'Driscoll observed tightly as they drove off.

"I would say so too, unless AMADO now supplies hard hats to water companies." Bartley answered him. "But what about Major Mbuta, what's he doing down travelling down here with that lot?"

"I don't know. But obviously whatever AMADO is up to, he's tied in. And that can't be good." O'Driscoll looked grim.

TWENTY-NINE

They reckoned that until Farka turned up they could safely visit the village that O'Driscoll had talked about. Already, they were able to see it out in the distance lying off to the east. They left the road and approached across a flat stony plain. The village comprised several dozen miserable rondavels, the daub walls reddish brown and the roofs crudely thatched with tired grasses. Several had encircling stockades formed from misshapen branches driven into the ground supporting thorny brushwood tightly woven and lashed to the uprights with some plaited, hemp-like material. Bartley wondered where the branches and grass thatch might have come from. There was no sign of either growing anywhere he could see. The plain was barren and bare, save for rocks and, as they drove up, for a bright yellow water container discarded on the ground, its plastic base split open.

Two young girls, the smaller dressed in a dark, tattered tee-shirt carrying a red basin and the second in a long white smock, hands resting on her hips, stood by the entrance of the nearest stockade. They watched the Landcruiser drive toward them. Off to their right in front of a line of cattle, half a dozen men had also turned to look. They approached warily as Bartley and O'Driscoll stepped out. The nearest of them, his arms looped over a stick resting on his shoulders, cackled upon recognising O'Driscoll and shuffled over to greet him. The others followed with much bowing and shaking of hands. Bartley noticed that they all appeared elderly. There were no young men.

Bartley stood to the side while O'Driscoll went through a ritual of greetings in the course of which he pointed several times in his direction. He could make out his own name – Ryan – and the word "Ireland" repeated several times. Despite their obvious joy to see O'Driscoll, there was something reticent or reluctant in the men's behaviour, but after a few minutes two of them strode off purposely. The first shooed away the two little girls who continued to watch open-mouthed. The old man motioned to Bartley to enter the stockade.

"We have been invited in to talk," O'Driscoll explained. "They are frightened of strangers because of what might happen if the authorities or the army finds out they have been talking to outsiders. But I have asked them to talk to you and said they can trust you. I said you'll tell no-one they have been speaking to you. I also told them you know people more important and stronger than the army and that you can tell them what's happening in Guseni. They're going to gather a few more elders from other villages to meet us. They all live together here now and are prevented from returning home. It seems the army can more easily control them if they're all cantoned in the one place.

"But we shouldn't leave our car here where Farka will see it if he comes. Fumbe," he called the driver over, "you should take the car around the back of the village. You'll see the dam over there. Park the car nearby and wait for us. If Farka comes, we should make it look like we have been at the dam all along and not in the village."

The stockade enclosed a hard earth compound in which Bartley and O'Driscoll sat side by side on a short wooden bench that barely raised them off the ground leaving their knees jutting up in front. It took little time for the stockade to fill with almost a dozen men, again all of a certain age except for a single young man, perhaps in his twenties, but with a stump where his right arm had once been. They either squatted on the ground close to the visitors or stood further back along the edges of the enclosure.

O'Driscoll spoke briefly when they appeared all to be assembled and again pointed to Bartley, finally inviting him in English to say a few words. First at a loss as to what he might say, Bartley surprised himself for the second time today in losing his fear and speaking up, but now he really wanted to win the trust of these people.

"I come from a small country where for a long time the people had to live on what they could grow in the earth and the animals they could raise, so I know it is always a difficult life. You have to be strong to survive even in the best of times when the rain comes and you have water for your cattle to drink and water in the earth for your crops to grow." He paused to look over at O'Driscoll who nodded encouragingly and then began to interpret. "But you also have to live in bad times when there is no rain and no water. I know that you are living in bad times now. I can see that there is drought and that there is little water. You need to be even stronger than before." He paused until O'Driscoll had translated.

"But I have heard that being strong is no longer enough because of other things that are happening. I have heard stories that the army has been doing bad things here – things that even the strongest of you cannot live with. I have heard that the army will not allow you to move around with your cattle. I have heard that some of you have been forced from your homes and villages. I have heard even, that that some of your homes and villages may have been destroyed and burnt by the army. You can tell me if any of this is true. I would like to hear from you in your own words what the army has been doing. If you tell me, I promise I will tell others about everything that is happening here. If people outside Guseni, and outside Kutaba itself, find out what is wrong here, maybe it will be possible to make changes and put an end to the things that have been done to you."

O'Driscoll smiled and finished interpreting and then he too spoke. "My friends, you know me and you have always trusted me. I have brought you another friend today. I tell you again that you can trust him also. Before you speak remember that you have not seen anyone else from outside Guseni for so long. You have had no-one to tell your stories to. Now, today, you have someone who will listen. Help him to understand your troubles and he will try to help you. I know it is dangerous for you if the army learns you have talked to him, but he will tell no-one any names of those who speak to him. He will not tell them that he has been in this village."

When O'Driscoll finished there was some murmuring among the men as he translated for Bartley's benefit. Then one elderly man who had been standing on the periphery moved forward and began to talk in a sing-song voice. The priest struggled to keep up with a translation until several of the others gestured to the speaker to stop every so often and then to talk in brief sentences. The man told that he was the chief elder of one of two villages that had been moved by the army as part of the programme to clear the area.

"The soldiers tell us there is to be a wildlife park for animals here and we must move to protect the animals. But we have lived here for a long time, back to the time of our father's fathers, as long as we can remember and the animals have always lived with us. Why should we now leave?

"We did not leave when they told us, so the soldiers came to my village. They destroyed everything even the cooking pots of our women. They set fire to our houses. They forced us to come to live here in this village where there is not enough food for those who already live here. We have no food for our children. We have no grazing or water for our cattle. Our young men have great fear of the soldiers and so they run off into hiding in the far south. Before they ran off, some young men tried to go out at night with our cattle to find grazing and to return to our old water holes. But the soldiers saw they were gone and they went out looking for them. From my village six young men have been found. The soldiers have shot them with their guns and killed them. Their bodies still lie out in the bush where the hyenas and vultures now eat them. The soldiers will not let us near to bury them. They say it is a warning to any who will disobey them.

"In this village now we are people from three villages living here. We cannot leave, but we will all die soon if we stay. We cannot live without help."

As he spoke others occasionally shook their heads, muttering in agreement. When he had finished it was if a floodgate had opened as others clamoured to tell their stories. The owner of the stockade in which they had gathered had to stand up and act as moderator. As senior elder of this village, the elders of the other villages deferred to him.

O'Driscoll waited until three more had spoken. They all told the same story of being driven from their villages. They told of soldiers poisoning their watering holes and wells to prevent them from returning. When the last had finished the priest stood up to signal they should end their meeting. He thanked those gathered for their courage in speaking to his friend and asked if they could now walk together through the village and out to the dam.

The village elder and several others led the way past several similar huts, some with surrounding stockades and some with adjoining shelters for livestock. Passing one of these, one of the men ahead of them stopped. It was his home and he steered them over to a grass thatched lean-to that was open at the front with rough wooden fencing closing in the three other sides. As they walked over, Bartley was able to see two cows inside under the shade, their white hides discoloured red from the earth on which they lay. The closest one was flat on its side, its back toward him and its neck stretched out, gaunt and lifeless, the head reaching out almost touching one of the upright wooden supports. Beyond it the second cow, barely alive, was resting on its belly. Its legs were tucked in underneath and it was patiently holding its head up. It looked that it too would soon draw its last breath. A plastic container had been left on the ground beside it. Perhaps it had been used to offer some last little water before the effort of trying to keep the animal alive had finally been recognised as futile. Bartley's gaze took in the scene. For some reason his attention settled on a hardy bush that had struggled to grow out of the ground alongside the rear wall. It too had died, its tangle of thin branches dried like twigs of a sweeping broom. Somehow the bush, as much as the dying cow, epitomised the misery and helplessness of the scene.

They walked on wordlessly, there was nothing to say. They cleared the last of the huts and started over the open ground in the direction of lines of cattle that had been drawn up to wait their turn to drink from the dam. The group halted for a moment by some further wizened bushes behind which they could see the remains of another half dozen cows. They resembled so many grotesque balloons suddenly deflated, empty hides tenting over protruding bones. Several carcasses had been picked clean and leg bones shone white where they had been stripped bare. The rear legs of one remained strangely untouched, lying casually one crossed over the other and attached incongruously to the collapsed sack of the cadaver.

Looking over at O'Driscoll, squinting through the viewfinder of his Olympus, Bartley heard the steady click, click of the shutter.

There must have been, he reckoned, at least a couple of hundred cattle waiting for water. They allowed themselves to be lined up silently and without protest, as if they understood the need to conserve what strength they had left. The herdsmen were again elderly, carrying sticks but otherwise completely un-warrior-like - no guns, no spears. Bartley wondered were these the dangerous cattle raiders he had been warned might threaten his safety?

The dam was no more than a rectangular depression somewhat smaller in area than a football pitch dug out by hand with the excavated earth heaped into sloping banks on three sides shored up with a lining of flat rocks. The depression angled gently down toward the rear bank near where twenty or so cattle stood, heads lowered to drink what little muddy water remained.

The slope was churned with the passing of so many cattle, their dung mixed in with the rancid water. Already men were driving out the cattle that had only barely begun to drink. They waded through the slimy green mess and beat the beasts back with long sticks that thwacked cruelly on white rumps. The next few cattle were lumbering down, lethargically unenthusiastic despite their thirst.

Farka's Toyota appeared just after O'Driscoll had finished another roll of film. They were already walking over to where the Landcruiser was parked when they saw it driving fast over the flat plain toward them. Farka was angry and suspicious, but when he saw the cattle and the dam close behind he had to accept Bartley's assurance that had been their sole point of interest. The village elders had by then melted away, mixing in with those moving between the cattle. Farka reasserted his authority, commanding now that Bartley had seen the dam, that he and O'Driscoll should begin their drive home. Farka's wheel had been replaced with the help of the Major Mbuta and the drilling team that they had encountered earlier. The Lieutenant now intended to complete his original assignment of seeing Bartley safely back to O'Driscoll's house in Shole before nightfall.

There were no farewells to the villagers as they drove away. It was best, O'Driscoll warned, not to allow Farka any impression that they had talked or engaged with any of them other than to have stood watching silently as they led their cattle down to water. Farka's Toyota sped ahead and Fumbe kept close behind. There seemed no further reason to hold back and indeed both Bartley and O'Driscoll would be happy to get back to the relative comfort of the priest's home. They soon passed the old Irish mission at Kuranata and settled down to the jarring rhythm of the rough road and the roar of the engine.

It came as a surprise, at most two hours later, as Bartley was beginning to fall asleep, his head dropping forward and his neck uncomfortably straining with each jolt, that the car began to slow and drew to a halt.

Blinking open his eyes, it was surely too soon to have arrived? He looked out and saw the reason for their stopping was a herd of cattle aimlessly straggled across the road. Two cows stood directly in front staring stupidly at their radiator grill. The Toyota was somewhere ahead, its driver weaving his way round the cattle blocking the road. Fumbe turned the wheel hard to the left to inch forward.

In the back seat O'Driscoll was craning out the window, alert and his camera bag open.

"Stop the car now!" he shouted suddenly to Fumbe and already he was jerking open his door and jumping out, his camera in hand. He ran back down the road some little distance toward a single large acacia bush. He heard Bartley starting out of the car behind him and turned, calling urgently, "Get back in the car and keep moving! I'll catch up!" He disappeared behind the bush. Confused, Bartley got back in beside Fumbe.

"He says to drive on and he'll catch up. Just go slow."

Fumbe glanced behind over his shoulder but did as he was bid. In front the Toyota was barely visible through a cloud of dust as it drove off the right side of the road to clear the last of the cattle. A moment later O'Driscoll came hurrying back, leaning in a crouch. He wrenched open the door, his head still down and his body obscured on this side of the Landcruiser from Farka and his men. He threw himself into the back seat.

Bartley looked at him enquiringly, but O'Driscoll shook his head, "Later, when we get home, but not now." His normally ruddy complexion had gone pale and his hand shook as he packed away his camera and stowed the bag on the floor beside his feet.

It was only much later that evening, finishing off the last of the open bottle of Jameson, that O'Driscoll was ready to speak. He seemed finally to be coming out of a state of shock.

"It was the cattle that warned me something was wrong. The army has long since cleared any herders and their cattle from the area we were in. The cattle we saw had therefore to be there illegally, but their herders should have been keeping them under close control. Instead they were scattered and wandering loose. I knew the herders should be somewhere, maybe hiding, but there was no cover except for the single piece of bush we had passed and I thought I saw something lying behind it.

"That's what I went to look at. There were two bodies there, two young men. I didn't have time to get close, but it looked like they had each been shot in the back of the head. I took photographs that will tell us for sure. Their hands were tied behind their backs with barbed wire. I'd guess they were dead no more than a couple of hours otherwise the cattle would have been long gone. I'd say they were killed just about the same time that drilling team and army truck were passing.

"I don't know if we can prove anything, but maybe the photos I took will help. I don't know if they're in focus or even if they will come out at all, my hands were shaking too much. I'll develop them tomorrow along with the others I took earlier. I've got the pictures of Charity's old home too. But please, let's not talk about it anymore tonight. Let's just finish our whiskey and go to bed. Let's sleep on it and tomorrow we can decide what to do."

THIRTY

Monday, 10 February

It had come as an unpleasant surprise when Michelle phoned Bartley at home early on Saturday morning. The Ambassador had arrived back unexpectedly in Bamgboshe on the Friday evening flight. When Michelle met him at the airport he was none too pleased to learn that Bartley had gone to visit Fr. O'Driscoll in Bakooli.

Although nervous, Bartley had nonetheless been impatient to meet with Clendenning. He had spent the weekend writing a full report of his trip down into Guseni and was hoping for the Ambassador's support to send it home. But the meeting was not going as well as he had hoped. Clendenning had finished reading. He held onto the pages, pointing them accusingly in Bartley's direction.

"I don't know what you're thinking of, but it's obvious to me that you've fallen completely under your priest friend's spell. First, you go off half-cocked and without my permission to Bakooli and then you come back over-excited, with some fantastical story involving the Kutaban army murdering local herdsmen, villages starving to death and wells being poisoned as part of some improbable conspiracy to do with oil exploration. It's all too much to be credible. I'm shocked that you have actually seen fit to commit it to writing and don't realise the folly of sending something like this back to HQ.

"The trouble with you, Bartley, is that you are far too impressionable. You're too gullible to be exposed to the likes of O'Driscoll. The danger of people like him is that they seem to exist only to challenge the established order and to look for conspiracies. Why couldn't you be more like Michelle Finn? She's young and may be inexperienced, but I doubt she would have been taken in by O'Driscoll. She would have made a much more reliable observer.

"I can't stop you sending this so-called report of yours back to Iveagh House, but I warn you, HQ will at best be sceptical of any overly exaggerated accusation of wrongdoing by the Kutaban government. More likely, it will agree with me that you have totally lost your grip on reality. Look, you have no concrete proof and you have to admit it. All you have is the word of a few old men in some village you visited."

"What about Fr. O'Driscoll's photographs?" Bartley argued. "He has photos of the two dead herdsmen who had been shot and also pictures of dead cattle and of the girl's burnt-out homestead."

"Does he really have photos of dead bodies? Have you seen them? Didn't you say he had been gone from the car for no more than a few short moments? In his haste he could have imagined seeing anything. For all you know, he could have seen a couple of dead goats and mistaken them for human remains."

"Alright, I haven't seen his photos yet. He hadn't developed them when I left on Friday. We agreed as soon as he had them and was able to drive up to Bamgboshe that he'd bring them straight to the Embassy."

"And when will that be?"

"I don't know. He wasn't sure when he could get away. He said it could be a few days, but he hoped it would be before the weekend."

"So, there you are then. Why don't you wait to see what he comes up with and, if the photographs prove you right, which I doubt, I'll endorse your report and write a recommendation that will make sure Dublin follows up. But if the photographs don't show conclusive proof, I expect you to forget this whole damned business and shred this." He tossed Bartley's report back across the desk. "What I'll do now is make a few discreet enquiries among my more knowledgeable colleagues. I'll ask if they have heard any rumours about army activities in Guseni.

"Meanwhile, you're to get on with your real work – the annual report on developments in the Kutaban economy for last year is due. There's another reminder about it from Iveagh House. Then tomorrow morning, for Independence Day, I want you to represent the Embassy at the official celebrations in the National Stadium. Do you understand?"

"Yes, I understand Ambassador. I understand that I will wait only until Fr. O'Driscoll arrives and then I *will* send this report home, with or without your approval."

"If that's what you want, but I warn you..." Clendenning waved him away without finishing.

Having thus dismissed Bartley, the Ambassador called Grace and asked her to get the American Ambassador on the phone. The latter had no trouble confirming that there was no way the Kutaban government could be involved in any type of what the American called "extra-judicial killings". The US had sources throughout the country but had received no reports that suggested anything vaguely like what Bartley claimed could be going on.

"Just as I thought," Clendenning muttered to himself as he hung up.

THIRTY-ONE

Kutaban Independence Day, Tuesday, 10 February.

The Ambassador had no desire to waste a good part of his day forced to endure the so-called annual 'celebration' of Kutaban Independence Day. His colleagues had warned him it was an ordeal that could last up to five hours, during which the crowds attending would be entertained by distinctly tacky cultural displays and lengthy speeches of inestimable boredom. He had decided, as indeed had a number of other heads of Mission, to be indisposed and to send an underling to fly the national flag. He had no qualms about inflicting this ordeal on Bartley. He had been furious that he had gone off on a wild crusade with that priest O'Driscoll when he should have been looking after the Embassy in Bamgboshe.

Thus at 7.15 in the morning, Bartley found himself dropped by Fumbe at the entrance reserved for diplomats outside the National Stadium. He showed his ID to the guards at the gate and proceeded through a turnstile, then through a short tunnel, coming out at the bottom of the stands. He was ushered along to his right and up the steps into the area reserved for the diplomatic community. He recognised a number of Ambassadors and several more junior diplomats already crowded into the uppermost rows of seats. There were places left only among the bottom rows and he squeezed his way toward an empty seat in the middle of one of these, thanking those who stood up to let him pass and waving a polite greeting at those who acknowledged his arrival from higher up. The Nunce was in the seat directly behind him, wearing dark glasses and despite the early hour already perspiring in his long white cassock. He stood up and first shook Bartley's hand warmly with both of his before leaning forward over the seat to hug him first on one side, then the other. Further to the back at the end of one of the higher rows, Bartley caught sight of Otto, but the Dutchman seemed not to notice his arrival despite the minor commotion caused by the white garbed Nunce. Otto had his head down, engrossed in reading *The Economist.*

The invitation Clendenning had passed on to him read that the diplomatic entrance would be open from 7.00 am and would close precisely thirty minutes later. Bartley thought his own arrival at 7.15 was early and was therefore surprised that so many members of the usually tardy diplomatic corps, and Otto in particular, had already arrived before him. He sat down, introducing himself to the Turkish Chargé on one side and greeting the Moroccan Ambassador, whom he knew slightly, on the other. The Moroccan seemed to have bathed that morning in a tubful of some overpoweringly cloying aftershave.

Sitting down, Bartley looked around. Not much was happening. A large stage had been erected to the left at one of the narrow ends of the stadium. Tiered seats rose toward the rear of the stage which had been covered over with a large canopy. A single row of red plush armchairs stood on a dais centred in front of the tiers with a red carpet leading up to them from the left side. A podium had been set up to the right of the line of armchairs. There was really little else of interest to hold his attention. After fifteen minutes of gazing at the stage, he was thoroughly bored. Only the arrival of some late-coming members of the diplomatic corps, the last of them the Czech Ambassador, offered some brief relief from the tedium. Across to the far side of the stadium the stands were beginning to fill with Kutabans jostling for seats, as always keen to witness a free show. The tiered seating below the diplomatic section and down to the left was being filled by wealthier looking Kutabans among whom Bartley spotted Professor Ballo and several other opposition politicians. It seemed they were not required to arrive at the same ungodly hour as the diplomats.

It was half past eight by the time the first in a series of cars started arriving, driving directly into the stadium from the tunnel entrance opposite. They proceeded clockwise around the circumference before stopping off to the left of the stage where a line of soldiers had drawn up and military ushers waited to open car doors and point those getting out in the direction of the seats behind the dais. The arrivals included a number of impressively uniformed military officers. Others seemed to be important officials. Bartley recognised Regional Governor Awale arriving in a silver S Class Mercedes. He was wearing a traditional dress of long robes, while his wife was swathed in a billowing yellow wraparound and matching headscarf. The other dignitaries were members of the governing party with their wives - there were few females in the party ranks.

The public address system echoed some incomprehensible announcement and a ragged troupe of 30 or more dancers and drummers came running out onto the central grass pitch. It was followed throughout the morning by a number of other troupes offering a succession of cultural displays ostensibly demonstrating the different traditions and cultural customs of each and every corner of Kutaba. The troupes leapt around with great enthusiasm and shrieked as the drummers tried to outdo each other in frenzied decibels. The packed stands opposite roared their appreciation. While most of the troupes were dressed in garish, tie-dye costumes that made it difficult to tell them apart, Bartley was able to make out a group from Guseni close to the side of the stage nearest him. The men's distinctive white painted legs and striped torsos and the long, greased braids of the women singled them out as they performed a rather sanitised version of their traditional dance. An elderly figure sporting a tight fitting skull cap adorned with what looked like balls of white wool atop his shaved head waved a spear to and fro to conduct their roughly choreographed movements. Somehow he looked vaguely familiar. Squinting more closely Bartley tried to make out his features. Yes, the figure was familiar, and he was almost sure it was Goodness' brother – what was his name? Ngule, yes, Ngule.

The sun had risen to make its way past the overhang of the roof so that it no longer afforded shade to the seats in the lower front end of the diplomatic section. Bartley now found himself in its glare, its rays not in the least deflected by the fine strands of his comb-over. He could feel his scalp burning from the unaccustomed exposure. Beside him the Moroccan seemed to have been overcome by the evaporating alcohol of his aftershave and was making low whimpering sounds in between wiping his forehead with the pitifully small blue handkerchief that had earlier decorated his breast pocket. Bartley now understood why Otto and the other old hands who had previous experience of attending Independence Day celebrations had been such unusually early arrivals. They had bagged the seats in the higher terraces where the sun was unlikely to penetrate until well into the day. Meanwhile, comparative latecomers such as he risked severe sunburn, dehydration and heat exhaustion.

It was precisely ten o'clock when a further procession of Mercedes and Landcruisers entered the stadium. These were the most senior VIPs: the Lord Mayor of Bamgboshe, Mrs Okeke, the Prime Minister's wife, and the various ministers of government. Bartley recognised the gold coloured Landcruiser of Minister Gabi as it pulled up and Gabi himself, looking impressive, not in a tailored western suit, but also in colourful, flowing national dress, emerged.

The Minister was making for the steps leading up to the platform when some commotion broke out somewhere among the performance groups out front. Gabi stopped and turned to see what was happening. There was some altercation among the members of the Guseni group. Several of them appeared to be tussling with their erstwhile conductor, Ngule - Bartley was now sure it was he. Ngule held out his spear and swung it round in an arc to drive them back. Free for the moment, he let out a wild scream and bounded off toward the stage. Taken by surprise, Gabi was slow to move, but his face showed horror. Two soldiers reacted more quickly and rushed forward. Seeing them, Ngule raised his spear and with another yell launched it at Gabi. The old man's throw was much weaker than his voice. The spear fell well short, skittering harmlessly along the ground. The next moment Ngule was sprawled, face-down, pinioned by the two soldiers while others moved swiftly to surround them. Gabi leaned forward, a hand placed across his chest and turned slowly back to face the platform. Slowly, hesitantly, he climbed the remaining steps. Bartley caught a final glimpse of Ngule, his skull cap askew, before he was bundled off.

If the crowd had been startled by this incident, it was even more startled as the conductor of the army brass band immediately launched his musicians into a raucous blare. The sound of La Paloma Blanca, of all tunes, boomed out just as an open topped Mercedes stretch-limo emerged on cue from the tunnel. It was led and followed by an escort of half a dozen police motor-cycles, blue lights flashing. Standing in the limo's back, recognisable from his moustachioed pate and round glasses, Prime Minister Okeke held onto a bar in front of him with one hand and waved languidly with the other in appreciation of the welcoming chant of "Okeke Wa, Okeke Wa!" that filled the stadium. Ngule was seemingly forgotten, but not, Bartley guessed by Gabi, or by himself as he worried about his earlier role in freeing the elderly Guseni.

The rest of the *celebration* ground exceedingly slow as Bartley only wished to escape what he nervously felt was the scene of a crime somehow of his making. The cultural groups left the stadium and were replaced by formations of troops representing the different arms of the military. Okeke spoke – at length. The military marched around the field. At last the brass band belted out the ridiculous *Itsy Bitsy Spider* national anthem, followed by a booming salute of cannons that signalled the end of proceedings.

As the diplomats queued to leave, Bartley edged over to Otto in the line and tapped him on the shoulder. Otto turned, but instead of his usual hearty greeting, glanced nervously around.

"Bart, hi, how are you? I guess I haven't seen you for a few days."

"No, not since I got back from my trip. How're things?"

Otto looked around him once more.

"Look Bartley, let's get outside. We should talk."

Diplomats were now filtering out through the tunnel and looking for their drivers. Puzzled, Bartley followed behind his friend. Otto drew him over behind a dusty yellow bus parked near the exit.

"Bart, I think you're in trouble. We were in the PM's office yesterday - me and my Ambassador and a bunch of guys from home. We had a meeting with Okeke himself. Look I shouldn't be telling you this, but there might be a big deal going down here. We're front runners and have it almost sewn up, but we need to keep schtum in case the Chinese try to take over...."

"Otto," Bartley interrupted, "What the hell are you talking about. What's this to do with me? Why do you say *I'm* in trouble?"

"Listen. The thing is when we were talking with Okeke he started on about the need for firm political backing from any country involved in the deal. He won't do business with any country if there's any possibility of its government coming into conflict with Kutaba. Okeke knows how the EU works and he's afraid a problem with one member state could escalate into a problem with all. He said that some EU diplomat has been meeting with rebels in Guseni who are a threat to national security. He wants us to give a guarantee that the EU will prevent any further contacts with the rebels. Everyone knows you've just been to Guseni. No other diplomat has been near the place, so it has to be you that Okeke is getting at. My new Ambassador is furious that we might lose an important deal over this. The monthly EU Ambassadors' meeting is on Thursday and I guess my guy could well give yours a rough time. And since shit always falls, that doesn't look too good for you."

Bartley was stunned. His first reaction was amazement that someone in his lowly position might have come to the Prime Minister's attention.

"Look, I don't know how Okeke might know I was in Guseni and I don't know why he or anyone else should say I was meeting rebel leaders." He paused, the image of Ngule brought down by guards flashing through his mind. *But that had nothing to do with anyone I met in Guseni.* "I met a few villagers who are herdsmen, nothing more. Christ, there are no fucking rebels!" He spat out the words, indignant anger replacing his earlier nervousness. "How is it Otto that a country like yours that's always banging on about its commitment to democracy and international human rights values, can suddenly turn around to put the interests of an oil company before the lives of poor villagers of a place like Guseni?" He was leaning forward, a finger raised almost in Otto's face.

"What oil company? What the fuck are you talking about?" Otto recoiled from the finger.

"Forget it, Otto. I *know* you know – AMADO, American and Anglo-fucking-Dutch Oil. But I tell you, if there's any shit to fall, it's going to come down on you and Okeke and anyone that's involved in this dirty business."

"Bart, what the hell? I don't know what AMADO has to do with this!" Otto hesitated before continuing in a more conciliatory tone, "Look, Bartley, my Ambassador is still feeling his way round and all and I am in a very delicate position. I don't want him to hear that I've been talking to you. In fact, it's probably best we not be seen together for a while. You know I've already said way more than I should."

He offered his hand. Bartley looked at it, before slowly shaking his head. "I never thought you would lie to me about something like this."

Not trusting himself to speak further, he turned quickly away to look for Fumbe. Already he realised his outburst had been an empty threat. He also knew he had better get back to the Embassy and speak to the Ambassador.

Although it was a local holiday, both Clendenning and Michelle were at their desks when he arrived. He made his way directly to the Ambassador's office. Clendenning looked up, surprised – it was a rare occurrence for Bartley to visit him without a summons.

"Ambassador, could I have a word. I've had a conversation with my Dutch colleague and I'm afraid his Ambassador might cause some problems for you at your next meeting..."

As he told his story, Clendenning listened with that peculiar, unblinking stare that Bartley always found disturbing.

"So you see, that's why he might say something or have a go at you," he finished. "He might accuse the Embassy of having behaved or acted inappropriately."

"My God, Bartley, but you do manage to fuck things up not just for yourself, but now for everyone else, don't you?"

Bartley's grip tightened on the arm of his seat. He was not prepared to take this from Clendenning, but before he could say anything, the Ambassador continued, "You've put me in an awkward position, but I'm not about to allow any outsider to say that my Embassy or any of its staff is guilty of inappropriate behaviour, no matter what! I'm especially not going to allow any gay newcomer get away with it!"

Bartley was stunned by Clendenning's vehemence. Maybe the old bastard had some streak of honour hidden deep inside after all. Would he really defend one of his staff from attack from outside? And that reference to a *gay newcomer*? Where did that come from? Bartley had heard some rumours about the new Ambassador but had discounted the possibility of a gay Ambassador being sent to a country where homosexuality was still a crime and where gays were constantly under attack by the Prime Minister.

As he was about to leave the office, Clendenning stopped him.

"Have you any further news from your priest friend? Has he got photographs and when is he coming to Bamgboshe?"

"Yes, that is, yes, he called me last night. He'll be here sometime Thursday evening. He's bringing his photographs."

"Alright, let me know as soon as he arrives."

Bartley had become increasingly uneasy since talking to O'Driscoll and his arrival could not come soon enough. The priest had been cryptically guarded on the phone as if worried that someone might be listening in on their conversation. *"I have those cost estimates we discussed and they've worked out better than I hoped. I've made two copies and I'll bring one to the Embassy and keep the other in a safe hideaway."* Presumably he had been talking about photographs of scorched huts and starving or dead animals, but if they had *worked out better* than hoped and included pictures of bodies of young, murdered herdsmen their effect would be explosive.

THIRTY-TWO

Thursday, 12 February.

The Ambassadors of the EU generally met on the first Thursday of each month and followed up with lunch hosted in rotation. Last week's meeting had been postponed at the French Ambassador's request because he had been preoccupied with arrangements for a concert in the National Theatre by a visiting quartet of young prize-winning French musicians. After the concert he was planning to host a large reception in the Theatre's eccentric Bauhaus-inspired foyer. It was a matter of some regret to the Ambassador that he lacked a budget to support some newsworthy development project for, like Adrian Clendenning, he welcomed any opportunity to raise his country's - that is his own - profile in Bamgboshe. Fortunately however, he never had any difficulty obtaining funds to promote French culture and the Embassy was often busy arranging exhibitions of paintings or sculpture by French artists or classical concerts by French musicians. It was a considerable consolation that he could sponsor a regular round of glittering social occasions - insofar as anything glittered in Bamgboshe apart from the cheap gold and tanzanite stones in the Asian jewellers' shops. Invariably, any public gathering of the diplomatic community and prominent members of local Bamgboshe society attracted extensive coverage in the otherwise drab and dreary local media and, just to make sure, the Embassy's Press Officer always issued an advance press release. If Prime Minister Okeke graciously accepted the Ambassador's invitation to attend, a headline would be guaranteed. More than others, the French Embassy understood that the Bamgboshe press could be relied upon to reproduce its press releases verbatim, since any actual editing called for skills far beyond the capacity of any of local journalists who made their living almost entirely by slavishly regurgitating the turgid and convoluted language of government propaganda notices. Journalists and their editors welcomed the elegant Gallic-inflected prose offered by the French Press Officer. The fact that identical articles would appear in several newspapers simultaneously under different by-lines caused the Kutaban press absolutely no embarrassment. The Ambassador kept a scrapbook of cuttings of such articles and took considerable satisfaction in leafing through the pages of headlines, lingering on those pages where the story was accompanied by photographs of himself and Prime Minister Okeke standing side by side, beaming for the cameras. He imagined one or more of these pictures being reproduced in his published memoirs at some later date.

Bartley impatiently threw aside the paper in which he had just finished reading a report of the concert. Normally he would have derived a certain amount of amusement from the French Ambassador's posturing and machinations, but since Tuesday he had been filled with an increasing sense of dread. He had heard nothing further from O'Driscoll and could only wait with his nerves increasingly on edge until he arrived sometime later today. Meanwhile, he worried what might transpire at the Ambassadors' meeting. He was nervous also that something might come out about his connection with Ngule, Minister Gabi's would-be assassin – a connection he had kept hidden from Clendenning. But surely it was unlikely that any connection would be made? Unlikely, yes, but Mbuta knew.

He picked up the agenda for the Ambassadors' meeting and read it yet again. It was rather run of the mill: A brief review of domestic economic affairs and trade relations with the EU; A discussion on the outlook for local elections later in the year. Finally, the French Ambassador was due to introduce his proposal for the first "European Union Film Festival of Bamgboshe". He could imagine this would take some time. He knew that several French films were already in the frame, so to speak, and the French would urge other Ambassadors around the table to come up quickly with names of films they might present so that suitable advertising posters could be commissioned. Bartley had been pessimistic when he had briefed Clendenning on the possibilities of procuring an Irish film. *The Commitments* and *The Guard* were now really dated and the Embassy would have difficulty getting round copyright issues if it wanted to show anything more recent.

Bartley ran his hand over his head, his scalp still tender from sunburn on Kutaban Independence Day. His rare exposure to the sun, he realised, had helped clear the eczema on his forehead. He dropped the agenda on top of the newspaper and opened his computer to look at the draft economic report on which he was supposed to be working. He had still not got beyond the introductory paragraph. He stared at it blankly for a few minutes until finally admitting he was too keyed up even to make the pretence of working. He stood up and left the office, stopping off at reception to tell Grace he was off for a haircut.

It was early afternoon after he returned when Grace called to say Clendenning had just come in from lunch and wanted to see him.

"You'll be glad to hear that my Dutch colleague didn't even hint at any difficulty with you during our meeting this morning." Clendenning was surprisingly relaxed – a consequence, Bartley surmised, of his having had a good lunch. "Even though I was sitting beside him at the Czech Ambassador's, he said nothing untoward. However, I did find it strange that he did not once mention meeting the Prime Minister the other day."

He stopped and looked at Bartley again. He had refrained from commenting on his First Secretary's rather startlingly altered appearance. Bartley's skull was shaved smooth and sunburned. Somehow it gave him...an almost athletic look? His glasses had also been cleaned to reveal a pair of deep brown eyes. It was a remarkable change and one Clendenning found a considerable improvement.

"I'm beginning to wonder if there really is some substance to at least some part of what you claim. Maybe there is some major oil deal in the offing. The Dutch and the Brit seemed to be having a very intimate conversation and were definitely put out when I went over to say *Good morning*. You could say they looked more than a tad put out. It could be that they are working together on a deal and don't want any of the rest of us to know at this stage.

"Apart from that, we had a very routine meeting. The French are getting excited about the EU Film Festival. You need to follow up with Dublin to see if there is even the remotest chance of showing an Irish film."

Clendenning leaned back in his chair.

"I don't think there was anything else that came up that would be of interest to Iveagh House. The Czech Ambassador hosts a surprisingly excellent table. He knows his wine. He was also telling us he has only now got the Mercedes he bought last October on the road. It's taken him that long to order a new door. Would you believe someone stole one just before it was delivered? It really is amazing what these Kutabans will steal. It's an E Class Mercedes, same model as mine. Thank goodness mine arrived in one piece."

Bartley had been about to leave but found himself riveted to his seat. He was conscious his mouth must be hanging open. Before Clendenning could notice anything amiss, there was an urgent knock on the door and the Ambassador looked up. A pale and visibly shaking Michelle stumbled in.

"There's been an accident," she stopped, making an effort to catch her breath. "The Foreign Ministry has just phoned. Yesterday in Bakooli...Fr. O'Driscoll's car ran off the road and crashed. He's dead."

THIRTY-THREE

Monday, 16 February.

Bartley found himself once more with Fumbe driving down the now familiar road to Bakooli. They had set out at first light. Bartley dozed fitfully for the first couple of hours, exhausted after yet another long, sleepless night. The journey no longer offered the same fascination and sense of adventure he had experienced when he had first passed this way. It had become simply long and tedious. The present circumstances only added to his wanting to get it over with.

The days since Michelle had walked into Clendenning's office with the news of O'Driscoll's death had been frustrating, not least because O'Driscoll's death seemed too convenient to be an accident, yet all Bartley could do was go through the tiresome and to him, at times ridiculous, ritual associated with *offering consular assistance* to the deceased's family. It had proved difficult to obtain much information as to what precisely had happened other than that O'Driscoll must have been driving at speed as he rounded a bend and swerved to avoid a herd of goats that suddenly appeared in front. His pickup had left the road, rolling down a steep bank and ended up lying upside down with O'Driscoll sustaining head injuries that had killed him instantly. A passing truck driver had called the police on his cell phone and they had arrived and initially arrested both the truck driver and the goatherd. However, after surveying the scene and taking statements, the police released the pair some hours later. The authorities remained vague as to the location of the accident or even the exact time of day at which it had happened. The priest's body had been taken to the hospital in Bakooli and his pick-up towed to the police compound in the town.

There had been contacts with the O'Driscoll family, his elderly mother and two sisters in Ireland, who had asked that arrangements be made for the repatriation of the remains so that *our Frank* could be buried at home in the same plot as his father. Minister Canavan had broken a prior engagement to drive to Waterford to console Mrs. O'Driscoll. He had appeared on the six o'clock television news on Friday visiting the weeping but grateful mother. In a subsequent interview outside her modest little bungalow, the Minister paid fulsome tribute.

"Fr. O'Driscoll was a true example of the Irish missionary spirit that has contributed so much to the education and development of Africa and to Ireland's wonderful reputation on that continent. I had the privilege of meeting Fr. O'Driscoll when I visited Kutaba last year. I was truly impressed by his work among the poor and even after our short meeting would count him as a friend. He will not soon be forgotten. It is a tragedy that he should have died in an accident in the course of carrying out his pastoral work.

"Diplomats on the ground in our Embassy in Bamgboshe are in touch with local officials and are facilitating arrangements to have his remains returned to Ireland so that he can be laid at rest in his native home.

"As I have said to his mother, Mrs. O'Driscoll," he looked solemnly straight into camera, "our Embassies, as long as I remain Minister for Foreign Affairs, will always be on hand, will always be ready, to respond to any and every request for protection or assistance from Irish citizens abroad no matter where, or under what circumstances."

The Minister was always particularly keen to publicise the assistance his Department was ready to offer any Irish citizen in difficulty abroad. It was only his officials who might have some misgivings about having to go to the assistance of an alleged child rapist in Thailand or a jihadi fighter detained in Lebanon. In the present case Bartley was upset to read about the Minister's visit to Waterford. He could not help feeling that Canavan was much more interested in Frank O'Driscoll dead than he had been in Frank

O'Driscoll alive. Especially that Canavan should claim him as a friend rang rather false.

He had spent the weekend unsuccessfully trying to comply with the various bureaucratic formalities required before any airline would agree to fly the corpse out on one of its aircraft. He still needed a death certificate, not to mention a doctor's certificate and radiological report that the body contained no potentially explosive devices such as a pacemaker. Then, on Sunday morning came the news that the hospital in Bakooli had no refrigeration plant and thus no proper mortuary facilities. O'Driscoll's corpse had already been lying for a couple of days in a box in an overheated back room and was rapidly deteriorating. Although it was not said in so many words, Bartley was given to understand that the smell was pretty horrendous. The hospital administration had approached the police; the police had approached Governor Awale. Governor Awale had approached the Catholic Bishop of Bakooli and the Bishop had granted permission for the early burial of his priest. The bishop himself would offer a funeral mass in Bakooli on Monday morning, after which the body would be immediately interred.

Mrs. O'Driscoll was inconsolable when, after considerable effort, Bartley succeeded in making phone contact with this news. As soon as she hung up she wept even more as she told her daughters that *Frank* would not be coming home after all, that they intended to bury him in the pagan earth of Africa. Her daughters had thereupon called Minister Canavan's Private Secretary, Eddie, whose private cell phone number the Minister had generously supplied on the occasion of his visit. Eddie dutifully relayed the news to Canavan who instructed that he should phone Secretary General McNamara telling him to get on to the Ambassador in Kutaba and tell him to get his finger out so that Mrs O'Driscoll could give her son a final farewell kiss no matter how badly decomposed the cadaver might be.

There had followed a flurry of urgent calls around Bamgboshe and to Bakooli. At one stage Clendenning had even phoned the Nunce asking if he could intervene. The Nunce had suggested that the bishop was well within his rights burying one of his priests, particularly one whose rotting corpse was causing nuisance and presenting a public health hazard. He reminded Clendenning that here appeared to be no facilities for keeping the body in storage, far less transporting it hygienically or otherwise to Bamgboshe. The road trip would probably result in a thorough mulching of the remains to the point where no airline would be willing to agree to fly them. As it was already, the Nunce cheerily pointed out, the bishop would need a considerable amount of incense to get through the funeral mass on Monday.

Clendenning called back to report to the Secretary General on Sunday evening. He suggested that the O'Driscoll family be told that the Embassy was doing everything possible and that the First Secretary had been dispatched to Bakooli in a last ditch attempt to arrange the return of the remains to Ireland. In reality, both men knew there was no real possibility of achieving such an outcome. The Minister also privately acknowledged as much when McNamara later phoned him.

Minister Canavan tried to reassure Mrs O'Driscoll, when he called her some fifteen minutes later, that everything possible was being done and that there was nothing to be gained by her daughters complaining to the Sunday Independent of complacency on the part of his Department. He repeated that the Embassy had already dispatched an experienced diplomat to Bakooli in an attempt to stop the burial and to repatriate *Fr. Frank.* He failed to add that the 'experienced diplomat' was unlikely to arrive in Bakooli until sometime after local labourers had finished filling in his grave. Nor did he mention that Bartley was actually still in Bamgboshe and would not in fact be setting off until tomorrow morning – the Minister and his Department took a very literal definition of *dispatch* to mean to *instruct someone to go somewhere* to carry out a task. In that sense Bartley had indeed already been dispatched.

Looking out at the dusty landscape, Bartley pondered the unreality of all this posturing. It was no more than game playing. His friend was dead and no-one had really explained how or why.

Yet again he agonised that the *when* of O'Driscoll's fatal accident was all too convenient, given what he was engaged in at the time of his death.

THIRTY-FOUR

Passing the turn-off for Lion's Rock Lodge Bartley looked at his watch. The funeral would already be over and those attending would all be back at home or work. He had agreed with Clendenning that he should first call on Governor Awale. It was important that the Embassy should be able to report that it had gone straight to the top man in the Region. Also, even if nothing could be done about the funeral, Awale might be able to provide further information that could offer some comfort to O'Driscoll's mother. Bartley should also try to gather up any of his personal effects that the family might wish to have, if necessary driving on to the priest's house in Shole to do so.

Bartley was already feeling weak from hunger when Fumbe drew up by the steps of the old colonial building and he got out, heading inside and straight for the staircase that led to the Governor's office. He was only halfway up the first flight when he saw Awale and an entourage of officials on their way down. The Governor stopped as they came level.

"Mr. Ryan, how are you? Your Embassy phoned to say you would be arriving today, but unfortunately I have a most pressing engagement. Colonel Uba....?" Awale looked behind for the RS. "Yes, Colonel Uba, Mr. Ryan has come at the direct request of the Irish Foreign Minister to enquire about the unfortunate accident of the priest, Fr. O'Driscoll. Please assist Mr. Ryan and then join me later when you are finished."

Uba looked less than delighted to receive this abrupt instruction but managed a smile, "Of course Governor, I will be happy to offer Mr. Ryan our full assistance. Mr. Ryan, I condole you on the death of Fr. O'Driscoll."

"Ah yes," added Awale, "Allow me also to condole you and the family of the deceased. Please assure your Minister that we will fully investigate this dreadful tragedy and if anyone is at fault we will get to the bottom of it. Yes? But please excuse me now, I must hurry."

He offered his hand to shake, at the same time condescendingly patting Bartley's shoulder with the other before continuing downstairs leaving Bartley and Uba standing alone together.

"Well Mr. Ryan, perhaps you can let me know how we can help. I was unable to attend the funeral this morning but a number of our officials were there."

Bartley was taken by surprise not to be invited into a private office and that the RS seemed to expect him to conduct his business standing casually on the stairway.

"We were hoping for some further information about the accident. Where and when exactly did it take place? Are there any witnesses I could talk to? Was Fr. O'Driscoll conscious at any time after the accident, did he say anything? Then of course, I need a death certificate and would like a copy if possible of the police report. I should collect any personal belongings that he might have in his house that his family might like to have. And I presume the police have taken charge of any personal belongings he may have had with him at the time of the accident."

He was burning to ask specifically whether anything that might contain photographs had been found in the priest's car, but he held back. He could not trust Uba.

"I do not know about any belongings he may have had, but I am sure we will be able to have all your questions answered at the police station. My car is outside so you can follow me there. Afterwards, a death certificate should be available at the hospital if you wish to go there."

They headed back to the outskirts of town and pulled up in front of a whitewashed single storey building that stood some way back off the road. A Kutaban flag hung pale and wilted from a pole in front. Bartley had not noticed the nondescript building when he had passed it earlier. The POLICE sign above the door was faded and there was no other indication that this was a police station apart from, now that he looked, what appeared to be a car compound to the left with a couple of police pick-ups and several wrecked cars behind a wire fence.

Inside, Uba led the way past a high wooden reception counter and, after a cursory knock, into an office at the rear of the building. A police officer sitting behind one of three metal desks that occupied most of the floor space looked up and seeing Uba jumped to attention, saluting. He remained standing, looking occasionally at Bartley as he and Uba spoke.

Reverting to English, Uba explained. "This is the officer completing the report into Fr. O'Driscoll's accident. Unfortunately he is unable to finalise the report until the two officers who first arrived on the scene sign their statements. This is not possible at the moment since one has been assigned on temporary duty to another station and the other had to travel to his village where his mother has died. However, he is able to confirm that the accident took place last Wednesday morning, perhaps around nine. It happened on the main road down into Guseni some kilometres north of the turn-off to Shole where Fr. O'Driscoll lived. There was only one witness, a goat herder who did not see the car go off the road but heard the crash. He found Fr. O'Driscoll lying inside the car. He was already dead. Soon after a truck came along the road and stopped. The driver called the police.

"That is all that will be in the report apart from the formal description of the scene by the two police officers, but you already know that the car had rolled over and that Fr. O'Driscoll was found dead inside. I think this is all the information you need, is it not?"

"What about personal belongings? What was in the car?"

Uba spoke again briefly to the police officer, "Nothing, he says they found nothing personal in the car except a passport and driving licence and some small money in a back pocket, and of course, a watch."

The police officer opened a drawer in his desk and took out a large brown envelope resting on a clipboard. He tipped out the contents of the envelope. There was an Irish passport in surprisingly pristine condition, a flimsy Kutaban driving licence that was much creased, several small denomination banknotes and O'Driscoll's watch with a cheap plastic strap. The policeman tapped each in turn with a pen and ticked them off a list on the clipboard. When he was finished he returned them to the envelope and gave it to Bartley asking him to sign the sheet attached to the clipboard.

"But surely there must be something else?" Bartley persisted. "Fr. O'Driscoll told me he would be coming up to Bamgboshe for several days. If he had left Shole and was on the Bakooli road he must have already been on his way to Bamgboshe. Surely he would have been travelling with a bag and some clothes? What about a camera? Fr. O'Driscoll never went anywhere without his camera."

Uba gave Bartley an enquiring look before conferring once more with the police officer. The latter was shaking his head.

"No, there is definitely nothing else," Uba confirmed. "Now you will wish to visit the hospital to pick up the death certificate. I think you can find the hospital yourself, can you? I have to join the Governor and will say goodbye here. I am sorry we had to meet again in such circumstances and again I condole Fr. O'Driscoll's family."

"Thank you, Colonel Uba. We will find the hospital ourselves. I wouldn't want to delay you any further. But before I leave, I wonder could I use the toilet here?

Uba looked dubious. "I am afraid you would not find the toilet here too pleasant. It is very basic. Perhaps you would wait until you arrive at the hospital?"

"Eh, I'd rather not. It's just that I've been on the road driving a long time. I'm sure the one here will do perfectly well."

"If you wish, you will find it at the back of the building through the door at the end of the corridor."

"Well, thank you again, Colonel Uba."

"Yes. Goodbye."

Bartley made off down the corridor and out the back of the building. Just as he had guessed a hut serving as the toilet stood off to his right, immediately recognisable from the smell emanating from that direction. There was no-one else in sight. It was unlikely that anyone would want to linger to smoke a cigarette in the vicinity of the outhouse. Over to his left was the compound fenced off from the front of the police station that he had noticed when they arrived. Looking behind to make sure he was still unobserved, he strode over. Immediately in front of him were two wrecks, one a rusted pick-up with its front end crumpled and the engine block smashed back into the cabin. It was without wheels and looked like it had been sitting there for some years. Beside it were the remains of what he recognised as a 1980's Peugeot 507, its roof flattened to sill level where it must have rolled over. Beyond them, but sitting behind the two police vehicles at the front of the compound so that it was not immediately visible, was a pick-up that very much resembled the one Frank O'Driscoll used to drive.

He pulled out his cell phone as he approached and took a quick picture from a distance. Coming up to the car, he was surprised that the roof looked undamaged with none of the dents or scratches he expected if it had rolled upside down as he had been told. The windscreen was intact, but the driver's window was shattered. He looked through the opening and saw a thick spattering of brown stains on the inside of the windscreen that he immediately took to be dried blood. Leaning forward he could see the ceiling was similarly sprayed and that there was there was massive staining on the bench seat backrest and on the gearstick. But there, in the door panel opposite was what to even his inexperienced eye looked undoubtedly like a bullet hole. He withdrew his head and checked once more to see he was still alone. He raised his phone and reached inside the cab, taking several quick pictures, pointing the camera in a different direction each time.

He pocketed the phone and hurried back to the rear door of the station. It was opening just as he reached it. The police officer he had been dealing with earlier emerged. He was looking toward the toilet hut to his right until he saw Bartley approaching from the left. A surprised expression appeared on his face, but he said nothing, holding the door open for Bartley and then following him through the building to the front where Fumbe was waiting.

They drove back toward town before taking a right turn that led them past the Catholic church - another long single storey building not unlike the police station but identifiable as a church from the single wooden cross fixed to the gable above the door. The hospital lay a short distance beyond.

"Fumbe, I think I saw Fr. O'Driscoll's pick-up parked in the compound beside the police station. It didn't seem to me to be a car that had rolled over on its roof, but it looked like there was a lot of dried blood on the inside. I took some pictures on my phone."

They were pulling in to the front of their hospital. An ambulance, no more than a converted pickup with a red cross painted on the sides, was parked by the entrance and Fumbe drew up on its far side. As soon as he killed the engine, Bartley pulled out his phone.

"Just a moment before we go in, let me see what these pictures look like." He fiddled briefly to call up the picture menu and then angled the screen between himself and Fumbe so they both could see.

"There's the pick-up. This one's the back of the car seat. You can see it is stained heavily with what looks like blood." He scrolled forward again. "This is the dashboard and windscreen. It's a bit over-exposed, but you can still see blood stains. Fuck it, this isn't very good! It's rather out of focus but you can just about make out what has to be a bullet-hole in the door."

"It looks like the Father's car, but I think we cannot be sure. Let me see." Fumbe reached to take the phone from him and started scrolling through, peering closely at each picture again in turn. He reached the last, stopped and then abruptly ran his finger across the screen to return to the previous one.

"See, Bartley! Look!" he said excitedly. "This one, you can see there, on the dashboard, it is the little statue that Father had sitting in the front of his car."

Bartley took the phone back and stared.

"You're right! It's his St. Christopher. I remember it looked like it had broken off and he had glued it back on. You can just make out it's the same. We have to go back to the police station. But let me collect the death certificate. I also need to have a word with the doctor who issued it."

He got out of the car and with Fumbe beside him made toward the hospital entrance. After a couple of steps, he halted, the full awful realisation only now hitting him.

"Fumbe, it just isn't possible that O'Driscoll died in a car crash the way they say. There's no sign that his car rolled over, but there's all that blood and then the bullet-hole. Someone killed him. I'm sure of it now."

"Shshh," Fumbe warned as a diminutive man in a white coat came out of the hospital and approached them, his arm extended.

"Mr. Ryan, I am Dr. Irosha. The RS has called me to expect you. Please allow me to condole you. It is very sad that Fr. O'Driscoll has passed. I did not know him, but many people say he was a good man. Please come to my office. I have the Father's death certificate to give you."

Bartley followed the doctor and found himself stretching his stride to keep up with Irosha who despite his stature appeared to move at considerable speed. Arriving at his office he made no offer to Bartley to take a seat. He bustled to the far side of his desk and, still standing, picked up a brown envelope that lay alone on its surface.

"Please, this is the death certificate. Can I do anything more for you Mr Ryan?"

His tone suggested that he hoped he was done with Bartley. He seemed nervous and somehow anxious to be rid of him.

Bartley took the envelope. It was not sealed and he reached inside to pull out a sheet of paper. Irosha looked at his watch, twisting the armband nervously between his thumb and forefinger.

It was a simple piece of paper attesting in the briefest of terms to the death. The individual particulars had been written in by hand using a black ball-pen. These included the date of death and the name of the deceased. The cause of death was startlingly brief, "Cardiopulmonary arrest following traumatic brain injury".

But when Bartley scanned further, he came to a halt when he read the name of the witness to the deceased's identity: Major K. Mbuta, Military HQ, Bamgboshe.

"It says here, Doctor, that the body was identified by a Major Mbuta. How was that? What was he doing here?"

"I am sorry I do not know. I was not here. It was my colleague Dr Kafuni who issued the certificate. I myself did not see the deceased."

Bartley looked at Irosha, "Can you tell me what sort of brain injury Fr. O'Driscoll suffered? What caused it exactly?"

The doctor looked uncomfortable and shrugged.

"Again, I am sorry. I do not know. You would have to ask Dr Kafuni."

"Alright, is Dr Kafuni here now? Can I speak to him?"

"I am sorry but he has travelled and will not be back for some weeks."

"Well then, is there some other report he wrote? Is there a post mortem report?"

"Oh no, there is no post mortem. We do not have the facilities. If you want a post mortem you must send the corpse to the state hospital in Bamgboshe. Here we do not carry out the post mortem examination. In fact we do not have a proper mortuary."

"So there's nothing more you or anyone else here at the moment can tell me? Perhaps there is someone from the ambulance or a nurse?"

"No, I am sorry there is no-one. The corpse was brought here by the police and there was nothing to do except to hold it until someone came to claim it. I understand that Major Mbuta spoke with Fr. O'Driscoll's church and made the arrangements that were needed with the coffin maker."

Irosha seemed better informed of the detail than he admitted, but this still told Bartley little. It was a mystery how Major Mbuta could have come to identify the body. It also seemed an unlikely coincidence, if not suspicious, that everyone else immediately involved, from the two policemen who arrived at the scene of the supposed accident to the doctor who had issued the death certificate, seemed at this very moment to have travelled out of town for one reason or another. It was obvious Bartley was not going to find anyone who had seen or would admit to having seen O'Driscoll's body at any time following the accident. There seemed no point trying to quiz Dr Irosha further. But perhaps he would have better luck in finding out what really might have happened if he and Fumbe went back to the police station.

Approaching the church on their way, he asked Fumbe to stop. He wanted to see where O'Driscoll had been buried. He should at least visit his grave. He had seen two headstones with crosses standing off to the left of the door when they had passed by earlier and now as he got out of the car he could see a mound of freshly turned earth beyond them. The two headstones were white painted concrete with faded black lettering. He stopped momentarily to read the inscriptions. They marked the graves of two priests, one described as the former parish priest. It seemed this plot was reserved for clergy and that the third mound must therefore be where O'Driscoll had been laid only hours earlier.

There were no flowers, but a small temporary wooden cross had been placed at one end. The mourners, whoever they had been, had long since left and the church and its grounds were completely deserted. Bartley walked up to the small cross. There was no doubt that this is where his friend lay.

He regretted he had not been present for the funeral. He wondered who had attended and what they might have said about this priest. He was sure that there must be a good number of people throughout Bakooli and Guseni who would miss him very much. His mother had wanted him home, but Bartley wondered whether Frank would not prefer to rest here in the dusty earth near the people he had loved and helped, rather than in the wet, cold clay of an Irish graveyard.

"But what the fuck happened?" he asked. "Where are those photographs you took? And where the hell is your camera? I don't suppose you can tell me now. I'm going to look for them, be sure of that. And I am going to find out what happened."

He was losing time getting back to the police station, but he owed O'Driscoll this visit.

"You poor bastard, I'll come back and see you again."

There was a low cough beside him. He had not noticed Fumbe following him up to the grave. He realised he must have been talking aloud, but he did not mind being overheard. He was happy to have Fumbe share the moment.

"Thank you, Fumbe. Yes let's go. First we should look at the car at the police station. Then we are going to drive to Fr. O'Driscoll's house in Shole. There's something I have to find there."

Arriving back at the police station, Bartley first peered through the fence, but to his dismay he could no longer see O'Driscoll's pick-up on the far side of the two police vehicles. He hurried inside, bringing Fumbe with him to interpret.

The same police officer as before was still there. He did not look too happy to see him again but did not appear unduly surprised.

"Yes", he admitted, "there was a pick-up outside, but now it has been taken away for examination. It has been used in a robbery and is being kept safe for evidence. No it is not Fr. O'Driscoll's car. I don't know where that car is. I have never seen it."

Bartley felt weak as they left. He was shaking from everything he had seen and heard. He realised he must also be weak from not having eaten for so long. He had felt hungry when they had first arrived in Bakooli, but events since had made him forget and indeed had killed his appetite. However, if they were to continue on to Shole it would be evening before they reached O'Driscoll's house and Fumbe too, would need some food if he was to drive that far. Also now, he really was in urgent need of a piss.

They stopped to fill up with diesel at the truck stop on the main road and went into the adjoining restaurant where they ordered two cokes and a plate each of rice with stringy chicken in a yellow sauce. They started the cokes as they waited for the food to arrive, the first few gulps offering a reviving sugar rush. Bartley took out his phone and once more began scrolling through his pictures. He took a paper serviette and wiped dry the puddle of water from his cold bottle on the plastic table cloth before leaning across to show Fumbe the screen once more.

He had stopped at the picture that showed the St. Christopher figure that had been glued clumsily back on its broken base.

"It was definitely O'Driscoll's car. That policeman must have guessed I had seen it. I think he saw me when I said I had to use the toilet. He must have told Uba and they decided to get rid of it in case I came back. This whole affair stinks. I just hope I can find something at the house in Shole."

Fumbe drove as fast as the old Landcruiser would allow over the bumpy, unpaved road that led south, but he was forced to slow down as they turned onto the rougher track that branched off toward Shole. It was dusk as they drew near the priest's house.

"The people, they have gone." Fumbe broke the silence they had maintained wrapped in their own thoughts..

"What people?" Bartley puzzled.

"Over there," Fumbe motioned to his left. "You know the houses of the small village near to Father's house. I think the people are gone."

"What makes you think that?"

"At this time every day women are cooking. You will see smoke and smell it, but tonight there is no smoke, no smell."

"I think you're right. I wonder why they might have left. Fr. O'Driscoll did say that people move their villages every so often to find a new grazing area for their cattle, but I didn't think they would do that up here in Shole."

They had arrived at the entrance to O'Driscoll's house and Fumbe pulled in to draw the car to a halt. There was no sign of a housekeeper as they got out, but they could see the front door was ajar.

Bartley led the way inside. The living room was in some disorder as if someone had rummaged or searched through the contents. It was hard to say if anything was missing. The dusty television and ancient video player still stood on a low table in the corner with a few video cassettes on the floor underneath. The single shelf bookcase had been emptied and O'Driscoll's meagre collection of books and a couple of old National Geographic magazines were scattered beside it. They moved on. In what had been O'Driscoll's room, the mattress had been pulled half-way off the bed onto the floor. A few items of clothing, a couple of shirts and pants, had been thrown carelessly on top. They peered into the second bedroom. Here again, the mattress had been thrown off the bed and the door of an empty wardrobe hung open.

Bartley left Fumbe still standing at the door and hurried to the back of the house to the little cupboard-sized room that he knew O'Driscoll used as his dark room. It had been stripped bare. Everything, even the plastic jars, the small developing tank, the different sized packs of print paper, anything that might give evidence of its former use had been taken away. It seemed that whoever had been through the house had been most interested in what might be found here.

"It doesn't look like we're going to find anything here, Fumbe. Can you get our things in from the car and I'll light some lamps while we can still see what we're doing."

Fumbe went out and carried in what little they had, a couple of packets of biscuits, bottled water and a torch. Bartley found some matches and lighted two paraffin lamps.

Later, wandering around with the torch, eating a dry biscuit, he carried out a more thorough search.

"I don't see anything here that can help us. There don't even seem to be any personal possessions that we might send back to the family. Do you remember O'Driscoll had some wonderful photo portraits of local people that he showed us when we stayed here before? There's no sign of them. They've been taken too."

"Maybe the village people have taken them when they were leaving," Fumbe sounded doubtful, "but I think maybe your friend Colonel Uba has been here."

"I think you're right, but there's nothing we can do about that now. We should get some sleep and start off in the morning as soon as it gets light. I'll sleep in the guest room I stayed in last time. You can have Fr. O'Driscoll's room."

Fumbe looked at him askance, "No, that is the room of a dead man. That is not good. I will sleep in the boys' room outside."

In truth the prospect of sleeping in O'Driscoll's room also disturbed Bartley, but he had not counted on Fumbe rejecting his proposal and leaving him with the even less welcome alternative of sleeping in the house alone.

"OK, I'll sleep in O'Driscoll's room, but you take the guest room. I think it would be better we both sleep in the house tonight."

Fumbe still looked doubtful, but agreed. Bartley handed him one of the lanterns and took the other off to his room. He laid the light on the floor, replaced the mattress back on the bed and tidied the scattered clothes. He sat on the side of the bed and took a sip from a bottle of water.

"Here's to you, Frank. I hope you don't mind a heathen taking your bed. Sorry I don't have any Jameson's this time. He lay down without bothering to take off his clothes. He knew it would be a long, uncomfortable and melancholy night.

THIRTY-FIVE

Wednesday, 18 February.

"Still, all you have are suspicions." Clendenning insisted. "Granted, some of what you say does sound strange, but you have no actual proof that any official or agency of government is guilty of foul play. Your own photographs in themselves prove nothing and without the photographs you say Fr. O'Driscoll may have had there's indeed no proof of anything. Frankly, I have to say that I was always sceptical that O'Driscoll had anything of real substance to show us, much less photographs of the bodies of murder victims lying by the side of the road."

Yet again, this was not how Bartley had hoped things would work out. The previous evening, by the time he arrived back from Bakooli, Clendenning had already left the office and gone home. Exhausted from his travels and conscious that he had not had a wash or change of clothes since Monday morning, he had been thankful to have the evening to recover and gather his thoughts. But he had not imagined Clendenning would be so negative.

"In summary, Bartley, I have to say that I'm simply not convinced that your account of what you saw in Bakooli and Shole amounts to very much."

"But surely the pictures I have of O'Driscoll's pick-up count for something?" Bartley persisted.

"Well, neither you nor I know exactly how his accident happened or what damage may or may not have been caused to his car. Obviously it's no surprise to see bloodstains in a car that's been involved in a fatal accident, is it? In any case, you have to admit that your pictures are rather unclear and don't explicitly point to murder. Why, you can't even prove that it was O'Driscoll's car you saw and now you no longer know where it is. What I suggest you do now is to go off and write a *factual* account of your visit to Bakooli. You must keep it strictly factual – I want none of your theories. You have to remember that anything you write might later come out if there is a Freedom of Information request, so make sure you commit nothing to paper that might embarrass us later. Bear in mind that the primary purpose of your visit was to try to arrange repatriation of O'Driscoll's remains. You will have to give some thought to explaining why this proved not to be possible. Meanwhile, I'll speak to the Secretary General and let him know about all this. I'm sure he'll agree with me that there's nothing more we can do and that it would be best for all of us, including O'Driscoll's family, whom we don't want to upset any further, that we not try to dredge up something we can't prove."

Bartley rose despondently, leaving the room without a further word. He considered banging the door behind him, but instead left it ajar knowing that Clendenning hated it sitting open.

Back in his own office, he tapped his computer to life and entered his password. He sat silent for a moment and then called up a Google search. When he found what he was looking for, he jotted down a number. He hesitated a moment, but then grabbed his phone and dialled.

Most unusually the Kutaban international network seemed to be working for he made an almost immediate connection and heard an Irish voice answering, "Good morning, *The Independent.*"

"Yes, put me through to the news desk, please..."

He stayed at his desk throughout lunchtime. He had no appetite and preferred to keep his own company. He was trying to write an account of his visit to Bakooli and Shole, sticking to the facts, not because Clendenning had ordered him to do so, but rather because he thought it might help him find a way forward. He was a little light-headed from dehydration and lack of food when he heard the others returning from their break. Almost immediately, his phone rang. It was Grace.

"Bartley, I have Professor Ballo on the line. He would like to speak to you."

"Fine, put him through" He wondered what Ballo might want. He hadn't heard from him since he turned up at the Malingas' orphanage during the Minister's visit.

"Mr. Ryan," He recognised Ballo's voice. "I hope I am not disturbing you, but I understand you have recently returned from Bakooli and were making enquiries about the death of Fr. O'Driscoll. Is that correct?"

"Yes, I was asked to see if his remains could be repatriated and also make some general enquiries about his accident." Bartley decided not to volunteer more information.

"Yes, it was a most unfortunate accident."

"Indeed, if it was an accident." Immediately Bartley regretted his words, but then if anyone were to share his doubts surely Ballo would?

"Mr. Ryan, you think it was maybe not an accident? Is there something you know?" Ballo paused, waiting for Bartley to continue.

"No, Professor, I'm sorry. I just don't know. Please forget I said anything."

"But no, Mr. Ryan, there are things that happen in Guseni that others do not like to believe. There are things that I know. Perhaps we could meet? It would be good if we could talk in private and not on the telephone."

"Well, I'm not sure, but..."

"Mr. Ryan I think it is important we should. Can you meet me tonight? Let us say seven o'clock at the Joly Bar. Do you know it? It is near the abattoir."

Bartley hesitated. He was nervous but anxious to learn whatever information Ballo might have. He did not see that he had any choice but to agree to a meeting.

"Eh, I guess. Alright, I'm sure I can find it. I'll be there."

As soon as Ballo hung up, he called Fumbe to ask if he could drive him later.

"Yes, I can drive you. But you know this Joly Bar is not a good place." Fumbe cautioned. "It is a place where some drug addicts go. It is also far, on the other side of the city. We will need to leave immediately after I drive the Ambassador home."

"That's fine, but don't worry about the bar, I won't be staying long." Bartley promised. "I'll meet Ballo and if it looks like he wants a long talk, I can always suggest we drive somewhere else. You can stay outside in the car. But, Fumbe, one thing, don't tell anyone else about this."

The bar was indeed close to the city abattoir, actually just alongside where it perched at the top of a hill. The site may well have been chosen to allow for the convenient disposal of unwanted offal and bones by simply tipping them down the slope. The corrugated iron roofs of its buildings were constantly black with vultures and it was these scavengers that ensured a certain degree of hygiene, devouring the dumped offal and stripping the bones clean. Their efforts did not however help with the smell of putrid decay. Depending on the direction of the wind, passing down the adjoining highway in slow moving traffic was often an ordeal.

Fumbe had turned off the highway just before reaching the abattoir and drove down a sandy track strewn with the remains of torn cardboard boxes and crushed plastic bottles. The abattoir loomed dark beyond a wire fence to the left. To the right an occasional light shone from a row of hovels, wires hanging loose from poles showing where the overhead electric lines had been illegally tapped. Between the hovels a few rickety vegetable stalls had been abandoned for the night.

About one hundred and fifty metres down the track on their right, two naked light bulbs marked an open entranceway and Fumbe turned into a surprisingly spacious yard at the far end of which was a low brick building. A few plastic chairs and tables were ranged haphazardly outside under a red neon sign that announced they had arrived at Joly Bar. An old Toyota Corolla sedan and a pick-up were already parked in the yard to the right and Fumbe pulled in alongside them.

"You see now. You do not want to stay in this bar." Fumbe could not hide his ill ease.

Bartley nodded agreement. It did not look like his kind of place either.

Inside, the bar was not quite as bad as he expected. A barman talking to two girls, hookers by the look of them, stood behind a counter at the far end. Half a dozen customers, all men, shabbily dressed, sat on more plastic chairs at rough wooden tables that looked like they had been made from packing cases. They were drinking bottles of Hippo and there was a strong smell of dagga.

Professor Ballo looked very much out of place, dressed neatly in a light grey suit that matched the colour of his hair and beard. He was sitting alone off to the left, up near the bar where he offered a wave that was no more than the opening of a hand, his elbow still resting on the table. Bartley wondered at the unusual choice of venue. The two hookers turned to take him in, but lost interest as soon as he crossed the room and sat down with Ballo. The barman tapped the counter, as if telling them not to leave, and came out from behind the bar and over to the table. Bartley ordered a Hippo, Ballo declined his offer of anything, pointing to his coffee to say he was fine.

"Thank you for coming Mr. Ryan," Ballo had taken out a handkerchief and was wiping beneath his collar at the back of his neck. He looked nervous. "It has been some time since we met. I think it was when your Minister was here on a visit? I have heard the visit was a great success. Of course that must be because of your excellent preparations."

Before Bartley could reply, the politician raised his hand to gesture silence as he watched the barman uncap a Hippo and return with the bottle and an empty glass. He proceeded to pour the beer, filling the glass until foam rose to the brim. He placed it down on the table and walked off without a word of acknowledgement of Bartley's muttered thanks.

They waited until he was back behind his bar before Bartley leaned across the table.

"Professor, you said we could talk about Fr. O'Driscoll. You seemed to suggest that you might know something about how he died. I for one don't believe his death was an accident."

Ballo twisted sideways in his chair, glancing at the door before replying.

"Yes, I understood you were suspicious. You must understand that the situation is very delicate. That is why I had to ask that we meet in this unlikely place where I thought we would be private. It seems you and your Fr. O'Driscoll have upset some people and they will go to any length to protect themselves. Believe me, I admire what you are doing, but you must be very careful. You may want to reconsider your own position before you enquire too deeply. " He paused and again looked toward the door.

"Which people are upset? How will they protect..."

Bartley was cut off by a dazzling glare of headlights flooding the yard outside and the loud crunch of tyres on sand and gravel. The dagga smokers were suddenly throwing their glowing wraps across the floor away from where they were sitting. The two hookers edged closer together and made to move to the end of the counter, one of them adjusting her cleavage so that her glittery top rested marginally higher. Like the barman, they were staring at the door. Bartley followed their gaze and then looked back at Ballo, but the Professor's head was down and his eyes fixed on his coffee cup. His right hand played nervously with the handle.

At once a group of black uniformed police burst through the door, filling the bar and outnumbering its customers. They were eerily silent as they moved to take positions guarding each table. Three stood in a line facing the bar counter. Two stood next to Bartley and Ballo, automatic weapons held low, pointing at the floor. The Joly Bar's patrons remained frozen in their places.

A police officer with a lieutenant's stripes came swaggering into the room and looked around. He paused to toe the butt of a discarded dagga wrap that still smouldered where it had landed next to the open doorway. He crushed it under his shoe and pointed to each of the tables of drinkers in turn giving them some order in a quiet but menacing voice. While he did not understand the words, Bartley understood their import for the men now rose slowly, raising their arms to lock hands behind their heads and file out followed by three policemen. The officer approached the bar and again spoke quietly. The two hookers looked immediately relieved and squeezed past him, teetering gratefully in their oversized heels to the door. The barman shuffled from behind his counter. A policeman grabbed his arms from behind and frogmarched him out to join the others.

Only now did the lieutenant seem to notice Bartley and Ballo, still sitting at their table off to the left. He walked over.

"Identity documents, please." He spoke in English.

Bartley removed his wallet from his back pocket and pulled out the small laminated diplomatic ID card with his photograph. He held it out. The officer looked at it briefly before reaching over to take the Kutaban identity card that Ballo offered. He examined it carefully and then nodded to Ballo.

"Professor Ballo, I know you. I am surprised to see you in a place like this. Please wait outside."

He returned Ballo's card and the Professor stood up, leaning heavily on the table. He walked slowly to the door, his eyes on the floor averting Bartley's gaze.

Bartley looked up at the officer, butterflies now playing havoc in his gut.

"Mr. Bartley Ryan, you are from the Embassy of Ireland." He was reading from Bartley's ID.

"Do you know this bar and what kind of place it is? It is a bar where criminals smoke dagga. It is not a bar where diplomats should be drinking. I hope you do not smoke dagga, it is illegal in our country and the penalties are very strict. So what are you doing here?"

Bartley collected himself sufficiently to protest his rights.

"Officer, as you can see I was having a quiet beer and talking to my friend Professor Ballo. It is quite natural that diplomats and politicians such as Professor Ballo should meet to talk. You know we're not obliged to go only to the Hilton. Sometimes we prefer to go elsewhere. Professor Ballo suggested we meet here. I presume it was convenient for him and it was no problem for me."

The lieutenant did not reply for a moment, as if considering his options.

"Very well, you may leave."

He offered back the plastic card and Bartley once more fished out his wallet to slip it back in place beside his other cards. He took his time in an effort to look confident, in control. He had nothing to fear, but the suddenness of the police invasion had rattled him. He worried that he might shake if he got up too quickly. He reached out, lifted his glass and took a token sip of his almost untouched Hippo before getting up and heading out, followed closely by the police officer.

A police pick-up and truck together with a green Nissan Pathfinder were now parked in the yard, the latter straddling the entrance. Bartley could see the barman and his clientele had been herded up into the rear of the truck where they now stood sullenly, guarded by police. He did not see Ballo or the two hookers. Fumbe was standing with his hands clasped in front between two policemen next to the front passenger door of the Landcruiser. Seeing the lieutenant coming out, one of them called to him, urgently waving something he was holding in his hand.

The officer hurried over and as Bartley caught up with him he saw that what the policeman held was a large manila envelope. At the same time Fumbe tried to push forward raising an arm in protest but the second policeman roughly pushed him back with the butt of his weapon. The lieutenant also motioned him back while he talked to his subordinate. He glanced quickly at Bartley before peering into the envelope and then levelling him a steady look. He gingerly took hold of the envelope and raised it directly in front of Bartley.

"Is this your property, Mr Ryan?" he asked.

Bartley felt an instant foreboding as he stared at it. He could clearly make out his name and the Embassy address printed on the cover.

"What? I don't know. It looks like my name on it. Is it important?"

"It is important. It is also very serious Mr Ryan. My man found this lying on the floor of your car as soon as we arrived."

He pushed open the end of the envelope and withdrew a crumpled Rothmans box. A wave of horror swept over Bartley as he recognised the packet as the one Fiona had left in his house. He watched frozen as the officer opened the packet and displayed the wraps nestling inside.

"This is dagga, Mr Ryan."

The loud diesel rattle of the green Nissan starting up roused him. Looking across he watched it reverse and turn to head out the gate. As it passed he could see two figures in the rear seat. Major Mbuta was looking out, a smile of smug satisfaction visible though the open window. On the far side Professor Ballo's head was bowed and turned away so that his face could not be seen.

THIRTY-SIX

Thursday, 19 February.

"At least the police made no attempt to arrest him and there was no need to claim diplomatic immunity, but of course it is extremely embarrassing to have the Embassy's First Secretary found in possession of drugs." Ambassador Clendenning found himself having to engage in a most unwanted and difficult phone conversation with Secretary General McNamara.

"The thing is," he continued, "Ryan remains dogged in insisting that he has been set up as part of some conspiracy that involves Fr. O'Driscoll being murdered rather than being killed in a road accident. He also says that the police must have planted the drugs in the car. The drugs themselves were apparently found in an official envelope with his name on it. However, as he points out, he has dozens of similar used envelopes in his desk drawers and elsewhere and it would also be easy to steal one from any number of places.

"I'm afraid I don't know the truth of it. I've been worried about his state of mind for some time, particularly since he went off to visit Fr. O'Driscoll. He came back here full of outlandish conspiracies involving the Kutaban government and genocide in the Guseni area in the south of the country. He even suggested there was collusion on the part of a number of western countries and international oil companies. He wanted to send a report home about it, but since he had no proof for any of his allegations, I persuaded him to hold off unless he came up with some hard facts.

"What is also worrying is that whatever he had been up to with O'Driscoll in Guseni before O'Driscoll's accident has somehow come to the attention of Prime Minister Okeke himself. I understand that Okeke mentioned him, albeit not by name, in the course of a meeting with the Dutch Ambassador, although the Ambassador has as yet said nothing to me about it."

"I don't like the sound of that." McNamara was finding the story going from bad to worse. "But first, how the fuck does Ryan explain what he was doing in this place where they found drugs in his car? From what you say, it's some sort of drugs den."

"He says he got a phone call yesterday afternoon from Professor Ballo - you might remember he's the leader of the opposition party here? Anyway he says Ballo called him and led him to believe he had some information that O'Driscoll's death wasn't an accident. He says Ballo said they should talk in person and it was he who proposed where they should meet."

"I presume you've spoken to Ballo to confirm this?"

"Eh no, I've tried, but his office says he's out of town and his cell phone isn't answering. There's also something else..."

"For god's sake, what now?"

"Well, Ryan claims the call was put through to him by our receptionist, Grace, but I've spoken to her and she swears there was no call from Ballo yesterday."

There was a silence on the line for a moment before Clendenning heard the Secretary General sigh.

"Fuck this for a can of worms! We'll have to try to make the best of this bloody mess but be prepared for the worst. It's already beginning to unravel in the press. Have you seen this morning's *Independent*?"

"No, not yet. We can only get it on-line here and I haven't had a chance to look yet."

"Then I can tell you the front page has a story, I have it here... yes, the headline is, **Foul Play Suspected in Death of Irish Priest in Kutaba**. Where do they get this stuff from? Anyway read it."

If Clendenning suspected that Bartley might be *The Independent's* source he refrained from hinting as much to the Secretary General. It seemed at that moment that whatever Bartley did, part of the blame would inevitably attach to his Ambassador.

"We have to consider our options here." McNamara continued.

"On the one hand, we can't entirely discount that there might be some substance to Ryan's theories, however unlikely that might be. We could choose to make a demarche to the Kutaban Foreign Ministry on the basis of some suspicion that Fr. O'Driscoll's death was not accidental and that it is somehow connected with illegal activities on their part in this Guseni area.

"Realistically, without any hard evidence, a demarche on those lines would achieve little result other than to lead to a very public breakdown in relations between us and Kutaba. It could also damage our relationship with any other EU country that has a particular economic interest in maintaining friendly relations with the country. No-one's going to be too happy with us appearing to try and dish the dirt."

"I have to agree," Clendenning was horrified at the thought of being instructed to confront Minister Roble on such a dubious basis. "I'm sure the Kutabans would react very badly and I'm sure the British, probably the Dutch, and certainly the Americans would be very critical."

"Even if we could live with that," McNamara opined, "I'd also be afraid of what might happen here at home. Doubtlessly it would add fuel to speculation about the circumstances of Fr. O'Driscoll's death. This could throw up some very undesirable consequences for the Department and Government too. There could well be demands for a public enquiry. O'Driscoll's family might decide to sue for compensation. The affair could rumble on for years and in the end no possible good would come of it. Meanwhile the Department's integrity and competence would be called into question."

"Yes, indeed that's also an important consideration." Clendenning was relieved that the Secretary General's thinking seemed to incline against a demarche, but he was still unsure where this was leading.

"The obvious alternative is to bring Ryan quietly back to HQ. If any questions are asked, we can suggest that he may have some private health issues that are best attended to at home rather than in Kutaba. From what you say that's probably true in any case. As far as our options go, it's essentially a no-brainer that Ryan comes home. How soon can you get him on a flight?"

"There's a flight to London tomorrow, it's probably too late to get him on that. It's usually fully booked. Realistically the best chance is to get him on a flight early next week, on Tuesday."

"Hmm, tomorrow might also be a problem if it gives him less than twenty-four hours' notice to pack and clear out. It's the kind of thing he could go to his union about. Giving him until Tuesday will give less grounds for complaint. Just keep him under wraps until then. With the weekend coming up, hopefully he will have no opportunity to get into any more trouble. Let me know when his flight's arranged."

Clendenning considered keeping Bartley under *wraps* was probably the least desirable of options, but once more refrained from enlightening McNamara. However, another thought occurred to him.

"I'll do that, but I wonder what about replacing Ryan here in Bamgboshe? I really do need a First Secretary here."

"I don't see that as a possibility what with the pressures on staffing at present. Don't you have a Third Secretary there?"

"Yes, Michelle Finn, but she's due promotion at home any day now, leaving me even with no Third Secretary when she goes."

"Well, if she's on the promotion list, we can leave her there in Bamgboshe for a while. Until her promotion comes through she can act-up at First Secretary level, but don't then expect a Third Secretary replacement."

Clendenning conceded inwardly that this was as good an outcome as he could hope. All he needed now was to get rid of Bartley before anything else came up.

Unfortunately something did come up. No sooner had he ended his call to the Secretary General, than he received one from the Foreign Ministry. Minister Roble was requesting an urgent meeting with him, preferably at once. Clendenning told Grace to instruct Fumbe to get ready. Before he left he called into Bartley's office.

"I've been speaking to the Secretary General. He wants you out of Kutaba. You're to leave on Tuesday, so you'd better start making arrangements. You can clear up your things in the office today and then stay at home until you leave. That will give you time to pack, but keep out of any further trouble."

The news came as no surprise. Bartley had been half expecting to be ordered out on the Friday flight, especially after reading the story in the Independent and guessing Clendenning would suspect him as the source. In preparation for his departure he had already started deleting the hundreds of out-of-date e-mails that had accumulated in his mailbox.

"That's fine. So we just allow the Kutaban government to get away with murdering an Irish citizen and I get shipped home out of the way?" He no longer cared what Clendenning might say.

"You're damned lucky you haven't been arrested or formally expelled, which you just still might be. The Foreign Ministry just phoned and I've been called in to see Roble immediately. In all my years, I've never heard of any of my colleagues receiving a summons from a Foreign Minister to come in to apologise for the conduct of one of his staff."

"Or, *her* staff?"

"Don't get gender cute with me. Just clear out your desk and make sure you're on that plane on Tuesday."

As Clendenning stormed off, Bartley felt some satisfaction at having gotten under his skin, but despite himself he hoped Roble would not give him too much of a hard time. On the other hand while Clendenning thought him lucky not to be expelled, he would prefer formal expulsion. That would make headline news at home, inevitably offering opportunities to air his side of events. However, now that his own Department had decided to bring him quietly home, no-one would notice. He would probably end up hidden away, forgotten in some anonymous cubbyhole in Iveagh House. And then there would be no chance of ever uncovering the truth.

THIRTY-SEVEN

The Ambassador had been waiting in the anteroom to Roble's office for fifteen minutes when he was ushered into the Foreign Minister's presence.

"Ambassador, thank you for coming to see me," the Minister rose from behind his desk to shake hands before inviting Clendenning to take a seat on a sofa. He meanwhile, positioned himself in a considerably higher armchair opposite. A young assistant in an overly tight suit and tartan tie who had been hovering in the background sat behind the Minister on an upright chair. It was a configuration that reminded Clendenning uncomfortably of an exasperatingly unsuccessful meeting in Secretary General McNamara's office about a year earlier when he had gone in to request he be posted somewhere more salubrious than Kutaba.

"When did we last meet, Ambassador? I think it must have been during your Minister's visit, was it? We really should meet more frequently. I think it would be very useful to have a regular exchange of views.

"So, how are things in Ireland? You seem to be doing remarkably well despite all that Brexit nonsense, but I think that best a matter we not discuss. Suffice to say we admire your efforts and value the relationship between our two countries."

The Minister settled back in his armchair, silently steepling his fingers to tap his chin as if deep in thought. He leaned forward again, as if only having come to a decision.

"We should thus avoid anything that might put our good relations at risk. We have as you know a very regrettable incident involving one of your staff being found in possession of dagga. You are aware, Ambassador, this is a very serious offence in our country. Some of our worst and most violent crimes have been committed by those who are under the influence of drugs. Our government is engaged in what I would say is a full scale war to eradicate all trade in drugs. We cannot therefore ignore it when we find a member of the diplomatic community is actively involved in this despicable trade. If he has diplomatic immunity, we cannot arrest him, but we cannot allow him to remain in our country.

"Now in our present case, we have, as I say, very good relations with the Irish and with you personally, Ambassador. I do not wish to make a formal expulsion order for your First Secretary, but I would ask you, informally to avoid embarrassment, that you should now immediately call him home from Kutaba and that we can then forget this affair as if it had never happened."

To emphasise his point he waved at the young note-taker, as if only now realising his presence. "There is no need to write any of this down. We will keep this off the record." He returned to Clendenning, "Are we agreed, Ambassador?"

This was milder than anything Clendenning might have hoped for and offered what he and McNamara most wanted: the possibility of moving on without further publicity. He was not going to take issue with Roble's assumption that Bartley, having been found in possession of two or three marijuana cigarettes, was somehow *actively involved* in the drugs trade. But he could not help wondering why the Kutabans were being so helpful and obliging when they could have made life so much more difficult. They could have challenged Bartley's diplomatic immunity or they could have gone public with a formal expulsion order. Instead they seemed only to want Bartley quickly and quietly removed and then the whole affair forgotten. This did not seem to be typical Kutaban behaviour. At this point, despite himself, he found himself beginning to question whether the whole affair was as straightforward as it first seemed. Could it be that Roble was open to the possibility, as Bartley continued to insist, that the police *had* planted the drugs?

"Thank you Minister, your understanding in this matter is much appreciated. I agree that what you suggest would be the best way forward and indeed arrangements are already in hand to this end. I have spoken to my Secretary General in Dublin and agreed that Mr Ryan's posting here in Kutaba is to end with immediate effect. I have instructed Mr Ryan to pack his belongings over the weekend. He is to fly out on the London flight on Tuesday, if that is acceptable to you?"

"Certainly, that would be most satisfactory. I am glad we understand each other, but I must not take any more of your time." Roble stood up and extended his hand again, "We really must meet more often."

*****

At that moment, back in the Embassy, Bartley was also getting up from his seat for what he expected was the last time. He had a look around his office and at his desk. He had surprisingly few personal possessions to take with him and they had all fitted into his briefcase. He saw no reason to remain until the end of office hours and he had already logged out of his computer. Leaving the room, he passed Michelle's office and looked in, but she appeared to be off somewhere. He then sought out Goodness, in the little kitchenette. Word of his imminent departure seemed somehow to have already spread and Goodness' eyes brimmed with tears when she saw him. They said goodbye and she gave him a hug. He presumed she knew her brother Ngule stood no chance of early release this time, but there was an unspoken understanding between them not to discuss it.

Grace looked up from her desk as he walked wordlessly past her in reception. He felt more pity than anger toward her, wondering what pressure she might have come under to lie about there being no phone call from Ballo. He was less forgiving of Ballo who had been instrumental in stitching him up. He wondered where he was now and what Gabi or Mbuta might have on him to coerce him into helping set him up.

THIRTY-EIGHT

Bartley was sitting on his verandah, a Hippo in hand, as Michelle's car drove in through the gate. She got out and approached tentatively, somewhat shyly perhaps because it was her first time to set foot in Bartley's home.

"Hi Michelle, welcome to my humble, if quite temporary abode." He was surprised to see her. She was wearing a tight blue tee-shirt and shorts so she must have gone home after the office to change before coming to visit. He noticed her legs were well tanned - another surprise since he had never seen her other than encased in one of her business-like pants suits.

"Hi Bartley, are you all packed or can I help?"

"So you've heard, then? No, thanks, I don't have much to pack anyway and I'll leave it until tomorrow. But come on in. Would you like a drink? I have some cold Hippo, but I have a couple of bottles of reasonable red wine that I don't intend to leave behind unfinished."

"A glass of wine would be lovely."

Bartley led her inside to his sitting room.

"The mosquitos have been eating me on the verandah again, so it's probably just as well to move inside. I was just having a last nostalgic drink out there. Have a seat, I'll open the wine." He finished off his Hippo and walked off to the kitchen.

"Bartley," Michelle raised her voice so he could hear, "I'm sorry you're being sent home like this. Look if there's anything I can do, maybe something you need shipped, even after you're gone, let me know."

"I don't think I'll bother shipping anything. Any of the bigger stuff I have isn't worth keeping. I'll just leave it here. Maybe one of the local staff would be interested in a large but pretty decrepit TV set."

"Look, I have to let you know that Adrian has told me that I'm staying on here in Bamgboshe to replace you. I'll be acting-up as First Secretary until my promotion comes through."

"Are you happy with that?"

"Yes very. I hope you don't mind."

Bartley had returned and proceeded to pour them each a large glass of wine.

"No, actually I'm glad it's worked out for you. Still, I don't envy you working with Clendenning for any length of time."

"Yes, I know what you mean. At least he doesn't have it in for me as he always seemed to have for you."

"So you noticed?"

"Actually," she ignored the question, "he was looking for you when he came back from the Foreign Ministry this afternoon. Apparently his meeting with Roble went off quite well. It was about you - obviously. Adrian says Roble agreed that you're to fly out on Tuesday and there will be no repercussions or recrimination on either side."

Bartley snorted. "Yeah, I'll bet Roble and company are delighted that there will be no recrimination – especially against them."

"I thought you'd feel like that. But I do have some good news for you." she grinned. "Adrian said it was unlikely that he'd see you before you leave, but he wishes you the best."

He lifted his glass toward her and laughed. "I'll drink to that," and she joined in his laughter. He topped up their glasses. She gave him a strange look as she took a sip.

"What?" he asked, "What's wrong?" he asked.

"Nothing, it's just that you look quite different with your head shaved. It suits you." She laughed again, "But there's something else you might find funny. No, I don't mean about you, something else, funny weird. It's just that Adrian got a call before I left. It was from your friend, Minister Gabi in person, inviting him to join him on a hunting safari next month. The Minister's cousin has apparently opened another luxury lodge somewhere up north and Gabi is inviting some people up. I don't suppose the timing is coincidental."

"Neither do I."

"I was talking to a friend at HQ this afternoon. The rumour mill already knows you're being taken out of here."

"No surprise there either, I suppose."

"They're also speculating where you might end up at home. Have you heard that Jim McAnespie is retiring?"

"What that old codger? It's about time he went out to grass."

"Yes, well the story is that you're the hot favourite to take over from him since no-one else is volunteering."

"Oh God! No!" Bartley groaned. "But he's in charge of the SMaP Unit! They can't put me in there. I hate SMaP, I think that it's all nonsense. Don't they realise that in putting me in charge, I'll find it next to impossible not to do my worst to bring the whole stupid scheme come crashing down?" He took a large gulp of wine.

"I'll drink to that!" she laughed and raised her glass. "But have you thought that maybe that's exactly what they hope you will do? The Third Secretary grapevine has it that the powers-that-be secretly agree that SMaP is an inane, if not plain daft, box-ticking exercise and would be happy to see it buried. My guess is that they see you as the perfect person to dig its grave. Meanwhile, the SMaP Unit is already a big enough hole to keep you out of sight for a year or two."

He could not help but admire her logic.

"So, I might have a useful role after all." he chuckled. "And you had this all sussed before I even knew what was happening."

"Sorry, I didn't mean to put you down."

"No problem, you've actually cheered me up. So tell me, what other news have I been missing that's passing round your soon to be ex-Third Secretary grapevine?"

They finished off the wine as she related the latest gossip and he brought in a second bottle. He sat down on the sofa beside her. He remembered the occasion when Fiona had turned up with the marijuana wraps and he had fobbed her off when she offered to stay the night with him. He found himself gazing at Michelle's tanned thighs – a pity she always wore long pants.

"Bartley?"

"Huh, sorry!" Too late, he averted his gaze.

"Bartley, what are you looking at?" She laughed lightly at his embarrassment, but then turned serious and deliberately placed a hand on his knee, looking him straight in the eye. "Bartley, I have to tell you that I really am sorry how you've been treated." He caught the tone of genuine sympathy in her voice. "It's dreadfully unfair. I know we haven't always been the best of friends, but I believe you about Fr. O'Driscoll and what's happening in Guseni. I admire what you've been trying to do. I've also been talking to Fiona. She told me the marijuana they found belonged to her and that she'd left it in your house. She's feeling very bad about it and blames herself for your getting in trouble."

"If it wasn't the marijuana, it would probably have been something else. It would have been no trouble to arrange anything they wanted. They already squared Ballo, then Grace at the Embassy and, I guess, my housekeeper too. Aida must have found the stuff and told them about it. I haven't seen her since I got back from Bakooli. Not that she's any loss. She was a rotten cook and not much better at cleaning."

"Yes, but it seems she was pretty good at snooping around. I imagine you had the marijuana hidden well away. Anyway, tell me," she was now looking into his face, "about you and Fiona. She's very fond of you, more than fond I would guess. Have you ever....I mean, have you two ever....?"

It was his turn to laugh as she faltered. "Hell no, you mean have we ever bonked? No, we have not. She's a friend."

"So you don't bonk friends?"

"That's not what I meant."

"Only enemies?"

"Yes, well maybe enemies, when they're no longer the enemy." He put his hand to the side of her head and drew her toward him. She did not resist as he kissed her. Her mouth opened and she tickled his tongue with hers before pulling back and looking at him with a mischievous glint in her eyes.

"Isn't there something in the regulations about a senior officer not being allowed to seduce a junior?" she asked. His hand had moved down to stroke her breast under her tee-shirt.

"I don't think the regulations come into it, now that you're Acting-First Secretary and we're effectively the same grade." Her eyes widened as he circled her nipple. "Christ," he thought to himself, "she isn't wearing a bra and I didn't even notice until now."

She gave his belt buckle a quick tug. "You know I haven't had a shag since I arrived here."

"Why, Miss Finn, there's a coincidence. Neither have I." He had unbuttoned the top of her shorts and was sliding his hand inside. She pressed toward him, her mouth inviting his again. As he leaned back she pulled his pants open and lay on top, her back arching as he eased down her shorts. Her hand reached up inside his shirt, her fingers entwining in his chest hair just as he made to enter her. She gasped. Her grip tightened involuntarily and her hand jerked down, tugging painfully at his hair.

Bartley yelped and his head shot up, knocking into her forehead. She recoiled in surprise and fell heavily against the back of the sofa, releasing her grip, but now digging her nails into his chest. He howled again and tried to wriggle free. The sofa trembled as the stack of books propping up the corner wobbled and gave way, sending the books skittering across the room and dumping Bartley precipitously on the floor, with Michelle on top of him giggling furiously. He reached up and rolled her roughly over.

It was there, on the bare tiles of his floor that they continued, with Bartley in full admiration of Michelle's pert bum spread deliciously before him.

When they finally collapsed, side by side, Michelle's face wore an amused, satisfied smile. "Wow, Bartley Stud!"

"Hmm?" he seemed vaguely miles away.

"I said 'Bartley Stud'," she grinned.

He turned his face toward her, then all of a sudden pushed up, propping himself on one elbow.

"Fuck, Michelle. Thank you!"

"You're welcome, Bartley. But is that what you always say to a girl after sex?"

"No, no, it's not that. It's what you said earlier about the marijuana. You said I must have had it *hidden well away*. But when I last spoke to Frank O'Driscoll he was very careful about his use of words. For instance, he didn't mention '*photographs*' or '*pictures*'. Whatever it was he had, he had made two copies. He was bringing one to the Embassy but he said the other was in a safe *hideaway*. You see, he was telling me where the second copy was in case anything happened to him. The time I stayed with him he told me about a hut, a special place he had. He called it his *hideaway*, and that's where his photographs are."

THIRTY-NINE

Friday, 20 February.

Michelle had left sometime after 10 o'clock the previous night, but arrived back now at Bartley's house shortly before six in the morning. He was waiting and jumped in the car beside her, throwing his bag and a blanket onto the back seat.

"There's a cool-box for you in the boot. I've filled it with water and made some sandwiches. There're some biscuits too, if you need them."

"Thanks, Michelle, I really appreciate this."

"Are you sure you want to drive to Shole alone and won't ask Fumbe to drive you?"

"There's no point getting Fumbe in trouble. As it is, Clendenning can't wait to have an excuse to fire him. Besides, I seem to have been down this road so often in the last few months that I could almost drive it blindfold. I just might just not be driving at the same pace as Fumbe and it could take me an hour or two longer."

They pulled up at the gate outside the Embassy compound. The night watchman, surprised to see them at this hour, hurried out of his hut to open up.

"You'd better not hang around. I'll get the keys for the Landcruiser and move this stuff into it," he jerked his head toward the back of her car. "Then I'll be off."

Michelle left first and moments later Bartley followed her out the gate, driving the Landcruiser.

It took him considerably more time than Fumbe would have needed to reach Shole. He had stopped twice on the way. Once to eat a sandwich and stretch his stiff back, the second to tank up with diesel at the filling station on the outskirts of Bakooli city. The sun was low in the sky behind him when he found himself driving along the last stretch of road before O'Driscoll's house, scanning the acacia hedge to his left, looking for the track O'Driscoll had pointed out that led to his *hideaway*.

He was afraid he might have missed it and the light was fading fast when, at last, he found the opening for the track between the bushes. He turned on his lights to better follow it. After about a kilometre when he thought he must be coming close to the now abandoned village it twisted back in a westerly direction to curve round a low hill beyond which it seemed to peter out. He stopped and looked around. To his right, just a little way up the hill, and facing due west, was a small rondavel.

He got out and opened the rear door of the Landcruiser, lifting up Michelle's cool-box, the blanket and his own bag and trudged up toward the hut. As he drew close, he saw a rough wooden bench leaning against the front wall under the overhanging thatch. He could imagine Frank sitting there, alone, gazing out over the plain toward the setting sun. There was a door, simply a few planks nailed together and less than five foot high, to the left of the bench. A horizontal wooden crosspiece fitted into slots on either side and kept the door closed on the outside. He lifted the crosspiece and bent down to push his way inside. It was dark and at first he could see nothing. He fumbled in his bag and drew out a torch.

He could make out that the thatched roof was high enough to allow him to stand upright in the centre of the hut. He swung the torch round. The interior was spartan to the point of being almost completely bare. To his left about three feet off the ground, a narrow shelf had been tacked onto the wooden uprights of the wall. There was nothing on the shelf save an inverted brown earthenware mug and a small kerosene lamp. In front of him at an angle to the door was a low cot with coarse webbing stretched across the frame. The legs stood in empty shoe polish tins that O'Driscoll must have filled with paraffin to keep ants at bay. The tins were now dry and Bartley noticed one of the legs appeared to have been recently gnawed by some rodent. He shivered. And that was that, apart from a small Irish flag tacked to the wall above the head of the cot. He shook his head ruefully - O'Driscoll's small nod toward patriotism seemed somehow entirely in character.

Disappointed that there was nothing else, he sat down on the cot, testing that the string webbing would support his weight. He rummaged through his bag until he found a box of matches. He took down the lamp from the shelf and lighted it, placing it afterwards on the floor.

Back on the cot, he played the torch around the walls once more and then onto the floor. He got down on his hands and knees and examined under the bed for any sign of disturbed earth that might conceal a hidden hole. There was nothing. He could not believe he was wrong, but he needed to think this through. Frank's photographs had to be here somewhere, but where? Perhaps they were outside, maybe buried under the bench or some other obvious feature? If so, there was little he could do before daylight.

The best he could hope for was to try to get some rest after his long drive and then carry out a thorough search around the outside in the morning. He sat down again and pulled the cool-box toward him. He lifted out a sandwich and a bottle of water, then from his bag, a bottle of Jameson's. "Here's to you Frank," he murmured, raising the bottle in salute toward the ceiling, "But could you tell me now, where the fuck have you hidden your photos?"

Finished with his sandwich, he gathered his blanket from the floor. He stood up and gave it a good shake to clear off the dust before throwing it over the bed. As it settled over the frame it created a small draft and the flag fluttered - just a little, but enough to make something catch his eye. He leaned forward and lifted it from the bottom. There behind, the wall had been hollowed out leaving just enough space to allow a canvas wallet, perhaps eight by six inches, to be wedged inside. He pulled it out, greedy to see what it might contain. He moved over the lamp from the floor and placed it on top of the cool-box.

The first few photographs were of the scene around Charity's home. Next came a series of pictures recording their encounter with Major Mbuta and the American drilling team. He had no idea how O'Driscoll had managed to fire off those shots. There was one picture of the driver who had worn the white helmet. The AMADO logo was clearly visible. Then, there was a picture of Mbuta and the unusual-looking pick-up truck the team had been driving. There was even a photograph of the army truck behind, with two soldiers peering over the side to see what was going on.

The next few pictures appeared all to have been taken around the village they had later visited. They showed cattle, both dead and dying and the pitiful dam on which the villagers hopelessly depended.

But it was the last two photographs that were truly shocking. There was no longer any mistaking what O'Driscoll had claimed to see. He had captured images of two young men, bullet wounds clearly visible on the back of their heads, lying together on their sides with their hands bound with wire behind their backs.

Bartley returned the photographs carefully to the wallet and placed it beside the lamp on his makeshift table. He reached forward for the Jameson's to take one celebratory sip, "You did it, Frank. Thank you. You did it!"

He recapped the bottle and placed it on the floor between the cot and the cool-box. He blew out the lamp and leaning back, pulled up his feet to settle down to sleep.

He closed his eyes, he should assess the consequences of what he had found and how he should handle it - it needed careful thinking over. But he was exhausted and dozed off almost immediately.

*****

He woke with a sudden start.

All was quiet - the quiet that O'Driscoll had described as loud. But then the noise that must have woken him started again, a furtive scratching somewhere at the end of his bed. He sat up and the cot creaked. He could hear something scurrying away.

"Fuck, it's a rat!" He was fully awake now, his hatred and fear of rats kicking into play. He fumbled beside him, almost knocking over the whiskey bottle, before he found his torch. He sat up and lighted the lamp, but there was no sign of any rodent.

He needed to pee. He heaved himself upright and headed outside. He played the torch around the side of the hill, looking for a suitable place, preferably one where he would not be surprised by any rat or, now that it crossed his mind, a snake. He chose a spot some little distance away where he felt he could safely admire the stars while he did his business. He then returned to the hut.

He did not relish the thought of once again being left in the dark. He considered leaving the kerosene lamp lighted, there was ample fuel left, but then he decided it would be dangerous to leave it burning while he slept. He blew it out and turned off his torch, laying it down on the blanket beside him, close to hand if needed. His wanderings inside and outside the hut, he told himself, must surely have frightened off any rodent - at least for a while.

In spite of this attempt at self-assurance, he found himself listening closely for the sound of further scurrying.

He was so intent on concentrating his effort on any possible noise inside the hut that he almost did not hear the soft scraping outside. He leaned up on one elbow. Had he really heard something? Then, distinctly, he caught the sound of a stone skipping across the ground as if it had been kicked aside. At once, there was a flash of light at the door and it came crashing open.

FORTY

Bartley was sitting on the edge of the cot with Professor Ballo and Major Mbuta crouched in the centre of the hut looking down on him. Mbuta was shining a torch in his face and through the dazzle Bartley could just make out that he held a gun in his other hand.

"Let's have some more light in here," Ballo picked up the oil lamp from on top of the cool box and lighted it. As he returned it back in place, he noticed the canvas wallet. "What's this?" He lifted it up and peered inside, "Photographs?"

He pulled them out and Mbuta redirected the torch beam so they could both see as he riffled through them.

"Very interesting, Mr Ryan, but I've already seen these photographs and don't think that these prove anything that I or my friend, the Major, whose picture I also see here, could not deny. Still, they could be an unnecessary embarrassment."

"So you've already seen them?" Bartley was beginning to recover from the shock of Ballo's appearance. "I suppose you saw the originals that Fr. O'Driscoll was bringing to Bamgboshe. Was that before or after you shot him?"

"Shot him? Indeed, but that's another story. However, the problem we seem to have now is that you have continued to meddle. I thought we had arranged that you would have left Kutaba by now, but still here you are. The question is what to do with you now that you have upset everything that was already working out so well.

"So Major, what do you think? Do we have to arrange another *accident*", he stressed the word, "for our friend here or would another *accident* seem to be one too many? Perhaps we need to come up with something quite new. I suggest you get your driver to bring the car over here while I look after Mr. Ryan and then we can work out the details."

"Alright, but we have to get rid of him." Mbuta grunted, offering Bartley an angry scowl.

"Yes, yes, but go and get the car. Here, give me your gun."

Ballo hunkered down on his haunches aiming the gun loosely at Bartley as the Major went off.

"I suppose you are wondering what I am doing here?" Ballo offered a self-satisfied smile that was in sharp contrast to Mbuta's glare of a moment earlier. "Perhaps you might be less surprised if I were Minister Gabi? But you should know that Mbuta and I are good friends and share a common interest in a certain oil company."

Now he laughed. "Yes, I can see from your face that you thought it was Gabi that has been dealing with AMADO. In a way he has been, but my good friend the Major has been the go-between so that Gabi really does think the AMADO people are only searching for water here. How ridiculous! Why should an oil company look for water? Poor Gabi is counting on finding water to set up his wildlife park and to earn a cut from the development costs he is trying to worm out of some Dutch group. But when it turns out that there is no water, only oil, well that will be the end of his park. And that is where I come in to help convince the good people of Guseni to agree to the exploitation of their land. For which help, of course, I expect considerable reward, far more than Gabi could possibly make from his pitiful little scheme. You see Gabi thinks small and has no vision. In effect he is a fool, admittedly a fool with a rather flamboyant lifestyle, but still a fool. Whereas, Mr. Ryan, you have absolutely no style but turn out to be not such a fool - except, of course you were foolish enough not to go quietly home so that now we have no choice but to deal with you once and for all."

"So you were behind everything all along?" Bartley had first been stunned by Ballo's appearance, but his shock had soon turned to anger. "Even the night at Joly Bar and the police raid - that was all your doing and a way to get me sent home."

"Yes, indeed, and I thought it had worked until today when I was told you had been seen stopping for fuel outside Bakooli. Happily I was already in the area attending to some unfinished business. When it turned out you were nowhere in town, I guessed you must have come down here to Shole in connection with that damned priest. We were rather surprised not to find you at his house and were just looking around the village when we saw your light flashing over here. Really, it was very considerate of you to show us where you were otherwise we might never have found you."

As Ballo spoke Bartley became conscious of some furtive shadow on the ground next to the wall. He squinted until he could just make out a large rat to the left of Ballo. It was cautiously edging forward, now coming up almost to Ballo's right leg.

"Ah, you and Fr. O'Driscoll have..."

"Rat!" Bartley yelled, cutting Ballo off and pointing to the floor.

"Really, Mr Ryan, how pathetic can you be!" Ballo glanced calmly down. But then, seeing the rat already against his leg, he tried to leap upright, but from his squatting position he lost balance and lurched to his left, knocking against the cool-box and upsetting the oil lamp. Bartley's hand was already on the neck of the Jameson's bottle swinging it like a club as Ballo tumbled toward him. It smashed broken on the side of Ballo's head leaving only the jagged neck in Bartley's grip. Ballo groaned, dropping the gun and collapsed to the floor.

The flame from the lamp flared up in the mix of spilt paraffin and whiskey. Seeing the wallet on the ground just in front of him, Bartley dropped the remains of the bottle and snatched it up, bolting for the door where he paused an instant to see Ballo still slumped prone.

"Sorry about the Jameson's, Frank," he muttered and then he was out the door, scrambling down the hill and jumping into the Landcruiser. The keys were still in the ignition. He was grateful he had seen no reason to remove them earlier.

He drove off, revving the engine as high as it would go through the gears and turned his headlights on full. There was no need for stealth as the car rattled along the track. Mbuta would be after him as soon as he returned with his car and found Ballo. Bartley kept the accelerator pressed down hard and almost too late saw looming up ahead the gap in the acacia hedge where the track joined the road.

The Landcruiser skidded, the rear end swinging out behind as he struggled to keep control over the uneven surface. He succeeded in regaining a straight line and again floored the pedal. He hoped he could put some distance between himself and any pursuit, but already he could see the lights of another car behind. The whine of the diesel engine was drowned by a deafening throbbing as the Landcruiser's wheels hit a stretch of washboard surface. The steering juddered in his hands and he could feel loose stones skittering under the tyres. He risked a fast look in his mirror. The lights behind were gaining.

At that instant a further flash of car lights somewhere ahead startled him. Their dazzle blinded him so that he saw the bend in front too late. In panic he stamped down hard on the brakes, the Landcruiser losing traction so that the back end came swinging around. He overcompensated, wrenching the steering to his left. The front end followed, but the back was still pushing forward and the car slewed into the bend, the two right wheels lifting off the ground. The car rolled heavily and slewed along on its side with a screech of gashing metal until it finally ground to a jarring halt.

Bartley found himself hunched against the driver's door on the ground. He seemed to be unhurt. He looked up at the passenger door above him. It seemed unlikely that he would be able to open it to escape. His best hope was the rear. He wormed his way between the two front seats, then over the back seat to where he could reach the tailgate. He pulled the handle toward him, pushing outward at the same time. The door was jammed and he had to squeeze back to wedge against the backseat to plant his feet against it to push as hard as he could. The door began to shift, the edge scraping along the ground. He gave one final heave and it opened just enough to let him wriggle through.

He was picking himself up off the ground as the car chasing him pulled up. He looked around to see if he could run for cover. There were a few acacia bushes growing on a slope at the bend. He thought he might make it that far and started running, but a second car was pulling up ahead, its lights again blinding him.

Behind, he heard a shout. "Ryan! Ryan! I'm going to kill you, Ryan!"

He twisted around to see Ballo coming toward him, Mbuta and another soldier just behind. They were now floodlit from the lights of the second car. Ballo had a crazed look on his face. His hair, darkened by blood stood up in a wild clump where a massive gash had cut through his scalp. Bartley watched, as if in slow motion, as he stumbled toward him. Mesmerised he stared at the burnt, suppurating side of Ballo's face, unable to move even as he caught the reek of paraffin and saw the gun pointed directly at him.

A shot rang out and Ballo staggered. His head dropped as if to look down at the splattered stain across his chest. Trying helplessly to raise his gun arm he seemed to mumble something, but then pitched headlong forward.

"Stop, give up or we will shoot!"

Another shout brought Mbuta to a halt in front of Ballo's burnt and bloody body. Immediately the soldier beside him threw down his weapon, but Mbuta let out a groan, abruptly turning at the sound of a car door crashing open behind him. His gun swung up, but a burst of automatic fire rattled out throwing him back to land with a slow, empty thump on the ground.

Bartley sank to his knees winded, clasping his belly as he leaned forward. He looked up in shock at Mbuta's Nissan. Frank O'Driscoll, in handcuffs and his mouth taped, was lumbering out the open back door.

And then Col. Uba was helping him to his feet and Lt. Farka was hurrying over to the priest.

FORTY-ONE

"Lovemore, another Hippo for Fr. O'Driscoll, please." Bartley ordered as he, O'Driscoll and Col. Uba sat late in the bar of the New York Palace which the RS had ordered to open for the occasion. Lt. Farka had gone off with the bodies of Ballo and Mbuta and to lock up their driver.

"I must say I'm sorry to have missed my own funeral, I would have very much liked to hear what the bishop had to say about me." Although bruised, bloodied and considerably thinner than a couple of weeks earlier, O'Driscoll was very much his old self. "Instead, I was being held by Ballo and Mbuta at Lion Rock Lodge."

"Yes, but they said you were dead and someone must have been buried in your place. Who was it?"

"I'm sorry to say it was Luuk, the Dutchman who used to own the Lodge. It seems Ballo and Mbuta had found out that I had something on them and that I was on my way to Bamgboshe with it. They stopped me on the road and brought me to Lion Rock. It's completely deserted now and nobody else seems to come near it. Of course, they found all the photographs I had on me. I was sitting, tied up in the dining room while they went off to discuss what to do with me when Luuk came in and found me.
"Apparently he was hoping to get back some papers he said had been stolen from him and thought they might still be at the Lodge. He was sure there would be no-one there, but just in case he had hidden his car down the road and sneaked up on foot. He was just beginning to untie me when Mbuta walked in. Luuk made a run for it and somehow got as far as my car.

I heard the engine start and then there were shots. Mbuta had shot him before he could get away.

"After that, Ballo and Mbuta came in and had a huge row. At first Ballo was furious at what Mbuta had done, but then they decided they couldn't have let Luuk get away after seeing me."

"But they didn't kill you. They kept you alive all this time?" Bartley quizzed.

"Well yes. A couple of things helped me. First, they knew if they killed me they would never find the second set of photographs. They seemed to know all about that. Mbuta, as I was afraid, was tapping my call to you. Second, they seemed to think they might still be able to use me if they didn't get you, Bartley, out of the country and you kept making trouble."

"Well they have succeeded in getting me thrown out alright, but just not fast enough."

"I thank God for that. But, poor Luuk – it turned out that killing him suited their purposes. When Mbuta identified his body as mine it meant they could hold me as long as they wanted. No-one would look for Luuk. Even his own Embassy would think he'd simply left the country."

"I still don't see how they managed to pass off Luuk's body as you." Bartley wondered.

"That was no problem." It was Uba who explained. "Mbuta said he had identified the body as Fr. O'Driscoll and the doctors at the hospital took his word for it. They didn't know O'Driscoll but seeing it was a white man had no reason to think otherwise. Mbuta then ordered a casket as quickly as possible and had the body sealed in it before anyone else could see."

"Yes, but the death certificate didn't say anything about a bullet wound."

"No, you're right, Mr Ryan. However, the cause of death was factually correct and Major Mbuta, with his connection to a powerful Government Minister, would have had no trouble persuading the doctors to write no more than what he considered necessary."

"There's another thing I have to ask, Colonel. When I came down here the day of Fr. O'Driscoll's 'funeral', I saw his car at the police station. When I came back, it was gone. You must have moved it. Why?"

"Mr Ryan, I had my own suspicions about there being no accident when I saw there was a bullet-hole in the car. But Minister Gabi – and I still thought then that it must be Gabi - and Major Mbuta were not men I could easily challenge. I had to investigate quietly or not at all. I removed the car so that I could proceed."

Bartley sat back and ran his hand over his shaved head. He was alive, his friend was alive. But an innocent Dutchman had died.

"Poor Luuk, he lost everything, even, when he died, his identity."

FORTY-TWO

Monday, 23 February.

"So after all, Gabi didn't know was going on in Guseni and if he suspected anything he might have found it convenient not to ask questions." Bartley was finishing his account of events to Clendenning. He had not expected to see the Ambassador again, far less the stuffed Thompson's gazelle that haunted his study, but here they were again, eyeball to glass eyeball.

Secretary General McNamara had ordered the Ambassador to debrief Bartley and deliver a verbal report over the phone. With Freedom of Information requests a certainty, he wanted as little as possible committed to paper. The unexpected resurrection of Fr. O'Driscoll was already causing a sensation in the Irish press and the Irish Government, as much as the Kutaban, was anxious to limit any reputational damage that might result if the full story came out. It was intended that the erroneous reports of O'Driscoll's death be written off as a case of mistaken identity in a botched kidnapping of a businessman carried out by a rogue army officer. Unfortunately, a local politician had been shot and killed in the course of a rescue operation.

"Yes, it seems Gabi has been taken for a ride and I doubt if his career will survive." Clendenning sounded wistful. "The Dutch Ambassador isn't too happy either. It seems he had staked much of his reputation on getting a few Dutch businesses together to bid for supplying the infrastructure and then the running of Gabi's national park. Apparently it would have been a lucrative contract. He was keeping it hush-hush, didn't tell anyone, even his European colleagues, for fear the Chinese would get wind of it and come swooping in."

"What about Guseni, what happens there now?"

"Well according to my British colleague this morning – who, incidentally is none too convinced of AMADO's claim that this was a rogue operation by one of its teams and it had no idea what it was up to - the initial geological tests have proved rather disappointing. There is some oil, but not in presently commercially viable quantities. Also there's no water, it turns out they did actually do some water prospecting. So that's the end of the national park."

"Does that mean that the land clearances will end? There's no reason to move people now."

"No, again the British Ambassador says Okeke claims he knew nothing about this and there is no reason that the locals should not be able to lead their usual nomadic lifestyle. After all they are the only ones who know how to survive in the area."

"That's good, that's as much, if not more, than Fr. O'Driscoll hoped. You know he wants to go back to Shole and go on working in Guseni." Bartley's pleasure at how things were turning out showed on his face. "Still, I guess everyone's still keen that I should leave Kutaba?"

"Yes, Bartley, you could say that. You're to go home as planned tomorrow. You acted in a very unorthodox and irresponsible manner and put the reputation of the Department at risk. However, the Secretary General has instructed me to tell you that the Department very much appreciates your initiative and integrity throughout this whole affair and that there will therefore be no repercussion as regards your future career." Clendenning's eyes hooded, "Personally, I would not have been so generous."

"Well, thanks for that," Bartley stood up. He let his hand fall onto the gazelle. "I suppose with Gabi gone that safari trip of yours has been cancelled?"

He patted the stuffed head and walked out, leaving the door ajar.

FORTY-THREE

Tuesday, 24 February.

Standing at the check-in desk at the airport, Bartley examined the boarding pass he had just been handed: seat 53A - well to the rear but at least beside a window. He stuffed the ticket into his inside jacket pocket and was lifting his briefcase when he felt a tap on his shoulder. Looking round he found Fiona with a big grin on her face.

"I promised I'd see you before you left!" She grabbed him by the shoulders and kissed his cheek before letting go and stepping back to give way to Otto. The Dutchman came forward to crush him in tight bear hug.

"Sorry Bart, I know I've been a prick this last while. I should really have told you what was going on, but I had no idea that you thought we were helping AMADO in some oil deal. But hell, I had to see you before you go."

"Thanks Otto, and thanks for coming. I don't know if I would have acted any differently in your shoes - dealing with someone like me. It's good to see you..."

"Excuse me, can you please stand aside and let me through!" An angry shout interrupted them. An oversized Kutaban lady in traditional dress directly behind abruptly shoved forward, one of her two massive suitcases forcing him to jump aside. She glared at him. For one desperate moment he feared that she would be given seat 53B. He imagined he would already be more than sufficiently constricted during the long overnight flight without having to share a portion of his seat with her ample overspill.

The three friends made their way toward the exit for security and passport control. Michelle was standing there, alongside Fumbe.

"Fumbe thank you for everything. You've been a true friend. We've had some good times together and I'll miss you. But can I ask you one last favour? Maybe someday you'll bring Fr. O'Driscoll a bottle of Jameson for me. Tell him I'm sorry I wasted the last one – he'll understand. Take care of yourself and remember never to let the Ambassador close that car door on his own."

Michelle gave a puzzled look as Fumbe winked. "Sure, I will remember, but I will miss you. It will not be so much fun when you go."

"Fiona, I have something for you." Bartley remembered. He reached in his briefcase and pulled out a key. "This is for my RAV. It's all yours now, so you can get rid of your old wreck of a Suzuki. I left Michelle a paper signing over ownership."

"I don't know what to say. Thank you, Bartley. I'll miss you." Her eyes misted, hugging him.

Bartley turned toward Michelle. "Thanks for coming to see me off, Michelle." He hesitated, "And for everything else."

"You're welcome." She gave him an amused smile that failed to escape Fiona whose turn it was now to look quizzical.

"Give me a call if you're ever back at HQ, maybe we could have a glass of wine."

"I'll do that, Bartley. Sure, we might even share a bottle?"

He hefted his briefcase and, grinning, headed out to security.

All named characters, with the exception of Ken Saro Wiwa, are fictitious.

There is no greater compliment than your having given time to read THE KUTABA EMBASSY. If you enjoyed it, please be kind and leave a review with Amazon so that others may hear of it and also read it.

Thank you,

Ronan Corvin

Printed in Great Britain
by Amazon

85525771R00198